Born in New Zealand, Heather Morris is an international number one bestselling author, who is passionate about stories of survival, resilience and hope. In 2003, while working in a large public hospital in Melbourne, Heather was introduced to an elderly gentleman who 'might just have a story worth telling'. The day she met Lale Sokolov changed both their lives. Their friendship grew and Lale embarked on a journey of self-scrutiny, entrusting the innermost details of his life during the Holocaust to her. Heather originally wrote Lale's story as a screenplay – which ranked high in international competitions – before reshaping it into her debut novel, *The Tattooist of Auschwitz*. Her second novel, *Cilka's Journey*, follows on from this international bestselling work.

Cilka's
JOURNEY

Cilka's
JOURNEY

HEATHER MORRIS

ZAFFRE

First published in Great Britain in 2019 by
ZAFFRE
80–81 Wimpole St, London W1G 9RE

Copyright © Heather Morris, 2019

Afterword © Owen Matthews, 2019

Map design by Sophie McDonnell

This is a work of fiction. Names, places, events and
incidents are either the products of the author's
imagination or used fictitiously.

A CIP catalogue record for this book is
available from the British Library.

Hardback ISBN: 978-1–78576–904–7
Trade Paperback ISBN: 978-1–78576–913–9

Also available as an ebook

1 3 5 7 9 10 8 6 4 2

Typeset in Simoncini Garamond by
Palimpsest Book Production Ltd, Falkirk, Stirlingshire

Printed and bound in Great Britain by Clays Ltd, Elcograf S.p.A.

MIX
Paper from
responsible sources
FSC® C018072

Zaffre is an imprint of Bonnier Books UK
www.bonnierbooks.co.uk

To my grandchildren
Henry, Nathan, Jack, Rachel and Ashton.
Never forget the courage, the love, the hope
given to us by those who survived
and those that did not.

This is a work of fiction, based on what I learnt from the first-hand testimony of Lale Sokolov, the tattooist of Auschwitz, about Cecilia 'Cilka' Klein, whom he knew in Auschwitz-Birkenau, from the testimony of others who knew her, and from my own research. Although it weaves together facts and reportage with the experiences of women survivors of the Holocaust, and the experiences of women sent to the Soviet Gulag system at the end of the Second World War, it is a novel and does not represent the entire facts of Cilka's life. Furthermore, it contains a mix of characters: some inspired by real-life figures, in some instances representing more than one individual, others completely imagined. There are many factual accounts that document these terrible epochs in our history and I would encourage the interested reader to seek them out.

For more information about Cecilia Klein and her family, and about the Gulags, please turn to the end of this novel. I hope that further details about Cilka and those who once knew her will continue to come to light once the book is published.

Heather Morris, October 2019

CHAPTER 1

**Auschwitz Concentration Camp,
27 January 1945**

Cilka stares at the soldier standing in front of her, part of the army that has entered the camp. He is saying something in Russian, then German. The soldier towers over the eighteen-year-old girl. *'Du bist frei.'* You are free. She does not know if she has really heard his words. The only Russians she has seen before this, in the camp, were emaciated, starving – prisoners of war.

Could it really be possible that freedom exists? Could this nightmare be over?

When she does not respond, he bends down and places his hands on her shoulders. She flinches.

He quickly withdraws his hands. 'Sorry, I didn't mean

to scare you.' He continues in halting German. Shaking his head, he seems to conclude she doesn't understand him. He makes a sweeping gesture and slowly says the words again. 'You are free. You are safe. We are the Soviet Army and we are here to help you.'

'I understand,' Cilka whispers, pulling tight the coat that hides her tiny frame.

'Do you understand Russian?'

Cilka nods yes. She grew up knowing an East Slavic dialect, Rusyn.

'What's your name?' he asks gently.

Cilka looks up into the soldier's eyes and says in a clear voice, 'My name is Cecilia Klein, but my friends call me Cilka.'

'That's a beautiful name,' he says. It is strange to be looking at a man who is not one of her captors and is so healthy. His clear eyes, his full cheeks, his fair hair protruding from beneath his cap. 'Where are you from, Cilka Klein?'

Memories of her old life have faded, become blurred. At some point it became too painful to remember that her former life with her family, in Bardejov, existed.

'I'm from Czechoslovakia,' she says, in a broken voice.

Auschwitz-Birkenau Concentration Camp, February 1945

Cilka has been sitting in the block, as close as she can get to the one stove that provides heat. She knows she has already drawn attention. The other able-bodied women, her friends included, were forcibly marched out of the camp by the SS weeks ago. The remaining prisoners are skeletal, diseased, or they are children. And then there is Cilka. They were all meant to be shot, but in their haste to get away themselves, the Nazis abandoned them all to fate.

The soldiers have been joined by other officials – counter-intelligence agents, Cilka has heard, though she's not sure what that means – to manage a situation the average soldier has no training for. The Soviet agency is tasked with keeping law and order, particularly as it relates to any threat to the Soviet State. Their role, she's been told by the soldiers, is to question every prisoner to determine their status as it relates to their imprisonment, in particular if they collaborated or worked with the Nazis. The retreating German Army are considered enemies of the State of the Soviet Union and anyone who could be connected to them is, by default, an enemy of the Soviet Union.

A soldier enters the block. 'Come with me,' he says, pointing to Cilka. At the same time, a hand clutches her right arm, dragging her to her feet. Several weeks have passed and seeing others being taken away to be questioned has become part of the routine of the block. To Cilka it is just 'her turn'. She is eighteen years old and she just has to hope they can see that she had no choice but to do what she did in order to survive. No choice, other than death. She can only hope that she will soon be able to return to her home in Czechoslovakia, find a way forward.

As she's taken into the building the Soviet Army are using as their headquarters, Cilka attempts a smile at the four men who sit across the room from her. They are here to punish her evil captors, not her. This is a good time; there will be no more loss. Her smile is not returned. She notices their uniforms are slightly different to those of the soldiers outside. Blue epaulettes sit on top of their shoulders, their hats, placed on the table in front of them, have the same shade of blue ribbon with a red stripe.

One of them does eventually smile at her and speaks in a gentle voice.

'Would you tell us your name?'

'Cecilia Klein.'

'Where are you from, Cecilia? Your country and town.'

'I'm from Bardejov in Czechoslovakia.'

'What is the date of your birth?'

'The seventeenth of March, 1926.'

'How long have you been here?'

'I came here on the twenty-third of April in 1942, just after I turned sixteen.'

The agent pauses, studies her.

'That was a long time ago.'

'An eternity in here.'

'What have you been doing here since April 1942?'

'Staying alive.'

'Yes, but how did you do that?' He tilts his head at her. 'You look like you haven't starved.'

Cilka doesn't answer, but her hand goes to her hair, which she hacked off herself weeks ago, after her friends were marched from the camp.

'Did you work?'

'I worked at staying alive.'

The four men exchange looks. One of them picks up a piece of paper and pretends to read it before speaking.

'We have a report on you, Cecilia Klein. It says that you in fact stayed alive by prostituting yourself to the enemy.'

Cilka says nothing, swallows hard, looks from one man to the next, trying to fathom what they are saying, what they expect her to say in return.

Another speaks. 'It's a simple question. Did you fuck the Nazis?'

'They were my enemy. I was a prisoner here.'

'But did you fuck the Nazis? We're told you did.'

'Like many others here, I was forced to do whatever I was told by those who imprisoned me.'

The first agent stands. 'Cecilia Klein, we will be sending you to Kraków and then determining your fate from there.' He refuses, now, to look at her.

'No,' Cilka says, standing. This can't be happening. 'You can't do this to me! I am a prisoner here.'

One of the men who hasn't spoken before quietly asks, 'Do you speak German?'

'Yes, some. I've been in here three years.'

'And you speak many other languages, we have heard, and yet you are Czechoslovakian.'

Cilka doesn't protest, frowning, not understanding the significance. She had been taught languages at school, picked others up by being in here.

The men all exchange looks.

'Speaking other languages would have us believe you are a spy, here to report back to whoever will buy your information. This will be investigated in Kraków.'

'You can expect a long sentence of hard labour,' the original officer says.

It takes Cilka a moment to react, and then she is grabbed by the arm by the soldier who brought her into the room, dragged away, screaming her innocence.

'I was forced, I was raped! No! Please.'

But the soldiers do not react; they do not seem to hear. They are moving on to the next person.

Montelupich Prison, Kraków, July 1945

Cilka crouches in the corner of a damp, stinking cell. She struggles to register time passing. Days, weeks, months.

She does not make conversation with the women around

her. Anyone overheard speaking by the guards is taken out and brought back with bruises and torn clothing. Stay quiet, stay small, she tells herself, until you know what is happening, and what the right things are to say or do. She has torn off a section of her dress to tie around her nose and mouth in an attempt to minimise the stench of human waste, damp and decay.

One day, they take her out of the cell. Faint from hunger and exhausted by the effort of vigilance, the figures of the guards and the wall and floors all seem immaterial, as in a dream. She stands in line behind other prisoners in a corridor, slowly moving towards a door. She can lean, momentarily, against a warm, dry wall. They keep the corridors heated, for the guards, but not the cells themselves. And though the weather outside must be mild by now, the prison seems to trap cold from the night and hold on to it through the whole next day.

When it is Cilka's turn, she enters a room where an officer sits behind a desk, his face bathed in greenish light from a single lamp. The officers by the door indicate she should go over to the desk.

The officer looks down at his piece of paper.

'Cecilia Klein?'

She glances around. She is alone in the room with three burly men. 'Yes?'

He looks down again and reads from the paper. 'You are convicted of working with the enemy, as a prostitute and additionally as a spy. You are sentenced to fifteen years' hard labour.' He signs the piece of paper. 'You sign this to say you have understood.'

Cilka has understood all of the officer's words. He has been speaking in German, rather than Russian. Is it a trick, then? she thinks. She feels the eyes of the men at the door. She knows she has to do something. It seems she has no choice but to do the only thing in front of her.

He flips the piece of paper and points to a dotted line. The letters above it are in Cyrillic – Russian script. Again, as she has experienced over and over in her young life, she finds herself with two choices: one, the narrow path opening up in front of her; the other, death.

The officer hands her the pen, and then looks towards the door, bored, waiting for the next person in line – just doing his job.

With a shaking hand, Cilka signs the piece of paper.

It is only when she's taken from the prison and pushed onto a truck that she realises winter has gone, spring never existed, and it is summer. While the warmth of the sun is a balm to her chilled body, her still-alive body, the glare of it hurts her eyes. Before she has a chance to adjust, the truck slams to a stop. There, in front of her, is another train carriage, on a cattle train painted red.

CHAPTER 2

A Train Bound for Vorkuta Gulag, Siberia, 160 km North of the Arctic Circle, July 1945

The floor of the closed railway wagon is covered in straw and each prisoner tries to claim a small space on which to sit. Older women wail, babies whimper. The sound of women suffering – Cilka hoped she'd never have to hear it again. The train sits at the station for hours, the heat of the day turning the inside of the compartment into an oven. The bucket of water left to share is soon gone. The infants' cries turn wretched and dry; the old women are reduced to rocking themselves into a trance. Cilka has placed herself against a wall and draws comfort from the small wisps of air that make their way through the tiny cracks. A woman leans on her from the side and a back is shoved up hard against her raised knees. She leaves it there. No point fighting for space that doesn't exist.

Cilka senses that night has fallen as the train makes its first jolting movement, its engine struggling to pull the unknown number of carriages away from Kraków, away, it seems, from any hope of ever returning home.

So, she had allowed herself just one moment of hope, sitting in that block back in that *other place*, waiting. She shouldn't have dared. She is destined to be punished. Maybe it is what she deserves. But, as the train gathers speed, she vows she will never, ever end up in a place like Block 25 again.

There must be more ways to stay alive than to be witness to so much death.

Will she ever know if her friends who were forced to march out of the camp made it to safety? They had to. She can't bear to think otherwise.

As the rhythm of the train rocks the children and babies to sleep, the silence is broken by the howl of a young mother holding an emaciated baby in her arms. The child has died.

Cilka wonders what the other women have done to end up here. Are they Jewish as well? The women in the prison mostly had not been, as she gleaned from overhearing various conversations. She wonders where they are going. By some miracle, she dozes.

A sudden braking of the train throws its passengers around. Heads bang, limbs are twisted, and their owners cry out in pain. Cilka braces herself by holding on to the woman who has spent the night leaning into her.

'We're here,' someone says. But where is here?

Cilka hears train doors clanging open up ahead, but no one leaves their compartments. Their carriage door is flung open. Once again, brilliant sunshine stings Cilka's eyes.

Two men stand outside. One hands a bucket of water to grabbing hands. The second soldier tosses in several hunks of bread before slamming the door closed. Semi-darkness once again envelops them. A fight breaks out as the women scramble for a piece of the bread. A too-familiar scene for Cilka. The screaming intensifies until, finally, an older woman stands up, raising her hands, saying nothing, and even in the semi-darkness the stance takes up the space, and is powerful. Everyone shuts up.

'We share,' she says, with a voice of authority. 'How many loaves do we have?' Five hands are raised, indicating the number of loaves of bread they have to share.

'Give to the children first, and the rest we will share. If anyone doesn't get any, they will be the first to eat next time. Agreed?' The women with the bread begin breaking off small quantities, handing them to the mothers. Cilka misses out. She feels upset. She does not know if it's the best idea to give the food to the children if where they are going is like where she has been. It will only be wasted. She knows it is a terrible thought.

For several hours the train sits idle. The women and infants fall again into silence.

The silence is broken by the screams of a girl. As those

11

around her attempt to quieten the girl, to find out what is wrong, she sobs, holding up a blood-covered hand. Cilka can see it in the flickering light coming through the gaps.

'I'm dying.'

The woman nearest her looks down at the blood staining her dress.

'She has her period,' she says. 'She's all right, she's not dying.' The girl continues sobbing.

The girl sitting at Cilka's legs, a bit younger than her and wearing a similar summer dress, shifts to standing and calls out, 'What's your name?'

'Ana,' the girl whimpers.

'Ana, I'm Josie. We will look after you,' she says, looking around the compartment. 'Won't we?'

The women murmur and nod their assent.

One of the women grasps the girl's face between her hands and brings it towards her own.

'Have you not had a monthly bleed before?'

The girl shakes her head: no. The older woman clutches her to her breast, rocking her, soothing her. Cilka experiences a strange pang of longing.

'You're not dying; you're becoming a woman.'

Some of the women are already tearing pieces off their garments, ripping sections from the bottom of their dresses, and passing them along to the woman caring for the girl.

The train jolts forward, dropping Josie to the floor. A small giggle escapes from her. Cilka can't help but giggle too. They catch each other's eye. Josie looks a bit like

12

her friend Gita. Dark brows and lashes, a small, pretty mouth.

Many hours later, they stop again. Water and bread are thrown in. This time, the stop brings additional scrutiny and the young mother is forced to hand over her dead infant to the soldiers. She has to be restrained from trying to leave the compartment to be with her dead child. The slamming of the door brings her silence as she is helped into a corner to grieve her loss.

Cilka sees how closely Josie watches it all, with her hand against her mouth. 'Josie, is it?' Cilka asks the girl who has been leaning against her since they first got on the train. She asks her in Polish, the language she has heard her using.

'Yes.' Josie slowly manoeuvres her way round so they are knee to knee.

'I'm Cilka.'

Their conversation opener seems to embolden other women. Cilka hears others ask their neighbours their names, and soon the compartment is filled with whispered chatter. Languages are identified, and a shuffling takes place to put nationalities together. Stories are shared. One woman was accused of aiding the Nazis by allowing them to buy bread from her bakery in Poland. Another was arrested for translating German propaganda. Yet another was captured by the Nazis and, being caught with them, accused of spying for them. Amazingly, there are bursts of laughter along with tears as each woman shares how she ended up in this predicament. Some of the women confirm the train will be going to a labour camp, but they don't know where.

Josie tells Cilka that she is from Kraków, and that she's sixteen years old. Cilka opens her mouth to share her own age and place of birth, but before she can, a woman nearby declares in a loud voice, 'I know why she's here.'

'Leave her alone,' comes from the strong older woman who'd suggested sharing the bread.

'But I saw her, dressed in a fur coat in the middle of winter while we were dying from the cold.'

Cilka remains silent. There's a creeping heat in her neck. She lifts her head and stares at her accuser. A stare the woman cannot match. She vaguely recognises her. Wasn't she, too, one of the old-timers in Birkenau? Did she not have a warm and comfortable job in the administration building?

'And you, you who wants to accuse her,' says the older woman, 'why are you here, in this luxurious carriage with us going on a summer holiday?'

'Nothing, I did nothing,' comes the weak reply.

'We all did nothing,' Josie says strongly, defending her new friend.

Cilka clenches her jaw as she turns away from the woman.

She can feel Josie's gentle, reassuring eyes on her face.

Cilka throws her a faint smile, before turning her head to the wall, closing her eyes, trying to block the sudden memory flooding in of Schwarzhuber – the officer in charge of Birkenau – standing over her in that small room, loosening his belt, the sounds of women weeping beyond the wall.

* * *

The next time the train stops, Cilka gets her ration of bread. Instinctively she eats half and tucks the rest into the top of her dress. She looks around, fearful someone might be watching and try to take it from her. She turns her face back to the wall, closing her eyes.

Somehow, she sleeps.

As she floats back awake, she is startled by Josie's presence right in front of her. Josie reaches out and touches Cilka's close-cropped hair. Cilka tries to resist the automatic urge to push her away.

'I love your hair,' the sad, tired voice says.

Relaxing, Cilka reaches up and touches the younger girl's bluntly chopped hair.

'I like yours too.'

Cilka had been freshly shaved and deloused at the prison. For her a familiar process, as she saw it happen so often to prisoners in that *other place*, but she supposes it is new for Josie.

Desperate to change the subject, she asks, 'Are you here with anyone?'

'I'm with my grandma.'

Cilka follows Josie's eyes to the bold older woman who had spoken up earlier, still with an arm around the young girl, Ana. She is watching the two of them closely. They exchange a nod.

'You might want to get closer to her,' Cilka says.

Where they are going, the older woman may not last long.

'I should. She might be frightened.'

'You're right. I am too,' Cilka says.

'Really? You don't look frightened.'

'Oh, I am. If you want to talk again, I will be here.'

Josie steps carefully over and around the other women between Cilka and her grandmother. Cilka looks on through the slats of light coming through the carriage. A small smile breaks free as she sees and feels the women shuffle and shift to accommodate her new friend.

* * *

'It's been nine days, I think. I've been counting. How much longer?' Josie murmurs to no one in particular.

There is more room in the compartment now. Cilka has kept count of how many have died, sick, starving or wounded from their prior interrogations, their bodies removed when the train stops for bread and water. Eleven adults, four infants. Occasionally some fruit is thrown in with the dry husks of bread, which Cilka has seen mothers soften in their own mouths for the children.

Josie now lies curled up beside Cilka, her head resting on Cilka's lap. Her sleep is fitful. Cilka knows of the images that must be racing through her mind. A few days ago, her grandmother died. She had seemed so strong and bold, but then she'd started coughing, worse and worse, and shaking, and then refusing her own ration of food. And then the coughing stopped.

Cilka watched Josie standing mutely at the compartment door as her grandmother's body was roughly handed down to the waiting guards. Cilka experienced a physical pain so intense she doubled over, all her breath leaving her. But no sound, and no tears, would come.

Auschwitz, 1942

Hundreds of girls are marched from Auschwitz to Birkenau on a hot summer day. Four kilometres. A slow, painful march for many who have ill-fitting boots, or worse, no footwear. As they enter through the large imposing brick archway they see the construction of blocks. Men working there pause to stare in horror at the new arrivals. Cilka and her sister Magda have been at Auschwitz for around three months, working among other Slovakian girls.

They are turned from the main road through the camp and into a fenced-off area, with several buildings complete, and others underway. They are stopped and held, standing in lines, as the sun beats down upon them for what seems like hours.

From behind, they hear a commotion. Cilka looks back to the entrance of the women's camp to see a senior officer, with an entourage of men following, walking up the row of girls. Most of the girls keep their heads down. Not Cilka. She wants to see who warrants such protection from a group of unarmed, defenceless girls.

17

'Obersturmführer Schwarzhuber,' a guard says, greeting the senior officer. 'You'll be overseeing the selection today?'

'I will.'

The senior officer, Schwarzhuber, continues walking down the line of girls and women. He pauses briefly as he passes Cilka and Magda. When he gets to the front of the row, he turns and walks back. This time he can see the turned-down faces. Occasionally he uses his swagger stick pushed under the chin to raise the face of a girl.

He is coming closer. He stops beside Cilka, Magda behind her. He raises his stick. Cilka beats him to it and lifts her chin high, looking directly at him. If she can get his attention he will ignore her sister. He reaches down and lifts her left arm, appearing to look at the numbers fading on her skin. Cilka hears Magda's sharp inhalation of breath behind her. Schwarzhuber drops her arm, walks back down to the front of the line, and Cilka notices him speak to the SS officer beside him.

* * *

They have been sorted, again. Left, right; hearts banging, bodies clenched in fear. Cilka and Magda have been chosen to live another day. They are now in the line to be painfully marked again – to have their tattoos re-inked so they will never fade. They stand close but not touching, though they desperately want to comfort each other. They whisper as they wait – consoling, wondering.

Cilka counts the number of girls in front of her. Five. It will soon be her turn, and then Magda's. Again, she will *hand her left arm over to someone to have the blurred blue numbers punctured into her skin. First she was marked on entering Auschwitz three months ago, now again after being re-selected for the new camp, Auschwitz II: Birkenau. She begins to shiver. It is summer, the sun blazes down on her. She fears the pain she will soon experience. The first time, she cried out in shock. This time, she tells herself she will remain silent. Though she is still only sixteen, she can no longer behave like a child.*

Peering out from the row of girls, she watches the Tätowierer. *He looks into the eyes of the girl whose arm he holds. She sees him place a finger to his lips and mouth, shhh. He smiles at her. He looks down to the ground as the girl walks away, then looks up to watch her moving on. He takes the arm of the next girl in line and doesn't see that the previous girl turns back to look at him.*

Four. Three. Two. One. It is now her turn. She glances quickly and reassuringly back at Magda, then moves forward. She stands in front of the Tätowierer, *her left arm by her side. He reaches down and gently lifts her arm up. She surprises herself by pulling it free, an almost unconscious reaction, causing him to look at her, to look into her eyes, which she knows are filled with anger, disgust, at having to be defiled, again.*

'I'm sorry. I'm so sorry,' he whispers gently to her. 'Please, give me your arm.'

Moments pass. He makes no attempt to touch her. She raises her arm and offers it to him.

'Thank you,' he mouths. 'It'll be over quickly.'

With blood dripping from her arm, though not as much as last time, Cilka whispers, 'Be gentle with my sister,' before moving on as slowly as she can so Magda will be able to catch up. She looks curiously around for the girl who'd been in front of her. She glances back at the Tätowierer. He has not watched her walk away. She sees the girl who'd been five in front of her standing outside Block 29 and joins her and the others waiting to be admitted into their 'home'. She studies the girl. Even with her head shaven, the baggy dress hiding whatever curves she may have, or once had, she is beautiful. Her large dark eyes show no signs of the despair Cilka has seen in so many. She wants to get to know this girl who made the Tätowierer stare. Soon, Magda joins her, wincing from the pain of the tattoo. They're temporarily out of sight of any guards and Cilka clutches her sister's hand.

That evening, as the girls in Hut 29 each find a space in a bunk to share with several others and cautiously enquire to one another, 'Where are you from?' Cilka learns the girl's name is Gita. She comes from a village in Slovakia, not too far from Cilka and Magda's town of Bardejov. Gita introduces Cilka and Magda to her friends Dana and Ivanka.

The next day, following rollcall, the girls are sent to their work area. Cilka is pulled aside, not sent like the others to work in the Kanada, where they sort out the belongings, jewellery and heirlooms brought to Auschwitz by the prisoners, and prepare much of it for return to Germany. Instead, by special request, she is to report to the administration building, where she will work.

CHAPTER 3

Vorkuta Gulag, Siberia

The temperature is dropping. It hasn't been sudden, more a gradual change noticed at night when Cilka and the others have found themselves snuggling into each other. They are all in summer clothing. Cilka doesn't know what month it is, though she guesses August or September, and she does not know where they are going, though the language at each stop is Russian.

One day bleeds into the next. Illness creeps through the carriage. Pitiful coughing drains the women of what little energy they have. Conversations become fewer and shorter. At the last few stops, men had taken pity on the cargo, had stripped and thrown in their *kal'sony*, as they called it, off their own bodies. Cilka and Josie had pulled

21

the loose, still-warm undergarments up over their goose-bumped legs, waving a weak thank you.

It has been three days since they last stopped when the train screeches to a halt, the heavy doors flung back. A vast, unpopulated landscape of dirt and yellow-green grass lies before them.

This time it isn't one or two guards greeting them. Dozens of men in uniform, rifles at the ready, line the length of the train.

'*Na vykhod!*' they yell. *Get out!*

As the women struggle to their feet, many collapsing on legs no longer capable of bearing weight, the shouting continues.

Cilka and Josie join the others outside for the first time in weeks. They link arms with two older women who are struggling to stand. They don't need to be told what to do; with a line forming in front of them they know which way to face. They can see some crude buildings in the distance, on the broad, flat plain. Another camp, thinks Cilka, surrounded by nothingness. But the sky here is different – an impossibly vast grey-blue. They trudge along with the flow of the others towards the far-away buildings. Cilka tries to count the number of carriages, some disgorging men, some women and children; people of all different ages, in varying states of ill-health and distress. Some who'd been on the train since the beginning, some who'd been added along the way.

Time stands still for Cilka as she remembers lining up to go into the *other place*. That line led to an existence that bore no end date. This time she knows her end date, should she survive to see it. Fifteen years. Will having an end date make the labour more endurable? Is an end date even to be believed?

Before long, Cilka is standing in front of a large woman dressed in a thick khaki uniform. Her own clothing is still too light for this weather. They must be far north. She can barely feel her hands and feet.

'*Imya, familya*?' the woman barks at Cilka, scanning a list on a clipboard. *Name.*

'Cecilia Klein.'

Her name ticked off, Cilka follows the line into a large concrete bunker. Immediately she looks to the ceiling for the tell-tale signs of showers. Will it be water or gas? Her relief at not seeing anything threatening is palpable and she holds on to Josie to steady herself.

'Are you all right?' Josie asks.

'Yes, yes, I'm fine. I thought we might be going to have a shower.'

'I'd love a shower – it's what we need.'

Cilka forces a small smile. There does not seem any point in explaining what she had feared. Looking at the bafflement on the faces around her, it dawns on her that few of them will have gone through something like this before. Only survivors from that *other place*, or those from other camps, carry the burden of knowing what may be in store for them all.

As the room fills, several male guards enter.

'Clothes off. Now.'

Women look around for guidance. The words are whispered through in different languages, and they catch on as several slowly start removing their clothes.

Cilka whispers to Josie, 'You have to take your clothes off.'

'No, Cilka, I can't, not in front of men.'

It seems Josie had only had her head shaved in prison, not the full ordeal. Cilka knows that all the hair on their bodies will be shaved.

'Listen to me. You have to do as you're told.'

Cilka starts undoing the buttons on the front of Josie's dress. Josie pushes her hand away, confused, looking around at the other women in various stages of undress. The naked women hold their hands in front of their pubis and across their breasts. Slowly Josie begins to undress.

'Hurry up,' Cilka says. 'Just drop your clothes where they are.'

Cilka looks up at the men standing in front of the doors, yelling out instructions. The smirks and nudges between them sicken her. She looks down at the pile of her clothes at her feet. She knows she will not see them again.

The men in front of the doors part as four other guards enter, each dragging with them a large hose. The blast of freezing water sends the women crashing into each other, screaming, shouting, as they are knocked down, bundled together by the force of the water. The smell of chlorine becomes overpowering and the screaming changes to gagging and coughing.

Cilka is smashed up against a cracked tiled wall, grazing

her arm as she slides to the ground. She watches as sadistically the guards target older, frail women who attempt defiance by trying to stand firm. They go down fighting. Cilka curls up in the foetal position and stays there until the hoses are turned off and the laughing guards leave.

*　*　*

As the women pick themselves up and shuffle towards the door, several grab at a dripping article of clothing to cover themselves. They exit the building and are handed a thin grey towel to wrap around themselves. Barefoot on the gritty cold ground, they walk to a nearby concrete building identical to the one they have just left.

Cilka sees Josie in front of her and hurries to catch up.

'Will they give us new clothes now?' Josie asks.

Cilka looks at Josie's drawn, desperate face. There is much worse to come, she thinks. Maybe, momentarily, she can cheer her.

'I hope so – grey is not my colour.' Cilka is pleased when Josie stifles a snigger.

They are roughly pushed into four lines and screams of protest inside are heard by those waiting to enter. Several terrified women break from their line, scared by the screams ahead. They become game for the warders to fire at. The shots miss but send the women scurrying back into line. A source of entertainment.

She feels Josie trembling beside her.

Cilka and Josie enter the building and see what is happening to the women in front of them. Four men stand behind four chairs. Several strong, large women, also dressed in khaki uniforms, stand nearby.

She watches as the woman in front of her approaches the chair and is forced to sit down. The woman's hair is roughly gathered together and swiftly cut close to her head with a large pair of scissors. Without missing a beat, the man exchanges the scissors for a shaving blade and scrapes it across the woman's scalp. Blood trickles down her face and back. One of the nearby women is yanked to her feet, turned around and placed with one of her feet on the chair. Josie and Cilka watch in horror as the man, with no sign of emotion or care, shaves her pubic area. As he lifts his head, indicating he is done, the female guard pushes the woman away and motions for Josie to come forward.

Cilka quickly moves over into the next line so she is next to be shaved. She can at least be beside Josie as this humiliation is played out; she has been through it all before. Together they walk to the chairs. Without instruction, they sit. Cilka keeps her eyes on Josie as much as she can, wordlessly offering comfort, her heart aching as she sees tears falling helplessly down Josie's cheeks. She can tell this is the first time Josie has been subjected to anything this brutal.

Their heads shaved, Josie is slow to stand and the back of a female guard's hand slaps her across the face as she is pulled to her feet. Cilka places her own foot on the chair and stares at the man in front of her. Her glare is met with a thin toothless grin and she knows she has made a mistake.

As Cilka and Josie walk away, grey towels their only cover, blood trickles down Cilka's inner thigh, her punishment for daring to be brave. Josie begins to vomit. Gagging, bile and watery liquid is all she can throw up.

They follow others down a long corridor.

'What next?' Josie sobs.

'I don't know. Whatever it is, don't argue, don't fight with them; try to be invisible and do as you are told.'

'That's your advice? Just take it, whatever it is, take it?' Her voice rises, anger replacing shame.

'Josie, I've been here before, trust me.' Cilka sighs. But she also feels relief at Josie's display of strength and defiance. She will need that fire in a place like this.

'Does this have something to do with the numbers on your arm?' Josie asks.

Cilka looks at her left arm, which is holding the towel across her body, tattoo exposed for all to see.

'Yes, but don't ever ask me about that again.'

'All right,' Josie says. 'I trust you. At least no one is screaming ahead of us now, so it can't be so bad, right?'

'Let's hope it's getting something warm to wear. I'm frozen. I can't feel my feet.' Cilka tries to bring lightness to her tone.

As they approach a room at the end of the corridor, they see piles of grey towels dropped at the entrance. Once again, blank-faced female guards stand nearby. Ahead of them they hear male voices.

'*Ty moya,*' *You are mine*, Cilka hears a guard call to one of the women just ahead of them in the queue. The woman

27

behind her, older, shuffles forward. Cilka and Josie are coming up to their turn.

'Move on, you old hag,' a guard shouts at the woman. Cilka's heart thumps. What is happening?

'Hey, Boris, what are you waiting for?'

'I'll know when I see her.'

The woman in front of Cilka turns back to the younger girls with a look of pity, whispering, 'The bastards are picking who they want to fuck.' She looks Cilka and Josie up and down. 'You'll have no problem.'

'What does she mean, we'll be picked?' Josie asks.

Cilka shakes her head in disbelief. Can this be happening again?

She turns to Josie, looks her in the eyes. 'Listen to me, Josie. If one of the men chooses you, go with him.'

'Why? What does he want?'

'He wants your body.'

She hopes she will be able to explain to Josie later that he can have her body and that is all; he cannot have her mind, her heart, her soul.

'No, no, I've never been with a boy. Cilka, please don't make me. I'd rather die.'

'No, you wouldn't. You have to live. We have to live. Do you hear me? Do you understand?'

'No, I don't understand. I didn't do anything, I shouldn't be here.'

'I'm sure most of us shouldn't be here, but we are. If you get chosen to be the property of just one man, the others will leave you alone. Now do you understand me?'

Josie's face is tight, puzzled. 'I-I think so. Oh, Cilka, this has happened to you before, hasn't it?'

'Lift your head up, don't look afraid.'

'A moment ago you told me to be invisible.'

'That was then, this is now; that's how quickly things can change.'

Cilka raises her own eyes towards the men.

Birkenau Administration Block, 1942

Cilka is sitting beside Gita, each working diligently, their eyes meeting fleetingly, small smiles shared. Cilka was pulled out of the selection line, and chosen for this work, rather than the Kanada. And she is grateful Gita is now working here, too. But she hopes she can also get Magda into the warmth, somehow. Gita's hair is still cropped close to her head but for some reason Cilka has been allowed to grow hers. It feathers down over her neck and ears.

She doesn't see the two SS officers approach them and with no warning she is grabbed by the arm, jerked to her feet. As she is dragged away, she looks back at Gita, her eyes pleading. Every time they are separated it could be the last time they see each other. She sees an officer approach Gita and strike her across the head with her hand.

She tries to resist as she is dragged outside and across to the women's camp. She is no match for the two men. It is quiet in the camp – the women all out at work. They walk

29

past the barracks where the women live until they come to an identical building, but this one is surrounded by a brick wall. Cilka feels bile rise in her throat. She has heard that this is where women go to die.

'No . . . Please . . .' she says. 'What's happening?'

There is a shiny car parked on the dirt road outside. The officers open the gate and go into the courtyard. One of the officers knocks loudly on the door to the left-hand building, and as the door opens they throw her inside, slamming it behind her. Cilka is sprawled on a rough dirt floor and standing in front of her, in front of rows of empty crude wooden bunks, is the man she recognises from the selection, the senior officer, Schwarzhuber.

He is an imposing man and is rarely seen in the camp. He taps his tall leather boot with his swagger stick. From an expressionless face he stares above Cilka's head. She backs up against the door, feeling for the door handle. In a flash, the swagger stick is hurled through the air and strikes her hand. She cries out in pain as she slides down to the floor.

Schwarzhuber walks to her and picks up his stick. He stands over her, dwarfing her. He breathes heavily as he glares at her.

'This will be your new home,' he says. 'Stand up.'

She gets to her feet.

'Follow me.'

He takes her behind a wall where there is a small room and an individual wooden-slatted bed with a mattress on it.

'You know each block has a block leader?' he says.

'Yes,' she says.

'Well, you are to be the leader of block twenty-five.'

Cilka has no words, no breath. How could she – how could anybody – *be expected to be the leader of this block? This is the block where women spend their final hours before being sent to the gas chamber. And will she ever see Magda, see Gita again? This is the most terrifying moment of her life.*

'You are very lucky,' Schwarzhuber says.

Taking off his hat, he throws it across the room. With his other hand he continues to hit his leg firmly with his stick. With every whack Cilka flinches, expecting to be struck. He uses the stick to push up her shirt. Oh, Cilka thinks. So this is why. With shaking hands, she undoes the top two buttons. He then places his stick under her chin. His eyes seem to see nothing. He is a man whose soul has died and whose body is waiting to catch up with it.

He holds out both his arms and Cilka interprets this gesture as 'undress me'. Taking a step closer, still at arm's length, she begins undoing the many buttons on his jacket. A whack across her back hurries her up. He is forced to drop his stick so she can slide his jacket off. Taking it from her, he throws it after his hat. He removes his own singlet. Slowly, Cilka begins undoing his belt and the buttons beneath it. Kneeling down, she pulls his boots off from over his breeches.

Pulling the second one off, she becomes unbalanced, falling heavily on the bed as he pushes her. He straddles her. Terrified, Cilka attempts to cover herself as he tears her

shirt open. She feels the back of his hand across her face as
she closes her eyes and gives in to the inevitable.

* * *

'They're the trusties,' a guard with a cigarette clenched between her teeth whispers.

The voice brings Cilka back to the present.

'What?'

'The men you're about to be paraded in front of. They're the trusties, senior prisoners who have high positions in the camp.'

'Oh, not soldiers?'

'No, prisoners like you, who have been here a long time and work in the skilled jobs, with the administrators. But these ones are also of the criminal class. They have their own network of power.'

Cilka understands. A hierarchy between old and new.

She steps into the room, Josie behind her, both of them naked and shivering. She pauses to take in the rows of men she must walk between. Dozens of eyes look back at her.

The man first in line on her right takes a step forward and she turns to meet his stare, boldly sizing him up, making the judgement he would have been the leader of a gang wherever he came from. Not much taller than her, stocky, clearly not starving. She thinks he must not be much older than in his late twenties, early thirties. She examines his face, looking beyond the body language he is throwing her way. His face betrays him. Sad eyes. For some reason she is not afraid of him.

'At last,' is shouted out somewhere amongst the men.

'About bloody time, Boris.'

Boris puts his hand out to Cilka. She doesn't take it but moves closer to him. Turning back, she encourages Josie to walk on.

'Come here, little one,' another man says. Cilka looks at the man ogling Josie. A large brute, but hunched. His tongue darts in and out of his mouth, revealing badly coloured and broken teeth. He has more of a feral energy than Boris.

And Josie is chosen.

Cilka looks at the man identified as Boris.

'What is your name?' he asks.

'Cilka.'

'Go and get some clothes and I'll find you when I need you.'

Cilka continues down the row of men. They all smile at her, with several making comments about her skin, her body. She catches up with Josie and they find themselves outside again, being ushered into another concrete bunker.

At last, clothing is thrust at them. A shirt with missing buttons, trousers in the roughest fabric Cilka has ever felt, a heavy coat and a hat. All grey. The knee-high boots several sizes too big will come in handy, once she's wrapped her feet in whatever rags she can get to help with the cold.

Dressed, they leave the bunker. Cilka shades her eyes from the glare of sunlight. She takes in the camp resembling a town. There are clearly barracks for sleeping, but they are not neatly lined up like those in Birkenau. They differ in size and shape. Beyond the perimeter she sees a small hill with a large, crane-like piece of equipment rearing above it. The fence enclosing them is scattered with lookouts, nowhere near as threatening as she has experienced in the past. Cilka looks closely at the top of the fence. She does not see the tell-tale insulators that would indicate it is electrified. Looking beyond the fence to the barren, desolate terrain stretching as far as the horizon, she accepts no electric fence would be needed. There could be no survival out there.

As they trudge towards the buildings that will become home, following the person in front, unaware who is leading them or directing them, a woman with a broad, weathered face sidles up to them. The sun might be attempting to shine but the wind chill bites into any exposed skin – they are so far north that even though it is late summer there is snow on the ground. The woman is wearing layers of coats, strong-looking boots, and has her hat pulled down and tied beneath her chin. She leers at Cilka and Josie.

'Well, aren't you the lucky ones! Got yourselves men to protect you, I hear.'

Cilka puts her head down, not wanting to engage in or encourage conversation with her. She doesn't see the leg extended in front of her, tripping her, so that with her hands in her pockets she falls flat on her face.

Josie reaches down to help her up, only to be hit in the back and sent sprawling herself. The two girls lie on the damp, frosty ground, side by side.

34

'Your looks won't get you anywhere with me. Now get moving.'

Cilka pulls herself up first. Josie stays lying on the ground, eventually taking Cilka's hand as she is helped to her feet.

Cilka risks looking around. Amongst the hundreds of women, dressed the same, heads shaven, faces buried in coats, it is impossible to identify the others from their train carriage.

As they enter a hut, they are counted off by the gruff woman. Cilka had thought maybe she was a guard, but she's not in uniform and as she walks past her Cilka notices the number sewn on her coat and hat. Must be like a block leader, Cilka thinks.

The room has single beds lining one side, a space in the middle with a stove throwing out a version of heat. The women ahead of them have run to the stove and push and shove, hands extended towards it.

'I'm your brigadier, and you belong to me,' the leader says. 'My name is Antonina Karpovna. An – to – ni – na – Kar – pov – na,' she repeats slowly, pointing at herself, so no one can misinterpret her meaning. 'All right, you lucky *zechkas*, I hope you realise you have one of the best prisoner huts in the camp.' Cilka thinks she must be right. No bunks. Actual mattresses. A blanket each. 'I'll leave you to sort yourselves out,' the brigadier says with a wry grin, before departing the hut.

'What's a *zechka*?' Josie whispers.

'I don't know, but it can't be a good word.' Cilka

shrugs. 'Probably means prisoner or something like that.'

Cilka looks around her. None of the beds have been claimed; the women ahead of them ran straight to the stove. Grabbing Josie's arm, Cilka pulls her away to the far end of the hut.

'Wait, let's find beds first. Sit on this one.'

Cilka claims the end bed, pushing Josie onto the one next to it.

They both examine what they are sitting on. A thin grey blanket over an off-white sheet covering a sawdust-filled mattress.

Their rush to find somewhere to sleep doesn't go unnoticed by the other women who now also scramble for beds, pushing and shoving each other as they too claim the place they will sleep tonight and for however many more nights they survive.

It becomes obvious there is a bed for everyone. Hats are taken off and placed where a pillow would be, had one been provided.

Cilka glances to the space across from the end of their beds.

Two empty buckets look back at her. Toilets. She sighs. For as long as she remains in this hut, she will be reminded of her greed to secure what she considered the best place to sleep. She thought she would have a little privacy: a wall on one side of her, Josie on the other. There's always a catch to a good position, to comfort. She should know that by now.

Having established their place, Cilka nudges Josie and they move towards the stove, hands outstretched. Cilka senses she has made some enemies already, on day one.

Josie is shoved in the back by a large, tough-looking woman, her age indeterminate. She sprawls forward, smashing her face on the hard, wooden floor. Blood seeps from her nose.

Cilka helps Josie to her feet, pulling the girl's shirt up to her face, covering her nose, staunching the blood.

'What did you do that for?' a voice asks.

'Watch it, bitch, or you'll get the same,' the bully says, getting in the other girl's face.

The other women observe the exchange.

Cilka wants to react, to defend Josie, but she still needs to know more about how the place works, and who these women are, whether there's a possibility of them all getting along.

'It's all right,' Josie splutters to the girl who defended her, a young, slight woman with fair skin and blue eyes. 'Thank you.'

'Are you all right?' the girl asks in Russian-accented Polish. She keeps touching her own shaved head.

'She will be,' Cilka answers.

The girl examines Josie's face with concern.

'I'm Natalya.'

Josie and Cilka introduce themselves.

'You are Russian?' Josie asks.

'Yes, but my family was living in Poland. For many

decades. Only now they decide that is criminal.' She lowers her head for a moment. 'And you?'

Josie's face crumples. 'They wanted to know where my brothers were. And they wouldn't believe me when I told them I didn't know.'

Cilka makes soothing sounds to Josie.

'I'm sorry,' Natalya says. 'Perhaps let's not talk about it now.'

'Or ever,' the bully says from her bed, turned away from the rest of them. 'It's all just variations on the same sob story. Whether we did something or not, we have been branded enemies of the state and we are here to be corrected through labour.'

She stays facing away from them. Sighs.

The fire crackles in the stove.

'Now what?' someone asks.

No one is prepared to suggest an answer. Some of the women wander back to their chosen beds and curl up, going deep into their own silent thoughts.

Cilka takes Josie by the arm and leads her to her bed. Pulling the blanket back she urges the girl to take off her shoes and lie down. Her nose has stopped bleeding. Cilka goes back to the stove. Natalya is carefully placing more coal from a nearby bucket into the red-hot cavity, using the end of her coat to open and close the door.

Cilka looks at the coal pile. 'There's not enough to get us through the night,' she says, as much to herself as to Natalya.

'I'll ask for more,' Natalya says in a softly spoken whisper. She is rosy-cheeked and delicate-limbed, but looks strong. Cilka can see in her eyes she thinks everything is going to work out. Cilka knows how quickly that feeling can be taken away.

'We could perhaps just watch and see what they do. Ask for nothing and you lessen the risk of a beating.'

'Surely they won't let us freeze,' Natalya says, hands on hips. The whisper is gone. Several other women push themselves up onto an elbow in the beds where they lie, listening to the conversation.

Cilka takes a moment to look around at all the faces now turned to her. She can't accurately tell all the women's ages but thinks she and Josie are amongst the youngest. She remembers her own words spoken only a matter of hours ago. Don't stand out, be invisible.

'Well?' is thrown at her from the bully at the front of the hut.

All eyes are on her.

'I don't know anything more than you. I'm just guessing. But I think we should go easy on what coal we have left in case we don't get any more today.'

'Makes sense,' says another woman, who lies back down and turns her head away.

Cilka slowly walks back to the end of the hut to her bed. The small drop in temperature from the middle of the room to the end, only a matter of a few metres, has Cilka rethinking the decision she made in placing perceived privacy over warmth. She checks Josie, who appears to be asleep, before lying down.

The sunlight goes on and on. Cilka has no idea what

time it is. She watches as Natalya approaches the fire, which is cooling, throwing a small amount of coal into the stove. Funny how people naturally fall into roles.

She falls asleep at some point, while it is still light, or light again . . . she's not sure.

Cilka is startled awake by the loud clanging outside. The door to the hut opens and the brigadier, Antonina Karpovna, is back.

'Up and get out, *zechkas*.' She gestures with her head, her hands staying firmly entrenched in the pockets of her coat.

Cilka knows the drill. She is the first to stand but doesn't move, hoping those at the front of the hut will leave first. She knows that standing somewhere in the middle is the safest place to be. She helps a drugged-looking Josie to her feet and pulls the blankets up on their beds.

Pushing her way forward, she guides Josie along with her and out of the building.

They see others like them exiting the huts all around.

Where were they when we arrived? The women from Cilka's hut huddle together outside in a ramshackle manner until they observe orderly rows of women walking around them. Copying, they form into two rows of ten.

With the hut empty, they follow the lead of the others slushing through thick mud towards a larger building. The rough fabric of her new clothes is chafing Cilka's skin. Mosquitoes bite at her exposed neck.

She notices the stares, both sorrowful and threatening. She understands. Another hut filled with inmates, more mouths to feed, more people to fight with for the better jobs. It is the newest arrivals who will have the hardest time adjusting and finding their place in the pecking order, until they are no longer the newest arrivals. She had been a long-timer in that *other place* – her and the other surviving Slovakian girls. They had seen it all. They had stayed alive. She wonders if she can find a way to advance her status, and Josie's, without standing out. Or maybe she is here because of thoughts like that. Maybe hard labour is what she deserves.

They enter the mess building, observing the established tradition of lining up, accepting what is given to you, finding a bench to sit on. *Eyes down, don't stand out.*

A tin mug is thrust into her hand. She checks on Josie. Her nose is swollen, bruising beginning to appear. Shuffling along, something resembling soup, full of little white unidentifiable bits, is slopped into the mug, a chunk of stale bread thrust at her. Josie's hands shake and she spills half her food in her attempt to grab it. Soup and bread lie on the floor. Slowly Josie bends down and picks up the bread. Cilka has a horrible urge to yell at her. How much these small portions are worth!

There are not enough tables and benches for all to sit. Many women stand around the walls looking, waiting for someone to finish and vacate their seat. Several eat while they stand, too hungry to care about table manners.

One of the women from Cilka's hut sees a space being vacated and hurries to reach it. She is met with a back-hand from the person sitting next to the vacated spot, sending her mug flying, its contents splattering over both the floor and nearby diners.

'Wait your turn, *novichok*! You haven't earned the right to sit with us.'

The pecking order is on display for the newcomers to observe and learn. Just like in Birkenau, with the swarms of new arrivals. She and Gita and the other Slovakian girls had dwindled from thousands, having lost all of their friends and families. And the new ones didn't understand, couldn't understand what their bodies and minds had been through, what they had done in order to survive.

'Eat your soup, then have your bread or save it for later,' Cilka says to Josie. 'Sometimes it is better to save it, just like we did on the train, until we know how often and how much we are going to be fed.'

She can see from looking at some of the women's sunken faces that it won't be frequent or nutritious.

The two girls slowly sip the brown liquid. At least it is hot. There is no real substance to it. Josie notices others sitting at the table with spoons, scooping out what look like bits of potato or possibly fish.

'They didn't give us a spoon.'

'I think that might be something we have to obtain for ourselves,' says Cilka, seeing the beat-up-looking utensils some of the old-timers are using, 'when and however we can.'

Soon, Cilka and the other newcomers are gathered by their brigadier. Antonina Karpovna corrals the women together and leads them back to their hut.

As the last woman enters the room, Antonina watches them wander either to their bed or to the stove in order to be comfortable.

'In future, when I enter the room you will immediately go and stand at the end of your bed. Do I make myself clear?'

Women jump from their bed or scurry to it, and all stand to attention at the foot.

'You will also turn and face me. I will give instructions once only and I want to look into your eyes and know you have all understood. Who understands what I am saying?'

Several hands meekly rise, including Cilka's. The rest had seemingly just followed what the other women were doing.

'Then those who understand better teach the rest, quickly.'

She pauses to watch the women look to the person standing next to them and a few of them pass on what had been said, mostly in other Slavic languages.

'These are the rules you will live by while you are here. We have already determined when and how you will work, receive food and how long you will sleep. Lights will go out at 9 p.m., though in summer you won't really notice . . . Between now and then is when you will clean the floor in here, restock the coal for the next day, shovel any snow away from the front of the building, do any mending of your clothes, whatever is required for you to live here. I will not stand for this place looking like a pigsty – I want to be able to eat off the floor. Do you hear me? You will hear the wake-up call, you won't be able to sleep through it. Two of you will empty the toilet buckets, I don't care who does it, just make sure it is done. No one will eat until it is.'

Not a word is spoken, but all heads nod.

'If you fail to do any of this, but especially if you fail to do your share of work – letting down *my* brigade – you will be thrown in the hole.' She sniffs. 'The hole is a solitary confinement cell in the *lagpunkt*. It is a dank, mouldy place where your body is forced into a crooked shape whether you stand, sit or lie down. There is no stove, and through a barred open window the snow will come in on you from outside. You'll be lucky to get a bucket for your waste, as there's a ready-made stinking hole in the floor. You will receive barely a third of your normal ration – and a black, hard piece of bread at that. Do you understand?'

The heads nod again. A shiver runs down Cilka's spine.

From a bag draped over her shoulder Antonina produces strips of rag, and a crumpled piece of paper from her pocket.

'When I call your name come and get your number. You have two: one you must put on your hat, the other on whatever outer garment you wear. You must never be seen outside without your number visible on at least one garment.'

As names are called out the women respond and take the two rags handed to them, examining the number roughly written in paint.

Another number. Cilka subconsciously rubs her left arm; hidden under her clothing is her identity from that *other place*. How many times can one person be reduced, erased? When her name is called, she takes the fabric handed to her and examines her new identity. **1-B494.** Josie shows Cilka hers. **1-B490.**

'Sew the numbers on, and do it tonight, all of you. I want to see them all in the morning.' She pauses, lets the translations come through, looks at the confused stares. 'I expect to see some interesting needlework, it will tell me a lot about you,' she sneers.

A brave voice pipes up, 'What do we use for needle and thread?'

From her bag the brigadier produces a small piece of fabric with two needles punched through. They look like they've been fashioned from wire and sharpened to a point. She hands them to the nearest woman.

'So, get to it. I'll be back in the morning. Tomorrow, you work. Six o'clock wake up.'

'Excuse me,' says Natalya, 'where do we get coal from?'

'Work it out for yourselves.'

As the door shuts behind her the women gather around the stove. Cilka is relieved no one received a beating for their questions.

Josie offers, 'If we go outside, we might see the others getting their coal; then we will know where to go.'

'Knock yourselves out,' says the bully, Elena, lying back on her bed. 'This could be our last day off.'

'I'll come with you,' says Cilka.

45

'Me too,' says Natalya. 'The rest of you start sewing.'

'Yes, master,' says Elena coldly.

Josie has placed the remaining few pieces of coal beside the stove and picks up the empty bucket.

The three of them cautiously leave the hut, looking around. Darkness is closing in, and searchlights light the yard. It is cold. They can see prisoners darting here and there between buildings, and a group of young women walking quickly towards the hut near them, carrying buckets brimming with coal.

'This way,' says Cilka.

Natalya steps in front of the women. 'Can you tell us where the coal is, please?'

'Find it yourself,' is the reply.

Natalya rolls her eyes.

'They came from here,' Josie says, pointing to a building. 'From behind there somewhere, let's go and look.'

They arrive back in the hut after taking turns carrying the heavy bucket. Natalya goes to place it on the floor. Her soft hands slip from the handle, the coal spilling on the floor. She looks at the other women, apologising.

'It's all right, I'll sweep up,' volunteers Josie.

Two women are quickly sewing their numbers to their hat and coat.

'Where did you get the thread from?' Natalya asks before Cilka gets the chance.

'From our sheets,' says the older woman, speaking a halting Slavic, close to Slovak, and repeating it in Russian. Possibly the oldest in the hut, a lifetime of hard work and

46

making do evident in her abrupt words. She tells them her name is Olga.

Cilka looks around and sees other women carefully stripping away thread from the end of their sheets.

'Hurry up. What are you doing taking so long with the needle, Olga?' Elena asks, looming over the older woman.

'I'm trying to do a good job. If you do it properly the first time you won't have to do it again.'

'Give me the needle now, you stupid bitch. There's a time and place to show off your embroidery skills and it's not here.'

Elena reaches her hand out impatiently.

'I'm nearly there,' Olga says calmly. Cilka admires the way she's dealing with the hot-tempered Elena, but she also understands the urge to lash out when all is not going as planned. This must be Elena's first camp. Olga increases her sewing speed, snapping off the end of the thread with her teeth before handing the needle over. 'Here you go, *Tuk krava*.'

Cilka suppresses a grin. Olga has just called Elena a fat cow in Slovak in an endearing voice. She winks at Cilka.

'My father was Slovakian,' she says.

Elena scowls, snatching the needle.

Cilka sits on her bed, looking at Josie, who forlornly fiddles with her number patches. She seems to go from capable to overwhelmed in a matter of moments.

'Hand it over,' she says.

Josie looks pained.

'One day at a time,' Cilka says. 'All right?'

Josie nods.

Cilka starts stripping threads from her sheet. When a needle is handed to her, she quickly sews the numbers on Josie's and her own garments.

Each time she stabs the needle through the fabric she feels the pain of a needle stabbing into her left arm. Another number. Another place. She grimaces.

To have lost everything. To have had to endure what she has endured, and be punished for it. Suddenly the needle feels as heavy as a brick. How can she go on? How can she work for a new enemy? Live to see the women around her tire, starve, diminish, die. But she – she *will* live. She does not know why she has always been sure of that, why she feels she can persist – keep picking up this needle even though it's as heavy as a brick, keep sewing, keep doing what she has to do – but she can. She starts to feel angry, furious. And the needle feels light again. Light and quick. It is this fire, then, that keeps her going. But it is also a curse. It makes her stand out, be singled out. She must contain it, control it, direct it.

To survive.

CHAPTER 4

The fearsome clanging of a hammer on metal wakes the newest arrivals at Vorkuta Gulag at 6 a.m. Antonina was right – it is an unmissable wake-up call. The women have taken turns putting coal in the stove throughout the night, just enough to keep it burning. Though the sun still shines through most of the night, there had been frost on the ground when they walked back after their meagre evening meal in the mess. They had all slept in the clothes they had been given the previous day.

The door opens, sending in a blast of cold air. Antonina Karpovna holds the door open, watching the women run to the foot of their beds, their eyes turned to her. She nods approval.

She walks up the hut inspecting the newly sewn numbers on the women's coats. Pausing at Elena, she barks, 'Do it again tonight. That's the worst needlework I've ever seen.'

When she is back at the door, she turns to the two nearest girls. 'Grab the buckets and I'll show you where to empty them. Tomorrow, one of you take another *zechka* and show her where to go and so on, you follow?'

The two girls scamper to the toilet buckets at the rear of the hut, directly opposite Cilka's bed.

While Antonina and the two girls with the buckets disappear, the rest of the women stay standing, no one prepared to move. When the girls return, ashen-faced, Antonina tells them all to head to the mess for breakfast and be back by 7 a.m. for rollcall.

Outside, the two girls who emptied the toilet buckets bend down and rub their hands across the frost in an attempt to wash the stench and urine away.

If this is the end of summer, Cilka thinks, as she walks with Josie over to the mess hut, and there is already light snow on the ground and air like ice, then none of them will be prepared for what is to come. Working outdoors will be unbearable.

Breakfast is a thick, tasteless gruel. Josie remembers to place her precious piece of bread up her sleeve. Like the day before, there are no vacancies at any of the tables. This time, the newcomers know what to do, and lean against the walls.

It is obvious the gruel cannot be drunk. The women look around. There are others using two fingers for a spoon. That will have to do for now.

*　*　*

Rollcall. This is very familiar to Cilka. She only hopes with the twenty of them it will go quickly. That no one has gone missing in the night. She remembers a night standing out in the cold – all night – until an inmate was found. The ache in her knees, her ankle bones. And that was not even the worst night in the *other place*. Not even close. Antonina Karpovna starts calling out names. Names. I'm not a number. And yet I have a number. Cilka looks at her covered-up left arm and the number now emblazoned on her brown, scratchy coat. I have a name. She answers loudly, 'Yes,' when it is called. They are told to get into four rows of five.

Groups of women file past them, each headed by a brigadier. Groups of men are also coming from the other side of the camp. Cilka and her hut fall in with them as they march to the gates that lead out of the compound. From what Cilka observed on arrival, there was only one way in and one way out. A simple barbed wire fence defines the boundary. Groups of men and women swarm forward.

They slow down, coming to a halt as they near the exit and see for the first time the ritual of going to work each day. As Antonina's turn comes, Cilka observes her approaching a guard or administrator and showing him the list of names. Antonina then beckons for the first row of women to approach. The guard walks along the row, counting out five, roughly patting them down in a search,

51

and then pushing them onward, before doing the same with the next three rows. He nods to Antonina, who goes along with the women, telling them to keep walking behind the others. They follow a train line, occasionally tripping over the rails, thinking it will be easier to walk on them than pull their feet through the sucking mud that drains them of energy they know they will need for work.

Guards walk up and down the rows of men and women trudging to the large mine that looms ahead of them. It looks like a black mountain with an opening that disappears into hell. Piles of coal tower beside small ramshackle buildings. At the top of the mouth of the mine they can see the wheel that is drawing coal up from the depths below. Open train carts line the track as the women get closer.

As they reach the mine, those in front peel off, going to jobs and areas they are already familiar with. Antonina hands the new arrivals over to a guard before following some of the women from the other huts, who are also part of her brigade.

Walking amongst the women, the guard pushes several to one side, separating them out.

'Hey, Alexei,' he calls out, 'come and get this lot. They look like they can swing a pick.'

Another guard comes over and indicates that the fifteen women should follow him. Cilka, Josie and Natalya remain behind. The guard looks at them.

'Couldn't swing a bloody pick with all of ya hanging on to it. Follow me.'

They walk over to one of the mountains of coal, arriving just as the crane dumps a load on the top. They are showered in dust and small chunks of the hard, sharp coal.

'Grab a bucket each and start loading. When it's full, take it over to one of the carts and dump it in,' he says, indicating the carts sitting on the train rails. Others are already at work, and again it seems a matter of following their lead.

The women pick up a bucket each and start filling them with pieces of coal.

'You better go faster or you'll find yourselves in trouble,' a woman says. 'Watch me.'

The woman takes her empty bucket and uses it as a scoop, half filling it. Steadying it on the ground, she uses her cupped hands to fill it to the top. The women attempt to copy her with varying degrees of success. They all fill their buckets before attempting to pick them up. None of them can; they are too heavy.

'Empty some out and just put in as much as you can carry. You'll toughen up the longer you do it,' they are advised.

Cilka and Josie can only manage half-filled buckets, which doesn't go unnoticed by the guard standing at the cart. It was one thing to carry them, another trial to lift and empty them.

The guard monitoring them looks at the half-empty buckets.

'You lot don't get a break. You have to make up for being such weak bitches, and get moving.'

At various points, Cilka sees Antonina writing in a little book, conferring with the guards, answering for her brigade's productivity.

* * *

The work is so gruelling that Cilka, Josie and Natalya are beginning to groan and huff out loud. They watch enviously when the others get ten minutes to down tools and take a break. There is a burning sensation across Cilka's shoulders, neck and back. When the next clanging bell sounds several hours later, buckets, picks and other tools are dropped where they are. Men and women trudge over to the train tracks, sorting themselves out as they find the others from their brigade – those they share a hut with and those from the surrounding huts. They stand, waiting to be led by their brigadiers, waiting for the signal to walk.

Once they are allowed, they silently trudge back down the track, stopping again outside the compound gates. Antonina Karpovna hands her piece of paper to the administrative guard, who counts the women in. They follow Antonina back to their hut, shuffling and sore, where a few embers glow without giving off any heat. Natalya throws some coal into the stove to reignite it. Cilka is amazed she can find the strength to even look at the coal, let alone lift a scuttle of it. They all fall onto their beds, pulling blankets up over their heads. No one speaks.

What passes for their dinner does nothing to restore

their energy. Returning to their hut, many retreat back to bed, but some hover around the stove.

'What are you looking at?'

Cilka, lying on her bed, recognises the voice. Elena.

'Not your ugly face,' she hears Natalya reply.

Cilka pushes up on one elbow to see where the exchange of words will go.

'I'll take you out, bitch, if you don't keep out of my face.'

'Leave me alone, you bully. Leave all of us alone,' a defiant Natalya snaps back, standing up from her bed

'Natalya, sit down. She's not worth it,' Olga says.

Elena gives out a hiss.

Exhaustion has flattened Cilka. She understands the anger, the lashing out. When the rage can't be targeted at your captors, for fear of death, it finds other ways out. She wonders how old Elena is, what has happened to her. Maybe it is that nothing has happened to her before. Like Cilka, before that *other place*. She'd had all the love, food, clothing, comfort she could possibly need. When it is all taken away overnight . . . Well, no one knows how they will react.

She must stop herself from thinking back. Tomorrow . . . Tomorrow will be a repeat of today, and the next day, and the next week, and for Cilka the next fifteen years.

Despair overwhelms her.

Auschwitz-Birkenau, 1943

Wrapped in a warm, full-length coat, Cilka stands in the snow outside Block 25. As she had feared, her block contains women who are spending their last days on earth, often too sick to move, the life already gone from their eyes. This is Cilka's world now, and she exists within it in order to stay alive. Similarly dressed kapos approach her with women and girls trailing behind – emaciated, wraith-like figures, many holding each other up. Each kapo tells the women they have escorted that Cilka is their block leader, they are to do as she says. They are instructed to wait outside in the cold for the SS officer who will do the roll call.

Cilka feels as inanimate as the snow. Her eyes blur over the bony, bowed bodies, but her feelings have been taken away. It started when Schwarzhuber placed her in that tiny room at the front of Block 25 and began his regular visits. She found she could become just a series of limbs, just bone, muscle and skin. She didn't choose it. It just happened. She thinks it might be a bit like when she was a child and badly scraped her knee – though she saw the blood it took a long time to register the hurt.

Cilka stands there, saying nothing as she waits to be told that all the women coming into Block 25 that evening are present. Tomorrow, or maybe the next day if the Nazis decide they have something better to do, they will all be taken to the gas chamber that looks like a little white house. And they will be killed.

A senior SS officer approaches, along with the last group

of ten women. His swagger stick strikes out, randomly hitting unsuspecting women. Something breaks through Cilka's glazed state and she hurries over to meet them.

'Hurry up, you lazy good-for-nothing bitches!' she calls out. 'I've got them,' she says to the SS officer, stepping in front of him as he is about to bring his stick down on the head of a nearby girl. Cilka gives her a hard shove, sending her sprawling face first into the snow.

'Get up and join the others,' she screams at the girl.

The SS officer watches, nods to Cilka and walks away. He doesn't see Cilka bend down and hoist her arm under the girl's armpit, helping her to her feet.

'Quickly, join the others,' she says more gently.

Cilka sees the SS officer turn back, and screams out at the women.

'Get inside now! I'm staying out here freezing because you're too slow and lazy to move. Go, go!' she calls.

Turning to the SS officer, she gives him a big smile.

She follows the women inside, shutting the door behind her.

The women have found places to sit or lie down, though there is barely room. Sometimes they spill over into the courtyard, stacked like animals. Gaunt faces stare at Cilka – looks of terror and helplessness. She longs to explain that if she screams at them the SS won't come in.

The words won't come.

She is sixteen. Possibly the youngest person in the room at that moment. And she will live longer than them all.

She sees one woman with sick crusted across her cheek.

Whatever feeling she let in a moment ago closes back over. She is as flat and blank as the snow, as the walls. As the women's noises rise – the wailing and crying and the beating of palms on walls, the praying and calling the names of the loved and lost, Cilka turns and goes to the front of the block, into her room, and lies down.

* * *

The days have been long and achingly difficult. Cilka is having to draw on reserves of physical strength she never knew she had. Cilka and Josie have been trialling different methods for how they parcel out their bread ration across the day for best energy efficiency. At night the women often talk about food. When they broach topics of family, home, they stay close to this – of meals shared. Sauerkraut and mushrooms, cottage cheese, sausages, pierogi, fresh fruit. Cilka has to reach back years into her memory to join in, and she has to fight a feeling of envy that comes from knowing these memories are much closer for the women around her.

It doesn't seem that any of them are ready to go into great detail about their arrests, about recent events, about where their families are now. Or perhaps they haven't worked out whether they can really trust one another. Though they do wonder aloud about the missing. Margarethe, in particular, a young Russian woman with a round face and dimples, who Cilka instinctively likes, cannot stop worrying about her husband. Josie thinks of her brothers; and Olga, though she knows where her children are, worries she will not hear from them, will not know whether they are all right. Cilka thinks about everyone she has lost, but she cannot even begin to express it.

One night, Olga says to Cilka, 'Klein . . . that's quite common as a Jewish surname, isn't it?'

Cilka nods. 'I suppose it is.' She stands. 'I'll go and get the coal.'

* * *

As the women return from work one week into their stay, Elena announces that Natalya is to empty the shit buckets tomorrow, for the second day in a row. The first heavy snow has begun, and as Elena says this, she snuggles down tighter into her coat.

'I'll do it,' Josie says. 'It's been a while since my turn.'

'I'm in charge here,' Elena says, standing. 'I'll say who does what.'

'No, you're not,' Josie fights back. 'No one put you in charge. We'll share the work.'

Cilka is surprised when Elena doesn't continue the exchange. She simply narrows her eyes and sits back down, huddled in the coat.

The women stand around the stove, letting the heat ease their aching muscles, waiting for the clanging on metal to indicate that it's time to go to the mess for dinner.

From behind, Josie is violently shoved in the back.

She reacts by raising her hand, reaching for something to brace herself against, and it lands on the stove flue. Her scream echoes off the walls.

Josie holds her arm out, like it's something she wants to shake off. A thousand thoughts run through Cilka's head, images of sick and injured women and what happens to them. No, not Josie. Cilka grabs her, propelling her out of the building, burying her burnt hand in the snow that now covers patches of the ground outside. Josie hisses through her teeth and starts crying audibly.

'Shush now,' Cilka says, a little harsher than intended.

After a few minutes, she pulls the hand from the snow and examines the damage. The palm and all four fingers on Josie's right hand are an angry red, her thumb the only untouched part.

Cilka pushes the hand back into the snow and turns Josie's face towards her. It is starkly pale, as white as the ground.

'Stay here, I'll be right back.'

Cilka storms back inside, pausing, staring at the women gathered around the stove.

A plaintive, 'How is she?' goes unanswered.

'Who did this? Who pushed her?' Cilka had only seen the quick movement of Josie ejected from the huddle, falling. She has her suspicions though.

Most of the women look away, but Cilka notices Natalya glance towards the culprit.

Cilka walks up to Elena sitting snug on her bed.

Elena snarls at Cilka, 'I could break you in two.'

Cilka understands the difference between an empty threat – a display of power borne of helplessness – and a true intention to harm others.

60

'Plenty of people scarier than you have tried to break me,' Cilka says.

'And I've fought men ten times your size,' Elena says.

The women around them move away, giving them space, certain a fight is about to start.

'Get up,' Cilka demands.

Elena continues staring defiantly. A fire is flaring inside Cilka.

'I will ask you one more time. Get up.'

The two women face off for several moments before Elena slowly stands up, pouting her lip a little, like a child.

'Elena, I am going to take your blanket off, hope the sheet underneath is not riddled with lice, and tear the end off. You will not try to stop me. Do you understand?'

Elena huffs, but nods slowly. The other women have closed the space again, standing behind Cilka now that the dynamic has revealed itself to be in her favour.

With one eye on Elena, Cilka pulls the blanket free. She takes the bottom of the sheet and brings it to her mouth and tears at it with her teeth until she has made a small rip. Using her hands, she pulls a strip free.

'Thank you, Elena. You can remake your bed.'

Cilka turns to the doorway.

Antonina Karpovna is standing there, her arm against the door frame barring Cilka from leaving.

'Am I going to have trouble with you?' she asks.

'*Nyet.*' Cilka answers her in Russian.

Antonina removes her arm. Cilka walks back outside, where Josie sits in the snow as the sun goes down, her body rocking from the cold and pain. Cilka wipes the snow from her injured hand before wrapping it in the torn sheet. Helping Josie to her feet, her arm around her, she steers her back inside. It feels strange to be so close to someone. The last person she had voluntarily touched like this had been Gita. Those gathered around the stove move aside to let them get as close as they can to the warmth.

The dinner alarm sounds. Josie refuses to leave her bed. Cilka feels a beat of frustration, anger, at her helplessness. She almost leaves her there. Then she thinks of how much worse it will be if Josie doesn't eat, loses strength.

'Josie, come on,' she says, and helps her up.

In the mess, Cilka hands Josie her mug of soup. She takes it in her left hand. When a chunk of stale bread is thrust at her Josie can't accept it. It falls onto the floor.

A mess guard watches, waiting to see what Cilka, next in line, will do. If she helps, she can probably expect to be punished. If she doesn't, Josie's strength will suffer. Josie bends down, holding tight to her mug, looking pleadingly to Cilka to help. With their eyes connected, Cilka places her own piece of bread between her teeth, holding it there – a silent instruction. Josie carefully puts her mug on the floor, picks up the piece of bread, and grips it between her teeth before picking up her mug and moving on.

Once they find a place to stand, away from the guard's stare, Cilka takes the piece of bread from Josie's mouth and helps her tuck it up the sleeve of her coat.

* * *

Back in the hut, the subdued women all ask Josie how her hand is. She bravely tells them it will be all right. Cilka is glad that eating has made her more hopeful.

Sitting on her bed, Cilka watches as the snow turns liquid on the outside of the window, tears running down the glass. She asks Josie to show her her burned hand. Carefully she unwinds the makeshift bandage, the last layer sticking to the blistered skin. Josie shoves her other hand in her mouth to keep from crying out in pain.

'It looks better,' she says, trying to comfort Josie with the words she doesn't believe herself. She knows how important it is to not give up.

Natalya comes over and sits down beside Cilka, looking at the wound.

'I'll ask Antonina tomorrow if there is a hospital or sick bay here. If there is, they will be able to help you and put a proper dressing on it.'

Cilka knows anyone wanting to get out of work won't be looked kindly upon. But if Josie's hand doesn't heal, things will be much worse. She nods.

'Thanks, Natalya,' says Cilka.

They all settle in their beds. The night envelops them, but dawn still arrives early and Cilka wakes with a jolt, heart racing, before the silence and stillness puts her back to sleep.

* * *

Antonina arrives in the morning, looking tired. She word-lessly indicates for them to get moving. Natalya goes to say something about Josie but catches Cilka's shake of the head. As they walk, Cilka whispers, 'Let her have break-fast first, otherwise she might miss out.' She's also very aware of Antonina's mood. She has learned to read the faces of captors, guards, those with power over the rest.

When all names have been checked off at rollcall Natalya looks over to Cilka. Cilka and Josie have had their gruel, and both have bread tucked up into their sleeves. Antonina's face has a little more colour too. Cilka nods to Natalya.

'Excuse me, Antonina Karpovna,' says Natalya. Cilka hears the formal use of first name and patronymic.

The brigadier gives Natalya her full attention.

'As you may know from your visit in the evening, Josie has acquired an injury on her right hand. Is there a sick bay she can go to?'

'How did it happen?' asks Antonina.

Natalya looks reluctant to reveal who is at fault. Despite the nastiness of the act, they don't want to get anybody thrown in the hole – the punishment cell. Starvation, disease, madness could result. Despite Cilka's fury at Elena – particularly at her cowardice; a push in the back – she thinks she deserves another chance.

It seems Josie does too.

'I tripped near the stove,' Josie says, 'and put my hand out to break my fall.'

Antonina beckons Josie over to her, chin raised.

Josie approaches the brigadier, her bandaged hand outstretched.

'How do I know you're not just trying to get out of work?'

Josie understands her. She begins unwrapping the bandage. She can't stop the tears that accompany the pain as she removes the last layer, revealing the raw blistered hand.

Cilka steps forward so she's beside Josie, not wanting to stand out but wanting her to know she is there, to comfort her. Antonina looks at the two of them, sizing them up.

'There's not much to either of you *zechkas*, is there?' She looks at Cilka. 'Take her back inside. I'll be back for you.'

Cilka is startled. Worried. But she does what she's told. They hurry back inside the building, Cilka casting a backward glance at the others as they shuffle off to work. The snow whips up, enveloping them, and they disappear from sight. What has she done now?

Cilka and Josie huddle by the stove, blankets wrapped around their shivering bodies. Cilka desperately hopes they will acclimatise. It's not even winter yet. An icy blast smacks them from their contemplation. Antonina stands in the doorway.

Cilka nudges Josie and they walk quickly to the door and follow Antonina out, Cilka making sure the door is securely closed behind her.

She has often seen Antonina with another brigadier – with whom she shared a hut in the cluster of huts that make up their brigade – so she supposes they must share responsibility for the women. Or perhaps the other woman was an assistant to Antonina. Either way, she must be the one keeping track of the brigade in the field while Antonina takes on this duty.

While the distance to the sick bay and hospital is not far, the blizzard conditions make walking slow and painful as the snow is so deep they are forced to push their legs through it, rather than take steps. Cilka tries to gain an understanding of the size of the complex by the number of huts that resemble theirs. The other, larger buildings that stand a little apart must be administration or stores, but there is nothing to indicate their use. The hospital building Antonina points out to them also has no outward sign of its purpose.

A guard stands outside. Antonina, her eyes barely visible, is forced to remove the scarf wrapped around her face, and shout into his face. Cilka wonders what he can possibly have done to be punished with this duty. It doesn't seem much better than being a prisoner, though he probably has better living quarters and more food. With apparent reluctance, he opens the door and pushes the women unceremoniously inside. Presumably he is under instruction not to let any snow in.

The warmth of the building hits them immediately, and they unwrap their scarves, Josie using her good hand.

'Wait here,' Antonina tells them. They stand just inside the door, taking a first look at the room they have just entered.

It is some kind of waiting room. Prisoners – men and women – sit on the few available chairs, with more on the floor, hunched over, pain etched on their faces. Others are curled up, sleeping, unconscious, dead – it is not obvious which. Several groan quietly, a distressing sound, a too-familiar sound for Cilka. She looks away from them, up at the portrait of Stalin on the wall.

Antonina is at the desk at the front of the room, speaking quietly to the matronly figure seated behind it. With a nod of her head she returns to Cilka and Josie.

'You are number 509 when it is called.' She repeats the numbers slowly in Russian: '*Pyat'sot devyat.*'

Without further word, Antonina walks back to the door and is replaced by a sheet of fresh snow, which quickly melts into the puddle on the floor.

Cilka takes Josie's arm and steers her to a small patch of bare wall they can sit against. It is only as they slide down to the floor that Cilka notices several heads lift and fearful eyes appraise the newcomers. Is there a hierarchy even here? Cilka meets their stares. They look away first.

* * *

Cilka hears their number, accompanied by some yelling.

She startles from a daze. 'Last chance!' the matronly woman is saying.

Disorientated, she sees Josie is asleep, her head resting on Cilka's outstretched legs.

'Here! We're coming!' she calls as loudly as she can.

She shakes Josie and they scramble to their feet, heading quickly to the desk and the scowling woman behind it.

She stands, thrusts a clipboard at Josie, and walks to a door leading to the back of the room. Cilka and Josie follow.

Through the door, the woman leads them past beds that line both sides of the room. A ward. Cilka glances at them. The sheets are white. The blankets grey, but possibly thicker than those they have in their hut. Pillows are tucked beneath the heads of the men and women lying there.

Through the ward, they enter a clinical area screened off from the rest of the room. The smell of disinfectant assaults their nostrils.

Josie is shoved into a chair next to a table laden with bottles, bandages and instruments.

The woman indicates the clipboard Josie is holding, and hands Cilka a pen. Cilka understands that they are to fill it out. The woman turns away and is gone.

'I can't do this,' Josie whispers. 'I write with my right hand.'

'Let me,' says Cilka.

She takes the clipboard, pushes some of the instruments on the table to one side and places it down.

And then she sees it is in Cyrillic script. The letters are like tunnels and gates, with surprising added curves and flourishes. It has been a long time since she has read it. Writing in it will be difficult.

'Right then,' she says. 'The first entry is always your name. What is your family name, Josie?'

'Kotecka, Jozefína Kotecka.'

Cilka writes the name slowly, as best she can, hoping the doctors will be able to read it.

'Let's see, I believe this is date of birth?'

'November 25, 1930.'

'And this asks for your place of residence.'

'I don't have an address anymore. They arrested my father after he missed a day from work. He was a forest worker, and he went looking for my brothers, who had been missing for three days. They arrested my mother next. My grandmother and I were so afraid, all alone together in our house. And then they came and arrested us too.' Josie looks pained. 'No one in my family lives there now.'

'I know, Josie.' Cilka puts a hand on Josie's shoulder. She was the same age when everyone was taken away from her too.

'They put me in prison.' Josie begins to cry. 'They beat me, Cilka. They beat me and wanted to know where my brothers were. I told them I don't know but they refused to believe me.'

Cilka nods to show she is listening. It's strange how and when the past wants to reveal itself, she thinks. But not for her. There is no way she could find the words.

'Then one day, they loaded me and my grandmother onto a truck and took us to the train station, and that's when I met you.'

'I'm sorry that I've brought it all up, Josie. Let's . . .' She looks down at the form.

'No, it's all right,' Josie says. She looks up at Cilka. 'Will you tell me why you're here? All I know is that you are Slovakian. And that woman on the train said she'd been with you somewhere . . . Did your family get arrested too?'

Cilka's gut clenches.

'Perhaps another day.'

'And you knew what to do, when we got here.' Josie's brow furrows, puzzling.

Cilka ignores her, makes out she is studying the form again.

Cilka and Josie hear someone behind them and turn to see a tall, slim, attractive woman wearing a white lab coat, a stethoscope hung around her neck. Golden yellow braids encircle the back of her head and her blue eyes crinkle at the edges in a smile.

She looks at their faces and immediately addresses them in Polish, a language they can both understand. 'What is it I can help you with?' Her accent is unlike any Cilka has heard.

Josie goes to stand up.

'No, sit, stay sitting. I take it you are the patient.'

Josie nods.

'And you are?'

'I'm her friend. I was asked to stay with her.'

'Are you having trouble with the form?'

'We were getting through it,' Cilka says. And then, she can't help asking, 'How did you decide what language to address us in?'

'I've been a doctor for a long time in the camps and I've learned to make a good guess.' The doctor smiles warmly, and confidently, the first open face Cilka has seen since she arrived here.

'Let me look,' she says, taking the clipboard from Cilka.

'Well done.'

Cilka blushes.

'Why don't you finish filling it out? I'll read you the questions.'

'In Russian?'

'Do you know any Russian?'

'I can speak it but writing is a little more difficult.'

'OK, I think you should continue in Russian in that case, yes. The quicker you learn it the better in here. What other languages do you know?'

'Slovak, Czech, Polish, Hungarian and German.'

The doctor tilts her head. 'I'm impressed.' Though she says it quietly. 'The next question on the form is: what is the purpose of your visit to the hospital?' She asks it in Russian.

Cilka goes to write something.

The doctor looks over her shoulder.

'Hmm, close. Why don't you try asking the patient and then writing down what she says?'

Cilka feels panicked. She's not sure if the doctor is playing a game with her. Why is it that she always stands out, no matter how hard she tries not to? She asks Josie in Russian. Josie looks at her, puzzled.

Cilka tries to write 'burned hand' in Cyrillic on the form.

'Not bad,' the doctor says. 'Enough of that for now. I can take care of the rest. I had better take a look at the patient.'

Josie holds out her hand. The doctor pulls a nearby chair in front of her and gently starts unbandaging.

'Who wrapped this up for you?'

'Cilka did.'

The doctor turns to Cilka.

'And you're Cilka?'

'I made her hold it in the snow for a while first, then got some sheeting and wrapped it as best I could.'

'Well done, Cilka. Now let's have a look at the damage.'

With the bandage removed the doctor turns Josie's hand over, examining it closely.

'Wiggle your fingers for me.'

Josie makes a painful attempt to wiggle her fingers, the swelling preventing much movement.

'It was very lucky you had someone with you who knew to get something cold onto the burn straight away. That has saved you from a far worse injury. As it is, you have what looks like a first-degree burn to fifty per cent of your hand and eighty per cent of your four fingers. Your thumb seems all right.' She looks up into Josie's face. 'You'll need daily dressings for two weeks, and no work is to be attempted inside or outside.'

She turns to Cilka. 'Pass me that tube . . . the one that says *maz ot ozhogov*.' Burn cream.

Cilka hands her the tube of cream, taking the top off as she does so.

Gently, the doctor applies the cream to Josie's hand.

'Now look on the shelf behind you and find me a large bandage.'

Cilka does as she is told, handing back the correct item.

It is expertly wrapped around Josie's hand, the end placed between the doctor's teeth as she tears a small section in two, tying the ends together to hold it securely.

'Now, hand me that pad and pen on the table. I had better write a note.'

Cilka watches as she writes, folds the note and gives it to Josie.

'I have written here just what I said. You are not to work inside or outside and are to come here every day for at least the next two weeks to have the dressing changed. We will see how you are healing after that time.

'Now, Cilka . . .' the doctor says, 'I am impressed that you were so helpful to your friend, and your writing is not as bad as you think.' She studies Cilka. 'You have a capacity for languages. You know, we are understaffed here at the hospital with these new intakes. Would you like to work here?'

Cilka realises the opportunity. In a camp there are the bad jobs – the outdoor, manual labour jobs – and then there are the good jobs. In the *other place*, a 'good' job meant more food, and warmth, but in Cilka's case, it also meant being repeatedly and incessantly used, and witnessing the very worst conditions in the camp. Her role as leader of Block 25 was a punishment, but one she also still feels she needs to repent for. For surviving. For trading food for cigarettes for warm clothes. While the women came in and out and went off to die. And in and out and in and out, ceaselessly.

She is dumbstruck. Again, she wonders why she always

stands out. She looks at Josie, feeling that if she says yes, she will be betraying her friend. She will be betraying all of the women in the hut.

Josie says, 'Of course she will.'

Cilka looks at her. Josie nods encouragement.

'I . . .' If Cilka refuses, will she be put in the hole? Maybe, at least, the job would mean she can smuggle more food to those who need it, or trade it for cigarettes, boots, coats for the others.

The doctor looks confused. Cilka supposes no one would ever say no.

'I don't think I can,' she says.

'I'm sorry?' says the doctor. 'We all must work.'

'And I am happy to work at the mine,' she says, but she hears how flat her voice is. Once she had thought she deserved more, or better, but she knows there is always a very great cost.

'Well,' says the doctor. 'How about for the next two weeks, when Josie comes for her treatment, you help me, and then you can decide.'

Josie raises her eyebrows at Cilka, encouraging her.

Cilka slowly nods.

'Yes, thank you, doctor. But what about Josie?'

'Let's worry about Josie in two weeks. I'm sure we can find suitable work for her. In the meantime, I'm going to write you a note to give to your brigadier. You are to come here every day, bringing Josie; she will return to your hut after we have done her dressing but you will stay on and work.'

The doctor scribbles out another note, tears it off and hands it to Cilka.

'Now, both of you, go back to your hut and rest.'

'Excuse me,' asks Cilka, 'but what do we call you?'

'I'm Doctor Kaldani, Yelena Georgiyevna. You may address me by either,' she says.

'Thank you, Yelena Georgiyevna,' both girls chorus.

They follow her back through the ward. The moans and cries of the patients make the hairs on Cilka's neck stand up.

She will do what she's told.

They pass through reception, head back out to the cold and the slog back to their hut.

CHAPTER 5

'I know you're cold,' Cilka says to Josie. 'But I think we should save the coal until the others come home. I'll just add enough to keep it burning.' She wonders if she's already trying to make up, somehow, for the fact she will be warmer than the other women for the next two weeks.

Cilka ushers Josie onto her bed, tells her to wrap the blanket tightly around herself. After placing a small amount of coal into the stove, Cilka lies down and looks across the small gap separating her from Josie. She studies the young girl's face. Cold, fear, pain and confusion distort her features.

'Move over.'

Cilka sits and then lies down next to Josie, knowing it will be comforting to her.

Within moments she and Josie are both asleep.

They are woken by a gust of freezing air and the groans of the others returning. The women push and shove to get close to the stove, removing wet boots and wiggling toes in front of it.

'Well look who's spent all day in bed,' says Elena.

All the women look in their direction, sooty-faced. Cilka can feel their anger, their tiredness, their envy.

Natalya comes over to them. 'How's her hand?'

Cilka moves off the bed, reaches under the blanket and pulls Josie's hand out for Natalya to see.

'She will need the bandage changed every day for two weeks, the doctor said.'

'Does that mean she doesn't have to work?' Hannah, a newer arrival, a wiry woman who has been sticking close to Elena, calls out from the pack around the stove.

'Of course it does,' says Cilka. 'She can't even feed herself properly. How do you expect her to work?'

'Well, at least *you* have no excuse,' Hannah says. 'Back with a bucket of coal in your hands tomorrow, won't that be a treat for you?'

Elena says, 'I'm so tired I just want to sleep and never wake up.'

The door opens before Cilka can say anything and Antonina is standing there.

All eyes turn to the door. The women rush to the end of their cots. Josie struggles to her feet, taking her place.

Antonina walks past the women to Josie and Cilka's beds. All eyes follow her path.

'Well?'

Cilka says, 'Excuse me, Antonina Karpovna, can I get the notes from under my pillow?'

She nods.

Cilka produces the notes and hands them over. Antonina first reads the one describing Josie's condition and her need for daily dressings and no work. She pauses, squints at Josie's hand and nods. Then she reads the second note, looks at Cilka, and reads it again.

'You just scored the best seats in the house. Congratulations.' She passes the notes back to her, bemusement on her broad face. 'All out, line up.'

The women head back outside, falling into two neat rows. They follow Antonina to the mess. Dinner awaits. The snow has stopped falling but is thick on the ground. They trudge through it. Cilka is keeping her head down, and her hat low. But Elena and Hannah catch up to her.

'You're going to have to tell us what the note says,' Elena hisses through her scarf.

Cilka doesn't say anything.

And then Natalya says, in a more polite tone, 'We are curious, Cilka . . .'

'Well, I didn't say yes,' Cilka says, 'but they're short in the hospital and they asked me to work there.'

Elena gasps.

'You lucky bitch.'

Hannah glares at Cilka.

'She said no,' Josie says, 'but the doctor is making her do a trial.'

'Why didn't you say yes?' Natalya asks.

'Scared of needles?' Cilka tries – a joke to deflect the tension.

Olga, who has been watching all the while from a distance, sniggers.

Josie says, 'She didn't want to have a position higher than us – honestly, I heard her try to refuse.'

'That's madness,' Natalya says. 'Any one of us would say yes.'

They've almost reached the mess.

Cilka feels the knowledge sinking in for them all, even Elena and Hannah, that now she will have access to better food, warmth, materials. By accident, again, Cilka is in a position of more, unwanted, power.

'I'll try to save Josie's bandages,' she says, 'when they're changed. So you can wrap your feet, your heads, for work.'

'You better,' Elena says.

At the mess, the women all file off and eat their watery soup and stale bread. She notices that Elena keeps looking at her, whispering to Hannah.

Josie says to Cilka, 'It will be all right. Maybe we'll all find good jobs.' She is staring off into the middle distance, no doubt imagining a rosier future. Cilka is glad she can maintain this optimism. It will keep her strong.

* * *

Nine o'clock is observed by the lights going out; the women already in their beds.

The searchlight outside advances into the hut, along

with a shower of snow. The door is open. Several women raise their heads to see the cause. Boys and men, old and young, are pushing their way into their hut. Many of the women scream, burying themselves under their blanket. *If you can't see me and I can't see you, I'm not here.*

'We thought we'd give you a little time to settle in,' says the man Cilka recognises as Boris – the one who chose her. 'But it's bloody cold and we need some warming up. Where are you? Where's my pretty one? I've been waiting all day for my fuck. Come on, identify yourself so we can get started.'

He is walking in her direction, pulling the blankets from all the women as he approaches.

'I'm down here,' Cilka calls.

'What are you doing?' Josie cries out. 'Cilka, what's happening? I'm scared.'

Boris stands over Cilka, smiling down.

'Cilka!' yells Josie.

'Shut up, bitch, before I shut you up,' he says to Josie.

'It's all right, Josie, it's all right,' Cilka says, although she is shaking.

'Hey, Vadim, here's your one next to mine,' says Boris. 'Come and get her.'

Josie attempts to get out of her bed, screaming.

Boris roughly pushes her back down and holds her as Vadim makes his way over to Josie.

Then, stumbling, Boris sits on the edge of Cilka's bed and starts taking off his boots. The smell of vodka wafts off him. Josie is quietly sobbing, a sound that tears at Cilka's heart. She puts a hand on Boris's chest.

'If you let me just have a few words with her, I can quieten her,' she says flatly. Every other woman is screaming and cursing as they are slapped around and forced down on their cots, but she feels responsible for Josie. She was there when she was chosen for this. She has to do what she can to protect her.

Boris gives an uninterested shrug of his shoulders, which tells Cilka she can try and calm Josie. Vadim has his hand over Josie's mouth and is tearing at her clothes.

'Hold on a minute,' Cilka says to him firmly. He stops, surprised. 'Josie, listen to me. Listen.' Cilka leans closer to the girl and speaks quietly. 'I'm sorry . . . there is nothing you or I can do to stop this. Or if there is I haven't yet worked it out.' She blinks her eyes slowly. Time is distorting in the way it does when she becomes blank. Just limbs.

'Cilka, no, we can't let them—'

'I would murder them all if I could,' Cilka whispers. She turns to Vadim. 'Please, she has an injured hand. Be careful.' She turns back to Josie. 'Josie, I'm right here.' Knowing, though, that she isn't. Not really. 'I'm so sorry . . .'

She looks at Boris. 'She's just a child, can't he leave her alone?'

'Not my decision. Anyway, Vadim likes them young. So do I. You're not much older than her, are you?'

'No.'

Cilka begins to unbutton her shirt. She knows what to do. The noise of screaming women, and shouting men determined to do what they came here for, is overpowering.

For a moment Cilka wonders if the noise will bring guards, rescuers. None arrive. They are probably just doing the same thing.

As Boris explores her body with calloused hands, talking himself up, Cilka looks across at Josie. In the flickering light from the stove she sees Josie's face turned to her – a new level of fear in her eyes. Cilka reaches out her hand. A heavily bandaged hand is placed on hers. Hand in hand, with Josie quietly sobbing, their eyes never leaving each other, they survive their ordeal.

As Boris is putting his trousers and boots back on, he whispers to Cilka, 'No one else will touch you. And I can arrange that only Vadim will touch your friend.'

'Then do.'

'Come on, boys, if you haven't managed to fuck by now, you're not gonna get it up tonight. Out of here – let these ladies get their beauty sleep,' Boris calls out across the room.

Groans from the unsuccessful men mingle with the sniggering and laughter of the conquerors, only to be replaced by the sobs of the injured and distressed women. No one speaks. The stink of unwashed, vodka-soaked men is all that is left in the air.

* * *

As the clanging outside drags the prisoners into a new day, the women rise slowly. Heads down, no one makes eye contact. No chatter. Cilka risks a quick glance at Josie. The swelling and bruising on her cheek and around her eye is obvious from where Vadim pressed her down. She thinks about saying something, asking how she is, having a closer look at her facial injuries, asking if she has any others. Josie turns her back on her. She gets the message.

Breakfast plays out in the mess hall in silence. The old-timers throw a quick glance at the newcomers, registering the injuries, knowing the cause. They retreat into their own shame, grateful for the fresh bodies that will provide some relief from their assault.

As the others leave for work, Cilka and Josie remain in their hut. They have been told not to leave until Antonina returns and escorts them to the hospital. Josie returns to her bed and curls up, her face buried.

Ice forms on the inside of the windows as the stove cools. Their time alone is mercifully short. Cilka can't stand the tension between them.

As they enter the hospital waiting room, Antonina takes them to the reception desk.

'This one is here to work,' indicating Cilka, who catches the gist of her words. 'The other will have to stay here until the end of the day. I'm not coming back just to get one of them.'

The woman at the desk reads the pieces of paper handed to her.

'Come with me.' She beckons.

They follow her through the ward into the treatment area. Josie sits on the chair indicated, Cilka behind her.

The dozen or so beds are all occupied, along with several chairs holding those capable of sitting. Groans of pain escape from several of the patients. They seem to be mainly men, but there are a few women. Cilka challenges herself to examine these people, trying to work out where they are injured or what could possibly be wrong with them. For many it is obvious: visible wounds exist, blood seeps through scraps of material masquerading as a bandage or tourniquet. She feels the blankness sliding over her, cold as snow.

'Ah, here you are.' Cilka and Josie see Yelena Georgiyevna approaching. Josie glances up before returning her eyes to the floor in front of her.

'How are you today? How is the pain?'

Josie shrugs.

The doctor looks from Josie to Cilka, who turns away. Yelena gently places her fingers under Josie's chin, forcing her to look up. The injury on her face looks worse, having been stung by the icy walk to the hospital. The doctor brushes her fingers over the damaged area. Josie winces.

'Can you tell me what happened?'

Josie forces her head down, Yelena releasing her hold.

'It's her fault,' Josie spits. 'She made me do it, made me go along with it. She calls herself my friend and she did nothing to help me, just let them . . .'

'Men visited our hut last night,' Cilka whispers.

'Oh, I see.' Yelena sighs. 'Do you have any other injuries, Josie?'

Josie shakes her head.

'And what about you, Cilka?'

'No.'

'Of course, she doesn't, she just let him have her, didn't fight, didn't say no.'

The doctor stands. 'Stay here. I'm going to try to find a room I can take you both to, I want to examine you further.'

Cilka and Josie wait in silence. Cilka wonders about the doctor. Are people assigned this work in the camps? Or do they choose it? She can't imagine anyone wanting to be here. Yelena returns and ushers them into a nearby room, the occupant being taken out is arguing that he should be in a room by himself; he is a senior officer, not to be treated like a prisoner.

The bed in the room has the crumpled sheet and blanket of the former occupant, and the smell of an unwashed male, stale alcohol and cigarettes. Yelena has the two girls sit side-by-side on the bed.

'This is a brutal place . . .' says the doctor.

'I know,' Cilka whispers. She turns to Josie. 'Josie, I'm sorry, I should have warned you, told you what to expect, helped you understand—'

'You just lay there. You . . . looked at me. Cilka, how could you?'

Cilka is still not able to access any feeling but she notices, distantly, she has started shaking, her knees knocking up and down on the bed. She clutches her hands beneath them.

'I'm sure she didn't have a choice,' Yelena answers.

'She could have tried; a friend would have tried.' Josie's voice lowers and fades away.

There are always other things people think she should have done. But it is hardest hearing this from someone she has been trying to let in, become close to. 'I just hoped it wouldn't happen,' Cilka says. 'I knew it would, but I didn't know when, and I just hoped it wouldn't.'

She is truly sorry, but she also doesn't know what else she should have done, could have done.

The doctor seems to feel the tension. 'For now, I want to examine Josie, change her dressing, then I need to get you set up for work here, Cilka.'

Cilka slides off the bed. 'Shall I wait outside?'

Yelena looks at Josie.

'You can stay,' she answers, the chill still in her voice.

Cilka looks away, holding one hand in another, trying to quell the shaking, as Josie is examined.

Bardejov, Czechoslovakia, 1940

Cilka and her sister, Magda, walk down a street in their hometown of Bardejov, on a fragrant spring day. Magda smiles at two boys walking towards them. She is two years older than Cilka and Cilka admires the way she walks, her elegant wrists with her watch glinting in the sunlight, her hips gently swinging.

'They both like you,' Cilka says. 'Which one do you like the best?'

'They're just boys,' Magda says.

The boys position themselves in front of Cilka and Magda, forcing the girls to either stop or walk around them. Magda stops and Cilka follows suit.

'Hello, Lazlo, Jardin,' Magda says.

'So, who's this pretty little thing with you?' Lazlo says, his eyes wandering up and down Cilka.

'She's my sister, my younger sister. Take your eyes off her,' Magda snaps.

'No boy or man is going to want to take his eyes off her,' Lazlo sneers.

Cilka's stomach lurches in a confusing way. She looks down at the ground.

'Come on, Cilka, let's go.' Magda grabs Cilka's hand and pulls her away.

'Hey, Cilka, lose your sister and come and find me,' Lazlo calls out.

Magda squeezes Cilka's arm.

'Ow! Stop it, let me go. What's your problem?' Cilka says, shaking her arm free.

'You're only fourteen, Cilka,' Magda snaps back at her.

'I know how old I am,' she says defiantly. 'He's quite good-looking. How well do you know him?'

Magda stops, puts her face close to Cilka's.

'Don't be stupid, Cilka. You're just a child. He's a . . . well, he's not a man but he's not a boy either. You have to be careful.'

Cilka brings her arms across her chest. 'So, I'm never allowed to talk to a boy, is that what you're saying?'

'No, that's not what I'm saying. One day you'll grow up, then you'll know . . .'

'Know what? What do you know about boys? I've never seen you alone with a boy.'

Magda looks away, a dark cloud on her beautiful face. Cilka has never seen her look this way, shadows behind her eyes.

'Magda, are you all right?'

'Come on, let's get the shopping done and get home before curfew.'

'No, why can't we stay out? I don't want to obey such a stupid rule. We haven't done anything wrong.'

'You can be such a child, Cilka. Do you want to get Papa into trouble because you won't do as you're told? This is so like you, always wanting things your way. This time, little sister, you do as I say and we go home before the curfew.'

'And if we don't? What will they do to us?'

Cilka stands still in the warm, scented street. What could possibly happen to them, on such a soft spring day?

'The Germans? You don't want to know.'

'How much worse can it get?'

'Oh, Cilka, please, just once believe me when I say, we need to do as Papa asks.'

* * *

Cilka and Josie follow the doctor, Yelena Georgiyevna, to the end of the ward and are introduced to two nurses, both Russian, Raisa Fyodorovna and Lyuba Lukyanovna. They are instructed to teach Cilka what is required in

88

filing patient records, making notations and fetching medicine. Raisa is tall and strikingly pale, with large, full lips, and Lyuba is shorter, with almond-shaped eyes and sharp cheekbones. Both have long dark hair, indicating they are not prisoners. Cilka wonders again if they choose to be here, or whether they are assigned their positions. Cilka and Josie's hair is still short, beginning to curl lightly in the damp air. Both Raisa and Lyuba speak multiple languages too, and Cilka is told they will be her main overseers during the two weeks. Josie is told she will have to sit in the corner of the room and wait until the end of the day.

Two other male doctors are introduced to Cilka, told she is in training to be able to record their notes directly as they examine and assess patients. Cilka notices the glances they give her, liking what they see. She cringes. Is this place as threatening as Hut 29? Only time will tell.

Josie sits on the floor at the back of the large counter that has four chairs to sit and work from. One of the women offers her a chair, which she declines. She is soon curled up asleep. Tired. Traumatised. In shock. A combination of all three.

Cilka is a fast learner. She catches on to the format and rhythm of carefully identifying the correct notes for each patient and filing them. She is taken to a small room at the back of the ward and shown the range of medications she will have to correctly write down or collect. Left there to study the names and spelling of each, she works out their varied medicinal benefits.

When Raisa comes to get Cilka from the dispensary for a meal break, Cilka asks her to confirm what she has taught herself. Raisa tells her she is very impressed, particularly with her pronunciation.

Another nurse comes in and angrily demands to know what they are doing. Without waiting for an explanation, she orders them from the room.

Cilka doesn't yet understand the hierarchy but realises that here, as with anywhere, she will have to learn who to trust and who to avoid.

Taking a seat at the counter, she is handed a tin plate with a sweet bread roll, a piece of potato and a small quantity of dried green beans.

'Is this for me?' she asks.

'Yes, eat up,' Raisa says. 'We can eat whatever the patients don't. This is what is left over. Many of them are too sick to eat.'

'Don't they need it to get better?'

'Some of them won't get better and we can't force them. If we send it back to the kitchen the greedy pigs there would only eat it or sell it.' Raisa's lips draw tight in a thin line of distaste.

Cilka's stomach suddenly feels very small. It wouldn't be the first time she's eaten a dead person's food.

'Can I share it with my friend?'

'If you want.' Raisa shrugs.

Cilka takes the plate and sits down beside Josie, resting against the wall. She gently shakes her awake. Josie sits up, orienting herself to where she is.

'Here, eat some of this.'

'I don't want your food. I don't want anything from you.' Josie lies back down and closes her eyes.

Cilka breaks the bread roll in two and places one half on the floor in front of Josie.

Lyuba, the other nurse, comes and sits down beside her. 'It's great to have some help.'

'Oh . . . I don't know how much help I am yet.'

'You'll get there. Raisa said you are a fast learner and already can pronounce the names of the drugs better than she can.'

'I'm good with languages.'

'Excellent. When you start writing your own reports, you will need to have your spelling one hundred per cent. Mostly it doesn't matter, but every now and then we get audited and we all get in trouble if they find incorrect spelling, or something left out.'

'I don't want to get anyone into trouble. Can I show you what I write before it goes on the file?'

'Of course – that is what I am suggesting. Raisa and I will teach and supervise you, and I think Yelena Georgiyevna likes you, so you will be fine.' She glances at the clock on the wall. 'It's time to go back to work.'

Cilka looks at Josie and the uneaten piece of bread. It is good, she thinks, that Josie does not just accept her situation. It is a kind of strength. Still, Cilka feels the pang of distance.

* * *

That afternoon when Cilka and Josie are returned to their hut before the others arrive back, they find it in total disarray. All the beds have been stripped of their sheet and blanket and in many cases tipped upside down or on their side. The meagre belongings of the women lie in heaps on the floor of the hut.

Josie, Cilka and Antonina stand in the doorway surveying the mess.

'Hmm, looks like Klavdiya Arsenyevna has been here,' Antonina says.

Stepping into the hut, Cilka asks quietly, 'Are we allowed to clean it up?'

'You can fix your own bed.'

Antonina stands with hands on hips, and Cilka notices how strong she is, though with a small frame. The muscles – arms, chest, thighs – bulge roundly out from her joints.

'What about the others? Can we do them all while we wait for you to bring the women back?'

'It's probably better they see for themselves what happens without warning.'

'But why? Why has someone done this?'

'Klavdiya Arsenyevna is the senior guard for this hut and the larger brigade; she is looking for things you shouldn't have.'

'We had everything taken from us; how could we have something we're not meant to have?' Josie asks.

'She knows that. This is her warning to you. And it might be because she has found out about your job, Cilka. You have access to things others don't now. If she finds

92

something she doesn't like you can expect to be sent to the hole for punishment.'

Antonina turns and leaves the hut, letting the door stay open, the icy air being blown in. Josie closes it. But what does Klavdiya not want to find? Cilka thinks. They seem to be allowed to have some possessions. The rules here change day to day, she thinks. And though this camp has a different purpose – to get them to work for the Soviet Union, rather than kill them for being Jewish – in these conditions, and with constant rape, always the threat of violence and the 'hole', Cilka can see that she has gone from one cruel, inhuman place to another.

She goes to the stove and attempts to coax it back to life by gently placing small amounts of coal ash from the bucket on top of the dulling embers. What should they do about the upturned room, she wonders.

'I think she was right,' she says to Josie. 'We should leave it for the others to see and we can tell them what Antonina said.'

Josie ignores her and goes to her bed, struggling to right it with one hand.

'Here, let me help,' Cilka says.

'I don't need your help.'

'Fine,' Cilka says harshly. She looks away from the spectacle.

Eventually she turns round to see Josie buried under the blanket, her back to her.

* * *

93

Day has turned to night; the stove is pumping out as much heat as Cilka can get from it when the door opens and the other women stagger in. The solitary light bulb casts eerie shadows over the chaos, making it difficult, at first, for the women to see what they have arrived home to. Slowly, as they each make their way to their beds, it becomes evident. Several of them turn on Cilka, who is standing by the stove.

'What the fuck have you done?' says Elena.

It hits Cilka that she and Josie are about to be blamed.

'No, no, it wasn't us.' She fights the urge to scream at the woman. 'See, my bed is the same. This is how we found the place.'

'Then who did this?' says Hannah.

'It was a guard, a guard named Klavdiya Arsenyevna. Antonina told us about her.'

'And why?'

Cilka quickly explains.

Hannah looks very pale. 'Oh no.'

'What is it?' Elena asks her. Hannah throws her sheet and blanket and mattress around, looking for something.

Elena slaps her, hard and sudden. 'It's just a crust, Hannah!'

Hannah lets out a sob. 'I was saving it for you.'

The other women look away, set about restoring their beds, awaiting their call to dinner.

* * *

After dinner they return to the hut, a reluctance to go to bed obvious in the way the women linger over even the unsavoury chores. In the brighter light at the mess Cilka had been able to see other injuries from the night before on the faces of some of the women and noticed one held her right arm limply, supporting a painful wrist.

Josie still avoids Cilka, preferring to talk to Natalya. This fracture in their friendship must be obvious to the other women but no one comments.

'Do you think they will come again?' Olga whispers. She is whipping a needle and thread through a small piece of fabric, with hands crooked from overuse and cold. She will unpick her stitches and do them over, perfecting her work several times before bed.

No one attempts an answer.

With the light off, the outside searchlight throws a diffused shadow that dances around the room as falling snow plays within the beams. The women slowly move onto their own beds. They have learned already the need to be as well rested as possible for the labour they will have to endure tomorrow.

CHAPTER 6

The two weeks of treatment for Josie's hand pass quickly. It heals, with the ministrations of Yelena Georgiyevna, beyond the point at which she should have returned to normal work. The cold continues to intensify, along with the hours of darkness. The women in Hut 29 have got to know each other, or at least, become used to each other. Friendships have formed, and shifted, and re-formed. Fights have taken place. Josie remains distant, and Cilka accepts this. She understands that her role in the hospital might distance her permanently from her hut-mates. She supposes she ought to take the job and survive. The reaction of those around her is just something she has to deal with. Some, like Olga and Margarethe, have expressed gratitude and already say they are relying on the extra bits of food she brings, the bandages and fabric to keep them warmer. So far, only Elena has expressed hostility. But although she has yelled and hissed at Cilka, she hasn't laid a hand on her. The men still visit at night. The women are raped, abused, injured. And there are other indignities. Two have been sent to the 'hole' for misdemeanours, including Hannah, Elena's hanger-on, for simply looking at the guard Klavdiya Arsenyevna the wrong way. When she returned, for days afterwards, she was not even able to speak.

* * *

Yelena smooths cream into Josie's hand before placing it back in her lap. Josie looks down.

'I'm sorry, Josie, it has healed well. I cannot continue to bandage it. In fact, I might compromise it by continuing to wrap it up; it needs to breathe now.'

Josie looks around the room, her eyes coming to rest on Cilka, who is standing by the doctor.

Yelena notices. 'I am sorry, Josie. If I could give you work here I would, but they only allow so many prisoners to work with us.' She looks genuinely pained. Cilka has learned over the past two weeks that Yelena is a good person, always doing her best for everyone, but also having to make hard decisions. She can't be seen to be too favourable towards the prisoner patients, for example, in front of the other doctors, as it would be seen as being favourable towards counter-revolutionaries, spies, criminals. With Cilka, it can always appear that Yelena is instructing Cilka in her work. Raisa and Lyuba too. But Cilka does notice they often talk to her quietly, out of earshot of others.

She has seen other prisoner nurses and orderlies on the ward, and they are spoken to mostly politely, professionally and directly.

'If something changes, I promise I will have Antonina Karpovna bring you to me.'

'Yelena Georgiyevna,' Cilka says, 'please, isn't there any way she can stay on?'

'We have to be very careful, Cilka,' Yelena says, looking around. 'The administrators do not look kindly upon what they call "shirkers" – people who want to get out of doing their work.'

Cilka looks at Josie. 'I'm sorry.'

Josie huffs. 'Will everyone please stop saying they are sorry that I can now use my hand? This is ridiculous. We should be happy. We should be happy.' Tears roll down her face.

Startled by the tone in Josie's voice, Lyuba comes over. 'Are you all right?'

Josie displays her hand to Lyuba.

'I see. It has healed nicely.'

A small laugh escapes from Josie. 'Yes, Lyuba, it has healed nicely and from now on I am going to be happy that I can use both my hands.'

She stands up, pulls her coat tight around herself and turns to face the door. 'I'm ready to go.'

As Cilka opens the door for her, a tall man rushes in, with a piece of paper in his hand. He clips her shoulder.

'Excuse me,' he says, looking back at Cilka with an apologetic expression as he hurries past. He has dark brown eyes in a pale, elegant face. Cilka is not used to a man being polite to her and doesn't reply, but she holds his eyes for a moment before he turns to the desk, to his task. He's in prisoner clothing. As she and Josie head out the door, Cilka looks one more time at the man's back.

* * *

That evening the sight of Josie's unbandaged right hand receives mixed responses from the other women. Pleased. Indifferent. Some are glad of an extra person to help with the task of moving the coal dug from the mines into the trolleys that takes it to waiting trucks and places beyond.

In darkness. In snow.

At dinner Josie makes a big deal about holding a piece of bread in one hand, her tin mug in the other. She offers to fetch the coal and grabs a bucket to head out the door. She is stopped by Natalya and told to wait a few days – they don't want her struggling and spilling their precious supply of heat.

When the men invade the hut that night Vadim notices the unbandaged hand. He asks Josie about it. Strokes it gently. Kisses it. Cilka overhears this display of tenderness. These men only treat you with care in order to soften their own image, so you might be more open to them. It is still a selfish act, a trick.

CHAPTER 7

Cilka drags her feet the next morning walking through spotlit darkness to the hospital. She will tell Yelena again that she has been very grateful for this opportunity, but she should return to working in the mines, or digging, or building – anything as difficult as the work her hut-mates are being forced to do.

She watched Josie walk away from the camp this morning, her body nudging Natalya's. The two of them have become close. A pang of jealousy gripped Cilka. The small thaw in Josie yesterday as she showed her her unbandaged hand had given her hope they might regain the closeness they had.

In truth, the hospital work has been challenging and draining, despite her fortune in being indoors. Not only does she have to communicate in Russian and the Cyrillic script, and learn to understand the established ethics, relationships and hierarchies, but most of all, she has to deal with the unexpected reactions of her body and mind to being around the sick and dying. She has managed to hide – she hopes – what is going on, but Raisa did mention the other day that it was amazing how Cilka was not at all squeamish. That she could be around blood and bone and waste without ever flinching. Raisa, who had been sent here after graduating, Cilka found out, said it had taken her months to become used to seeing bodies in these various states of disease, injury and malnutrition. Cilka hated the mixture of horror and fascination on Raisa's face. She shrugged, turned away, said in a monotone: 'I guess some of us are just like that.'

But the job is distracting her from her troubles too. Always a new problem to solve, something new to learn. If she did continue working here it would almost feel like a life, a way of keeping herself shut off from the memories of the past and the horror of her present situation.

Yelena is occupied when Cilka gets in, and Lyuba and Raisa understand her mood and conspire to keep her busy and take her mind off Josie. Cilka is grateful for their efforts.

'Come with me.' Lyuba beckons Cilka to follow her to where a male doctor is standing at a bedside. She has seen him working around the ward and has been briefly introduced, by first name and patronymic – Yury Petrovich.

The patient is unconscious, his wounds obvious, the bandage around his head soaked with blood. Cilka stands silently behind doctor and nurse, peering round to watch the examination taking place.

The blanket is pulled up from the bottom of the bed. A needle is rammed firmly into the heel of one of his pale, lifeless feet; blood spurts out, covering the sheet. There is no reflexive movement from the man. The doctor turns to Cilka, handing her a clipboard, bypassing Lyuba. Lyuba nods encouragingly and stands beside her.

'No movement from foot on needle prick.'

Cilka writes, after first glancing at a clock at the end of the ward to record the exact time of her notation. Lyuba whispers to her whenever she pauses, uncertain. Cilka is concentrating hard.

The bleeding foot is covered, the doctor walks to the top of the bed and roughly stretches the patient's right eye open, then covers his face.

'Pupils fixed and dilated,' Cilka writes next.

'Slight pulse, irregular.' Again, noted.

Turning to Cilka, Yury Petrovich speaks quietly, 'Do you know how to feel for a pulse in the neck?'

'Yes,' Cilka replies with confidence.

'Good, good, show me.'

Cilka pulls the blanket away from the man's face, mimicking what she has seen. She places two fingers under the curve of the jaw, applying pressure. She feels the flutter of a faint pulse.

'Check on him every fifteen minutes, and when you can no longer feel anything, declare him dead and let the porter know. Make sure you note the time in the record.'

'Yes, Yury Petrovich, I will.'

He turns to Lyuba. 'She's a quick learner, we may as well use her. They don't give us enough nurses to have them checking on patients filling beds by taking too long to die. Make sure you sign off on what time she records.' He nods at Cilka and Lyuba and then moves off to another part of the ward.

'I've got to check on a patient,' Lyuba says. 'You'll be fine.' She walks off.

Cilka looks at the clock, working out exactly when it will be fifteen minutes since she noted the words 'slight pulse, irregular'. She is still standing by the bedside when Yelena walks up to her and asks her what she is doing. When she explains, Yelena smiles reassuringly. 'You don't have to wait by the bed. You can go and do other things – just come back every now and then and don't worry if it's not exactly fifteen minutes, all right?'

'Oh, thank you . . . I-I thought I had to stay here until he died.'

'You're really not afraid of death, are you?'

Cilka drops her head, the image of a pile of emaciated bodies flashing through her mind. Their desperate, final sounds. The smell of it. 'No, I've been around it enough.' The words slip out.

'I'm sorry to hear that.' Yelena pauses. 'How old are you again?'

'Nineteen.'

Yelena's brow furrows. 'One day, if or when you feel up to it, please know you can talk to me about it.'

Before Cilka can answer, Yelena walks off.

On her third visit to the dying patient, a prisoner who had an accident while working outside, Cilka writes the time and the words *'no pulse'*. She takes a moment to pause and force herself to look at the face of the man she has just declared dead. She flicks back through the paperwork, searching for his name.

Bending down as she covers his face, she whispers, 'Ivan Détochkin – *alav ha-shalom*.' May peace be upon him. She has not uttered these words in a long time.

Auschwitz-Birkenau, Summer 1943

'What did he say to you? We want to hear every word, and did he look at you while he was talking? Tell us, Gita, we need to hear.'

Cilka sits on the grass at the side of Block 25 with her friends Gita and Dana. Magda is resting inside. It is a Sunday afternoon, summer, with no wind to carry the ashes spewing from the nearby crematoria their way. Cilka, in her position as block leader, has been allowed some freedom of movement, but Lale is the only male prisoner they've ever seen inside the women's camp. That morning he had appeared. The girls knew what to do, to lessen the risk for their friends – encircle Gita and Lale, giving them just enough privacy for a whispered conversation. Cilka had strained to hear and had caught snippets; now she wanted the detail.

'He was asking me about my family,' Gita replies.

'And what did you say?' Cilka asks.

'I didn't want to talk about them. I think he understood. So he told me about his.'

'And? Has he got brothers and sisters?' Dana asks.

'He has an older brother called Max . . .'

'I love that name. Max,' Cilka says, putting on a gushy, girly voice.

'Sorry, Cilka, Max, is married and has two small boys of his own,' Gita tells her.

'Oh well, never mind. What else did he say?'

'He has a sister. Her name is Goldie and she is a dress-maker. I could tell he really loves his mumma and sister. That's good, isn't it?'

'That's very good, Gita. You want to love someone who is good to the other women in his life,' says Dana, mature beyond her years.

'Who said anything about being in love?' Gita throws back at her.

'Gita loves Lale . . .' Cilka sing-songs to her friends, letting the sunlight and their friendship momentarily block out the horror surrounding them.

'Stop it, both of you,' Gita says, but she is smiling.

Exhausted by hope, the three young women lie on the grass and close their eyes, letting the warmth of the sun transport them away from where they are.

* * *

That afternoon as Cilka is putting on her coat, readying to leave the warmth of the hospital and face the freezing temperatures outside, she sees Yelena.

'Yelena Georgiyevna, I need to talk to you—'

'Cilka! I've been looking for you. Yes, let's talk.'

Before Cilka can say anything, Yelena continues, 'My colleagues are impressed with you. They asked if you had any nursing experience.'

'No, I told you . . . I've never been a nurse.'

'That's what I told them. We chatted about you and we were wondering whether you would like to train to be a nurse.'

This was all happening so fast.

'I . . . How can I do that? I'm a prisoner here.'

'What better way to learn nursing than by doing it. I'll be your teacher. I'm sure the other nurses will help and be grateful for the extra pair of hands. What do you say?'

'I don't know . . . Yelena Georgiyevna. I don't know if I belong here.'

Yelena puts a hand on Cilka's shoulder. Cilka tries not to flinch at the intimacy of the touch.

'I know I don't know you very well, Cilka. But you are good at this, and we would like your help. Will you think about it?'

Yelena smiles warmly, like a sister. Cilka swallows. She can hardly bear it. The guilt she feels is overwhelming. She thinks of her hut-mates after they come in, huddling by the stove, unwrapping wet fabric from their frozen feet, groaning. But she also thinks of Olga's face when she hands her the real tea she has just boiled on the stove. This is a terrible decision and she doesn't know why, again, she has been singled out.

'Can I ask, Yelena Georgiyevna, why you are here?'

'You mean, what did I do to be assigned this position in Vorkuta?'

Cilka nods slowly.

'Believe it or not, Cilka, I volunteered to be here.' She lowers her voice. 'My family always believed in a . . . greater good.' She nods to the sky. It is forbidden to talk about religion, but Cilka understands what she is getting at. 'My parents devoted their lives to helping others. In fact, my father died doing so, fighting a fire. I try to honour them by carrying on their mission.'

'That's very good of you,' Cilka says. She feels over-whelmed.

'Although,' Yelena says, her brow creasing, 'I must admit I did believe, broadly, in the project of the Soviet Union – the Motherland calling, and all that – but it is quite different to *be* here.'

Cilka sees her turn to look back at the people lying in the beds behind them.

'I'd best stop talking now,' she says, and pulls her face back into a smile.

'Thank you, Yelena Georgiyevna, for telling me. And I just hope the women in my hut can find better work too. And soon.'

'I understand. I do too,' Yelena says. 'See you tomorrow.'

Yelena takes her hand off Cilka's shoulder, goes to leave. Cilka remains facing her.

'Is there something else, Cilka?'

'Josie – could Josie do my clerical job?'

Yelena thinks for a moment or two. 'Not just yet. Maybe if we can use you full time as a nurse, we will bring Josie here. But will she be able to learn . . . ?'

'I'll teach her. She'll be all right.' It is a risk, thinks Cilka. If Josie can't pick up the tasks, the language, as quickly as Cilka, will she be punished? A punishment worse even than going back to outside labour?

'We'll see,' Yelena says, and walks away.

CHAPTER 8

Long days and nights of darkness. The temperature drops to well below anything Cilka has ever experienced. She continues working in the hospital, never far from her guilt, trying to assuage it by smuggling back food for the women in the hut. Bread, vegetables, margarine. Real tea. Just enough for them to eat each evening, lest there is another raid by Klavdiya Arsenyevna. Antonina Karpovna gets a larger portion than Cilka's hut-mates each night.

Over the next few months, Cilka absorbs all that she is shown and told at the hospital like a sponge. She becomes so good at giving injections that patients start requesting her. They will often wait, desperate, until she is free to tend to them. The fact she is minimising pain rather than exacerbating it is a wonder for Cilka. She does still try to remember, as the ward overfills with desperate, frostbitten patients, that she cannot do more than she can do. And still, often, her mind goes blank and she runs on automatic, like an engine. Yelena notices, and tells her to take breaks, but if she could stay at the hospital twenty-four hours a day, she thinks she would.

Returning each night to her hut brings conflicting emotions. Not wanting to leave 'her' patients; needing to see Josie and the other women to know they have made it through another day of carrying, stacking, lifting, picking, their eyes streaming tears from the icy wind onto the fabric wrapped across their faces. She leaves earlier than the women and comes back later, so she does not have to sit idly while they wrap and unwrap themselves, aching, head to foot.

And then there are the frequent night-time visits by the men. Always outnumbered, the other women have very few 'nights off', the men coming into their hut changing often. Cilka and Josie's protected status as the 'camp wives' of Boris and Vadim keeps them from being brutalised by others, though not protected from the cries of their hut-mates. One evening Josie laments to Cilka that she is unhappy at Vadim's failure to appear, finding herself jealous that he has other women he prefers to her. This is difficult for Cilka to hear. She does not want to tell Josie how to feel – she knows how this abuse can affect a woman, a girl, in many unforeseen ways. But she does say that if she were her, she would feel only relief when he stays away.

After a five-day absence, Boris and Vadim enter the hut.

Josie jumps up, screaming at Vadim, accusing him of being unfaithful. Vadim slaps her hard in the face, before pushing her down on the bed. Cilka is shocked – is Josie losing her mind? She doesn't want Josie to be killed. She wants to hit Vadim herself, feels that fire burning inside her, but instead, later, she simply cautions Josie to be careful. It feels wrong, and inadequate, but she doesn't know what else to do. For the next few days Josie ostracises her, making comments to the others about the easy life Cilka has in the hospital. The thaw in their relationship has frozen back over. Elena, one night, loudly tells Josie to grow up – they are all benefiting from the extra food Cilka smuggles to them from the hospital, the uneaten patient meals she has become expert at hiding in her clothing.

Indeed, each night she comes in and empties her pocket on the edge of her bed, quickly breaking up the food so no one else has to do it and be accused of uneven portions, then turns away as the women leap forward and snatch at it. If Antonina is not there, she tucks her portion back in her pocket, as it's rude to leave the temptation out in front of starving eyes.

She turns away because it is so hard to see the women's unwrapped, bony fingers snatching. Their chapped, sore-encrusted lips opening. Their veiny eyelids closing as they take as long as possible tasting and chewing the food.

Cilka gives Elena a small, surprised smile for having come to her defence. Though Josie's words sting. Yes, Cilka is strangely lucky. But also cursed. If they knew of where she had been, for all those years, while they still

111

had an abundance of food and drink and warmth. While they still had families and homes.

Elena remains a complex character for Cilka. Angry, often uncaring, – yelling at the world and everyone in it – yet also showing compassion and tenderness on occasions when she is caught off-guard. She is just surviving, Cilka has often thought. There is no one way to do it.

Elena's friend, Hannah, speaking again now she has recovered from her time in the hole, remains more antagonistic. The two women are close because, Cilka has found out, they fought in the resistance together – the Polish Home Army. Fighting both the Nazis and the Soviets. Cilka is intimidated by their bravery. And it makes her even more unwilling to share her past.

* * *

The next day, Josie hands Cilka two small spring flowers she has managed to pick on her way back from the mine. Brilliant purple petals with a red and black centre. Wispy green fronds surround the delicate bloom. Cilka has seen them poking through the ice near the hospital, a sign spring is coming. The possibility of relief from the constant freezing, biting wind and snow gives a sense of hope that life might become a bit easier for all of them.

Cilka tries not to make too much of the gesture from Josie. Truth is, for the first time in here, she feels an aching in her throat like she is about to cry. She swallows. The flowers are placed in a chipped cup, now the pride of each woman in the hut. They have all learned the art of stealing anything not nailed down; smuggling mugs from the mess; a small table discarded from an officers' hut with a broken leg propped up on random bits of timber; a battered kettle of permanently boiling water on the stove. Antonina, sharing in the uneaten food Cilka brings from the hospital, has chosen to ignore the 'extras'. It seems that whatever contraband Klavdiya is looking for, it is not these items. The hut is taking on a cosy appearance. Olga, the embroiderer, who managed not to give the needles back on the first night, has been teaching several others her craft. Threads from the ends of sheets have been taken and turned into beautiful doilies which are strung about the hut. Cilka has continued to help herself to discarded bandages, cleaning them in boiling water and donating them to the embroidery group. Several of the scarves that cover the heads of the women have delicate embroidered edges.

On their monthly visits to the bath hut the women hand over their lace-edged scarves along with their other clothing for de-lousing while they quickly run a sliver of soap across their bodies, and rinse off from a vat of thankfully hot water. Their pubic area hasn't been shaved again, after the first time, and they are allowed to let their hair grow back, unless they are found to be infested with lice. Most of the women hack their hair short during the bathing sessions. Cilka lets hers grow a little longer. The clothes come back, warm and stiffly hung over a pole, and they have to grab them before they are unceremoniously dropped on the floor. Sometimes the stronger women elbow their way to a new scarf or warmer coat, and so the lace detailing begins to spread throughout the wider brigade.

* * *

Spring is sweet but too short. The snow that has covered the ground almost since Cilka arrived melts quickly as daytime temperatures increase. Now the sun is brilliant, reflecting off the nearby hills.

When summer arrives, darkness shrinks down until, one day, there is no night at all. There is no need for searchlights in the yard, unless it's very overcast. Some of the women in the hut from further south in Europe react to this phenomenon with panic – it seems to go against nature. The men enter the hut and now the women have to see them clearly, up close. Several of the women do not hold back, telling them what ugly pigs they are, and are punished for daring to say so.

Sleep becomes difficult for some as they struggle to shut their eyes in light as bright as day. Tempers flare, and the harmony of the hut is shattered with both verbal and physical fights breaking out.

When Cilka is caught with a nodding head by Yelena, the doctor asks how she is coping with the white nights.

'The what?' Cilka asks.

'The white nights. We will be in daylight for twenty-four hours each day for a while. Everyone adjusts differently.'

'I can't sleep, and when I do fall asleep it's only for short bursts.'

'And others in your hut?'

'Some are fine, most aren't. Fights seem to break out over nothing. How do you cope?' Though she imagines, in the staff quarters where Yelena sleeps, there may be adequate curtains.

'Your first summer will be your worst. Well, for many their worst. There are others who never adjust and struggle each year; some simply go mad. They can't cope with the sleep deprivation, the change in their body rhythms – it does something to their head.'

She seems very casual about this, Cilka thinks. 'Could that happen to me?'

'You will be fine, Cilka.' Cilka hasn't got used to Yelena's enduring faith in her. 'You need to make a blindfold and cover your eyes and slowly let your body adjust. Tell the other women to do the same,' she says. 'I'm sure if you look in the linen area you will find some old blankets that have been thrown out. Take a break, take a pair of scissors, go there and cut up enough strips for the women. All you can do is offer.'

Cilka doesn't need to be told twice. In the linen room she experiments with blankets and other materials she finds until she is happy with the comfort level of having something wrapped around her head. Not too itchy, not too smelly. Twenty lengths are cut and stuffed throughout her clothing. It's incredible to even be using scissors. In the hut, the women sometimes cut material by running a just blown-out match along it.

That night, a Sunday where they have only had a half-day

of work, Cilka distributes the blindfolds, and the women start to settle in their beds, the hut still lit up by daylight. The sound of voices talking outside is heard. They wait for the men to arrive but the door stays closed. The voices continue. Several women get out of bed and cautiously poke their heads outside. Elena opens the door and the voices grow louder.

'What's going on?' Cilka calls out.

'There are people just walking around and talking; it's like a party out there!'

They all jump out of bed and rush to the door and windows. Everyone fights to get a look. Slowly, they all venture out.

'What's happening?' Elena asks a group of women walking past, chatting away.

'Nothing. What do you mean?'

'Why are you outside in the middle of the night?' Elena asks.

'It's not the middle of the night yet, and we're outside because we can be. Is this your first summer?' one of the women asks.

'Yes,' Elena tells her. 'Well, most of us arrived right at the end of the last one.'

'If you have the energy, you may as well enjoy being outside for a while without having someone standing over you forcing you to work.'

'I didn't think it would be allowed.'

'Rubbish. You stay inside in winter because it's too cold and too dark to come outside. I could read a book out here, if I had a book to read, so why not enjoy it? It won't last for long.'

The women wander off.

'I thought . . .' Josie stammers.

'I guess this is something else our beloved Antonina Karpovna didn't tell us,' says Elena. 'Come on, let's go for a walk and have a proper look at our prison.'

For the first time in a long while Cilka sees smiles on the faces of some of the women. Despite their exhaustion from the work week, they walk, several arm-in-arm, outside. Cilka supposes this will only happen on Sundays, when the half-day off allows them to be slightly less exhausted. The prisoners gaze at the sky; see the mountains of coal darkening the horizon. They breathe in the fresh air, their enemy in the winter when it sears their throats, burns their lungs. For the first time they see men milling around together in the central area where the men's and women's camps meet, not posing a threat to them. Some respond to their smiles with a girlish giggle. A sense of freedom comes over them.

'Come with me, Cilka. We have to find them,' an excited Josie squeals.

'Find who?'

Cilka is surprised by the first face that comes into her mind: the messenger she has seen on the odd occasion at the hospital, the brown-eyed man who had been polite when he accidentally ran into her. They haven't spoken, though he has nodded hello a couple of times.

'Vadim and Boris. Let's find them and walk with them.

Won't it be lovely to just walk and talk to them, get to know them, not just—'

'I don't want to find Boris. Why can't we just be together? We don't need them, Josie.' Cilka has tried to be understanding of Josie's naiveté, her need to think of this as a real connection, but it disturbs her greatly.

'But I *want* to see Vadim. Are you coming or am I going on my own?' a petulant Josie says.

'I'm not interested,' Cilka says coldly.

'Well, if that's the way you feel . . .' Josie stomps off. Cilka watches her go, before wandering away on her own.

Cilka struggles with this freedom – it is so new to her. She keeps looking at the perimeter with its guard towers, looking for guards who could mow them down with their weapons. This is how on edge they felt in that *other place*. She doesn't know the rules here yet. She is one of the first to go back to what is, to her, the safety of Hut 29. She waits patiently until they all return, particularly Josie, whom she regrets leaving alone, before going to sleep, making sure they are all back. Then she ties on her blindfold. The women continue to murmur happily as they settle, this small freedom giving them a moment of contentment.

* * *

For eight weeks, the sun never leaves the sky. Cilka begins to relax and properly join in on the Sunday evening strolls around the camp. She, along with the other women in her hut, explores the environment. They keep their whole bodies covered, and wrap scarves around their faces, to ward off the mosquitoes. She struggles to convince Josie she doesn't need to find Vadim and be with him, that he is not her future.

One evening, Hannah begins to walk beside Cilka, pulling her away from Josie with a firm grip just above her elbow. Up close, Cilka can smell the stale sweat in her clothes, the grease in her hair.

'What do you want?' Cilka asks.

'You know, in the war, people like me and Elena worked to resist every oppressing force – the Nazis, the Soviets . . .'

'I know. You're a hero.'

'While some people just lay down and gave themselves over to them, even benefiting from this *coupling* while watching everyone around them die.' Her grip intensifies on Cilka's arm. Cilka feels sick. Hannah keeps walking, forcing Cilka to keep putting one foot in front of the other.

'I don't know what you're talking about,' Cilka says flatly.

'I'm not going to give away my source . . . but that's a nasty little secret you've kept from us.'

Cilka swallows, feeling fear, rage. It must have been that woman from the train, who had also been in that *other place.*

'So, is it true what this woman was saying? She seemed desperate to tell someone. She didn't seem long for this world.'

'I have nothing to say to you.'

Cilka spares a thought for the woman who, like her, had survived that *other place* only to end up here. And worse, who might never leave.

'So it is true. You're just a common whore who gets what she wants by sleeping with the scum of mankind. Well, well, well.'

'You can't hurt me, Hannah. Don't even try,' Cilka says, looking her in the eye.

'I bet you don't want your friends to know. Do you want me to keep your secret?'

'I want you to go fuck yourself. I couldn't care less what you do or say.' Cilka is bluffing to make the secret less appealing to Hannah. But she knows Hannah must be able to feel her shaking, under the tight clench of her hand.

'I can keep it secret, for a price . . .'

'How often do men come into our hut and rape you, Hannah?'

Hannah doesn't answer. Keeps her brows furrowed, breathing heavily.

'I didn't hear you,' Cilka says, her voice raised. 'One man, several men . . . how many different men have raped you since we've been here?'

'It's just what happens here.'

'Yes, it's just what happens here. It's what happened *there* to me. I was kept hidden away so the officers would not be seen to be *polluting* themselves. Do you know what that is like? For you and your family and friends, your whole race, to be treated like animals for slaughter?'

Hannah looks away, keeps her face blank.

'And did this person who claims to know so much about me say why *she* was here?' Cilka asks.

'Yes, I got that out of her. The Russians said they didn't like people who told on others without being asked, so sent her here too. It seems like you were all weak in the end, all turning on each other.'

'No one can judge us,' Cilka says through gritted teeth. 'You can't know what it was like. There were only two choices: one was to survive. The other was death.'

Hannah chuckles quietly. Cilka is seeing double with rage. She should be used to this by now – people creating hierarchies of good and bad, deciding where you fit in.

'But that's not all there is, is it?' Hannah says.

Cilka looks at her.

'Would you really want me to tell the others – Josie, Natalya, Olga, Elena – about your role in the death block?'

Cilka tries not to let her expression falter.

'I thought so,' Hannah says. 'I will tell you what I need, soon, and you will give it to me.' She walks away, across the patchy grass and dirt.

Cilka looks up at the women standing around in a circle, sharing a rare moment of leisure. Josie turns and smiles at Cilka. Cilka forces a smile back. She does not want to go back, in her mind, to that *other place*; she wants to take each day and get through it the best she can, with her new friends. She does not want Hannah to ruin this for her. Her gut churns.

* * *

121

All too soon, the women wake to frost on the ground. The air is thick and wet in their throats. Cilka has now been here a year. Their scarves are put away, their hats and heavy coats retrieved from under their mattress where they have spent the past two months.

Hannah does not yet seem to have decided on her 'price' for keeping quiet. But she reminds Cilka frequently, with a look or a gesture, of what she knows. Cilka tries, most of the time, to block from her mind her fear of the women finding out.

The transition from autumn to winter is swift. Seasonal rain dampens the ground and the mood. The evening strolls in the camp end and the women struggle to adjust to only having their own company once again.

The rain becomes sleet, the sleet becomes snow. There is constant darkness.

The hut feels small and close with Hannah's knowledge.

CHAPTER 9

A day for making plans. A day for thinking ahead. For most people, but not for Cilka.

For the first time today, she writes in a patient's file: January 1,1947.

Patient making good progress, expected discharge tomorrow.

She hears the words spoken by the doctor, transcribes them, forces a smile as she looks at the man lying in the bed in front of her, his eyes full of tears.

'Please, just a little longer. Can I stay a little longer? Two, three more days. I am still weak.'

The doctor looks at the man without compassion. Turning to Cilka – 'What do you think, Cilka? Shall we let this malingering piece of shit take up a bed some ailing fellow prisoner should have? Or kick his sorry arse out of here tomorrow?'

Cilka has learned the game some of the doctors like to play, involving her. Making her the person who determines whether or not a patient gets another twenty-four hours in a warm hospital bed with nourishing food. She has also learned which doctors might agree to her suggestion that a patient may have a day longer, and which will do the opposite.

This doctor often agrees with whatever Cilka says. She carefully grants days to the sick and infirm that she never could in her old life. Though in all of these places, it is always one person for another. One person's comfort, one person's food. Nothing is fair.

'It is the first day of a new year. Perhaps in the spirit of this—' She glances at the file in her hands before continuing. 'Georgii Yaroslavovich would benefit from an extra day with us. Shall I amend his file to say discharge in two days?'

'Amend.' The doctor walks away.

Cilka glances up at the poster on the wall above the bed. A smiling worker in a sunny field. *Liberation through honest toil.*

She amends the file.

'Thank you, Cilka Klein, thank you, thank you. You are an angel sent from heaven.'

Cilka winks at him. This time her smile is genuine, 'It's all right, Georgii Yaroslavovich, you know I'll take care of you.'

As she walks back to the desk to drop off Georgii's file and collect another, Yelena is waiting, having watched the game play out.

'Cilka, I have some good news for you.'

The smile returns to Cilka's face. She's almost too scared to ask what. She waits.

'I've spoken to the head of the hospital and convinced him you now qualify to be called a nurse.'

'Really? That's wonderful, thank you so much,' Cilka says. But she feels numb. Her position makes a marginal difference to her hut-mates' lives, but still she wishes she could do more. Behind Yelena, outside the frosted window, there is howling darkness. 'I don't know what else to say.'

'You don't have to thank me. You did the hard work – you've earned the right to be recognised for it.'

There is churning deep down inside her. Something like shame. Would Yelena feel differently if she knew everything about Cilka's past?

'I won't let you down,' Cilka says.

'I know you won't. And Cilka, one more thing.' She hands a note to Cilka. 'Give this to Antonina Karpovna tonight. It is my request for Josie to start work here tomorrow as a clerical assistant. She will learn some of your old duties to free you up for nursing.'

Taking the note with a shaking hand, Cilka turns away to compose herself. *Finally.* She has been agitating for this to happen for as long as she has been in the hospital. She stuffs the note in the pocket of her hospital apron; with a nod of thanks she picks up another file and walks briskly, with purpose, to another patient.

For the first time in a long while Cilka arrives back at

her hut before the others. She paces the small room, her nose still aching from the cold of the walk, waiting for Josie, for Antonina, to share her news. It is not the news that she is to be called a nurse that excites her so; it is that Josie will no longer be working outdoors, but in the comfort and warmth of the hospital. She knows it comes from a selfish place – she wants to be closer, physically, to Josie. So she can watch over her.

The women enter the hut in a state of fear and panic. Cilka's first thought is of Hannah, what she knows – or thinks she knows. Has she told the women and are they going to attack her? But then she realises it is something else entirely. One of the women is sobbing and groaning at the same time. She is being supported by two others, each holding her up by one arm as the woman doubles over in pain. The others are in a fluster, issuing instructions on what to do with no one listening, no one taking control.

Cilka grabs Elena, pulling her from the pack. She sees now that the groaning woman is Natalya, her blonde hair stuck with sweat and soot to her forehead.

'What's happening? What's wrong?'

Antonina has followed them in. As they place Natalya on her bed they step away and let the brigadier see her.

'How far gone?' Antonina asks.

Natalya shakes her head in pain and fear, 'I don't know.' Her scarf is still bundled around her neck. Her gloved hands clutch at it.

'Weeks or months?'

'Months, five or six, I don't know! Help me, please help me.'

'What's wrong with her?' Cilka asks Elena again.

'She's bleeding and she is pregnant. We think she is having the baby.'

Antonina looks up and sees Cilka standing back.

'Come here,' she says. 'You work in the hospital – take charge. The rest of you, get ready to go to dinner.'

Cilka opens her mouth to object, changes her mind. She has no idea how to deliver a baby, but she wants to be there for Natalya.

'Excuse me, Antonina Karpovna, can I have Josie and Elena stay and help me? I have a note here for you from the doctor, Yelena Georgiyevna.'

Cilka unfolds it and puts the note in Antonina's gloved hands. Antonina reads it and looks around to find Josie, says in monotone, 'Well, another one of you wins a prize, congratulations.' She looks back at Cilka. 'The two of them can stay with you. I'll have some towels and sheets sent over. The rest of you, get out.' She wraps her scarf back over her mouth, only her eyes showing.

Before the women leave for the mess, Cilka says, 'Can I ask if anyone here has had a baby or attended anyone giving birth?'

The brigadier looks around at the women, pushes her scarf down again. 'Well?'

'I've helped birth plenty of cows but no humans,' says Margarethe, matter-of-factly.

'You can stay also.'

Natalya's screams from the bed refocus their attention. Sweet, beautiful Natalya, Cilka thinks. Josie kneels down beside her, pushes the damp blonde hair off her face.

'How bad is the bleeding?' Cilka asks.

'There was a lot of it when I went to the latrine on the worksite. Help me, please, Cilka, save my baby.'

She wants the baby, Cilka notes. There is something within Cilka that understands, if this happened to her, she might cling to that idea of life too. But it won't happen to Cilka. She doesn't think her body is able to get pregnant.

Josie looks pleadingly at Cilka. 'You know what to do?'

Cilka keeps her face blank, serious. 'We will do all we can, Natalya. We need to take your clothes off so we can see how you are, all right?'

Fifteen women gather at the door, wrapped up, eager to get away, keen not to bear witness to tragedy. Cilka, Josie, Elena and Margarethe tend to Natalya as best they can.

A guard delivers two towels and two sheets. Greeted by the screams of Natalya, he throws them into the hut without a word.

While the rest of the hut is having dinner, Natalya gives birth to a baby boy. He makes no sound; he gives no movement. Taking one of the towels, Cilka wraps his little body in it and places him in Natalya's arms. The four women stand over her as she cries herself to sleep, clutching her son to her chest for what will be their one and only night together. Josie stays by her bedside all night.

The next morning Antonina tells Elena and Margarethe

to stay with Natalya. Cilka and Josie are to take the baby and report to the hospital for work. Josie looks pained.

'We'll look after Natalya, Josie,' Elena says.

Taking the dead baby from his mother's arms is one of the hardest things Cilka has done in her twenty years.

* * *

In the hospital, Josie is slow to catch on. Cilka finds herself spending more time teaching and doing the job herself at the expense of nursing. She perseveres, and Yelena looks the other way as slowly Josie learns the art of determining what information from a doctor needs to be in a patient file, what was only comment and not for recording. She can speak Russian well now but she struggles greatly with the Cyrillic, with the names and spelling of drugs. She is shy towards the medical and nursing staff, preferring to interrupt Cilka for help than ask for instructions to be repeated.

Cilka, however, excels at every task. She is now expert at drawing blood; her suturing, while not to the standard of Olga and the others in the embroidery class, is admired by her more experienced colleagues. She effortlessly combines caring for the emotional needs of her patients with their practical ones.

Josie is grateful and warmer to Cilka now, whispering to her in the hut as they lie side by side on the nights Boris and Vadim haven't visited. She is anxious, and overwhelmed. 'How will I learn? How will I keep up?'

Cilka sometimes does not have the energy to reassure

her, though she wants to be good to her. She just knows it's possible things will get even harder, that they have to take each moment as it comes.

One day, they return from work and Natalya is gone. Antonina Karpovna refuses to give them answers, which Cilka knows is not good. Usually, they know when a woman has gone to the hole, because it is a warning to the rest of them. Cilka cannot stop the images of women leaping onto electric fences in that *other place*, preferring a quick death to the hell on earth that was the camp, or the gas chamber they knew awaited them all. The blankness is coming over Cilka, cold and flat as snow on the ground, and she just wants to lie down. But she knows what Natalya meant to Josie. She sits by her and silently offers a hand for her to hold until she falls asleep.

Winter seems relentless, all-consuming in its freezing darkness, but weeks become months. The seasons make their dramatic changes and once again small flowers push their way through the melting snow and ice. The light in the hut goes out and the sun remains high in the sky.

A second white-night summer has arrived.

There are a few more changes in the hut, besides Natalya's departure. Two of the original women get involved in a fight. When a guard attempts to break them up he is struck. The women are sent to the hole, and do not return. Three young Ukrainian girls arrive and sleep in their beds. Olga, Elena, Margarethe and Hannah remain.

The walls of the hut are covered in the women's craft. When a piece deteriorates due to the damp conditions it is quickly replaced. The lace adorns the collars on the women's coats, their dresses, the edge of pockets, on their hats and scarves. It is a small reclamation of an identity, a femininity, an expression of something other than a functional body put to work daily.

* * *

Cilka has managed to avoid being alone with Hannah for months until, one evening, when they are all walking back from the mess to go straight into the hut. Cilka slows, telling Josie she'll be in soon.

'Are you all right?' Josie asks, frowning at Hannah standing next to Cilka.

'Yes, of course,' Cilka says, forcing a smile.

Josie shrugs and walks on, leaving Cilka and Hannah alone.

Cilka takes a deep breath.

To her surprise, Hannah does not look threatening, but vulnerable. She licks her dry lips, her eyes darting about.

'In the hospital . . .' she says tentatively, 'you have drugs for pain, right?'

'We do, but they are limited. We only use them when we really have to.'

'Well, you have to get me some,' Hannah says. Her eyes flare in their sockets, desperate.

'There's not enough—' Cilka says.

'You know the consequences,' Hannah growls, digging

her hand back into the flesh of Cilka's arm until it hurts. 'If you don't get me a steady supply, I will tell everyone in there—' she nods towards the hut – 'that you not only fucked the Nazis but you stood like an angel of death in a fur coat and watched, and did nothing, as thousands of your kind were killed before your eyes.'

Despite the mild weather, Cilka's insides turn to ice. She begins to shake. She wants to explain to Hannah: *I was sixteen! I did not choose any of it, any of this. I simply stayed alive.* But no words come. And she knows, too, how they would ring out hollow and desperate to her hut-mates. How they would not be able to stand to be around her. How she would seem cursed, wrong. She does not want to steal drugs badly needed by patients for Hannah. But she also can't lose her friends – her only solace. And what if Yelena found out about the death block too? Raisa and Lyuba? She might lose them, and her position. She wouldn't be able to bring extra food for her hut-mates, helping to keep them strong enough to do their gruelling work. Everything would unravel.

She sees on Hannah's face that she has guessed Cilka's thoughts.

'I'll see what I can do,' Cilka says in a flat voice, defeated.

As she is about to go back into the hut, to lie down and try to close her mind to this dilemma and all that it has brought up, she hears a voice call her name.

'Cilka, Cilka!' It is Boris.

She turns as the stocky, ruddy-faced Russian bounds over to her. How can she deal with him right now? Their

132

relationship has gradually changed. He tells Cilka often that he cares for her. She forces herself to tell him the same, for her safety, but she never means it. Many times, when he visits, he just wants to be held, cuddled. He tells her about his childhood, one of rejection, of never knowing the love and comfort of caring parents. She pities him. She wonders if her feelings for men are to be only fear and pity? Her own childhood was full of love and attention, her parents always interested in what she said, appreciating the stubborn, wilful daughter they were raising. There is a remnant of this sense of family, and belonging, tucked deep down, that cannot be touched. Her father was a good man. There must be other men like her father. Like Gita's Lale. Love against terrible odds is possible. Maybe just not for her.

She thinks again of the messenger she has seen in the hospital. His kind, dark eyes. But can a look of apparent kindness really be trusted? She doesn't even know his name. It is better that she doesn't.

'Walk with me,' Boris says firmly. She doesn't know what will happen if she protests. So she goes. He takes her to a part of the camp she and the others have avoided, an area full of men, often arguing, always fighting.

Boris tells her he wants her to meet some of his friends. He wants to show her off. For the first time since her arrival in Vorkuta, Cilka is genuinely scared. She knows Boris is a powerful trustie in the camp, but the vile comments of the men, who attempt to grab her and touch her as she walks past them, make her fear that he cannot protect her. One of the others has a young woman with him and is savagely having sex with her in full view of his comrades. The calls for Boris to prove his manhood and take Cilka the same way make her break from him and run. Catching up to her, Boris insists he would never do anything like that. He offers a heartfelt apology, confirming what she has suspected. He cares for her. But how can he care for her when he does not know her? He only knows her as a body: face, hair, limbs.

As they move away from the others, the girl's screams follow them.

Cilka begs Boris to let her go back to her hut. She wants to be alone. She is turning blank and numb. She assures him it is nothing he has said or done, trying to keep the fear out of her voice; she needs time by herself.

Alone, curled up on her bed, facing the wall, even with her blindfold on, sleep will not come. Absurd images appear and warp in her head. An SS officer, his rifle adorned in lacy embroidery; Gita and Josie sitting beside a mountain of crushed coal searching in the grass for a four-leaf clover, laughing and sharing a secret as Cilka looks on from a distance; Yelena leading Cilka's mother away from the truck as other women are piled on it, nearly corpses already, and bound for their death; Boris dressed in an SS commandant's uniform, his arms outstretched, dead flowers being offered to her. She sobs silently at the hopelessness she suddenly feels for her future and the people who will never be in it.

Auschwitz-Birkenau, 1944

Cilka steps foot outside Block 25. Four SS officers stand near the idling truck, just outside the gates of the brick courtyard, waiting to take the overnight residents of her block to their death. The women are slowly making their way out the gate, dead women walking. She pushes through them to approach the two nearest SS officers.

'Two have died overnight. Would you like me to have their bodies brought out for the death cart?'

One of the officers nods.

Cilka stops the next four women.

'Get back inside and bring out the two who have cheated the gas chamber,' she snarls.

The four women turn back into the block. Cilka follows them in, pulling the door behind her, not quite shutting it.

'Here, let me help you,' she says. The women look at her as if it's a trick. Cilka frowns. 'They would have stuck their rifles in your belly and dragged you back here if I didn't say something first.'

The women nod, understanding. One of them has died and is lying on a top bunk. Cilka climbs up to her, and as gently as she can, lowers her down into the arms of two of the waiting women. The body weighs nothing. Cilka climbs down and helps properly place her across their spindly arms, then adjusts the woman's meagre clothing to give her a degree of dignity in death.

Once the two dead women are carried outside, Cilka watches the truck drive away. She is left with the squeak

and scratch of hungry rats. She will go inside in a moment
and put on her clean nylons, bought with bread. If he comes
to visit, he likes her clean. And she has a favour to ask him,
for her friend Gita, concerning the man she loves. Cilka
finds 'love' a strange word – it bounces around in her mind
but doesn't land. But if Gita is able to feel it, Cilka will do
what she can to preserve that. Before going inside, she
glances in the direction of the gas chambers and crematoria.
When she started here in this hell on earth she had always
sent a prayer. But now the words will not come.

*   *   *

In her hut, desperate to drive away the memories, Cilka
wills sleep to come.

Thirteen years to go.

CHAPTER 10

A small child screams. Patients and staff turn as the door to the ward is flung open, and a woman runs in, holding a little girl. Blood covers the child's face and dress; her left arm hangs at an impossible angle. Two guards follow, shouting for a doctor.

Cilka watches as Yelena runs to the woman. She is well-dressed, clad in a warm coat and hat; not a prisoner. Her arm around the woman's shoulders, Yelena ushers her to the end of the ward. As she passes Cilka, she calls to her, 'Come with me'.

Cilka falls in behind the procession, the child still screaming. In the treatment room, Yelena gently takes the child. She places her on the bed and the child appears to go limp. Her cries subside to a whimper.

'Help her, help her!' the mother begs.

'What's her name?' Yelena asks calmly.

'Katya.'

'And what's your name?'

'I'm Maria Danilovna, her mother.'

'They are the wife and daughter of Commandant Alexei Demyanovich Kukhtikov,' one of the guards offers. 'The officers' hospital is at capacity because of the ward being rebuilt, so we brought her straight here.'

Yelena nods, asks the mother, 'What happened?'

'She followed her older brother up onto the roof of our house and fell off.'

Yelena turns to Cilka. 'Get some wet cloths and help me wipe the blood away so I can see the extent of the injuries.'

A small pile of towels rests on a chair next to a basin. Cilka drenches two of them. There is no time to wait for the water to warm up, cold will have to do. Handing one to Yelena, she follows her lead in wiping blood from the little girl's face. The wet, cold towel seems to revive her, and her screams resume.

'Please, help my *malyshka*, please,' sobs Maria.

'We are helping,' Yelena says softly. 'We need to clean some of the blood away to see where she is hurt. Be careful of her arm, Cilka, it's broken and will need to be set.'

Cilka glances at the arm hanging over the bed next to her and repositions herself to avoid it. Bending down, she speaks to Katya in a quiet, soothing voice, telling her she is not going to hurt her, she is just cleaning her face. Katya responds, her whimpering now accompanied by shivers that wrack her small body.

'Get a blanket, quickly, and cover her. We need to keep her warm.' Cilka grabs a blanket from the end of the bed. Folding it into two she carefully places it over Katya, again murmuring, telling her what she is doing.

'I can see the site of the wound, it's on my side of her head – it's quite a gash. Keep cleaning her face, Cilka. I'm going to get some supplies.'

Yelena drapes the end of a towel over the right side of Katya's head, covering her right eye.

Maria steps in front of Yelena. 'You can't leave her, you're the doctor. Send her.'

Cilka's heart races. At some point today she has to get to the dispensary that contains all the medicines and medical materials needed on the ward, though she dreads what she is planning to do.

'She won't know what to get. I'll be right back. In the meantime, Katya, and you too, Maria Danilovna, are in good hands with Cilka.'

Yelena leaves the room.

'You might want to hold her hand,' Cilka tells Maria, who nods and takes Katya's uninjured hand in her own.

Cilka wets a clean towel.

When Yelena returns, Cilka is talking to Katya.

'Katya, my name is Cilka Klein. Doctor Kaldani and I are going to take care of you. Do you understand?'

A small grunt comes from the little girl.

'Good girl. Now, Katya, can you tell me where you hurt? We know your head hurts and we know your arm hurts, but does it hurt anywhere else?'

'My . . . my leg,' splutters Katya.

'Good girl. Anywhere else?'

'My head hurts. Mumma, Mumma!'

'I'm here, my *malyshka*, I'm here. You're such a brave little girl; you're going to be all right.'

Yelena places the tray she has brought in on the bedside table. From the bottom of the blanket she lifts it gently to look at Katya's legs. They are covered in thick stockings, and no injury is visible.

'Cilka, help me take her stockings off so we can examine her legs.'

Whatever pain Katya is feeling in her legs is not significant enough for her to react as Yelena and Cilka each remove a boot and a sock. Yelena examines her legs. The right one is showing signs of early swelling and bruising around the knee. Yelena moves it carefully; Katya doesn't respond.

'I think it's not serious. Let's get back to her head.'

'What about her arm?' Cilka asks.

'We'll get to that. You're doing really well, Cilka; thank you for asking her about other injuries. Often children this young don't respond. You have to find the injuries yourself, so well done. Pardon me, Maria Danilovna, but how old is Katya?'

'She's nearly four.'

'A lovely age,' Yelena says quietly, as much to herself as Maria.

Yelena removes the towel from Katya's head. The gaping wound has stopped pulsing blood, but the red raw edges look nasty. She hears Maria gasp.

Yelena pours antiseptic over a wadded bandage and gently places it over the wound. Cilka continues to attempt to wash the blood from Katya's hair.

'You have beautiful hair, Katya. It goes with your lovely face.'

'Keep talking to her, Cilka. Maria Danilovna, this is what we have to do. I cannot take care of Katya's injuries while she is awake. I will give her an injection to put her under, examine her more closely, then move her to a more sterile room to stitch her head wound and take care of her arm. It is broken between the elbow and the wrist and will need to be pulled into place properly before it can be plastered. Do you understand?'

'I think so. Are you sure you need to put her to sleep though? What if she doesn't wake up? I've heard about people being put to sleep by doctors and not waking up.'

'She needs to be asleep, Maria Danilovna, you have to trust me.'

'Where are you from? Where did you get your training?' Maria asks Yelena, and Cilka senses the anxiety beneath her bravado.

'I'm from Georgia, and I was trained there.'

'I'm also from Georgia – they have good hospitals there.'

'We must talk some more, but for now, I need to take care of Katya,' Yelena says, and then quietly, 'Do you want to tell her she is going to have a needle and go to sleep or should I?'

Turning to Cilka, Maria says, 'Let her, she seems to be able to calm Katya.'

141

Although Cilka has heard the exchange, she looks to Yelena to repeat exactly what it is she is to say to Katya. She doesn't want to get it wrong and frighten the girl. She strokes Katya's face as she tells her what is going to happen. Katya doesn't flinch as Yelena injects the anaesthetic, and both she and Cilka watch as Katya's eyes flutter and close.

When Yelena is convinced Katya is deeply asleep, she removes the blanket and starts to cut away her clothes. Layer by layer is discarded on the floor. With only a singlet and underpants remaining, Cilka becomes aware of the two guards in the room.

'Leave,' Cilka says to them firmly.

They don't need to be told twice.

As the door closes behind them, bellowing can be heard in the ward. 'Where is she, where is my *malyshka*, Katya?'

'My husband,' whispers Maria. Cilka watches as the relief on her face at hearing her husband's voice is replaced by what looks like fear. Maria backs away from the bed.

The door bursts open and Commandant Alexei Demyanovich Kukhtikov storms into the room. Scrambling behind him, a senior doctor enters, squawking, 'Alexei Demyanovich, Alexei Demyanovich, I am in charge.'

The commandant arrives at the bed and registers his daughter's broken, bloodied body. He looks to his wife.

'What happened, Masha?'

'Alyosha—'

Yelena comes to Maria's defence. 'She was just playing, Alexei Demyanovich, and had a fall. It looks worse than it is. I have put her to sleep so I can take care of her, but I assure you she will be fine.'

The commandant listens without interrupting, but the doctor who followed him intervenes.

'Alexei Demyanovich, I am in charge here. I am so sorry I didn't know your daughter was here.' Turning on Yelena, he shouts, 'No one told me the commandant's daughter was here. I will now take over.'

Maria cautiously walks towards her husband. 'These two angels have taken care of our little girl. Let them finish what they have started.'

Alexei looks at his wife. 'And are you all right?'

'Excuse me,' pipes up the doctor. 'I am the most experienced doctor here and it is my duty to take care of your daughter, Alexei Demyanovich.'

Without looking at him, the commandant answers. 'If my wife says she trusts these two to look after Katya then they will, with my thanks.'

He turns to Yelena. 'You look like the doctor.'

'Yes, Alexei Demyanovich. I am Yelena Georgiyevna, or Doctor Kaldani.'

Turning to Cilka. 'And you, the nurse?'

'She is not even a nurse, she's a—' the male doctor interjects.

'A nurse in training, Alexei Demyanovich, but a very good one,' Yelena says.

The commandant attempts to run his hands through the matted, bloodied hair of Katya. He bends down and kisses her gently on the cheek.

'I'll go back to my office and leave her in your hands. Have someone report to me when you have finished and I will organise where she is to stay; she's not staying here.' He turns to Maria. 'Stay with her, my dear.'

'I was never leaving.'

Cilka and Maria follow the bed with Katya on it as it is pushed by Yelena to the operating room. Cilka has not been in this part of the hospital before. The door at the end of the ward always seemed forbidden territory to her. A short corridor leads to two small anterooms feeding into a slightly larger room with a big overhead light. Cilka heard about such rooms in Auschwitz. Chills overcome her, her breathing quickens.

'It's all right, Cilka,' Yelena says, 'this is where we operate. Now come on, I need your help.'

While Yelena stitches and bandages Katya's head, manipulates and plasters her arm, examines the bruises which have now appeared on her legs and small body, none of which require medical attention, Cilka stands with Maria. At the sound of the bones in the girl's arm crunching back into place, Maria buries her head in Cilka's shoulder. Cilka takes a sharp breath, then places a loose arm around the distressed mother.

In the recovery room, Cilka stands beside the chair while Maria sits with her head on the bed beside her daughter. When Katya wakes, crying, her mother comforts her as Cilka runs to get Yelena.

A quick examination by Yelena determines that Katya has come through her procedures well. Cilka notices Katya looking at her quizzically, as if she doesn't know who she is.

'Hello, Katya, I am Cilka.'

Katya registers her voice; a small smile crosses her lips.

'These are the two angels who took care of you,' Maria tells her daughter.

Katya continues to look at Cilka through one opened eye, the other partially covered by the large bandage encircling her head. Cilka is uncomfortable with the attention from the girl. Now the action is over she's much more aware of the child's smallness, her vulnerability, how it could all have gone so wrong.

'There's a truck outside waiting to take the girl home,' says a guard from the doorway. Cilka is glad she cannot hear the idling truck, a sound from her nightmares, a sound she would hear from her room in Block 25 – the death cart waiting for its passengers. The guard steps aside as two men enter, carrying a stretcher between them. Yelena lifts Katya from the bed. The stretcher is placed on the bed and Yelena lowers Katya back down, carefully placing her broken arm across her small body. Blankets are piled on top of the delicate little frame.

As the men lift the stretcher and walk towards the door Maria turns back to Cilka.

'If there is anything I can do for you, please ask. I mean it.'

'Thank you,' Cilka says. *My freedom.* That is an impossible request, she knows. 'Thank you for letting me care for Katya.'

'I wouldn't let anyone else care for my children or myself but you and Yelena Georgiyevna.' She smiles.

Cilka smiles back.

'Goodbye,' Maria says.

As she is leaving, Cilka studies the elegant woman she has spent the past few hours with. The delicate lace collar on her dress and the silver locket and chain hanging around her neck. The colourful belt that pulls her dress in to her tiny waist, and the shiny buckles on her shoes. It has been many years since she saw a woman dressed so beautifully. Images of her mother dressed similarly come into Cilka's head. A memory to cling to. But that is followed by thoughts of her mother at the very end. A memory she can't bear.

It takes until the final hour of her shift for Cilka to find an excuse to go to the dispensary. She takes one container of the pills, slips it into the extra pocket sewn into her skirt where she normally puts food to take back to the hut. It is just one container, she thinks. She just can't face up to this relative peace – this position, these friends – being lost.

As she steps outside after her shift she glances over towards the administration building. She sees the messenger, the polite man with the brown eyes, walking across spotlit grass. He raises a cigarette to his lips, pauses his walk, closes his eyes and inhales. Despite his layers of clothing, his scarf and hat, his worn boots, there is an elegance to him, in the small pleasure he takes on the inhale, in the exhaled smoke rising above him and his gloved fingers poised in front of his mouth. Cilka feels something shift inside her.

She keeps walking.

CHAPTER 11

Name: Stepan Adamovich Skliar
Date: September 14, 1947. Time of Death: 10:44
Placing the blanket over Stepan's head, Cilka walks back to the desk area, slowly flicking through Stepan's file. A couple of recent entries catch her attention and she reads on.

Ukrainian prisoner, presented three days previously with stomach pain. Nothing identified on examination. Watch and wait. Aged 37 years.

She looks for the treatment plan. There isn't one. Investigations: nil. Pain relief: occasional.

A doctor is sitting at the desk nearby. She hands him the file.

'I've noted the time of death for this patient, Gleb Vitalyevich.'

'Thank you, just leave it there.' He indicates a pile nearby.

'If you would like to sign it, I can file it immediately.'

The doctor takes the record from her and flicks quickly through it. He scribbles something on the front page and hands the file back.

'Thank you, I'll file it.'

With her back turned to the doctor, Cilka looks at the entry. The doctor's illegible signature beside her notation. Then the words 'Cause of Death: unknown.'

Cilka looks back at the doctor, noting how little he is writing in any record, how he is not reading previous entries, and how the pile of records that was in front of him when she approached is now reduced to three or four.

With anger growing inside her, Cilka doesn't see Yelena approaching until she stops in front of her, blocking her path.

'Is something the matter, Cilka?'

Cilka takes several moments to think of how to respond.

'Why do you go to great lengths to save some people and not others? How do you decide who should live and who should die?'

Yelena frowns. 'We try and save everyone.'

'You do, not every doctor here does.'

Yelena takes the file from Cilka, scanning the last entries.

'Hmm, I see what you mean. It's possible that investigations were made and simply not recorded.'

'Possible, but I don't think so.'

Yelena looks at Cilka seriously. 'You need to be careful, Cilka. The administration needs functional bodies to work, and so saying anybody was deliberately hindering the sick from getting better so they can serve Mother Russia is a more serious accusation than you may realise.'

Cilka takes back the file with a little more force than she should have.

In the small filing room filled with boxes she goes to place Stepan's file in the current open box. Taking the last two files out she quickly looks at the entries. Both causes of death do seem valid to her untrained brain. She will keep her thoughts to herself and heed Yelena's advice not to pry. After all, it's not as though she is doing everything right by the patients. Though she tries her hardest, there is that one container of pills slipped into her pocket every now and then.

* * *

'Are you religious?' Yelena asks Cilka one day, standing near an unconscious patient in the corner of the ward who has just been looked over by Gleb Vitalyevich. It is dark outside, and snowing.

'No,' Cilka answers quickly, though it is not the full answer. 'Why?'

'Well . . .' She is keeping her voice low. As Cilka remembers, one does not talk about religion in the Soviet Union. Any religion. 'It's the season where some religions celebrate . . . I wasn't sure if it meant anything to you.'

'No, not me.' Cilka looks down at the patient. Talking

149

about this means talking about a lot of other things. Talking about the annihilation of her people. About how hard it is to have faith the way she once could. 'You?'

'Well, in Georgia, it was always a time when we would gather with family, and have food and music . . .' It's the first time Cilka has seen Yelena look properly sad, wistful. She is always forthright, practical, in the moment. 'Are you just not . . . Christian?'

'No, not a Christian.'

'Dare I ask, any other religion?'

Cilka pauses for a moment too long.

'It's all right. You don't have to answer. You know that if you ever want to talk about where you come from . . . just know I will not judge you.'

Cilka smiles at her. 'A long time ago, my family did celebrate . . . around this time of year. Also with food, lots of food, lights, blessings and songs . . .' She looks around her, fearing someone may overhear. 'But it is hard to remember.'

Deeply and instinctively, Cilka still often reaches for prayers. Her religion is tied to her childhood, her family, traditions and comfort. To another time. It is a part of who she is. At the same time, her faith has been challenged. It has been very hard for her to continue believing when it does not seem that actions are fairly rewarded or punished, when it seems instead that events are random, and that life is chaotic.

'I understand,' Yelena says, warmly.

'I wonder if anyone is lighting a candle tonight for this

150

poor fellow,' Cilka says, wanting to move the focus from herself.

'Let's hope so,' says Yelena. 'For all these wretches. But you didn't hear me say that.'

Cilka nods and takes a step away from the bed, before turning back to Yelena.

'If I was ever going to talk about my past, I would like it to be with you.'

She has surprised herself by saying it. It is too much of a risk, and too difficult. And even if Yelena – the most compassionate person Cilka has met – could handle it, what if she told others? Even the patients in the hospital wouldn't want her around. Someone who has overseen so much death.

'Whenever you're ready, come and find me,' Yelena says.

The ward is quiet for a moment, unusually so. Cilka stands by the window, watching the snow flurry in the blue-black sky. Closing her eyes, she sees her family sitting around the table. Her beloved father reciting blessings, the lighting of the *menorah*, the pure joy of being together. She can smell and taste the *latkes*, potato pancakes fried in oil, that will be eaten for the next eight days. She remembers the excitement of being a young girl given her first candle to light. How she pestered her father many times to be allowed to light the first one. How she never accepted his explanation that it was the man in the house who did it. Then the memory of the time he relented, telling her she had the courage and determination of any boy and as long as it was their family secret, she could light the first candle. She then remembers when that was. The last time she sat with her family to welcome and celebrate Hanukkah.

'*Hanukkah sameach*,' she whispers to herself. 'Happy Hanukkah, my family: *Ocko, Mamička*. Magda.'

Bardejov, Czechoslovakia, 1942

'*Happy birthday. Pack the new coat Mumma and Papa gave you for your birthday, Cilka. You may need it,*' *Magda whispers as the sisters each pack a small suitcase.*

'*Where are we going?*'

'*To Poprad. We have to catch the train there for Bratislava.*'

'*And Mumma and Papa?*'

'*They will take us to the train station and we will see them when we come home. We must be brave, little sister, keep Mumma and Papa safe by going to work for the Germans.*'

'*I'm always brave,*' *Cilka says firmly.*

'*Yes, you are, but tomorrow when we say goodbye, you have to be especially brave. We will stay together and . . . and you can look after me.*' *Magda winks at her little sister.*

Cilka continues putting her very best dresses into the suitcase.

She will make her family proud.

* * *

Cilka has contained all this for so long. She is not sure if it is the darkness or the quiet, or Yelena's open face, but she has to run to the nearby linen room. She closes the door, heart racing, and drops onto the floor, burying her face in dirty soiled linen so no one can hear the sobs that are escaping her.

With no sense of how long she has been down there, Cilka struggles to her feet. She smooths down her clothing, wipes her fingers under her lashes, making sure it is not obvious that she has been crying. She needs to get back to work.

She takes a deep breath and opens the door. As she leaves the room she hears—

'There you are. I've been looking for you.'

Cilka squares her shoulders. Striding towards her is the doctor she despises for his attitude and complete lack of compassion in treating his patients: Gleb Vitalyevich. She has often wondered if it would be possible to compare the survival rate of his patients with other doctors. She knows he would be the worst by far.

'Watch Bed nine for time of death. I'm going off for a while. I'll sign it off tomorrow.'

She watches him walk away. *I know about you*, she thinks, throwing silent daggers at his back.

Bed 9 is the unconscious wretch by the window. Cilka leans in and, with detachment, feels for the pulse in his neck. She is shocked to feel a strong, healthy *thud thud, thud thud* . . . She peels back his right eyelid and notes the pinprick-sized pupil, sees a flutter of movement.

Looking around, she observes that Yelena and the two nurses present are occupied. She can see Josie's back in the filing room.

The man's file lies at the foot of the bed. As she is about to pick it up, she hesitates, and pulls the blankets away, revealing his feet. She scratches her fingernail down his right foot. It twitches. She reads his file.

A single line. Name: Isaac Ivanovich Kuznetsov. December 24, 1947. Found unconscious in his bed, unresponsive, brought to hospital. Not for treatment.

Isaac. A Jewish name. Cilka tries to control her breathing. No. No. Not today, not this man. She will not sit by and watch him die if there is something that can be done to save him.

From the dispensary, Cilka finds the medication she has used many times before to wave under the noses of unconscious patients to try to bring them around. A foul-smelling substance she has often thought could wake the dead. Gently she slaps his face, calling his name. A small whimper escapes his lips. She holds the cloth containing the substance close to his nose. She pinches his nostrils shut for a moment or two before releasing them. Being denied oxygen briefly his nostrils flare open and inhale. Immediately, he responds; his eyes open as he gasps for breath, choking. She gently rolls him onto his side. Soothing words float from her lips to his ears as he turns his eyes upward towards her.

At that moment, Josie comes over to see if she can help.

'Is Yelena Georgiyevna available?' Cilka says.

Josie reaches out to Cilka, a look of concern on her face. 'Cilka, are you all right?'

Cilka has forgotten, already, about the linen room, though she does feel tired, emptied out.

'I am, Josie. I just need to help this man.'

Josie looks around. 'I'll find her,' she says.

Cilka is glad that she and Josie have become close again. Josie was quiet and subdued, and closed off, for a long time after Natalya disappeared. But she began to enjoy conspiring with Cilka to sneak food back to the hut, especially when winter set in. They have been pretty lucky with the food, and sometimes Cilka has to remind herself to be careful. Mostly the women do not leave so much as a crumb. But if the head guard, Klavdiya Arsenyevna, came in at the wrong time, it could be the hole or worse for Cilka and Josie. Not to mention Hannah, whose pills are swapped from pocket to pocket and then Cilka assumes sewn into something – her mattress, perhaps – by night.

Josie returns a few moments later with Yelena.

Cilka explains how she was meant to be watching the patient to record time of death but was concerned no attempt had been made to work out why he was here. When she did some tests of her own, she discovered he had a strong pulse and good reflexes. She used the smelling substance and he has regained consciousness.

Yelena listens intently. Reads the sole entry on his file.

She draws breath through her teeth. 'You have interfered here, Cilka. Gleb Vitalyevich isn't going to like this.'

155

'But—'

'I do think you've done the right thing, and I'll take a look at the patient, but I can't guarantee there won't be consequences for you. Remember what I said? You two go. It's time to finish up and I'll see you tomorrow.'

'You won't get in trouble, will you?' Cilka asks Yelena.

'No. I'll try and make it look like he recovered on his own,' she says.

Cilka looks down at the bewildered man lying in the bed.

'You'll be fine, Isaac. I'll see you tomorrow.'

Cilka and Josie go to get their coats, their scarves, their hats.

* * *

That night, Cilka hardly sleeps. How can saving a man be a problem? Why is it that her life always pushes her to be confronted by, or to embrace, the deaths of others? Why is it that, even if she tries, she cannot change this? Is there any point ever getting attached to another person – Josie? Yelena? They are always in danger.

* * *

When Cilka arrives on the ward the next morning, she is greeted by Gleb Vitalyevich and a bulky-looking trustie thug.

'I want her out of here,' he screams on seeing Cilka.

The trustie moves towards her.

'She's an interfering, mixed-up *zechka* who does nothing

here of any lasting good. She'd be of better use in the mines.'

Yelena and the other staff stand back watching the rant. Cilka looks pleadingly at Yelena. She shakes her head, indicating there is nothing she can do. Josie stands close behind Cilka, silently supporting her.

The trustie grips Cilka's upper arm, steering her to the door.

'It'll be all right,' Cilka calls out to Josie.

'She is going,' Gleb Vitalyevich says. 'Now, the rest of you get back to work.'

Cilka glances at Bed 9 and sees Isaac sitting up. She throws him a quick smile as she is forced out of the ward. The trustie follows her all the way to her hut.

CHAPTER 12

The next morning at rollcall Josie keeps looking at
Cilka, and then at Antonina Karpovna, as Klavdiya
Arsenyevna barks out their names. They stand in ankle-
deep snow. Cilka looks back at Josie's questioning eyes
beneath the lace detail on her hat. When Josie turns
back to Antonina, the searchlight casts a patterned
shadow across her pale cheek. Cilka knows Josie is
wondering when she is going to tell Antonina she has
to put her back on another work detail. As Josie leaves
the hut to head towards the hospital, Cilka falls into
line with her.

'What are you doing, Cilka? You can't come back,' Josie
says, worried. Cilka did not tell their hut-mates last night
why she'd been back early; she'd feigned illness.

'I assumed you just weren't ready to tell everyone

yesterday – I didn't know you would try to come back!'
Josie says.

'I am going to stand up for myself,' Cilka says. 'I did
nothing wrong, I deserve to have my job back.'

She is surprising even herself, but something became
clear to her overnight. She will no longer accept death,
which is all around her, as inevitable.

'You'll get thrown in the hole! Please, Cilka, go back.
Don't do this.'

'I'll be all right, Josie. I just need your help.'

'I can't. *I* don't want to go back to working at the mine,
I'll die there. Please, Cilka.'

'Just this one thing. I'll wait outside. You go in and find
Yelena Georgiyevna, ask her to come outside and talk to
me. That's all. I won't walk into the hospital with you. No
one but the doctor will know I'm here.'

'What if she's not there? What if she's busy?'

'I'll wait for a while, and if she doesn't come out, I'll
go back to the hut and think of something else.'

She has a good enough relationship with Antonina
Karpovna by now, having lined her stomach with hospital
food just like her hut-mates, so there's a certain amount
she can get away with. As long as Antonina also keeps the
guard Klavdiya Arsenyevna happy.

Cilka lets Josie get a few steps ahead of her. When
Josie enters the hospital, Cilka leans against the building,
grateful for once for the swirling snow that covers her,
blending her into the surroundings. She watches the
door.

It finally opens and two men walk away without noticing her. She waits. She watches. Time passes.

The door remains closed.

Back in her hut, Cilka flings herself onto her bed, beating the thin mattress, screaming at the world, screaming at her stupidity in losing a job that kept her safe and helped to feed her hut-mates. She falls asleep, face down, drained of energy, of emotion.

A hard slap across the back of her head brings Cilka back to time and place.

Klavdiya Arsenyevna stands over her, her hand raised to strike her again.

'What are you doing here? Get on your feet,' she screams.

Crawling to the end of her bed, scrambling to her feet, with her head down, Cilka stares at the foot tapping out a threatening tune on the wooden floor.

'I said, what are you doing here in the middle of the day? Answer me, *zechka.*'

'I-I work in the hospital, but I'm not needed there today,' Cilka mutters, trying to buy herself time to explain her dismissal.

'So you thought you could just spend the day in bed? In the comfort of a warm hut while everyone else is out working?'

In fact the stove is barely working, the temperature inside the hut is not much warmer than outside. Cilka is still in her coat and hat.

'No, I didn't know what to do after I left the hospital this morning so came back here, that's all.'

160

'Well then, let me put you to work.'

'Yes, Klavdiya Arsenyevna.'

Klavdiya pulls the blanket and mattress from Cilka's bed, throwing it into the middle of the room.

'Your turn.'

'I'm sorry, what do you want me to do?'

'Strip every bed into a pile. You can then explain to the others when they return how *you* trashed their tidy little home. You will do this and bear the consequences. Now get going.'

Josie's bed, being next to Cilka's, is quickly added to the middle of the room. And then the next, and the next, until mattresses and blankets cover the entire floor of the hut. Klavdiya positions herself next to the stove, enjoying the scene.

With the last bed stripped, Cilka looks back at Klavdiya, awaiting further instructions.

Klavdiya walks to the back of the hut next to Cilka's bedding and begins kicking it, looking for something that shouldn't be there. A letter, something smuggled into the hut.

Next to Cilka's bed, Klavdiya kicks the sheet that has clearly come from Josie's bed, before picking it up and examining what looks like another piece of fabric sewn onto the sheet.

'What's this?' she calls out to Cilka.

Hurrying to her side, Cilka examines the sheet with the attached piece of fabric containing words written in Cyrillic text, the names of medications.

161

'Who sleeps here?' Klavdiya demands to know, pointing at Josie's bed.

Cilka doesn't answer.

Klavdiya stares at her. 'You will sit here amongst this mess until the others have come back and then I shall return. Don't forget to tell them it was you who did all this,' she says, sweeping her hand around the room. 'You did a better job than I would,' she adds with a snarl. 'I want it to look just like this when I return, so don't go getting any ideas about fixing it up. Tell Antonina Karpovna to be here when I return also.'

Punishing herself for her foolishness, Cilka curls up on the wooden slats of her bed.

* * *

The blast of icy wind alerts Cilka to the arrival of the women, Josie coming in behind them. They enter slowly, stepping over the scattered bedding, shaking their heads in disgust at yet another violation of their space.

'Antonina Karpovna,' Cilka calls out as the brigadier is about to shut the door and leave. 'Please, Antonina Karpovna, Klavdiya Arsenyevna has asked that you stay until she returns.'

'Can we make our beds?' one of the women asks.

'No. And I have to tell you something.'

The women pause, all eyes on Cilka.

'It wasn't the guard who did this, it was me.'

'Why did you do this?' Elena asks.

162

'Because Klavdiya made her, obviously.' Josie jumps to Cilka's defence.

'Is that right?' Elena asks.

'Still, it was me who did it,' Cilka replies.

She flicks her eyes to Hannah, who is red-faced as she presses around the edges of her mattress, seeming to find her pills safe.

Antonina walks down towards Cilka.

'What's this all about? Why weren't you at work?'

'Well . . .' Cilka says, struggling to hold on to a voice that threatens to break.

She is saved by the door opening and Klavdiya stepping inside the hut, imposing in her uniform. She looks around with a wicked smirk on her face.

'Get this place tidied up, you lazy bitches.' To Antonina, she says, 'Come with me,' and the two of them walk to the end of the hut where Josie has been putting her mattress and sheet back on the bed. They stop beside the bed. Josie stops what she is doing. Cilka stands beside her unmade bed.

'Is this yours?' Klavdiya asks Josie.

'Yes, Klavdiya Arsenyevna.'

Klavdiya yanks the sheet away from the mattress, turning it over, revealing the sewn patch with writing. She shows it to Antonina and asks her, 'What is this?'

Antonina looks at the sheet with writing thrust at her.

'I don't know. I haven't . . .'

'I'm sorry, Josie, you have the wrong sheet. This is mine,' Cilka blurts out.

All eyes turn to Cilka as she reaches out and takes the sheet from Klavdiya.

'These are the names of medications we use in the hospital. I wrote them to practise spelling them. I didn't want to make mistakes in the patients' records.'

'Cilka, no,' Josie says.

'It's all right, Josie, I'm sorry you picked up my sheet. Please, Klavdiya Arsenyevna, this is mine, I'm the one to blame.'

Klavdiya turns on Antonina.

'You are responsible for what goes on in this hut. What have you got to say for yourself? When was the last time you inspected this?'

'I only did it today, this morning, when I returned,' says Cilka. 'Before you came. Antonina Karpovna couldn't possibly have known about this. She inspected our beds only yesterday.'

'Is that right?' Klavdiya asks, looking at Antonina.

'I haven't seen this before,' Antonina replies, looking at Cilka with concern.

'Cilka, no . . .' Josie wails.

'It's all right, Josie, make your bed. I'll be fine.'

Cilka is grabbed by the arm, marched from the hut.

* * *

Cilka lies curled up on the stone floor of a tiny cell. She wears only her underclothes. She is shivering so hard her hip and shoulder are turning to bruises. In front of her nose is a damp wall, smelling of mould. A barred window at neck height lets in the weather.

With no sense of time, she trains herself to sleep, inviting in the blankness. She wakes from nightmares, screaming, thrashing about, banging her limbs on the cold, hard floor and wall. She shivers more, the bruises blossoming all over her.

Sometimes a hand throws in a hardened chunk of black bread, sometimes a cup of soup so thin it could just be water.

The toilet bucket in the corner reeks; it is rarely changed.

When she wakes from her nightmares Cilka willingly invites the blankness back. But sometimes it will not stay. There is too much quiet, and a tight band of pressure around her head. Hunger, thirst, pain, cold.

She keeps seeing her mother, her hand slipping from Cilka's, the death cart being driven away.

Other women's faces. Shaved heads, sunken cheeks. They all had a name. They all had a number.

The images crackle, burn. The crying of the women permeates the silence. Or maybe it is her, crying. She is no longer sure.

At some point, a man enters. A blurred face. Gleb Vitalyevich. Cilka is too weak to protest when he takes her arm, feels for her pulse.

'Strong. Keep going,' the doctor says.

No. A wild, angry scream rises from within her. She

bucks on the floor, screaming. He closes the door. Her nails scrape the mould from the walls. She screams on.

Maybe this was where it has all been leading. But to go through all of that, and end here? *No.* Some part of her wills herself to go back to stillness, distance. *Do not give in to madness.*

She will survive, she knows that. She can survive anything.

The loud clanking screech of the door opening.

'Get up, get out,' a blurred face says.

Unable to walk, she crawls from the hole through the open door.

The glare of the weak setting sun bouncing off the snow blinds her, and she can't see the person screaming abuse but then recognises the voice. Klavdiya Arsenyevna kicks her in the side. She curls up in a ball only to find herself being pulled by the hair up onto her feet. Dragged like this, stumbling continually, Cilka is returned to her hut as the others are arriving back from their different work areas.

The women in Hut 29 look down on the frail, broken body of Cilka lying on the floor, Klavdiya challenging them to help her, waiting to strike out at anyone who attempts to do so. Cilka crawls through the hut to her bed at the end of the room and pulls herself onto the bed. The mattress feels almost unbearably soft.

'Anyone else who has material they shouldn't will get double the stay in the hole.' She leaves the door open as she departs, glaring at Antonina as she passes.

Antonina closes the door and hurries to Cilka. Josie has

already wrapped her in her arms, weeping as she rocks her, whispering, 'I'm sorry, I'm sorry.' Cilka can feel where every bone in her body meets skin, meets material, meets the other bodies, the bed.

The women gather around, curious to hear what Cilka has to say. She is not the first one of them to spend time in the hole, but she is the first to have been punished for someone else's error.

'Has anyone got some food they can give her?' Antonina says. 'Elena, get the kettle boiling and make her some tea.'

She turns to Cilka. 'Can you sit up? Here, let me help you.'

Elena does as she's told.

Cilka lets Antonina help her sit up to rest against the wall. Josie hands her a large chunk of bread, everyone grateful that Antonina has never objected to food being in the hut, having also been the beneficiary of the patients' uneaten meals. Antonina often trades this food for goods for Klavdiya. There is a network and the rules are murky. This is the prerogative of the guards and, beneath them, the brigadiers – to bend the rules or enforce them, at will, depending on how they will benefit.

Cilka nibbles on the bread and soon a cup of strong tea is in her hand.

'Do you think you can make it to the mess?' Antonina asks.

'No, it's all right. I just want to sleep in a bed.'

'I'll have Josie bring you back something. The rest of you, off to dinner.'

'Can I stay with her?' Josie asks.

'You need to go to the mess, eat, and bring back something hot for Cilka.'

The women head towards the door, pulling on layers of clothing. Hannah is the last of them. She stands by the door, looks back at Cilka.

'I know what you did,' she says.

'You don't know anything,' Cilka says flatly.

'No, I mean for Josie.' She sighs. 'But don't think this gets you off the hook with me.'

Cilka says nothing.

'I could have told them everything, while you were in there.'

Cilka rolls away, tries to block out the voice.

'You would have come back and been shunned. You only help people so you can feel better about having rolled over for evil.' She pauses. 'You're lucky, I have found another supply point for . . . what I need. For now. But you will keep doing whatever it is I ask you to. Because I will tell them.'

She closes the door.

* * *

The next morning Cilka struggles to get out of bed, her legs collapsing underneath her at first. Josie returns from the mess with breakfast for her. Antonina tells her not to report for rollcall, she will mark her as present.

As the women prepare to go to work Cilka limps out to join them, not knowing where she should go.

'Josie, take her to the hospital with you. I think she needs to see a doctor,' Antonina says.

Cilka looks at Josie. She doesn't want to tell Antonina, but it has occurred to her that the doctor who fired her, Gleb Vitalyevich, might have some connection to the guard Klavdiya Arsenyevna. That he may have told her Cilka would be in her hut, and to make things worse for her.

It would be risky to go to the hospital, when last time, Josie had not been able to get Yelena alone and let her know Cilka was waiting outside. But Cilka can't stay in the hut for fear of being accused of 'shirking' again, nor is she able to go to the mines and work – she is not strong enough. She will have to face the hospital and hope that she and Josie can get Yelena's attention, and not Gleb's.

* * *

This time, Josie leaves Cilka in the waiting area, leaning against a wall, and goes through to the ward. Cilka has her hat pulled low. Soon several staff members rush out to her and assist her into a chair.

'Get Yelena,' Raisa says to no one in particular.

'I'm right here,' Yelena says, pushing her way to Cilka.

'Hello,' says Cilka, forcing a smile.

'Come with me,' Yelena says, helping her to her feet. 'Gleb Vitalyevich is not in yet.' They enter the ward and go through to the nearby dispensary. Sitting her on the only chair in there, Yelena carries out a cursory examination of Cilka's face and hands, tenderly stroking her dirty face.

'We'll get you cleaned up and I'll take a better look at you. How do you feel?'

'Stiff, sore, worn out. I ache in bones and muscles I never knew I had, but I'm all right. I survived.'

She feels guilty sitting in this room though, remembering the drugs she's taken.

'I'm so sorry this happened, Cilka.' Cilka can see the regret in Yelena's eyes. 'We are all in danger from him, but I wish—'

'It doesn't matter,' says Cilka.

'What are we going to do with you?' Yelena asks, sighing.

'Can't you get me my job back? You know what I did was the right thing.'

'It doesn't matter what I know, I can't take you back here.' Yelena looks pained.

'Well, where else can I work? I want to help people. And I know I'm not currently strong enough for the mines.'

Yelena looks away, thinking. Cilka waits.

'I have a colleague who works in the maternity ward behind us. I don't know if they need anyone, Cilka, and I don't want to get your hopes up . . .'

A maternity ward, in this place? Of course, there would have to be, Cilka thinks. But what happens to the children afterwards? Perhaps it is better to not think of that, for now.

'I'll go anywhere I can help.'

'I will ask him,' Yelena says. 'Have you had any experience delivering babies?'

Cilka flashes back to the night she held Natalya's premature, stillborn son. How useless she felt.

'Well, I have helped deliver one baby here.'

'Ah yes, I remember. You brought his body to us. I can't promise anything, but I will ask.'

'Thank you, thank you. I won't let you down.'

'I can't keep you here today. You will have to risk going back to the hut. A note may not be enough, but I'll get a messenger to alert the relevant parties. He can take you back too. Wait here.'

Cilka's rests her head against a shelf, feeling lightheaded. She needs this job to work out. She thinks about how grateful she is to Yelena for the ways she has always tried to help.

The door opens and Yelena and the messenger enter. She looks up and another wave of dizziness overtakes her. It is the man with the brown eyes. He smiles gently as Yelena relays instructions to him. He looks at Yelena, nods, then reaches out a hand for Cilka's arm, just above the elbow. He helps to lift her from the chair and opens the door.

Outside the hospital, his grip remains firmly on her upper arm, and he keeps his body at a polite distance as they walk towards the huts in a light snowfall. Where is he from? Why is he here? Why does she even want to know?

'Your name is Cilka Klein?' he asks.

'Yes,' she says. She looks briefly up at his face. He is looking ahead, snow dusting his face, his eyelashes. His accent is recognisable.

'You are Czech,' she says.

'Yes,' he stops, looks down at her.

'What is your name?' She switches to speaking to him in Czech, to which he gives a delighted laugh, his eyes lighting up.

'Alexandr Petrik.'

Before they start walking again he releases his arm momentarily to light a cigarette. As he closes his eyes to draw in the smoke, Cilka studies his face – his dark eyebrows, his lips, his strong jawline above his scarf. He opens his eyes and she looks quickly away.

He takes her arm again, and she leans in a little closer to his side.

They arrive at the hut, and though Cilka is exhausted and needs to lie down, it feels too soon.

He opens the door for her, and she goes in. He remains outside.

'I will take my messages,' he says. 'And I . . . hope to see you again soon, Cilka Klein.'

Again, words get stuck in Cilka's mouth. She nods to him, then lets the door close.

* * *

The next morning Cilka walks with Josie to the hospital. As Josie enters, Yelena steps outside, taking Cilka by the arm.

'Come with me.'

Heads down, they fight against a blizzard, their progress slow. The snow-blast stings Cilka's sensitive skin, where it is uncovered. Behind the main hospital building, several smaller ones are barely visible. Yelena heads for one of them and they go inside.

A man in a white coat with a stethoscope around his neck is waiting for them.

'Cilka, this is Doctor Labadze, Petre Davitovich. He and I trained together in Georgia and he has been kind enough to agree to give you a trial. Thank you, Petre Davitovich. Cilka is a quick learner and patients love her.'

'If you recommend her, Yelena Georgiyevna, then I am sure she is good.'

Cilka says nothing, worried that if she opens her mouth, she will say the wrong thing.

'Look after yourself, Cilka, and do as you are told,' Yelena says pointedly. 'No doing things on your own.'

With a quick wink, Yelena leaves Cilka with Petre.

'Take your coat off, you can hang it on a hook behind you, and come with me.'

A nearby door opens into a small ward. Cilka hears the cries of labouring women before she sees them.

Six beds line each side of the room. Seven of them are occupied, one by a mother with a new arrival, the delicate cries of a newborn competing with the women's moans of pain.

Two nurses move quickly and efficiently between the women, three of whom have their knees bent, close to giving birth.

'Welcome to our world,' the doctor says. 'Some days

we have one or two women birthing, other days they fill the beds and can be on the floor. No predicting.'

'Are these women all prisoners?' Cilka asks.

'They are,' the doctor says.

'How many nurses do you have working each day?'

'Two, though you will make three, but one of them will probably move to the night shift.' Relief and gratitude run through Cilka. Clearly room has been made for her. 'I don't know why babies insist on being born during the night, but it seems to happen. Have you delivered babies before?'

'Just the one, a stillborn in our hut.'

He nods. 'No matter, you'll catch on. Really, there is not much for you to do, just catch the baby,' he says with a hint of humour. 'The women have to do it themselves. What I need you to do is look for signs of problems – the head is too big, the birth not advancing like it should – and let myself or one of the other doctors know.'

'How many doctors work here?'

'Just the two of us, one day shift, the other night shift. We swap around. Let's go and take a look at bed two.'

The woman in Bed 2 has her bent legs exposed, her face soaked in perspiration and tears as she groans quietly.

'You're doing well, nearly there.' He takes a peek at the bottom of the bed. 'Not long now.'

Cilka leans over the woman.

'Hello, I'm Cilka Klein.' In the absence of a patronymic name, which is used when the Russians greet each other, Cilka often uses two names – her first and last, when introducing herself, to make the person she is talking to comfortable. 'What's your name?'

'Aaaargh . . .' she grunts. 'Niiiina Romano . . . va.'

'Have you had a baby before, Nina Romanova?'

'Three. Three boys.'

'Doctor, doctor! Here, quick,' is shouted from the other end of the ward.

'Why don't you stay here and help Nina Romanova, she knows what she's doing. Give me a call when the baby is out.'

With that, he walks quickly to the nurse who called out. Cilka looks over and sees her holding a small baby upside down who appears lifeless. She continues watching as the doctor takes the baby and gives it a quick pat on the bottom before pushing a finger into the infant's mouth and down its throat. The baby splutters and the ward fills with lusty crying.

'Lovely!' Petre says. 'Another citizen for our glorious State.'

Cilka can't tell if he is just saying this for show or whether he believes it.

She turns her attention back to Nina. She wipes the woman's face with the corner of a sheet. Useless. Looking around, she sees a basin on the far wall, a small pile of towels beside it. She quickly wets a towel and gently wipes Nina's face, brushing her wet matted hair away.

'It's coming, it's coming,' Nina screams.

Cilka ventures to the end of the bed and looks in fascination as the head pops free.

'Doctor – Petre Davitovich,' she screams out.

'Cilka, let me know when the baby is out. I have my hands full here.'

'Pull it out!' screams Nina.

Cilka looks at her hands, bony and weak, and at the baby who now has one shoulder and an arm out. She pushes up her sleeves and reaches in to take hold of the little arm with one hand, cradling the head in the other. Feeling Nina bearing down, she gently tugs on the slippery baby. The one almighty push expels the baby completely and it lies between its mother's legs and in Cilka's hands, blood and fluid pooling around it.

'It's out, it's out,' Cilka cries.

From the other end of the ward comes the doctor's voice, calm and reassuring. 'Lift it up and give it a tap – you have to make the baby cry, make sure it is breathing.'

As Cilka lifts the baby up it begins to cry without the need of assistance.

'Well done – that's what we want to hear,' the doctor calls. 'I'll be with you in a minute. Wrap the baby up and give it to Nina.'

'What is it?' pleads Nina.

Cilka looks at the baby, then to the doctor, who is watching her.

'You can tell her.'

Cilka wraps the baby in the towel left for that purpose. Handing it to Nina, she tells her, 'It's a little girl, a beautiful little girl.'

Nina sobs as her daughter is placed in her arms. Cilka

176

watches, fighting tears that threaten, biting her lip – the emotion of the moment overwhelming. After studying her baby's face, Nina exposes her breasts and pushes the baby roughly onto a nipple. The baby does nothing at first, seemingly reluctant, and then she finally latches on and Cilka marvels at the little jaw working feverishly away.

The doctor appears beside her.

'Well done. If Nina was a first-time mother, she wouldn't know to put the baby to her breast as quickly as possible. In that case, you would need to help her. Do you understand?'

'Yes.'

'Go and get some towels. Nina's work isn't done yet – she needs to get the placenta out, and having the baby suckle will quicken that.'

'So much to learn,' Cilka mutters as she retrieves a handful of towels.

When Nina has delivered the placenta, the doctor takes it away in a basin he retrieved from underneath the bed.

'Clean her up,' is his parting comment.

One of the other nurses comes over and shows Cilka the procedure for caring for the mother post-delivery. She tells Cilka she and the other nurse are fine with the remaining patients and she should spend some time with Nina and the baby, making sure nothing changes in their condition.

Cilka helps Nina sit up and examine her baby from head to toe. They talk about names and Nina asks Cilka if she has any ideas.

One name comes directly into Cilka's mind.

'What about Gisela – Gita for short?'

Newborn Gita is placed in Cilka's arms and Cilka revels in her smallness, her smell. She goes to give her back and finds Nina sound asleep. Exhausted.

'Get a chair and sit with her,' the nurse who has identified herself as Tatiana Filippovna, suggests. Cilka is grateful. She is still aching all over. 'We don't often get a chance to cuddle the babies, as the mothers are very attached to them. Well, the ones who wanted them. A lot of them are all too happy for us to take them away and never look at them again.'

The idea breaks Cilka's heart, but it is also something she understands. How could anyone bear to think of what the child's life would be like, or their own life trying to protect them in a place like this?

'Nina will be transferred next door to the nursery hut in a little while,' Tatiana continues.

From Nina's bedside, Cilka cuddles little Gita while observing the other two nurses and the doctor at work. Always calm, they move from patient to patient, soothing them, offering words of encouragement.

When a guard appears to take Nina and the baby away, Cilka is upset to see them go. Helping Nina into her coat, wrapping the baby inside, she assists the unsteady new mother to the door, and she is gone.

When she thinks about it, she's never before held a newborn, healthy baby.

She doesn't dare hope that she has broken her curse.

That she could have a role in helping new life come into the world, rather than overseeing death.

'And now you clean up and get the bed ready for the next one, says Tatiana. 'Come on, I'll show you where the buckets and water are. Can't guarantee clean linen for everyone but we'll find the least spoiled.'

'Aren't there cleaners to do this?' Cilka asks. She wouldn't normally baulk at the work but she has mere threads of energy left.

Tatiana laughs, 'Yes, you. You are the cleaner. Unless you think the doctor should do it?'

'Of course not,' Cilka says, smiling, wanting to show she is happy to work. She will grit her teeth and be grateful.

Cilka cleans up after Nina and two others who give birth. Tatiana and her colleague Svetlana Romonovna concentrate on the other patients, and then Cilka, to show her dedication, cleans up after them, drawing from a hidden reserve of energy. Each patient is taken away mysteriously with their newborn, for life in 'the hut next door'.

* * *

'Who do we have here?'

Two new nurses enter the ward.

Cilka looks up from her mop, leaning on it. 'Hello, I'm Cilka Klein. I started work here today.'

'As a cleaner, I see. Just what we need,' one of them replies.

'Well, no, I'm a nurse . . .' She tries to steady her

breathing. 'I'm just helping Tatiana Filippovna by cleaning up.'

'Hey, Tatiana, got yourself a slave here.'

'Get lost, you pathetic excuse for a nurse,' Tatiana responds.

Cilka tries to work out if the exchange is in jest or seriousness. The thumb thrust through the middle and index fingers at Tatiana – a rude gesture – answers her question.

'Well, slave, we'll be on day shift next week; we'll see how good a cleaner you are.' The two newcomers go to the front of the ward to the desk area. Pulling up chairs they relax, talking and giggling. Cilka doesn't need to be told they are talking about her, their body language and calls of 'Get back to work' are clear enough. This surprising, joyous day seems also to herald a darker future.

Tatiana finds a moment to reassure her. 'Look, you are a prisoner. We are not, we are qualified and must work both day and night shifts. I'm sorry, but every second week you will have to work with those cows. Don't let them boss you around too much, you are here to work as a nurse.'

'Thank you. I shall look forward to every second week.'

'Our shifts are up,' Tatiana says. 'Come on, get your coat and go. We'll see you tomorrow.'

'Night.'

With mixed emotions, but relieved that her shift is over, Cilka wraps herself in her coat and steps out into the frigid air. In her pocket she feels the note Petre has written advising Antonina of her new position.

* * *

180

That night, Cilka tells Josie, Olga, Elena and anyone else interested about her day and her new role helping deliver babies. Though Hannah lies on her bed, facing the wall, Cilka can tell she is listening, too. She regales them with exaggerated stories of baby Gita's birth, and how she flew out from her mother and would have landed on the floor if Cilka hadn't caught her. She declares herself now an expert on all matters concerning childbirth and tells them about the support she received from the nurses and the one lovely doctor who couldn't be more caring. She doesn't mention the two night-shift nurses she will have to spend the next week with.

Questions of where the new mothers went and whether they were allowed to stay with their babies, and for how long, are brushed aside. She doesn't know that yet. And she's worried about knowing.

Elena says she has heard that they take the babies away from the mothers and force them back to work.

'I'll find out soon enough,' Cilka promises.

Cilka had been given the same food as the other nurses, twice as much bread as the usual ration, and she has been able to bring that back to share. She is relieved she can still be useful in this way, or the guilt of landing another inside job would be overwhelming.

Cilka is also grateful that the job will be so busy and all-consuming that she will have no time to think about Alexandr Petrik, the Czech man working as a messenger. Because no good would come of that.

As Cilka lies down, Josie pushes her over, crawling in

beside her. She sobs, 'I'm sorry about the sheet, Cilka. About you having to go into the hole.'

'Please, Josie, you don't have to keep saying that. It's over. Can we get back to being friends?'

'You are my dearest friend,' Josie says.

'Well, dearest, get out of my bed and let me get some sleep.'

Auschwitz-Birkenau, 1942

Cilka stares at a fly on the cold cement wall of her room in Block 25. He has not come for her today.

Women and girls stagger into the block to seek out a place to lay their head for the final time. She sighs, stands up from her bed and opens the door, watching the wraiths pass by her, holding her arms around herself.

A woman, being assisted into the block by two others, turns to Cilka – thick grey-brown locks, dark circles under her eyes, sunken cheeks. It takes Cilka a moment to recognise her.

'Mumma!' she screams.

Cilka pushes herself into the trio, grasping the woman in the middle.

'My baby, my beautiful dievča*!' the woman cries.*

The other women are too distraught, blank-eyed, to pay much attention to the reunion.

Cilka helps her mother into her own room, and onto the

bed. For a long time they sit there, holding each other, not saying a word.

The clanging of pans and shouts rouses Cilka. The evening rations have arrived. Gently removing her arms from around her mother, Cilka goes to meet those bringing in urns of watery coffee and small rations of stale bread.

She tells the women around her to come and get some food. She knows from experience that those who have the strength will. The others are too far gone.

Back in her room, she places her mother's portion on the floor as she attempts to prop her up against the wall. When this fails, she places a small piece of bread on her lips, encouraging her to open her mouth. Her mother turns her head away.

'You have it, my darling. You need it more than I do.'

'No, Mumma, I can get more,' Cilka says. 'Please, you have to get your strength back, you need to eat.'

'Your hair . . .' her mother says. It was still there, tucked behind her ears, falling over her shoulders. She reaches up and runs her fingers through it, like she did when Cilka was a child.

Cilka brings the food up to her mother's mouth and she opens it and allows Cilka to feed her. Pulling herself up, she drinks the foul-tasting liquid Cilka holds to her lips.

Cilka settles her mother on the bed.

'I'll be right back, just stay here and rest.'

'Where are you going? Don't leave me.'

'Please, Mumma, I won't be long, I have to find some-one . . .'

'Nobody can help us, please stay with me. We have so little time.'

'That's why I have to go and see someone, so we can have more time. I won't let them take you.'

Cilka reaches the door.

'Cilka, no.' The voice is unexpectedly firm.

Cilka returns to sit on the bed, cradling her mother's head in her arms. 'There is someone who can help us, someone who can have you put into another block where you can get better and we can see each other, be with each other. Please, Mumma, let me go and speak to him.'

'No, my darling daughter. Stay with me, here and now. There are no certainties in this place. Let us have this night together. I know what awaits me in the morning. I am not afraid.'

'I can't let them take you, Mumma. You and Magda are all I have.'

'My darling Magda! She's alive?'

'She is, Mumma.'

'Oh . . . thank Hashem. You must look after each other, as best you can.'

'And you, Mumma, I must look after you.'

Cilka's mother struggles to free herself from her child's arms. 'Look at me, look at me. I am sick, I am dying. You can't stop that.'

Cilka runs her hands over her mother's face, kisses her shaven head. Their tears mingle and fall together onto the bed.

'What about Papa, Mumma – was he with you?'

'Oh, my darling, we were separated. He was in a bad way . . .'

Overwhelming waves of sadness and hopelessness threaten to drown Cilka. 'No. No, Mumma.'

'Lie here with me,' her mother says gently, 'and in the morning kiss me goodbye. I will watch over you.'

'I can't. I can't let you go,' Cilka sobs.

'You must, it's not your decision to make.'

'Hold me. Hold me, Mumma.'

Cilka's mother embraces her daughter with all her might, pulling her down onto the bed. The two become one.

'One day, if Hashem is willing,' her mother says, stroking Cilka's face, 'you will know a child's love. You will know what I feel for you.'

Cilka buries her face in her mother's neck.

'I love you, Mumma.'

* * *

The sun has barely risen when Cilka, her mother and the others in Block 25 are roused by the screaming SS and barking dogs.

'Out, out, everybody out.'

Cilka's head rests on her mother's shoulder as they slowly leave the room and join the others heading outside to the waiting trucks.

Swagger sticks are being wielded at those too slow or in any way resisting the final few steps onto the trucks. Cilka pauses. A stick is raised in her mother's direction by a nearby guard.

185

'Don't you dare,' she hisses at him.

The baton is lowered as Cilka's mother takes the final few steps, Cilka still clinging to her arm.

'Mumma, no, don't get on the truck!'

The guards watch as Cilka's mother frees herself from her daughter, kisses her on both cheeks, on the lips and runs her fingers through her hair. One last time. She then accepts the hands reaching down from the truck to help pull her up. Cilka can still feel her mother's lips on her face. She sinks to the ground as the truck starts up and drives away. A guard extends his hand to Cilka and she smacks him away. The truck drives on.

CHAPTER 13

'You, what's-your-name.'

Pasting a smile on her face, Cilka turns to the voice. She will not respond, will make the nurse work for it.

'Come here.'

Cilka walks to the bed where the nurse stands. Every bed is occupied. If ever there was a day Cilka could be useful, today is it. Cilka smiles at the new mother holding her baby, just hours old.

'We need this bed, and no one has turned up to take her next door. You need to take them over.'

'I'll just grab my coat,' Cilka replies. It is spring now, but frosty outside.

'You don't have time for that; just get them out of here.'

'But where—'

The new mother tugs on Cilka's skirt.

'It's all right, I know where to go. I've been there before.'

The patient is already dressed, her baby swaddled in a blanket. Cilka helps her into her coat with the baby tucked inside. The patient looks for the nurse; she is nowhere to be seen. Grabbing the blanket off her bed, she indicates for Cilka to wrap it around herself. She does. The patient leads the way out of a back door.

The building they are headed to is only fifty or sixty metres away. Their feet crunch across the frosty grass. The sound of infants crying, jabbering and screaming reaches them before they open the door. Stepping inside, Cilka is confronted by a chaotic scene. A few cots crammed against one wall, small mattresses – more like mats – scattered around. Three staff to care for what looks like twenty babies and toddlers.

'We need to check in here and then go through the door at the end of the room to the dormitory where I will sleep.'

'And we have a full house again,' one of the staff members says as she walks towards them. 'Well, hello, Anna Anatolyeva. You're back.'

'I missed your charming face, what can I say. How are you, Irina Igorevna, still eating little children for breakfast?'

'Oh, Anya, of course, why are you back here?'

Cilka notices the switch to the diminutive and understands that these women know each other quite well.

'One of those ugly pigs looked at me and, you know, I

have another baby. This one you will look after properly, or I will send his ugly pig of a father to deal with you.'

'Yeah, yeah, heard it before. What have you got this time?'

'Another girl. Another victim for the cause.'

'Have you named her this time?'

'You did such a great job with the last one, you give her a name. Make it a strong one. She will need to be strong to survive this house of horrors.'

Looking around, Cilka tries to process the meaning of what she sees. The two other staff stand chatting, each with an infant on their hip, jiggling it up and down in an attempt to soothe it. They seem oblivious to the howling babies, the toddlers fighting over a ratty blanket. Several have no nappy on; the smell of urine and faeces is overpowering.

The new mother attempts to hand her newborn over.

'Look after her yourself for a while,' Irina Igorevna says. 'She won't bite, or maybe she will when she realises who her mumma is.'

She turns to Cilka and thrusts her chin at her. 'Who are you?'

'I'm one of the nurses. I was asked to bring her over here.'

'All right then. This one knows what to do – you can go.'

Cilka can't just yet. 'Excuse me,' she asks. 'How many babies do you have here?'

'Twenty is our maximum; there are only twenty beds next door for the mothers.'

'How long are they allowed to stay here? Some of them don't look like babies anymore.'

'New, huh? Well, *printsessa*, here's how it works. When Anya here produces another bastard, she gets to stay here until the kid is two then she gets sent back to a general hut to get knocked up again and it starts all over.'

'So she doesn't have to work? Just stay here and look after her baby?'

'Do you see any other mothers here? Do you? No. Anya will go next door and look after her bastard by herself for four weeks, then she will bring it here each morning and go off to work like the rest of the poor bastards.'

'And you three look after the babies during the day.'

'Got an education, have you? Worked that out by yourself, did you?'

'I'm sorry, I don't mean to offend,' Cilka says, not wanting to get on anyone's wrong side again. 'I had no idea how it worked, that's all.'

The woman's face softens a little.

'Are there more huts?'

'If you must know, the majority of the new arrivals go with their mothers to the big unit down the road, at Rechlag,' says Irina Igorevna. 'You're very nosy.'

'Can I have a look around?'

'Please yourself. I've got things to do, can't stand here chatting all day. Anya, get out of here.'

'Thanks,' says the departing mother to Cilka. 'See you around.'

190

'Anna Anatolyeva,' Cilka says tentatively. 'I think . . . Jozefína . . . Josie, is a nice name.'

The woman shrugs. 'Fine, whatever you want. I'll take little Josie and go and have a lie-down.'

An infant has crawled over to Cilka, plonking himself on one of her feet, and is staring up at her. Cilka bends down and picks him up. His little fingers poke her in the mouth, the eyes and up her nostrils. She giggles and tickles him on the belly. He doesn't respond, keeps wanting to put his fingers up her nose.

With the boy balanced on her hip Cilka walks around the room, looking at the other infants. She stops at a small baby lying on a blanket on the floor staring at the ceiling. Cilka moves her head to get its attention; only a small movement of its head shows it knows Cilka is there. Placing the boy on the floor she touches the baby; it is hot to the touch in a room badly in need of heating. She picks up one of its arms and lets it go. The baby makes no attempt to stop its arm flopping onto the floor.

Cilka calls out to the staff. 'Excuse me, this baby is sick, there's something wrong with it.'

One of the attendants wanders over.

'Yeah, been like that for a couple of days.'

'Has a doctor seen it?'

'Doctors don't come here, love. These little ones either make it or they don't. This will be one that probably won't.'

Cilka looks again at the tiny form, its large head and sunken cheeks, its ribs showing under the skin.

191

She has seen enough.

'Thank you,' she says to no one in particular. She leaves.

* * *

When Cilka returns to the maternity ward, Petre greets her.

'Hello. Where have you been?'

'Next door – to the nursery. I went with Anna Anatolyeva and her baby.'

Cilka offers no further explanation; she wants to get away from him, away from the images she has just seen, busy herself by cleaning.

'And what did you think of our nursery?'

'Do you ever go there?' she blurts out.

'No, my job is here, delivering babies. Why do you ask?'

'Because some of those babies you deliver safe and sound lie on the floor over there sick and dying.'

'And you know they are dying?'

'I saw it for myself. The staff there, I don't know what you call them, they're not nurses – they show very little interest in the babies. They told me only the strong survive, but they might just be sick. They could live if they got care and treatment.'

'All right, all right, Cilka, settle down. Why don't we talk about this another day?'

'When?'

'When we are not so busy.'

'Tomorrow?'

'When we are not so busy,' Petre repeats. 'Now you had better get back to work.'

* * *

Several weeks pass. The frost starts to thaw, the days get longer. Petre seems to be avoiding Cilka. She struggles. She has learned her lesson about interfering in medical matters, so she never mentions the building next door with the neglected babies. But it's pressing at her. To know something could be done. Once, she'd had to accept circumstances like these. How can she now?

One day she is working with Tatiana and they only have one patient labouring. Petre comes in and checks on the woman. He watches Cilka tidying the administration area, neatly stacking files, checking for entries; the tasks that can only be done when you aren't busy. Pulling up a chair, he says to Cilka, 'Let's talk about the babies in the nursery, shall we?'

'I . . . shouldn't have said anything, it's not my place.' She is clenching her jaw.

'True.' His face, with its bushy brows and moustache, is enigmatic. 'You know, I spoke to Yelena Georgiyevna about you. She asks about you all the time.'

'Really? How is she?' Cilka's chest aches. She doesn't admit to herself she is missing anyone, anything, until her body reminds her that is the case.

'She's good. Busy. I told her what you said about the babies.'

'What did she say?'

193

'She laughed and said, that sounds like Cilka, trying to fix everything.'

'It's just, well . . . you take good care of the mothers, making sure they have healthy babies, then they get sent over there and no one cares anymore.'

'I'm sure their mothers do.'

'Yes, of course, but they work all day and only return to the nursery at night. How are they ever going to get a doctor to check on their babies?'

'That is a very good point. Well, the State cares too, or should do. Those babies are our future workers.'

There does seem to be quite a contradiction about that in this place though, Cilka thinks. Such as the workers getting less food when their productivity drops – as punishment. There are always more people out there to arrest, to replace the dead. But of course she cannot voice any of this out loud.

'How about, given it is quiet here today, you and I go to the nursery and I'll have a look at any baby you think needs to see a doctor,' Petre says.

'I'll get my coat.'

Petre laughs, retrieves his coat and follows Cilka out the door.

The smile on Petre's face disappears the moment he enters the nursery. The three staff are sitting together sipping steaming cups of tea. Babies and infants lie on the floor; some crawl lethargically in circles. He stares in disbelief.

'You're back,' Irina Igorevna calls out before registering

Cilka is not alone. She puts her cup down and hurries over to Cilka and Petre.

'This is Petre Davitovich, the maternity doctor,' Cilka says. 'He has come to have a look at some of the babies, to see if any of them need medical attention.'

Wiping her grubby hands on her dress, the woman extends her hand.

'Irina Igorevna, I'm in charge.'

Petre doesn't take her hand.

'I'm glad you've identified yourself. I'm going to take a look at some of these babies. Show me your charts with their feeding regime.'

'Well, we don't have charts. We just feed them when we can with what we've got; there's never enough to go around so we give it to the strongest. They make the most noise,' she giggles.

Petre goes to the nearest baby, lying limply on a blanket, a thin smock hanging loosely on its body, eyes sunken. The baby doesn't respond when he picks it up. He carries it to the table the three women were sitting around, sweeps their cups to the side, gently places the baby on the table and begins examining it. Cilka stands beside him.

'How old is this infant?'

The three women look from one to another, none of them wanting to speak.

'Irina Igorevna, I said, how old is this infant?'

'I don't know, we just look after them during the day while their mothers are working; there are too many of them for us to get to know them – there are only three of us,' she says, waving her hand around at the others.

'This child is starving. When was the last time you fed him?'

'We would have offered him something a couple of hours ago, but I don't think he wanted anything,' Irina replies.

'Cilka, put him in a cot.'

Cilka takes the little boy and gently places him in a nearby cot. Petre picks up the next infant and repeats the examination. He asks no further questions of the nursery staff. Another baby is given to Cilka.

By the time all the sickly babies have had a quick examination, seven are lined up lying quietly in two cots.

'You two,' Petre points to the other two staff members, 'put your coats on, wrap up two of the babies and come with me. Cilka, can you take two, please?' He picks up the remaining baby, snuggles it inside his coat and heads out the door with Cilka and the nursery staff following.

Back on the ward, he has three babies placed on one bed, four on another. With a flick of his hand he dismisses the nursery staff, who beat a hasty retreat.

Tatiana and Svetlana gather at the beds, looking down at the babies.

'Oh my God, what's happened to them?' Svetlana wails.

'Do either of you know how we can get our hands on some milk?' Petre asks.

'I'll find it. Look after them and I'll be back,' Tatiana says as she grabs her coat and heads out.

'Svetlana, see if you can find the doctor called Yelena Georgiyevna and ask her if she can come here.'

'What can I do?' Cilka asks.

'Well, I could say you've done enough,' he says with a half-laugh. 'Get some charts and write down what I say about each one of these poor little things. We don't know their names so you will have to call them baby one, baby two, and so on.'

As Cilka walks past the only patient on the ward, returning with charts and pens, the woman softly calls out to her, 'What's going on over there?'

'It's all right, just some sick babies. Don't worry, we're going to take care of them.'

Petre is wrapping up the first baby he examined.

'Baby one,' he says. 'Male. Severe malnutrition, fever, infected bug bites, possible deafness. Four to six months of age, hard to tell.'

Cilka quickly writes down his comments below the notation 'Baby 1'. With a thicker pen she gently writes the number one on the baby's forehead, fighting to shut out memories of her own, permanent marking.

They hear the door open, followed by, 'Oh, Cilka, what have you done now?'

Yelena and Svetlana are back. Close behind them Tatiana runs in, carrying a box with baby bottles, each half-filled with nursing mothers' milk.

Petre fills Yelena in on what they are dealing with. She

immediately claims a baby, and strips the child bare to examine her.

'Make her number three, Cilka, I've got number two,' calls out Petre.

Tatiana and Svetlana set about warming up the bottles, holding them in a basin of boiling water. Yelena warns them not to let the babies drink too much; they must be given small amounts and often if they are to recover. The new mother whose baby is sleeping soundly offers to help with feeding and finds herself with a strange baby in her arms.

As the day ends, seven worried mothers appear on the ward, looking for their infants. Petre and Yelena talk to them, assuring them they do not blame them for the condition their infants are in. They are told to stay the night on the ward, food will be brought to them, and they will be shown how to feed their babies every hour – small quantities.

The nurses for the changeover shift appear. Tatiana sends them away saying she will stay the night. Cilka asks if she too can stay.

* * *

Over the next several weeks, the management of the nursery changes. The original staff disappear, replaced by carers approved by Petre and Tatiana. A recording system relating to each baby is put in place. Petre gives Cilka the responsibility of visiting the nursery once a week to identify any baby or infant she determines is in need of medical attention. Despite Petre's belief that these children are important to the system as future workers, Cilka thinks the system might also see them, for now, as a drain on resources. She wonders whether they are all at risk of punishment because of it, but she knows she will fight to keep these infants alive.

Lying on their beds one night, with the sun still high in the sky, Cilka says to Josie, 'Do you think this is to be my calling?'

'What do you mean?' Josie asks.

It is hard for Cilka to reveal her inner thoughts. She worries about what else might be opened up, might spill out of her. Josie looks at her expectantly. 'Am I not to be a mother myself, but someone who helps others who can be?'

Josie bursts into tears.

'Oh, Cilka, I think I'm pregnant.'

CHAPTER 14

To the sounds of snoring, Cilka rolls out of her bed. She pulls the blanket off Josie and runs her hands gently over the swollen body hidden by layers of clothes. She pulls the blanket back under her friend's chin.

'When did you suspect?' Cilka asks.

'I don't know, a month ago? Who can keep track of time in this forgotten place?'

'Josie, I felt the baby kick. You are well along. Why didn't you say something sooner?'

Josie's body shudders as she sobs, biting down on the blanket.

'I'm afraid, Cilka, I'm afraid. Don't yell at me.'

'Shhh, keep your voice down. I'm not the one yelling.'

'What am I going to do?' Cilka sees Josie glance at the

bed that used to be Natalya's. 'You have to help me, Cilka.'

'You are going to have a baby and I will be there with you. We need to tell Antonina tomorrow. Surely it's a risk for you to be working around sick people.'

'And the others?'

'They'll work it out. Don't worry, we will all help you.' Cilka tries to give Josie a look filled with warmth and hope. 'You're going to be a mumma!'

'What about Vadim? Do I tell him? What do you think he will say?'

'I'm surprised he hasn't worked it out,' Cilka says. 'Surely he felt you were getting bigger around your stomach.'

'He just told me I was getting fat. He's such a stupid boy – it wouldn't occur to him.'

'Yeah, you're probably right, but you need to tell him. Next time he comes.'

'What if he—'

'Just tell him. We will worry about his reaction when we get it. You do know they are not going to let the two of you go off and live a happy family life somewhere, don't you?'

'They might.'

'They won't.'

* * *

The next morning after rollcall Cilka approaches Antonina with Josie.

'She's having a baby.'

'Is she now? I wonder how that happened,' Antonina says with disgust.

Cilka chooses to ignore the comment. Josie keeps her head down. Ashamed, humiliated.

'Five months, I'd say,' Cilka tells the brigadier.

'I'll be the judge of that. Open your coat.'

Josie opens her coat, shivering against the wind and in fear of what she is being publicly subjected to. Rough hands press hard against her obvious baby bump. Feel all around her sides, pushing hard from top to bottom.

Josie cries out in pain. 'Stop it, you're hurting me.'

'Just making sure it's not rags stuffed up there; wouldn't be the first.'

Cilka pushes the brigadier's hands away. 'Enough. Satisfied?'

'Get off to work, you. As for the slut here, she can go too, there's no reason she can't continue in the soft job she has. I'll have to tell Klavdiya Arsenyevna about this. She won't be pleased.'

Cilka and Josie hurry towards the hospital buildings.

'I don't mind working, it's not as though it's difficult and it is a distraction for me, during the day; the nights, however . . .'

* * *

That evening, Josie is made a fuss of by the women. They want to feel the baby in her belly; some lucky ones receive a kick for their efforts. 'You're carrying just like I did with my boys,' Olga says, her eyes smiling but with tears in them.

Someone remembers Natalya, the only other pregnancy in the hut, and the tragic ending that was.

Olga notices the effect talking about Natalya is having on Josie and quickly changes the subject. She suggests they all get involved in making clothes for Josie's baby. She is immediately designated the designer; sheets are inspected to see who can afford to lose a foot or two, the embroiderers excited at having something meaningful to create for a new life.

Hannah is sitting at the back of the group, watching all the activity with a look of distaste.

'How do you all have the energy,' she says, 'to delude yourselves?'

'Hannah,' Olga says sharply, 'finding a little hope in the darkness is not a weakness.'

Hannah shakes her head. 'Like a nice fur coat, ha, Cilka?'

The women look at Cilka. Her face burns and there is bile in her throat. She can't think of any reply – an explanation or a retort. She coughs and clears her throat.

'Hannah's right though,' Josie says, putting down the strip of sheet in her hand. 'It's silly to forget where we are.'

'I don't think it is,' Olga says, determinedly unpicking some thread. 'I think it helps us to go on.'

* * *

It is well over a week before Vadim comes knocking. As he starts his groping and pawing of Josie, she stops him.

'I have to tell you something.'

'I don't want to talk just now.'

'I'm having your baby,' she blurts out.

Cilka has turned her head away from Boris to listen to the exchange.

'What's wrong?' asks Boris.

'Nothing, shhh.'

'What did you say?' Vadim growls.

'I'm having a baby, your baby.'

'I thought you were just getting fat.'

'No.'

'I don't want no fuckin' baby. What the hell do you think you're doing having a baby?'

'You did this to me. I didn't ask for it.'

'How do I know it's mine?'

Josie pushes him away, screaming, 'Because you made me your property, remember? No one else is allowed to touch me, remember? Get out of here, get out, get out!'

Josie's screams reduce to a whimper.

Vadim stumbles from the bed, hopping about as he looks for his discarded clothes. The exchange disturbs all the men in the room who scramble for their trousers and start retreating.

'I would never speak to you like that,' Boris says to Cilka, pushing a lock of hair back from her eyes. 'In fact, I'd be so happy if you had my baby.'

That's not going to happen, Boris, she thinks, but she

merely tells him it's time to go. Cilka has never been pregnant. Her period stopped in the *other place* for a long time, like so many of the women there, and now only comes intermittently. Poor nutrition, shock, she isn't sure. It is possible there is no going back from it.

'All right, I will, but I will be thinking about you.'

In the dark, the women find their way to Josie's bed, offering support and hugs. The slightly warped sense of humour the women have developed over the past few years serves them well as they share stories about what the men who have visited them lack, and their capacity to father a child. Josie finds herself laughing, between sobs. Cilka feels affection bloom for these women, with their hollow cheeks and gap-toothed smiles – a feeling that has only ever surfaced in brief moments surrounded by loss. For her sister. For Gita. She tucks the feeling deep inside, where nothing can harm it.

* * *

Over the next few weeks, Josie's moods swing wildly. In the morning she wakes, joins the others for breakfast and rollcall upbeat and keen to go to work, where she will be asked by medical and nursing staff how is she feeling. At the end of the day, tired and aching, she barely speaks, stays on her bed and often doesn't come to dinner. At first she had been excited about the small gowns the women were making for her; now she barely glances at them.

Cilka and Elena gently speak to Josie, to discover if it is the fear of the approaching birth causing her mood swings. The only clue she gives them relates to Vadim. How will she ever be able to tell her baby about its father? They comfort her as best they can, promising to be in her and her baby's life always. It is a promise they all know will be difficult to keep. Just words to keep her holding on, to get her through.

With little more than a month before Josie's expected birth date, Cilka wakes in the middle of the night, startled by the hut door slamming shut in the wind. She glances at Josie's bed. It is empty. She has spent many nights looking at her friend sleeping, her face pinched and troubled even in sleep, her growing stomach protruding underneath the blanket.

Alarmed, she reaches out to pat the bed, to confirm Josie has gone. Her hands rest on something soft and she realises it is an article of clothing. It is well below freezing outside. She sits up, grasps the coat and several more items of clothing she finds with it.

Cilka quietly locates her boots and shuffles along the row of beds until she gets to Elena's. She shakes her awake and tells her to get dressed quickly. Wrapping their faces, heads and hands as best they can, the two women head out of the hut.

It is bitterly cold. Snow is falling lightly. A chilling wind cuts through their layers of clothing to their blood and bones. The nearby searchlights cast a ghostly shadow around their hurrying forms. They see bare footprints in the snow leading away from their hut. Their feet squelch and squeak as they follow the trail.

Behind the mess hut, they find Josie. Naked, unconscious, barely breathing, curled up by the perimeter fence. Cilka gasps – *no*. And then feels the blankness closing over her.

'What do we do with her? I think she may be dead,' Elena whispers.

Cilka leans over and wraps Josie in the coat she has brought with her.

'We have to get her back to the hut and warm her up. Oh, Josie, what have you done?' Cilka cries.

Cilka lifts her by the shoulders; Elena takes her legs. Together they stumble back the way they came to the safety of their hut.

They are unable to open and close the door quietly, and soon the rest of the women are awake, demanding to know what is going on. Elena fills them in, and calls them over, for whatever they can do. Cilka seems to have lost her words for a moment. The women go about helping as they can. Two of them begin massaging Josie's feet, another two her hands. Cilka places her ear on Josie's stomach, tells them all to be quiet a minute, and listens.

Thump, thump, strong and loud, bounces back to her.

'She's still alive, and the baby is still alive,' Cilka says.

Elena shakes her head. 'Even a minute longer out there . . . Cilka, it's so lucky you noticed she was gone.'

'Come on,' Cilka says, 'let's get her warmed up quickly.'

She takes a mug of hot water, opens Josie's mouth and pours a small amount in. Blankets are piled on top of her.

Slowly, she begins to moan, low and guttural. Elena gently slaps her face.

'I saw someone do that once to someone who had fainted,' she explains.

In the dark they can't see if Josie has begun to open her eyes. Cilka senses that she is coming to and talks softly to her. Brushing Josie's face, she feels tears.

'It's all right, Josie, we have you.' It is an effort for Cilka to keep her voice gentle. A part of her feels enraged, helpless to the point of dizziness. She has seen too many naked bodies lying in snow. With no choice but to give in. But Josie has a choice. Maybe Cilka hasn't helped her enough to see that. 'Josie, you are going to be all right. We're not going to let anything happen to you.'

A chorus of support increases Josie's crying. 'I'm sorry,' comes out, choked with tears. 'I'm so sorry. I can't do this.'

'Yes, you can,' Cilka says with force. 'You can. You must.'

'You can, Josie,' Elena says, and the other women echo the words, reaching in to touch her.

Cilka says, 'She's going to be all right now. Take back your blankets and get some sleep. I'm going to spend the night with her.' She will curl up beside her, despite the dizzying rage. She will give her what she needs. She will hold her. She will make her see this is not the end. 'Thank you all,' Cilka says. 'We have to stick together, we're all we have.'

Many of the women hug both Josie and Cilka before going back to their beds, where sleep may or may not come for the rest of the night. Cilka doesn't respond to their affection, but feels grateful somewhere deep down.

Cilka moves Josie over and climbs into her bed. With her arms over Josie's large belly, their heads resting against each other, Cilka murmurs softly. Josie soon falls asleep. It doesn't happen for Cilka, who is still awake when the clanging sounds in the dark, signalling it is time to get up.

After rollcall, Cilka tells Antonina that Josie is having some pains and she thinks she should come to the maternity hospital with her in case the baby is coming. Antonina looks like she is just about out of patience with Cilka's requests, but says nothing, which Cilka interprets to mean she is allowed to take her. She will need to return with some extra tea or bread for the brigadier, or she will suffer the consequences.

Petre examines Josie. 'The baby is fine,' he says. 'It has a strong heartbeat, but it is not ready to be born.'

Josie, who has not yet said a word all morning, but has kept one arm clutched through Cilka's on the walk to the hospital, tells the doctor she just wants the baby to be born. Petre senses there is more to her story and has her placed in a bed for rest.

Cilka is grateful. There are no signs of frostbite, because they found her so quickly, but Josie had shivered all night, and now she needs to rest and stay warm. Petre takes Cilka aside and asks her if there is anything else going on with Josie. Cilka looks into the doctor's kind face and thinks she can risk telling him what happened last night, emphasising that Josie is not a shirker, that she is in fact unwell.

* * *

Josie sleeps the day away. When it is time for her and Cilka to return to their hut Petre tells them that he thinks he needs to keep an eye on Josie as her baby could come at any time. He hands Cilka a note to give to Antonina, stating that Josie is to come to the hospital for observation every day until the baby is born. Cilka tucks the note into her pocket along with the bread she has saved from her meal. Her stomach groans. She has not eaten enough herself today, and the fatigue has made the hunger worse, but she must keep the brigadier content.

For the next three weeks, Josie sleeps and helps out on the ward. She holds the hands of young women like herself as they labour and give birth. Cilka can see that being on this ward is helping Josie just as it helped her. While remaining fearful of the process she is yet to go through, Josie tells Cilka she thinks she can do it, and is now beginning to look forward to meeting her baby, holding her baby in her arms, and feeling what she has seen on the faces of many of the gaunt, tired, beaten women when they first look at their child. Cilka starts to smile a little again, realises how the muscles around her neck and shoulders have been bunched up – not from the cold but from holding the worry in her body that Josie would not find a way to make it through. Cilka herself does not know how she has always found a way, does not know where that comes from, within herself. She has never wanted to die, despite the horror.

Josie goes into labour on the first day of Hanukkah. She endures a long, painful birth, helped and encouraged by Cilka, Petre and Tatiana. Cilka brings the blessings and songs of this time of the year, their comfort and joy, secretly to the front of her mind. It is less painful to remember them in this small, contained environment of new life.

She gets permission to stay with Josie after the end of her shift. On the stroke of midnight, Josie delivers a tiny, squalling, precious baby girl.

When mother and baby are clean and the ward is quiet, Cilka asks, 'Have you thought of a name for her?'

'Yes,' Josie says, looking into her friend's eyes. 'I'm going to call her Natia Cilka. Do you mind if her second name is after you?'

Josie passes the baby to Cilka.

'Hello, little Natia,' Cilka says. 'I am honoured that you will share my name.' So many thoughts rush in for Cilka. How dangerous and unexpected the path ahead could be for this tiny new being. 'The story of your life begins today, Natia. My hope for you is that you will be able live your own life, with the help of your mumma and everyone who will love you. There is a better world out there. I've seen it. I remember it.'

Cilka looks up at Josie and realises the baby has allowed her to express something to her friend that she can't say directly. She hands the baby back and leans in to kiss them both.

211

The next morning, Natia is thoroughly examined by Petre, who declares her the healthiest and sweetest newborn he has ever seen, and he has seen a lot of them. Josie glows.

Later that day, Cilka takes Josie and Natia next door to the nursery and settles them in to what will be their home for the next two years. No mention is made of what will happen at the end of that time. Cilka has now heard from the nurses that the toddlers are sent to orphanages at two, but she doesn't tell Josie this. She'll find out soon enough. Two years is a long time in this place, and Cilka is determined to find a way to keep them together.

That evening, after Cilka fills the other women in on all the details of Josie's labour and birth, the loss they feel without Josie starts to sink in. Within days, a stranger will be sleeping in her bed. The little gowns so lovingly made by them all are bundled up and given to Cilka to take to her. They also send word that they will continue to make clothes for little Natia, in varying sizes as she grows, and they will run freely with the embroidered lace now they know it is a little girl they are sewing for.

Without Josie's presence Cilka allows herself a little thought of Alexandr, the messenger, finding that his face provides comfort. She wonders if she will ever speak to him again, hopes that she might.

* * *

212

Cilka and the others return to their hut the next day and find someone sleeping in Josie's bed. The newcomer winces as she sits up to face the women's scrutiny.

'I am Anastasia Orlovna,' she says, in a strong clear voice.

Elena walks over to her, looking her up and down. The bruises on the newcomer's face reflect beatings over a period of time. The older ones are a purplish blue, more recent ones still black. Her right eye is partially closed from swelling.

'How old are you?' Elena asks.

'Sixteen.'

The women crowd around the bed to get a closer look at their new resident, who holds her head high, refusing to hide her injuries, defiance written across her face and the body she struggles to hold straight.

Olga gently pushes her back down onto her bed. 'What happened to you?'

'Do you mean to get me here in the first place, or more recently?'

'Both,' says Olga.

'We were caught stealing from the bakery.'

'We? How many of you?'

Anastasia forces a small grin. 'Six of us. It was good while it lasted.'

'What was good?' Elena asks.

'The thrill of taking the bread as soon as it came out of the oven, right under the nose of the pig who made it.'

'Why were you stealing?' Elena asks. They didn't normally put political prisoners and thieves together, but the rules in Vorkuta had seemed to become a bit more relaxed on this front. Wherever there is a bed, Cilka supposes.

'Because, despite us all supposedly getting a fair share in the great Soviet Union, the kids were starving. Why else?'

'So you and your friends . . .'

'Yes, we were a gang of older kids – one or two of us would distract the shopkeeper while the others snuck in and took some food. We got some caviar once, but the children didn't like it. Neither did I.'

'Huh!' Hannah exclaims in frustration. 'What I wouldn't give—'

'And your bruises, how did you get them?' Elena asks.

'I could say I fell down some stairs.'

'You could,' Elena retorts. 'But you're acting like we're your interrogators.'

'The spies are everywhere,' Anastasia says. 'But yes, sorry, I have just come from prison where they tortured me and Mikhail, the only two of us who got caught. The police knew there were more of us and wanted names. I wouldn't give them.'

'Hence the bruises,' Elena says.

'Yes,' Anastasia says. 'But you can't talk. You all look like you haven't seen a piece of bread in a year. And definitely not a vegetable.'

Elena leans in, deliberately close, Cilka observes, so Anastasia can get the full force of her malnourished, rotten-teeth breath. 'Believe it or not, love, we're the lucky ones.'

The dinner alarm sounds.

'Are you able to walk?' Olga asks.

'Yes, slowly.'

Olga helps Anastasia to her feet, buttons her coat, pulling the collar up around her neck. Anastasia pulls her hat on. They join the others in their procession to the mess hall.

Sixteen, Cilka thinks. Another young, defiant woman to be ground down by suffering. But Elena is right. Their horror is marginally better than the next woman's. This hut, the extra rations and fabric, the fact they have a jug in which to boil water! The hard thing will be helping Anastasia to accept that, especially after her first visit from the men.

CHAPTER 15

'She smiled at me!' Cilka joyfully recounts her visit with her namesake to the women in the hut. 'She gurgled, looked me in the eyes and smiled.' *It tore my heart apart.*

'Is she putting on weight, is she healthy?' Elena wants to know.

'Yes, and yes. I think she has become a favourite with the nursery staff, but I'll need to make sure they're not feeding her another baby's lunch.'

Cilka looks around at the women's thin faces, chapped lips, dark circles under their eyes. Their clavicles protruding. She is glad she can give them some reprieve – something warm to think about and hold inside them during the hard, long days out in the snow.

'You'd know all about that, Cilka. Taking someone's lunch,' Hannah says.

Cilka's stomach flips.

'Shut up, Hannah,' Elena says. 'Who has given you more of their own lunch than anybody else here?'

'Well, she can afford to.'

'Well, so can you, now your "husband" has got you a job in the mess.'

'I will eat all of my lunch because I fought in a resistance against these bastards, and the Nazis, too. Unlike some people here.' She looks pointedly at Cilka.

'Keep your fucking voice down, Hannah,' Elena says. 'Attacking the only Jewish woman in here, one would think you were just like the Germans you fought against.'

Hannah looks indignant. Cilka's heart is racing. The blankness is coming over her.

'She . . .' Hannah points at Cilka. She goes to say more, then lets a smile come across her face. 'I could tell you about all the things she has done to preserve her own flimsy little life.'

'No life is flimsy,' Elena says.

Cilka feels sick.

'Do you know how Josie is doing?' Olga asks, cutting across the tension, her fingers darting in and out, weaving her spell, embroidering another gown.

Cilka finds her voice. 'I haven't seen her for a while now, not since they made her go back to work when Natia was four weeks old. I'm told she is doing well; she is working in the administration building, and she is feeding the baby herself, plenty of milk apparently.'

'That's probably why little Natia is getting fat.'

'I never said she is getting fat. Just chubby.' Cilka tries to smile.

'Please give her our love, however you can. Maybe one of the nursery staff will pass it on,' Olga says.

'I will,' Cilka reassures them. 'She knows how much you all care.' She looks pointedly at Hannah. 'But I will ask the staff to pass it on anyway.'

'What's going to happen when . . .' Elena whispers.

'Don't think about that,' Cilka says. 'Two years is a long way ahead.' The truth is, Cilka finds it incredibly hard to contemplate the separation. She knows too much about the pain of mother and daughter being forced apart. She knows too much about whole families being broken up, dehumanised, murdered. She cannot let herself think what might happen to Josie and Natia, or what might happen to Josie if Natia is taken away from her.

'Do you think there is some way we can see her and the baby, I mean, just for a minute?' Olga asks.

'Maybe in summer,' Elena suggests.

'That's an idea. When it's warmer and we can be outside on a Sunday. I love that idea, something to look forward to,' Olga says.

Hannah huffs. 'There's no getting through to you all.'

Smiles return to the other women's faces at the possibility of seeing the baby. The faraway look Cilka sees in their eyes tells her they are dreaming of, visualising, holding an infant. Cilka knows several of them have children waiting for them, including Olga. It's not something she is often able to talk about, but when she receives her limited letters she sometimes passes them around to share what her two boys – who are living with an aunt – are getting up to. She is often silent for days afterwards, with emotions playing across her face, no doubt picturing every little detail her sister has included in the letter.

* * *

Before the moon and stars disappear and the white nights return, the camp is struck down with typhoid. The accommodation hut nearest the hospital is emptied of its residents to create a new ward. The infectious ward.

In the washroom cleaning up after a birth, Cilka is joined by Petre. She hasn't seen him in this room before and immediately braces herself for news she suspects she doesn't want to hear. He leans against the door looking at her.

'Just say it,' she says abruptly.

'We—'

'Who's we?' she interrupts.

'Sorry, some of the other doctors you've worked with, here and on the general ward.'

'Go on.'

'We know you have spent time in another prison, another camp, and that maybe there you were exposed to typhoid.'

His eyes are focused on the ground.

'Do you want me to confirm or deny that?' she says, both terrified and exhausted.

'Have you?'

'Been exposed to typhoid? Yes.'

Auschwitz-Birkenau, Winter 1943

Ever since her mother died, Cilka has been spending less time in the main compound, too afraid of seeing the women who are starting to turn, the ones who will soon be sent to their deaths. The ones who will soon be coming to her, the ones she will have to force herself to feel nothing for. But her mother had told her to look after Magda. And she wants to.

But her strong, kind sister is just as vulnerable as the rest.

There is also the fact that the other women, besides her friends, have begun to give Cilka a wide berth. Those that dare spit on the ground when she walks past, call her the worst names they know. Death clings to her. And so do the SS.

One Sunday afternoon she has forced herself out, to check on Magda. Cilka and Gita are sitting beside Gita and Magda's block, away from the door. She can't bring herself to go in yet, as Gita has told her that Magda has been lying down all day, that she is worried. Cilka watches as Gita sifts through the new grass, searching for the elusive four-leaf clover. They are currency here: with a clover she can buy extra food or prevent a beating.

Gita is talking quietly about her latest stolen moment with Lale. He had walked beside her as she left the administration building, slowly going back to her block. They hadn't spoken, just exchanged stolen glances, which said a thousand words.

The quiet is broken by hysterical screaming. It starts inside the block and intensifies as a girl runs outside. Cilka and Gita look up; they both recognise the girl and jump to their feet, running towards her; she is heading to the edge of the women's camp and into danger.

'Dana, Dana,' they both scream.

Catching up to her, they grab an arm each as Dana collapses, sobbing.

'No, Cilka, no . . .'

Cilka's heart sinks.

'What, Dana? What is it?'

'What's happened?' Gita says.

Dana slowly lifts her red-rimmed eyes to Cilka. They are full of regret. 'She was so weak, it was typhoid . . . She hid it so you didn't have to . . . And then it happened so fast.'

'No, Dana, please, not Magda.' Cilka clutches at Dana's arm. Please, please, not my sister too.

Dana nods slowly. 'I'm sorry, Cilka.'

Cilka feels an intense pain course through her body and up into her head. She leans over and retches, feels arms around her, under her arms, helping her up. Gita is crying softly next to her.

'Cilka,' Dana says, her voice choked with tears. 'She told me just this morning how much she loves you. How brave you are. How she knows you're going to get out of here.'

Cilka lets Dana and Gita hold her, the way she held them when they lost their families. This is what they share – unfathomable losses.

'I have to see her,' Cilka says.

Her friends go into the block with her and help her to sit in the bunk across from Magda's body. Cilka wants to cry and scream but it comes out more like a yell, a fury. And then, as soon as it has come out of her, it goes back inside. Her crying stops. She stares, shaking, but feeling blank. She stays like that for a long time, and her friends stay with her. Then she stands and closes her sister's eyes, clutches both her friends' hands in turn, and leaves the block.

* * *

'Did you get the disease? Have you had symptoms?'

'No and no,' Cilka says, her mind numb.

'That means you probably have an immunity to it, meaning you can get exposed and not suffer the symptoms or become sick. Do you understand?'

'Yes, I understand. Why do you need to know?'

He shifts on his feet.

'We need nurses to work on the infectious ward, which is now overflowing with typhoid cases; we need nurses like you who can work there and not get infected.'

'Is that all?' she says, with a strange mix of fear and relief.

He looks surprised. 'What did you think we would be doing to you?'

'I don't know . . . injecting me with the disease to see how I fared?'

Petre cannot keep the shock from his face. He looks away, speechless.

'I'll go,' she says hastily. 'I'll work on the ward; there

222

are many days here I'm not really needed. If you need someone in my place, please . . . there are many capable women in my hut.'

He nods, but he is not really listening. 'I think Yelena Georgiyevna was right about where you have come from.'

'I come from Czechoslovakia.'

He sighs, knowing it is not the full answer. 'To think we would experiment on you, or on anybody for that matter, in the manner you just said.'

'It doesn't matter,' Cilka says, panicking. 'I didn't mean to say that. When do you want me to start?'

'Tomorrow is fine. I'll let them know you're coming.'

Cilka finishes cleaning up before dashing to the nursery next door. Natia is rolling around on the floor, attempting to snatch at a nearby rag doll. Her little face lights up as she hears Cilka call out her name. Cilka sweeps her into the air, and, hugging her tightly, she paces the room, whispering words of love and promises to return as soon as she can.

She hopes by saying these words they will come true.

* * *

A white surgical gown, face mask and thick rubber gloves are handed to Cilka as she enters the infectious ward. As she is tied into the gown at the back, she looks around the ward, trying to process the scene. Every bed has at least one patient, some two; others lie on the floor with no mattress, covered only by a dirty sheet or blanket. She tries to steady her breathing.

The nurse helping her into the gown introduces herself as Sonya Donatova.

'It looks as if we're going to be busy here,' Cilka says. 'Please tell me what you want me to do.'

'Very happy to have you, Cilka. Come with me, we're doing rounds. I'll introduce you to the others later.'

'Can we not get more beds in here? No patient should have to lie on the floor.'

'We move the ones who are not going to make it onto the floor; it's easier to clean the floor than a mattress. You'll get the hang of it.' Something turns in Cilka's gut. Bodies on the floor, on the ground, with no hope of living another day. So, she is back here again. Her curse.

Cilka watches as two nurses gently lift a patient from a bed and place him on the floor nearby. She overhears one of them say: 'He's on hourly time of death recording.' Once a blanket has been tucked under his frail shivering body, a note is made in his file and placed by his feet. Cilka sighs, feeling the familiar sensation of her body beginning to leave her, icing over.

She follows Sonya to a bed where a delirious, screaming woman thrashes about. Sonya dips a small towel in a nearby basin of water and attempts to place it on the woman's face. She is smacked in the hand and upper body by the flailing limbs.

'Help me cool her down. Take one of her hands and hold tight.'

Cilka grabs one of the woman's arms, forcing it down by her body. Sonya holds the other arm and with her free hand attempts to place the wet towel on her face and head, only partly succeeding.

'She only came in yesterday. She is young and has got to the delirious stage really quickly. If we can cool her down and break the fever, she has a chance of surviving.'

'Couldn't we just bring some snow or ice in and apply it to her skin?'

'We could, that's one way of cooling someone down quickly, but it could be too quick and would shock her system. No, I'm afraid we have to do it fast but not that dramatically.'

'I'm sorry, I didn't know.'

'No, you made a good suggestion, it's just not the right one. No one expects you to know what to do the minute you walk in, unless of course you have worked here before.'

She has not, but she has seen the final stages of typhoid enough times. And the aftermath.

'I came here from maternity. Does that answer your question?'

Sonya laughs. 'You are definitely not expected to know anything about treating typhoid, just as I would pretend I wasn't a nurse if someone came to me in labour – that's scary, two people to worry about.'

The cool towel is having an effect; the patient is becoming subdued, and the manic movements associated with fever subside. Was Magda like this in her final hours? She wonders now if Gita had been distracting her with the four-leaf clovers, sparing her these horrific images.

'I think you will be all right with her on your own. Just keep wetting the towel and running it over her face and head, her arms and legs; you're washing the sweat off and this will help cool her. I'm going to check on another one. Call out if you want help.'

As Sonya leaves, Cilka rinses the towel in the basin, noting that the water is in fact very cold – small bits of ice visible. She takes over washing the woman, talking to her in a soothing voice. This voice seems to be something that Cilka uses naturally, no matter what she is feeling – or not feeling – when she is looking after a patient. It's a low voice, a murmur, that tells a story beyond the moment of pain. Perhaps she does it just as much for herself.

After a short while, the woman's body changes from being drenched in sweat to being covered in goose bumps; her shivering changes, reflecting she is now cold, as she attempts to curl up in a ball. Instinctively, Cilka reaches for the blanket on the floor and wraps her up tightly. She looks around for Sonya.

'Sonya Donatova, she's now shivering with the cold. I've wrapped her in a blanket. What should I do next?'

'Leave her and find another patient who needs cooling down.'

'Where do I find more towels?'

'Is there a problem with the one you've got?'

'No, it's just that . . . well, I used it on her.'

'We don't have the luxury of new towels for every patient, Cilka,' Sonya says with an apologetic look. 'Take the towel you have to the next patient, and the basin of water. If you need more water get it from the sink at the end of the room.'

As her day ends, Cilka has seen six patients die, and fourteen new patients brought in. On two occasions, heavily gowned and masked doctors have come into the ward, walked around and spoken to the nurses in charge. It is clear to Cilka this ward is managed by nurses only. The doctors do not get involved with medical care. They visit to get the statistics on how many enter, and how many leave, either alive or to the mortuary.

Cilka arrives back at her hut every night exhausted. Her days are spent cooling down and warming up feverish patients; moving men and women from a bed onto the floor when it is deemed they will not survive; helping to carry the deceased patients outside where they are left to be collected by others, unseen. She carries the bruises unintentionally caused by delirious patients she is trying to care for.

She learns all there is to know about the disease, such as how to recognise the different stages and when to diagnose the more severe internal bleeding and respiratory distress that will likely lead to death. No one can explain to her why some patients get a nasty red rash over their bodies while others don't, or why this symptom is not necessarily an indicator of a poor outcome.

With the first flush of spring flowers and the melting of some of the snow the numbers of new patients presenting on the ward each day begins to decline. Cilka and the other nurses begin to enjoy caring for only a few patients each, giving them the attention they would have liked to have shown to all who went before.

One day, Yelena appears on the ward. Cilka is overjoyed to see the familiar face of the doctor.

'How are you?' Yelena asks warmly, wisps of blonde hair escaping from her braids and framing her face like a halo.

'Tired, very tired, and very happy to see you.'

'You and the other nurses have done an amazing job. You have saved many lives and you've given comfort to others in their final moments.'

Cilka tries to take this in. She still feels as if she should be rushing about, doing more.

'I . . . We did what we could. More medicine would have been helpful.'

'Yes, I know, there is never enough medicine here. We have to make hard decisions over and over about who gets them, who doesn't.'

'I understand,' Cilka says, that rush of guilt coming again for the medicine she has stolen.

'So, my girl, the question is . . . what do you want to do now?'

'You mean I have a choice?'

'Yes, you do. Petre will take you back on the maternity ward tomorrow. However, your friend Olga is also enjoying the work.' Cilka understands that what Yelena is saying is that going back may displace Olga from her now much better position in the camp. 'And I was wondering if you would like to come back and work on the general ward, with me?'

'But . . .'

'Gleb Vitalyevich is gone. He was transferred a few weeks ago. The administrators finally looked at his mortality figures and decided, in the interests of productivity, it would be best that he move on.' She smiles.

'Where to?' Cilka asks.

'I don't know, and I don't care. I'm just glad he's no longer here. So that means you can come back to my ward. If you want to, that is?'

'I do enjoy working with Petre Davitovich and helping the babies into the world.'

Yelena nods her head, thinking she has her answer.

'However, I would like to come back and work with you and the other doctors, where I can make more of a difference, if that's all right.'

Yelena wraps her arms around her. Cilka responds stiffly, moving one hand to Yelena's back, then pulls away.

'Of course it's all right,' Yelena says. 'It's what I want; you do make a difference. Petre Davitovich is going to be very angry with me for stealing you away though.'

'He's a good doctor. Will you tell him how much I appreciate what he has done for me, what he has taught me?'

'I will. Now go back to your hut and I don't want to see you for two days,' she says, taking a pen and paper from her pocket to write a note. 'Get some rest. What you have done here over the past few months, you must be exhausted.'

'I am. Thank you.'

Cilka looks out at the daylight, thinking of the coming short summer. 'Yelena Georgiyevna?'

'Yes?'

'You know Josie had a little girl.'

'Yes, I heard, and I hear both mother and baby are doing well.'

'I'd love to see little Natia. Is it safe for me to visit her, given where I've been working?'

'I wouldn't go near her for another two weeks; that is the incubation period of typhoid – maybe even three weeks to be safe.'

'I can wait another three weeks, but not a day more.'

CHAPTER 16

'It's like you never left. Welcome back,' Raisa greets Cilka on her return to the general ward.

'About time you showed up,' Lyuba calls out from the other end of the ward. 'Get your coat off and help us out.'

'Have you two not done anything to clean this place up since I left? I swear that dirty towel was lying there more than a year ago,' Cilka throws back at them.

'Has it been that long?' Raisa says.

'Long enough,' Cilka says.

Screams from the patient Lyuba is caring for divert their attention.

'Is everything all right?' Cilka asks.

'Come on, we've got plenty for you to do,' Raisa says. 'There was an explosion in one of the mine tunnels yesterday; quite a few men died, and we have several who are badly injured. Some have been in surgery and we have two who had to have limbs amputated.'

'Just tell me where you want me.'

'Go and help Lyuba. That poor chap was badly burned and she's trying to change his dressings; we've given him something for the pain but it's barely touching him.'

Cilka joins Lyuba, forcing a smile for the man lying in the bed, his arms and upper body wrapped in bandages, his face red raw from flash burns, his sobbing producing no tears.

'Tell me what to do,' she asks Lyuba.

'Cilka, this is Jakub. We need to change the bandages on your arms, don't we, Jakub? We don't want you to get an infection.'

'Hello, Jakub, that's a Polish name, isn't it?'

Jakub nods, despite the pain moving obviously causes him.

'Lyuba, is it all right if I speak to Jakub in Polish?'

She nods. 'Perhaps you can change the bandage on his other arm while you two are remembering old times.'

'I'm from Czechoslovakia, your next-door neighbour, but I am . . . familiar with Poland. I was about to ask you what you're doing here, but let's leave that conversation for another time.'

Cilka gently unwinds the bandage covering Jakub's left arm, chatting like a long-lost friend. With the bandage removed, she sees the damage. Lyuba hands her a new bandage soaked in a solution that makes it feel slimy.

232

Cilka asks Lyuba, 'How is his arm burnt worse than his hand? It doesn't make sense.'

'Jakub's clothes caught fire and the burns he received through his clothing are more severe because they kept burning for longer – until the clothes could be removed.'

'I see. Well, Jakub, can I give you some advice? Go to work naked in future.'

Cilka realises her comment is in extremely bad taste and starts to apologise. But she feels Jakub squeeze her hand and looks down at him; he is trying to smile, to laugh, he has appreciated her joke.

Lyuba regards them both. 'You have to excuse her, Jakub. Cilka has been away from us delivering babies. She's used to her patients being naked. In fact if it wasn't so cold, I'm sure she would walk around here naked.'

'Lyuba!' Cilka exclaims indignantly.

Lyuba laughs heartily. 'I've finished with your dressing, Jakub, so I'll leave you two. Call if you want anything, Cilka.'

'You've been a great help, Lyuba, I think Jakub and I can manage from here, can't we, Jakub?'

Cilka quickly finishes rebandaging Jakub's other arm, telling him she will be back to check on him in a little while. She joins Raisa and falls quickly back into the rhythm of caring for the patients Raisa allocates her. This feels natural, she thinks. And she knows what the complete opposite is like – when a role you are forced into feels unnatural, like your very soul has been contorted.

During a break, Raisa, Lyuba and Cilka sip on hot weak tea, eat bread and something pretending to be sausage.

Yelena joins them, waving away the offer of tea. It's well known the doctors have the premium tea in their lounge area.

'How's our girl doing?' she asks Raisa and Lyuba.

'It's like she never left! Thanks for talking her into coming back to us,' Raisa says.

'She didn't talk me into anything,' Cilka says. 'It is good to be back and helping out, even if I have to hear you telling patients I should be walking around naked.'

'Who said that about you?'

'It was just a joke,' Cilka quickly says. 'We were distracting a patient with nasty burns while we changed his bandages.'

'So long as it's effective.' Yelena smiles.

'Is there anything more I can do to help?' Cilka asks.

'Actually, Cilka, I was wondering if you would like to assist me in surgery tomorrow. It's the one area you haven't worked in. I'm doing some relatively straightforward procedures and thought it could be an extension of your training.'

'That's a great idea,' Lyuba says. 'I think she's ready for it. What do you say, Cilka?'

'I don't know what to say. Thank you. What do I have to do?'

'Just come to work tomorrow as usual. I'll meet you and we'll take it from there.'

Cilka watches Yelena walk away. She is in awe of her ability as a brilliant doctor and of her willingness to share her knowledge, particularly with someone who has had no formal training.

'It's amazing that she volunteered to be here,' she says to the others.

'Yes, most of the doctors have been sent here, usually because they have screwed up at whatever hospital they came from or got on the wrong side of someone in their hometown. Or, like us, it's their first assignment out of medical school. Yelena Georgiyevna genuinely wants to work where she can do the most good,' Raisa says.

'I've felt rude to ask, but does she have a family with her?'

'No, she lives with the other female doctors in their quarters, though I did hear a rumour about her being friendly with one of the other doctors. They've been seen together in the town at night,' Lyuba whispers.

The town of Vorkuta, outside the camp, has been built entirely by prisoners.

'Really . . .' *Love again*, Cilka thinks, even in a place like this. 'Do we know who? Which doctor?'

'The doctor in the maternity ward is all I know.'

'Petre – she and Petre Davitovich?'

'You know him?' Raisa says.

'Of course she does,' Lyuba adds. 'That's where she was working. Did you see them together?'

'No. Well, only the once, when she took me to meet him on my first day, but that explains why he was prepared to take me on when I got fired from here. That's wonderful,' Cilka marvels, 'because he is just like her, a really good doctor and a kind man.'

'Is he good-looking?' Lyuba raises her eyebrows.

Cilka thinks for a moment.

235

He is handsome, with a thick moustache and eyes that smile. 'Yes; they are perfect for each other.'

She can't help thinking, though, that he is not the most handsome man she has seen in her time in Vorkuta. Now she is back in the hospital, she wonders if she will see the messenger, Alexandr, again.

'I think we'd better get back to work,' Raisa says. 'I can feel the temperature rising around you two.'

Yes, work is what Cilka needs to do. She will not allow herself to wonder far too long, about the impossible.

* * *

The prospect of being in the operating room sends Cilka's brain working overtime. That night she cannot sleep. Thoughts whirl around inside her head as she replays all she has seen and done that day.

The next morning the sky is overcast but Cilka appreciates walking across the grass, with small weedy flowers underfoot, on the way to the hospital. Yelena is waiting for her and together they go through to the area designated for surgery. An assistant is standing by with a gown, gloves and a mask. Cilka reaches out to take the gown.

'You have to wash your hands thoroughly first,' Yelena says, leading her over to a nearby sink. 'Are you wearing anything under your shirt?'

'Just my slip.'

'Good, take your shirt off. You can't have a sleeve getting in the way.'

Cilka hesitates.

'It's all right, Cilka, there's only us women here.'

Slowly, Cilka unbuttons her shirt. The assistant takes it from her, handing her a bar of soap and turning a tap on for her. Cilka starts rubbing the soap up her arms. The assistant goes to arrange the room. Yelena stands beside her, lathering up and scrubbing her own hands and arms, past the elbows. Cilka copies her actions.

Focused back on the running water, rinsing the soap from her arms and hands, Cilka is startled when Yelena gently takes hold of her left arm. She turns it towards her, staring at the blurry blue-green numbers running down the inside of her forearm.

Yelena goes to say something, closes her mouth.

Cilka continues to stare at the running water, breathing deeply.

Raising her head, she looks directly at Yelena. 'Do you know where I got this?'

'Yes. I had suspected you had been there, but I . . . didn't really want to believe it.'

Cilka feels hot and cold at the same time.

'You must have been so young,' Yelena says. She lets go of Cilka's arm.

'Sixteen.'

'Can I ask . . . your family?'

Cilka shakes her head, looking away, reaching to turn off the tap. She wants this conversation to be over.

'Oh, Cilka,' Yelena says. Cilka looks at the doctor's compassionate face. Of course, she thinks. Everyone would know by now what that *other place* was. But not her role in it.

'Doctor, just tell me one thing.' Cilka says firmly. She can't look at Yelena.

'Yes?'

'Did they get them?'

Yelena pauses, then understands. 'Yes, Cilka. The commandants, the guards, the doctors. There have been trials. Their crimes are being exposed to the world. They are being imprisoned or executed for what they did.'

Cilka nods. Her jaw is clenched. She could scream, or cry. There is too much welling up inside her. It's still not enough. It took too long.

'I don't know what to say, Cilka, except that I'm so sorry you had to go through that, something unimaginable, and then, also, to end up here. Whatever the reason for that . . .' Yelena falters. 'Well, you were only sixteen.'

Cilka nods. Her eyes are hot with unshed tears. She swallows and swallows. She clears her throat. Takes a deep breath. Wills her racing heart to slow. Looks back at Yelena.

'The patient is waiting for us,' she says.

'Yes,' Yelena says. As they dry off their hands, and start to walk towards the operating room, where the assistant waits with their gloves and gowns, Yelena says, 'Cilka, if you ever want someone to talk to—'

'Thank you,' Cilka cuts her off. She can't imagine a time when she could ever put those memories, those images, into words. She clears her throat again. 'I am grateful, Yelena Georgiyevna.'

Yelena nods. 'Just know I am here.' As they near the

operating room, the conversation recedes in Cilka's mind. She has an important task to do, and it will distract her. Once her gown and gloves are on, the assistant pulls Cilka's mask down under her chin and then holds open the door leading into a small room.

A patient lies on a table and an anaesthetist sits at the end of the bed holding a rubber mask over the patient's nose and mouth.

'He's out,' he comments, with little interest or enthusiasm, before staring off at a point on the far wall.

Cilka follows Yelena and stands beside her.

'Go round to the other side: you can see and help me better from there.'

Cilka does as instructed, holding her hands out in front of her, afraid to touch anything.

'All right, here we go. You see all the instruments on the table beside you? Well, I'm going to say the name of the instrument I want, then point to it so you know which one it is. You'll soon get the hang of it.'

The assistant has followed them into the room and pulls the sheet covering the man away, revealing his naked body.

'I need to get into his stomach and remove whatever it is he has swallowed that he shouldn't have. Unfortunately, some people will go to extreme lengths to not work outside, including swallowing objects that could kill them.'

'You're joking,' Cilka says.

'No, I'm not. Coming into hospital and having their stomach cut open is seen as a better option than working, at least for a while.'

'How do you know for sure he has swallowed something?'

'The pain he was in when he was brought to us was real; when we couldn't work out what was wrong he finally admitted to having swallowed something.'

'Did he say what?'

'That's the funny thing – he wouldn't say, told us to go hunting for it and then we'd know.' Yelena gives a wry smile.

It is a different world here, Cilka thinks. Still very much a prison, as such desperate actions indicated, but in that *other place*, you would not want to draw any attention to yourself. In a selection, you would not want to attract the eye of the doctors. You would not want anything to do with them at all.

'Cilka, I need you to hand me a scalpel.' Yelena points it out on the tray. Cilka picks it up and places it in her outstretched hand.

'Slap it in my hand so I feel it. These gloves are so thick I won't know if I'm holding it unless you hit me with it, just make sure the blade is pointed at you and I get the handle.'

Cilka watches in fascination as Yelena quickly and expertly slices the patient's abdomen open, blood gently oozing from the cut.

'Grab some swabs – those pads that look like thick squares of bandage – and wipe the blood away; it will stop soon.'

Cilka catches on quickly, wiping the blood away so Yelena can see what she is doing.

Instruments are handed over, explanations given by Yelena, questions asked by Cilka, until Yelena raises her hand from the man's abdomen, holding up a metal spoon.

'I wonder if the owner misses this,' she says with humour. 'Let's see if it caused any damage in his stomach.'

She pokes around. Cilka leans over for a closer inspection and the two women bang heads.

'I'm so sorry, I shouldn't have—'

'It's all right, I'm glad you want to have a closer look; this is how you will learn.' Yelena is silent for a moment, considering the open cavity. 'Well, there doesn't seem to be any damage, so now we sew him back up.'

* * *

When the patient has been wheeled from the room, Cilka follows Yelena back into the washroom. The assistant is waiting for them. She unties their gowns, removes their masks and gloves, and hands Cilka back her shirt. Cilka wonders if she is a prisoner too.

'As usual, you learned quickly in there. I'd be happy to have you assist me any time. In fact, I think we should do more of it, so you become totally comfortable with what you are doing. What do you say?'

Cilka is wary for a moment. She hopes that Yelena is not just doing this because of what she knows; because she pities her.

But this is rewarding, challenging work. And Cilka does think she can do it.

'Yes, please.'

'Go back and tell Raisa and Lyuba the news. I'm sure they could do with an extra pair of hands for the afternoon.'

'Thank you,' Cilka says. She feels herself welling up again. There's no blankness coming to take over – to cover it – and so she hurries from the room.

She stops a moment in the hall to gather herself, then walks onto the ward.

A chorus of 'Well, how did you get on?' greets her.

'Well, very well.' She looks at their open faces. Wonders suddenly if they know, too. 'What do you want me to do here?' she asks quickly. 'I've still got half a day of work.'

'Can you check the charts and get any medicines that need to be handed out?' Raisa says.

Cilka dives into her work, relieved to push all thoughts away.

CHAPTER 17

Cilka has written down the names of five patients and the drugs they require. She strolls to the dispensary. As she approaches, she hears voices inside, one of them raised. Cautiously, she opens the door. Yury Petrovich, the kind male doctor Cilka remembers from her previous time working in the hospital, stands in the middle of the room with a knife held to his throat. On the other end of the knife is a man who looks capable of wrestling a bear and winning the fight. The big man turns to face Cilka.

'What the fuck do you want?' he yells at her.

She can't speak.

'Get in here and close the door.'

Cilka does as she's told, leaning her back against the shut door, staying as far away from the man as possible.

'Get over here and stand beside the doctor. Do it now, or I cut him.'

In three steps Cilka is beside the doctor, who looks at her, eyes pleading.

'What do you want?' she asks with a bravado she doesn't feel.

'You to shut your mouth. You picked the wrong time to come in here; now I'll have to deal with you too.'

Cilka glares at him. She knows enough about violent men to be able to judge the desperation in this one. His threats are a means to an end. 'What do you want?'

'I said shut your mouth. I'll do the talking.'

'Just do as he says,' the doctor whimpers.

'That's good advice,' the big man says. 'We can all leave here happy if you listen to the good doctor and do as I say.'

As he pushes the knife under the doctor's chin, a trickle of blood flows and the man smiles a toothless grin. 'Now give me the fucking drugs; the ones I got last time.'

Cilka is incredulous. She stares from the man to the doctor.

'All right, all right, but you need to put the knife down,' Yury Petrovich says.

The man looks from the doctor to Cilka. In a flash, the knife is now at Cilka's throat.

'In case you thought of making a run for it,' he chuckles.

The doctor takes several pill containers from the shelves. With the hand that is not across Cilka's neck, the man holds open a large pocket sewn in his coat and the doctor stuffs them in there.

'Keep them coming; I've got another pocket on this side.'

The doctor places more drugs in the other pocket.

'That's all, if I gave you any more there wouldn't be enough for the patients.'

'I don't care about the patients! When's the next delivery coming in?'

'I don't know.'

'Wrong answer.' The man presses the knife against Cilka's throat. She gasps.

'Don't hurt her! In two weeks, not for another two weeks.'

'Well, I'll see you in two weeks, then.'

He lets Cilka go, keeping the knife raised. He looks her up and down. 'And maybe I'll see you too; you're not bad.'

'You should get out of here before someone comes looking for me,' Cilka says, bravely.

'Yeah, you're right.' The big man points the knife at the doctor. 'He knows the drill – don't leave here until you know I will have cleared the building.'

Cilka and the doctor watch as the big man calmly walks to the door, tucking his knife inside his coat, opens it, pulls it shut quietly behind him.

Cilka turns on the doctor. 'Who is he? We need to get the guards, get someone and stop him.' She wants to say, 'How could you just hand over medicine to him?' But how can she ask such a thing, when she has taken some here and there, to protect herself?

'Slow down, Cilka.'

Cilka waits while he takes a moment, appearing to calm himself before he speaks further.

'He is one of the criminal trusties. He's a powerful person in the camp, with a lot of very strong friends. They cornered me a few months back when I was leaving one night and threatened to kill me if I didn't give them regular supplies of medicine.'

This may be where Hannah is getting them from now. Through the network.

'Why didn't you—'

'Tell someone? Who? Who do you think is running this place? It's not the guards, Cilka, they're outnumbered. You should know that. It's the trusties, and as long as the work is done here, the fighting and killing kept to a minimum, no one is going to challenge them.'

Cilka feels foolish to have been here so long and not have realised the extent of the trusties' involvement in running the camp. But she supposes stumbling across such knowledge is partly luck in a place like this – depends on where you are and what you can overhear, find out. It is better not to be so close to power, to not know too much.

She is still incredulous about what this means for the patients – that quantity going missing. 'I don't believe that they can just walk in here and demand you hand over whatever they want.'

'Afraid so,' he sighs, leaning against a bench as the

colour slowly returns to his face. 'They did it to my prede-
cessor, and I'm just the next person for them to threaten
and intimidate. And they will kill me, I have no doubt
about that.'

'Then I'll—'

'No, you won't. You won't say anything, you hear me?
Not a word. Or it will be the last thing you say. They
know I won't say anything, and if something happens to
that bastard who was just in here, they know it will have
been you that talked and they'll be waiting for you.'

Cilka won't say anything, for now, but she does need
to think about this.

'Promise me you won't say anything—'

'There you are.' Raisa appears in the doorway. 'I was
wondering what was taking you so long.' She looks at the
pale-faced doctor. 'Am I interrupting something?'

'No, no,' Cilka and the doctor chorus together.

'I'm sorry, Raisa, I shouldn't have kept Cilka from her
work. She was just helping me out.'

'You need to get some of the medication to the patients
right away, Cilka; they're asking for it.'

Cilka looks at the scrunched-up piece of paper in her
hand; she had forgotten she was holding it. Straightening
it out, she tries to read what she needs. She quickly locates
the medications and hurries from the room, leaving Raisa
looking at the doctor in disbelief.

As Cilka is handing medication to a patient Raisa steps
up beside her, whispering, 'Are you all right? Was he
trying something on with you?'

247

'What? No, no, nothing like that. I'm fine.'

'All right, but you will tell me if there is something I should know?'

'Don't worry, I will.'

As Raisa walks away, Cilka calls out, 'Raisa, did you see a large, ugly man leaving the ward about five minutes ago?'

'I see nothing but large, ugly men leaving here all day, every day. Was it someone in particular?'

'No, not really. Thanks for your concern.'

At the end of her shift Cilka steps outside and looks to the sky. Clear, blue, the sun shining brightly. The white nights have returned.

'You,' is spoken gruffly behind her.

Cilka turns round. Six or seven large men stand behind her. They take one step closer in unison.

'Have a safe evening,' one of them says.

'I will,' she defiantly throws back at them.

'See you tomorrow, same time,' he says.

From behind the pack the large, ugly brute who held a knife to her throat only a few hours earlier steps forward. Out of his pocket he pulls the knife and tosses it from one hand to another.

Cilka walks away slowly, not looking back.

CHAPTER 18

'You promised, Cilka, please make it happen,' Elena pleads one Sunday evening as they stroll around the camp, snatching this opportunity to enjoy the dazzling overhead display of sunlight poking through clouds.

'I know,' Cilka says. She wants to see Josie so badly, but she hasn't figured out what to do about the eyes of the trusties on her. Whether they might threaten anyone they see her close to. She has determined by now, though, that they only appear as she finishes work. She has never seen them after she returns to Hut 29. 'I'll go to the nursery tomorrow and get a message to Josie that it's time you met Natia.'

Though Olga has been working in the maternity ward, she hasn't yet crossed paths with Josie – only seen little Natia when delivering a mother and baby over to the nursery. Josie must finish later than her in the administration building.

'I'm sorry to keep pestering you,' Elena says, 'you've seemed worried about something for several weeks and, well, me and the others are concerned about you . . . and perhaps seeing Josie and Natia will help you.'

Cilka has been going straight to bed after nightly duties, not speaking much to the others, not wanting to endanger anyone. It isn't just the trusties who are worrying her, though. It is also the thought that some of them might already know, as the doctors did, what went on in that *other place*. And they know that she is Jewish, and that she never speaks about her arrest. The worry has brought images back to the surface. Made her blank and unresponsive.

'You've been talking about me?'

'We talk about all of us, behind our backs of course.' Elena smiles. 'Something has been bothering you. You don't have to tell us if you don't want to, but we might be able to help. You never know.'

'That's very nice of you, Elena, but everything is fine.' She tries to keep the sharpness out of her voice. 'I promise I will get a message to Josie tomorrow. I want to see them both too.'

Several of the other women from Hut 29 join them and Elena excitedly tells them Josie and Natia will be visiting next Sunday. Cilka must correct them. She will get the message to Josie, but she doesn't know when they will see her. Clearly Josie hasn't been wandering around on the white-night Sundays, whether by choice – for comfort or safety of herself and her child, from Vadim, from strangers – or because she's under a specific set of rules, Cilka is not sure. But hearing that a visit to Josie and Natia is a possibility is enough for the women, for now.

Anastasia walks up beside Cilka.

'Tell me more about Josie. Why is she so special?'

The sun pokes in and out of the clouds, throwing shadows across Anastasia's young features.

'No one has said she was special.'

'Look at them, look how happy they are just hearing her name.'

Cilka considers. 'We went through a lot together when we first came here. Josie was the youngest of us and I guess we all sort of mothered her. Then she got pregnant. That was hard on her and we all helped her get through her pregnancy. That's all. You can understand them now wanting to see her again with her baby – for them, part of that baby belongs to us. They have made clothes for her, and some of them have left their own babies behind, so they are desperate to hold little Natia.'

'I see.' She nods. 'I look forward to meeting her.'

They walk on in silence for a while.

'The man who visits your bed some nights,' Anastasia says, 'do you love him?'

Cilka is stunned by the question. 'What?'

'Do you love him?'

'Why would you ask such a question? Do you love the men who abuse you?'

251

'That's different.'

'In what way?'

'I hear your guy talking to you. He's in love with you. I just wondered if you loved him back. I don't hear you saying the same things to him.'

Cilka pulls Anastasia close.

'You will not ask me that again,' she says firmly. 'My business is not your business. You're young and still have a lot to learn about this place and your place here. Do you understand?'

Anastasia looks shocked. 'You don't have to get angry with me. I just asked a question.'

'I'm not angry,' Cilka says. Though she knows she is acting as she has in the past. Some indignation rising up, cracking through the blank surface. 'I need you to know your boundaries where I'm concerned. I'll do all I can to help you, but you need to stay out of my business.'

'I'm sorry, all right? Sorry I said anything.' Anastasia moves away from her. 'I just thought if you loved him back that would be really nice.'

Anastasia's questions rattle Cilka. She knows Boris feels differently about her than she does him. She has never considered their arrangement to be anything more than her providing him with comfort and her body. A transaction. Love! She is fond of the women in her hut, and Yelena, Raisa and Lyuba. She cares for them, would do anything for them. When she tries to connect these emotions to Boris she definitely can't. If he disappeared tomorrow would she miss him? No, she answers to herself. If he asked her to do something that could get her into trouble? Same answer. What he provides for her is safety from gang rape. She knows about being the property of powerful men and the protection it can provide, though she has also never had any choice in the matter. No, she cannot think of love.

'Hey, you, nurse.'

Cilka looks to her right, to where the voice came, not sure if it is aimed at her.

'Enjoying your walk?'

Cilka freezes. Her hand instinctively pushes Anastasia away, not wanting her to be part of any danger she now feels is imminent. The thug who held a knife to her throat is only a few feet away, surrounded by his shadows, all smirking, some leering at the two girls. The thug pulls his knife from his pocket, waving it at Cilka.

'I'm going back to the hut,' she fires at Anastasia. 'Go and find the others and meet me back there.'

'But—'

'Go, Anastasia, don't ask questions.'

Slowly, Anastasia walks away, towards the rest of the women. The hut is the jurisdiction of Boris and the trusties who protect 'their' women, so Cilka thinks they will be safe there.

'What do you want?' she asks, hoping to keep their eyes on her so the other women can get away.

'We just saw you and thought we'd say hello,' he smirks.

Cilka asks them more questions, hoping not to work them up but trying to stall them. She notices Vadim in the distance, watching.

'I am no threat to your . . . operations,' she says. And starts to walk away, the hairs rising on her neck when she turns her back to them. How easy it would be for the thug to lunge with the knife.

Collapsing on her bed back in the hut, Cilka looks at the bed beside hers, where Anastasia sleeps, the girl who moments ago was placed in danger because of Cilka; the girl who had asked Cilka about love. Still a girl, only sixteen, the age Cilka was when she entered the *other place*, she realises. Was that why Cilka had been so upset? Had she been that naïve at Anastasia's age? Had she believed in possibilities like love? Yes, she had.

Auschwitz-Birkenau, 1944

Cilka watches as hundreds of naked women file past her. The snow is several inches thick on the ground and continuing to fall, whirling around in the wind. She pulls her coat collar over her mouth and nose, her hat all but covering her eyes. Women march past her to who knows where, their death the only certainty. She is transfixed and cannot move. It's as if she must bear witness to the horror – she might survive this hell on earth and be the one who has to tell whoever will listen.

A handful of SS guards walk either side of the rows of women. Other prisoners hurry on, turning away. It is too much to fathom, too much pain.

As the last guard passes Cilka, she sees the commandant from Auschwitz, Anton Taube, walking behind him, his whip smacking against his thigh. He is Schwarzhuber's senior officer. She recognises him. He sees her. Before she can turn and run he has grabbed her by the arm, forcing her to walk with him. She doesn't dare speak or attempt to break free. Taube is the most hated and feared of all the senior officers, even more than Schwarzhuber. Already he has visited her in her room. Already he has let her know he too will come for her whenever it suits.

Out of the gates of Birkenau they march, into a nearby paddock off to the side of the road that separates Auschwitz from Birkenau.

The women are made to stand in a single line, pushed and shoved by guards until they stand shoulder to shoulder, shivering, freezing, weeping. Cilka stands beside Taube, looking at the ground in front of her.

'Walk with me,' Taube says to her.

They stop in front of the first woman. With the tip of his whip Taube lifts her breast. When he releases the whip, it sags down onto her chest. To the guard walking in front of him he indicates for the woman to be pushed back a step, out of line. Cilka watches as the next two women, after their breasts also sag, join the first on a back row. The fourth woman stays in line, her breasts having bounced back into place.

He is choosing whether they will live or die, depending on whether or not their breasts are firm.

Cilka has seen enough. She stumbles along beside Taube,

not looking above ground level, refusing to notice whether the next woman has remained in line or taken a step back.

Turning away, she projectile vomits, splattering the pristine white of the snow with her morning coffee and bread.

Taube laughs.

Blindly, Cilka allows herself to be grabbed by the arm by a guard and half dragged back to her block.

* * *

'You can take a break,' Raisa tells Cilka the next day. 'Put your feet up and have something to eat; there's plenty left over, many are too sick to eat today.'

'Will it be all right if I go out for a short while, just to the nursery? I want to see baby Natia and leave a message for Josie.'

Raisa considers. 'Don't be too long.'

* * *

Cilka has timed her visit deliberately to avoid the trusties. When she arrives, she stands near the door, watching Natia dragging herself along the floor, getting up onto all fours and attempting to crawl before collapsing as if a large hand has pushed her down. She waves to the staff, pointing to Natia. They nod their approval for her to visit.

Sitting on the floor a few feet away, she encourages the baby to come to her. With a mighty effort the little girl balances on her hands and knees and slowly moves first

256

one hand, then the opposing leg. She squeals with delight at her accomplishment. Cilka encourages her further. Another hand moves forward, she wobbles, a leg moves forward, one – two – three giant shuffles for a little girl who is then swept up into Cilka's arms, hugged so tightly she squeals and wriggles to be released.

'Well, there will be no stopping her now. Look what you've done, given us another one to chase after,' says the nurse, whom Cilka has learned is called Bella Armenova.

Cilka is not sure if Bella is seriously annoyed or making fun of her. She starts to apologise.

'It was going to happen sooner or later. I'm just glad someone who knows her was here to see her crawl for the first time.'

'It was very special, wasn't it?'

'We won't tell Josie what she did today, and I guarantee when she drops this one off tomorrow she will tell us how she crawled for the first time last night.'

'That's a really nice thing to do,' Cilka says. 'I was wondering if you could pass on a message to Josie for me?'

'If I see her, yes, certainly.'

'Tell her, her friends would love to see her and meet this little one, and if possible, can they come out this Sunday after lights out?'

'Hardly matters that they turn the lights out this time of year, but I know what you mean. Where do you want to meet?'

Cilka doesn't want Josie to have to stray too far from

comfort and safety. As a pack, with Cilka hidden in the middle, the women from the hut should be all right.

'We will wait between the maternity ward and the nursery.'

* * *

Anastasia stands back as the women she shares living quarters with cry, hug, push to get their hands on both Josie and the small infant clinging to her. It is too much for Natia, who lets the world know she is scared of so much attention from strangers. Josie turns her back on the women and gently rocks Natia, soothing and comforting her.

'One or two at a time might be best,' she says, turning back to them with a smile. 'She doesn't know you, but I want her to. I want her to know the people responsible for her being here, being alive.'

Elena pushes her way forward. 'Me first, can I have a hold?'

Josie softly touches Elena on the face, making sure Natia is watching. Slowly she hands her daughter over. Elena holds her at arms' length, not sure what to do with her. As she feels Natia relax, her little face never leaving her mother's, Elena brings the baby to her chest. They work out that as long as Natia can see her mother she will happily be held and cuddled by them all.

Cilka stays at the back, enjoying the rare, sweet scene playing out in front of her. She cannot remember the last time they were all smiling gap-toothed smiles, laughing and crying together. She marvels at the power of something so small to make a difference. But in a place like this, any tiny moment that shifts them away from the relentless, gruelling horror, from the reminder of the long years still ahead, is to be treasured. It's a shame, really, that Hannah has not joined them, too. Preferring to lie passed out on her bed.

When Cilka has determined that everyone has had a hold of Natia, except the reluctant Anastasia, she pushes her way forward. Natia sees her and immediately throws her arms at her, desperate to be with Cilka. The others grumble and complain good-naturedly. Cilka walks over to Anastasia. In Cilka's arms, Natia doesn't complain that she can no longer see her mother.

Cilka introduces Natia to Anastasia. The little girl looks at Anastasia in puzzlement, as Anastasia makes no effort to touch her. Natia reaches out and tugs at strands of Anastasia's growing hair that have sprung free from her scarf. They both giggle. Anastasia refuses the offer to hold her; she is quite happy just to look at her.

The others join them as Josie tells them they have now spoilt Natia and she probably won't sleep tonight. Reluctantly, Natia is given back to her mother and they say goodbye, promising to come back in seven days' time. Same place.

The women slowly drift back to their hut, chattering away about the evening, the embroiderers debating amongst themselves about the next size of gown they will need to make now they have met Natia. They all agree she is the most beautiful baby they have ever laid eyes on. Natia has been like a sun breaking through dark clouds. No one mentions the uncertain future that both Natia and Josie have, or the cruel surroundings Natia was born into. That's a conversation no one wants to start.

* * *

They see Josie and Natia a second and third time. The third time, in a moment with Josie out of earshot of the others, Cilka asks her if she has met a man called Alexandr while working in the administration building.

'The Czech man?' Josie asks.

'Yes, he works as a messenger. Or did, last I knew,' Cilka says.

'Yes, I don't have a lot to do with him day to day, but I see him. He is very friendly,' she says. 'Which is a rare enough thing around here.'

'It is,' Cilka says. 'I guess that's why he has stayed in my mind.'

Josie contemplates Cilka. 'I can try to talk to him for you.'

'Oh no . . .' Cilka says. 'I was just wondering if he was still there. I haven't seen him for a while.'

Josie nods. Cilka can see she wants to say more, but she turns away and calls out to little Natia, who is reaching out for her.

A fourth planned visit doesn't happen as autumn comes early; the temperature drops dramatically, and rain and sleet prevent all but the foolhardy and those forced to work from being outside. The trusties have curtailed their daily visits to Cilka, perhaps thinking she has received the message, or having found someone else to intimidate. Still, the drugs dwindle, and the doctor seems permanently rattled. A feeling of unease plagues Cilka, darkness and cold closing in on her with the weather.

CHAPTER 19

Daily life for Cilka plays out, the only thing changing being the patients in the beds. The gloom of another winter fifty miles from the Arctic Circle hits and settles on her.

Getting out of bed in the darkness is something she doesn't want to do. Often she doesn't go to the mess hall for breakfast. Her conversations in the evening have ceased. No longer does she gather around the stove, sipping hot tea and listening to the stories and complaints of the women, who now all trudge to different parts of the camp for work, with varying degrees of warmth, food, and physical challenge. More in the hut are able to aid the others now, and so the pressure is off Cilka – she is no longer the only one who can bring in extra rations or materials. But being less useful is not necessarily a state Cilka is able to embrace.

Her bed becomes her sanctuary, and she lies with her head turned to the wall.

On the ward, Raisa and Lyuba notice the change, comment on it and ask if something is wrong. Can they do anything to help her? With a forced half-smile she tells them she is fine, nothing is wrong. There is no other way to answer their questions. Cilka cannot articulate to herself, let alone anyone else, how she is feeling.

For the first time in many years she has allowed herself to be dragged down by the enormity of what she has seen, heard, and done – or not done – herself. What she no longer has and what she can never long for. It is like an avalanche – there seems to be no way now of holding it at bay. She doesn't understand how she kept it all back before, but suspects this may be happening because she has acknowledged aloud to Yelena that she survived that *other place*. Josie is also front and centre in Cilka's mind. With every day that passes, Josie comes closer to being separated from her daughter.

Cilka thought she had been saved from this feeling of despair by using her position to make a difference to many of the sick and injured. Now she knows that it will always catch up to her. She is filled with heaviness. Why go on?

'Get the midday medication,' Raisa tells her one day, seeking to jolt Cilka from her melancholy. Without response, Cilka trudges to the dispensary, shutting the door behind her.

She stares at the medications lining the shelves for a long time, disorientated. She picks up a pill bottle, the

Cyrillic script swimming in her vision. To take them all would bring back the blankness. She tips the pills into her hand.

She rolls them around.

She tips the pills back into the bottle and, trembling, spills some on the floor. She gets down on her knees and starts to pick them up. The door opens, startling her.

'Cilka, I've been looking for you,' Yelena says, putting her head round the door. 'Did you drop something?'

'Yes,' Cilka says, not looking up. 'I'll be out in a moment.'

Once the trembling has subsided, Cilka takes the medication to Raisa, and then finds Yelena. The doctor looks at her steadily for a while, as if guessing what has just played out in Cilka's mind – her dance with death, oblivion, freedom from the aching loss and the guilt and shame; and then her step back from the abyss.

'Are you ready for another challenge?' Yelena asks Cilka.

'Not really,' Cilka replies.

'I think you are,' Yelena says slowly, still watching her carefully. 'At least, you could try it and if you don't like it, well, we can always stop it.'

'Are you opening another ward?'

'No, not a ward. We need a new nurse on the ambulance. What do you say?'

'I've seen what the ambulance brings in. How can I help them? I need you and Raisa and Lyuba to tell me what to do.'

'No, you don't. Not anymore, Cilka. I think you would be a great asset at the scene of the accident. They need someone who can think quickly on her feet, do what needs to be done to get the patient here, then we can take over. Will you at least give it a try?'

What have I got to lose? Cilka thinks.

'All right, I will.'

'Don't forget, Cilka, I am here. Any time you want to talk.'

Cilka sways a little on her feet. Sometimes she does run the words in her head. But can she let them out?

'I need to get back to work.'

'What about at the end of the day?' Yelena persists. 'I'll make sure you get something to eat if you miss your dinner.'

Cilka is afraid to let it come up, come out. But talking about it is something she hasn't tried. She feels a glimmer of something, that survival mechanism; a sense of hope. Maybe she should. She nods, just a little. 'Not here. I don't want anyone we work with to see me talking to you.'

'I'll find an empty room for us.'

While they have been talking, a new patient has arrived. Blood is seeping through the bandages on his bare chest. He is groaning quietly, the deep, painful sound Cilka has come to recognise as coming from someone barely conscious and unable to scream out in pain. She is glad of the distraction.

'Do you need a hand?' she calls out to the men roughly transferring him from the stretcher to the bed.

'He's not going to make it,' one of them calls back.

Cilka walks over to the bed, picking up the man's file that has been dropped on his legs. She reads the brief notes. Multiple stab wounds to the chest and abdomen, extreme loss of blood. No active treatment.

A hand grabs at her apron. Strong and with purpose, the man pulls her towards the head of the bed, his eyes pleading, small gasps escaping from his bloodied mouth.

'Help.' Barely whispered.

Cilka takes his hand and looks down at the wounded man. Only then does she recognise him – it's the thug who threatened her in the dispensary, shadowed her, taunted her.

'You,' he says.

'Yes, me.'

'The drugs . . .'

Cilka can see his face is full of regret.

'I know it's this place that did that to you,' Cilka says.

The man manages to nod, squeezes her hand.

Cilka holds the man's hand between her own two until she feels the strength leave it. She places it on the bed, and she closes his eyes. She doesn't know what he did in his life, or in here, but he will not be harming anybody else, now, and she thinks she can spare him a thought. A prayer.

Picking up his file, she records the time of death.

She takes the file back to the nurse's desk and asks Raisa if she knows what happened to the man whose death she has just recorded.

'He was the loser in a fight. The trusties of the criminal

class are always wanting to be the top dog around here, this is the way it ends up.'

* * *

At the end of the day, Cilka takes a cursory look around but can't see Yelena. Gathering her coat, she walks from the ward, trying not to admit to herself that she is grateful she has escaped talking to her. As she steps into the waiting room, Yelena is there. She beckons Cilka to follow her to a small room off to the side of the ward.

A desk and two chairs are the only furniture in the room. Yelena places the chairs face-to-face.

She waits for Cilka to begin. Cilka takes her time folding her coat and placing it just so on the floor beside her.

Raising her head, she looks directly at Yelena. 'I *was* only sixteen when I went into that place. But I grew up fast.'

Yelena says nothing.

'They said they wanted people to go to work for them.'

Yelena nods.

'The Germans, the Nazis. I stood in a cattle train for days, peed where I stood, held up by people surrounding me, squashing me.'

'And it took you to the camp called Auschwitz.'

'Yes,' Cilka says quietly. 'My sister too.'

'How long were you there?'

'Three years.'

'But that's—'

'A long time to be there, yes. For three years I lived in hell – the abyss. Although I have been here just as long now.'

'Tell me about the number on your arm.'

'That was our introduction to Auschwitz. They took my small bag of belongings. They took my clothes. They took my youth, my identity, and then they took my name and gave me a number.'

'How . . . how did you . . . ?'

'Survive?' Cilka begins shaking. 'In a place that was created for one reason only, to exterminate us? I'm not sure I can tell you.' She holds her arms around herself.

'Cilka, it's all right. You don't have to tell me anything you don't want to.'

'Thank you, Yelena Georgiyevna,' Cilka says, and then forces herself to ask something. 'Do you know why I'm here?'

'No. I don't. I don't know why anyone is here, and I have no need to ask. I'm sorry if that makes me sound like a coward.'

Cilka clears her throat.

'I am here because I slept with the enemy, or that is what I was charged with. Sleeping with the enemy. Working with the enemy. For me, there was no sleeping. He – they – came into my bed and sometimes slept, after they . . .'

'Raped you?'

'Is it rape if you don't fight back, don't say no?'

'Did you want them to have sex with you?'

'No, no, of course not.'

'Then it is rape. I take it these men had some kind of power or control over you?'

Cilka laughs. Standing up she walks around the room.

'They were senior officers.'

'Oh. I see. This was in Auschwitz?'

'Yes and no. It was another camp down the road from Auschwitz but still part of it. It was called Birkenau.'

'And . . . for three years?'

'Two and a half. Yes . . . And I never said no, never fought back.'

'How could you fight a man? I'm sure they were bigger than you.'

'That's an understatement. One of them, I didn't even come up to his chin, and there was, there was . . .'

'Was what?'

'The gas chambers, where everyone went. Went in alive and came out the chimney. I-I saw them every day, every day that was my future if I didn't . . .'

'So, you're telling me you spent two and a half years being raped by the men in charge of the camp in which you were a prisoner, and for that you are now here?'

Cilka sits back down on the chair. Leaning forward, she stares Yelena in the eyes.

'I gave in.'

Yelena shakes her head.

There is more, Cilka thinks. Can she say it? Tell her all of it? Telling her this much has already exhausted her.

Yelena reaches out and takes Cilka's hands.

'The first day I saw you I felt there was something about you, a strength, a sense of self-knowledge that I rarely see. And now, with the little you've told me, I don't know what to say other than that you are very brave. There is nothing I can do to get you out of here, but I can look out for you as best I can and try to keep you safe. You have shown what a fighter you are. My God, how have you done it?'

'I just want to live. I need to feel the pain I wake up with every morning, knowing I am alive, and my family aren't. This pain is my punishment for surviving and I need to feel it, live it.'

'Cilka, I don't know what to say to you other than *keep living*. Wake up each morning and breathe. You make a huge difference here, and if you go with the ambulance you will be helping keep patients alive. I truly believe you will thrive in this role.'

'All right, I'll do it. I can be brave because of you. You're the most courageous of us all. I haven't said that before, but that is how I feel about you. So brave, being here when you don't have to be.'

'You don't have to say that. Yes, I choose to be here. I am a physician; I always wanted to help people, and here, well, here there are a lot of people who need the help I can provide. But we're not here to talk about me.'

Cilka smiles at Yelena.

'Well, I really appreciate this, Yelena Georgiyevna, thank you.' Cilka stands, thinking of the solace of her bed, of lying facing the wall.

Yelena stands, too, and Cilka looks at her, grateful to see no pity on her face. 'See you tomorrow then, Cilka.'

'See you tomorrow.'

As she steps outside she glances over towards the administration building. And today, he is there. Alexandr. Standing under a searchlight in the snow. Raising his cigarette to his lips, closing his eyes. Shifting his shoulders up and down for warmth. She holds the bright image in her mind as she walks away.

CHAPTER 20

All the next day, Cilka is on edge, distracted. She calls a patient by the wrong name, fumbles giving medication. Her eyes go constantly to the door, waiting for a head to pop round and announce that the ambulance is going out.

It doesn't happen, and she returns to the hut disappointed. Her melancholic state was meant to improve today, now she has released some of the burden and with the prospect of something new to focus on. She wants an instant fix to a problem she can't articulate.

To make matters worse, Hannah has cornered her again, saying that her supply has been cut off, and that Cilka must procure the drugs for her again. So, it must have been the trustie thug who died who was supplying Hannah all this time. And despite her conversation with Yelena, when Cilka looks around at the women in the hut, she still doesn't think she can face that moment when their faces change to horror, pity, fear, maybe even hatred.

* * *

The following morning, she has to force herself to concentrate, get on with the job at hand. When the call comes, 'Ambulance going out,' Cilka misses it.

'Cilka, you're needed,' Raisa calls out.

Cilka looks up at Raisa, to the door, and sees the man waiting for someone to acknowledge him.

Grabbing her coat, hat, scarf and gloves, Cilka follows him outside into the whirling snow and perpetual darkness of the Arctic winter.

'Hurry up, people are dying out here while you take your time putting your bloody layers on,' the driver yells, revving the engine impatiently.

The man Cilka followed opens the back door of the modified truck, indicating for her to get in. The ambulance takes off before the doors are closed, sending her flying. The passenger in the front seat leans round, smiling as Cilka tries to shove herself up against the side, bracing herself for more violent driving.

'Haven't seen you before. What's your name?'

With her hands planted firmly on the floor, her legs spread apart for support, Cilka checks him out. His friendly grin reveals a few large crooked teeth. He is wiry and olive-skinned, with heavy eyebrows framing bright eyes.

'I'm Cilka. This is my first time out.'

273

'Hey, Pavel, it's her first time,' the gruff driver says. He is bulkier and broader than Pavel. 'From what I saw of her, it'll probably be her last as well – look at the size of her.'

'She may prove you wrong there, Kirill Grigorovich,' says Pavel. The two men cackle away. Kirill winds down his window as he nears the closed front gates, which are lit up by the searchlights of the compound. Sticking his head out the window, he screams at the sentry as he speeds towards him.

'Open the fucking gates, you moron! Can't you see we're in a hurry?'

The gates are barely open when the ambulance races through, and a torrent of abuse from the sentry follows.

Crunching the gears, Kirill winds up his window and shakes the snow off his hat.

'Excuse me,' Cilka says loudly, ensuring she is heard over the revving engine.

'Find out what she wants,' Kirill says.

Pavel leans back over the seat, staring at Cilka.

'Pavel . . . is it? What can you tell me about where we're going? What kind of accident is it?'

'Yes, I'm Pavel Sergeyevich. We'll find out when we get there.'

'But surely you know if there is more than one patient?'

Kirill cackles away, his big shoulders shaking up and down in his coarse pea coat. They are prisoners, she thinks. Trusties with a good job, driving back and forth with cigarette breaks in between.

'That you can be sure of, honey, when any part of a mine collapses, there will be more than one casualty.'

'So, you do know what happened. Why couldn't you just say so?'

'Well, well, what do we have here, Pavel? A nurse with attitude. Listen, *printsessa*, you just do what you do when we get to the scene and we'll transport them.'

Cilka looks around her in the back of the ambulance. Two stretchers are stacked against the side of the truck, and two containers slide around the floor. One comes to rest against Cilka's leg.

Cilka edges the top off the container to examine the contents. An assortment of instruments bang against each other. Rolls of bandages, bottles of medication. Cilka lifts each one, identifying exactly what she has to work with. Dragging the other container over she finds the equipment for hanging a drip and two bottles of saline solution.

The road is pockmarked; the ambulance swerves round boulders, bounces against snow piled at the side of the road, visible in the headlights.

'Time for action, honey, we're here.'

The ambulance screeches to a halt, throwing Cilka against the front seat.

Before she can steady herself, the back doors are thrown open. Hands reach in and grab the stretchers. A hand is held out for her to take and she is helped down. Cilka notices the numbers roughly sewn on their jackets.

She takes a moment to have a quick glance around. At first she can see nothing in the dusk and sleet. Then she begins to make out figures: men moving about aimlessly, some screaming orders. Cilka, Pavel and Kirill make their way to the opening of the mine, towards the ladder-like structure with the wheel on top. A guard strides over.

'An upper tunnel is caving in; we're not sure when it's going to be safe to go down.' The wheel above them creaks to a stop as a lift cage full of soot-blackened men arrives at the top. The men spill out.

'There are still injured men down there,' one of them says, holding his hat in his hand.

'We have to go and get them,' Cilka yells.

'Who's this?' the supervisor asks Pavel.

'It's the nurse they sent with us,' Pavel answers.

'Not much to her,' the supervisor responds, looking Cilka up and down.

Cilka rolls her eyes. 'Let me go in and see if I can help,' she says.

'Didn't you hear me, girl? The tunnel is still collapsing. Do you have a desire to die?'

'No.' Cilka raises her chin.

She advances towards the now empty elevator cage, looking back at the men.

'If you want to go in, go, but I'm not coming with you,' the supervisor says.

'I can't go alone. I don't know how to operate this or where to get off.'

'I'll come,' Pavel says, without conviction.

'I'll take you to the level,' the miner with the hat in his

276

hand says. His teeth are chattering. Cold, or shock? Cilka wonders.

Wrapping her scarf over her mouth and nose, she steps into the cage. Pavel follows, loading the equipment in too. The miner clears his throat, then pushes a lever, and the lift jolts into action, lowering slowly into dusty gloom. Cilka checks the lamp Pavel handed her as they set off.

They go down, and down and down. Cilka tries to keep her breathing steady.

The lift stops at a tunnel entrance. Cilka clears her throat. She unlatches and pushes aside the lift cage door.

'It's a bit of a walk,' the miner says, indicating he will stay where he is. 'Just keep to the left.'

Cilka and Pavel do as he says.

'We're here to help you,' she begins to yell out. Debris enters her lungs and she coughs. 'Call out so we know where you are.'

'Here, over here,' she eventually hears from somewhere in front of her. The voice is weak, scared.

'I'm coming, hold on. Keep talking.'

'I'm here! Keep walking.'

By the light of her lamp, Cilka sees a hand waving at her. Scanning the area she sees three other men, not moving. She hurries to the man who had been calling out.

'I'm Cilka Klein.' She kneels and gently lays a hand on his shoulder. 'Are you trapped?'

'My legs, I can't move them.'

Cilka examines the man, seeing that his lower legs are pinned by a large chunk of rock. She gently pushes him

277

down flat and checks the pulse in his neck as Pavel arrives beside her, opening the container.

'What's your name?' Cilka asks the injured man.

'Mikhail Alexandrovich.'

'Your legs are under a boulder, but I think we can move it as it's not that big. You have a nasty cut on your head, which we can wrap up to stop the bleeding. Mikhail Alexandrovich, I need to go and see to the other men. Do you know how many of you were in here when the collapse began?'

'Four of us. The others had gone for a break. We were loading the last wagon.'

'I can see three others,' she says, waving her lamp around.

'I'm not going anywhere,' he says. 'Check on the others. I was calling their names but none of them answered.'

Cautiously, Cilka steps over the rubble covering the floor of the mine tunnel. On reaching the first man she checks for a pulse, finds one. Pulling back an eyelid, she holds her lamp above his eyes – one reacts. Running the lamp over his body she sees he is not pinned down, just unconscious.

'Pavel Sergeyevich, go back and convince that miner to come and help us. Take this one first. He's unconscious but you can move him.'

'Be right back,' she hears as Pavel heads back to the lift.

Cilka finds a second man. Immediately she can see he is trapped under fallen rock. She finds no pulse.

The third man groans as she holds her lamp above his face.

'My name is Cilka Klein, I'm here to help. Can you tell me where you're hurt?'

The man groans again.

'It's all right. I'm going to have a look and see if I can find your injuries.'

She quickly identifies a badly broken arm, twisted in an unnatural position. A large rock is pressed up against his side. Gently, Cilka pushes on the man's chest, from side to side, then further down his abdomen. He cries out in pain. With difficulty she pulls at his clothing, undoing his coat so she can see. Pulling his shirt and undergarments from his trousers causes him immense pain. Cilka sees the crush injury below his ribcage.

She hears the crunch of footsteps in the tunnel and Pavel is back with the miner, each carrying a stretcher. She scrambles over to the unconscious man.

'Load him up and get him out of here,' she says. 'And then there's another who can be taken out, but you need to go carefully. He's badly injured and in a lot of pain. Get both of them out of here and I will tend to him in the ambulance.'

As they take care of those two men, Cilka goes back to the first man she spoke to, the one who is trapped.

'I'm sorry – one of your friends is dead.'

'The others?' he asks.

'They're alive and we're moving them out. Now we have to think about how to move this rock off your legs.' She stands, looking around in the gloom, feeling helpless.

'Don't go, please.'

'I'm not going anywhere. I can't move it though, it's way too heavy for me and I don't want to roll it off. I think it needs to be lifted off, so it doesn't do any more damage. Hang in there, Mikhail Alexandrovich, I'll get something for your pain also.' She hunts for the supplies that Pavel had placed in the tunnel and finds the pain relief. She returns to Mikhail.

'Mikhail Alexandrovich, I'm going to give you an injection to help with the pain,' she says. 'And then, when the men come back, we're going to gently lift the rock from your legs and load you onto a stretcher. The ambulance is outside the mine and we'll take you to the hospital.'

Mikhail painfully raises a hand and brushes it against Cilka's face. She smiles reassuringly at him. She takes scissors from the container and cuts through his coat and shirt, exposing his upper arm. She injects him slowly and watches as he relaxes, his pain diminishing.

Cilka sits in the gloomy, quiet tunnel, waiting, coughing regularly. Eventually, Pavel and the miner come back.

'All right,' she says, 'you need to slide your hands under each end of the rock and when you have a good hold lift it off cleanly. Do not roll it or drop it on him.' She holds her lamp up for them. She holds her breath.

The men lift the rock, wobbling slightly, and drop it down to the side, panting with exertion. Cilka looks at Mikhail's legs – bone protrudes through the skin of his right shin.

Pavel and the miner place Mikhail on the stretcher and they all hurry back down the long tunnel to the lift and up and out of the mine. The dead man will have to be removed when it is safer.

With Mikhail loaded into the ambulance along with the other two injured men, there is no room in the back for Cilka.

Kirill leers at her. 'You'll just have to ride up front with us. Get in.'

Squashed between Kirill and Pavel, Cilka has to constantly remove Kirill's big hairy hand, which is attempting to creep up her thigh. She winces at the cries that come from the injured men in the back as they are bounced around, Kirill showing no compassion or care for their injuries. She offers up words of comfort, telling them they are nearly there, nearly at the hospital, where doctors and nurses will take care of them.

The drive cannot end soon enough for Cilka.

CHAPTER 21

Cilka reaches over and opens the passenger door before Pavel can. He finds himself pushed out of the ambulance, Cilka right behind him. Two orderlies approach and open the back doors.

'This one, take this one first,' she points to Mikhail. 'Then bring the stretcher back to get the other one.' She indicates the unconscious man lying on the floor.

'Give me a hand,' Pavel calls out to Kirill as he pulls the other stretcher free from the ambulance.

Cilka runs after the first patient, unbuttoning and flinging off her coat as she enters the ward. Yelena, another doctor and several nurses appear.

'This one, Mikhail Alexandrovich – small head wound, both legs crushed by a large rock.'

'I thought you said it was a small rock,' Mikhail whispers through clenched teeth.

'I've got him,' Yelena says. Two nurses tend to Mikhail, assisting.

'Over here, put him on this bed,' the other doctor calls out to Pavel and Kirill.

'There's one more coming. Unconscious but with a strong pulse, obvious head wound.'

'Thanks, Cilka, we've got it,' Yelena says.

The unconscious patient is brought in and placed on a bed. Kirill leaves immediately and Pavel wanders over to Cilka.

'You did great work, stupid and dangerous work.'

'Thanks, you too. I wasted too much time being angry with Kirill Grigorovich when I should have been helping the patients.'

'Kirill thinks he was born to rule.'

'Bad driver, bad attitude.'

'You'd better learn to get along with him, or he can make your life hard.'

This again, thinks Cilka. But she can't stifle a laugh. He is far from the most intimidating figure she has met.

Pavel looks puzzled.

'Let's just say, I've seen worse,' Cilka says. She looks around at the efforts being made to comfort and treat these three men injured just doing their job, a job with no proper safety measures. She has seen injuries like this too many times. The prisoners are here for their productivity, as part of a quota, and they are expendable and replaceable.

'But thanks for the warning, Pavel. I'll keep my distance from him.'

'Cilka, can you give me a hand over here?'

Pavel watches as Cilka goes over to Mikhail, cleaning and rebandaging his head wound as Yelena continues the examination of his lower legs. Cilka glances occasionally at the doctor, reading her expression as serious.

Yelena says quietly to the nurse assisting her, 'Find me an operating room, we need to get him there straight away.'

'What's going on? How bad is it?' Mikhail gasps, his hand reaching out for Cilka, grabbing her forearm, panic rising as he tries to lift his head to see his legs.

'I'm sorry,' Yelena says gently. 'I can't save your right leg; your left is not as bad, and we should be able to keep it.'

'What do you mean, keep one and not the other? Is that what you're saying?'

'Yes, we need to amputate your right leg below the knee, it is too badly crushed.'

'No, no, you can't chop off my leg! I won't let you.'

'If I don't, you will die,' Yelena says, keeping her voice steady. 'The leg is dead. There is no blood flow into the lower part; if we don't amputate it, it will poison you and you will die. Do you understand?'

'But, how will I . . . Cilka Klein, don't let them chop off my leg, please,' Mikhail pleads.

Removing his grip from her arm, Cilka holds his hand and brings her face close to his.

'Mikhail, if the doctor says she has to amputate your leg, then she has to. We will help you deal with this, help you recover. I'm sorry I could not do more.'

'The leg was crushed on impact, Cilka, there's nothing more you could have done,' Yelena says. 'I'm going to go and get ready. Cilka, will you prepare the patient and I'll see you in the operating room.'

That evening Cilka doesn't go to the mess for dinner. Exhausted, she drops onto her bed, and is instantly asleep.

* * *

Men and women in white coats waltz around her, laughing, some hold amputated limbs, tossing them to each other. Small children dressed in blue-and-white pyjamas wander aimlessly between them, their hands outstretched. What do they want? Food, attention, love?

A door opens, sun streams in. A man enters, a rainbow halo surrounding him. He is dressed in a suit of immaculate white, doctor's coat unbuttoned, a stethoscope around his neck. He holds his arms out. The adults lower their heads in respect, the children run towards him, excited.

'*Papa, Papa,*' *they cry out.*

Cilka wakes from her nightmare, but the memory that it awakens is just as horrifying.

* * *

Auschwitz-Birkenau, 1943

'Papa, Papa,' they cry out. Boys and girls run to the man who has stepped from his car. He is smiling warmly at them, his hands extended and full of candy. To the children he is a beloved father. Some call him uncle.

Cilka has heard the stories. Every adult at Auschwitz-Birkenau has heard the stories of what becomes of the children when they leave here, in his car.

Cilka watches from a distance, examining the slightly built man with not a hair out of place: his dark green tunic, without a crease or wrinkle, partially covers the white coat that indicates his rank of doctor; his clean-shaven face; his brilliant white teeth revealed by his big smile; his gleaming eyes; his SS cap tilted to one side.

The Angel of Death, that is what they call him. Twice, prior to being sent to Block 25 and given a layer of protection, she'd had to parade in front of him. She had barely dared to sneak a look at him whistling a tune as he flicked his hand to the left or the right. Both times she had escaped selection.

The children clamber around him. 'Pick me, pick me,' they squeal.

Four girls are tapped on the head and handed candy, and they climb into the car with him. The other children go back to playing. Cilka bows her head in silent prayer for the four souls being driven away.

* * *

286

Cilka cries out, sitting bolt upright in bed, shaking, terror etched on her face.

The women in the hut are all looking at her. Some from their beds, several others standing around the stove.

'Are you all right?' Olga asks with concern.

Cilka looks from one to the next, scanning the faces only partly visible in moonlight. Pulling herself together, she drops her legs over the side of the bed.

'Yes, I'm fine, just a bad dream.'

'This whole place is a bad dream,' Elena says.

They are being kind, Cilka knows. It is not the first time she has woken them by screaming. Anastasia has told her too, that sometimes she whimpers, and sometimes she hisses, like she is furious with somebody.

Cilka shuffles to the stove. A comforting arm – Elena's – is wrapped around her shoulders as she extends her hands to feel the warmth. She glances towards Hannah's bed, can't see whether she is awake and watching or not. Only she would know what the nightmares are really about. But she is probably more blissfully asleep than any of them, having collected her goods from Cilka's pocket when the women all came in.

There are layers of pain within Cilka. She misses Josie and Natia too. All winter it has been impossible to see them. Natia must have grown so much, may even be walking by now.

'You need to remember the happy times to dream about,' Olga says from her bed. 'That's what I do. Every

287

night before I fall asleep, I remember my childhood, on the beach in Sochi. It was a happy time.'

As Cilka closes her eyes for the second time that evening she decides she will try and remember a happy time in her life. It is not for a shortage of them, quite the opposite, her life up until the day she was loaded onto a cattle train had been blissfully happy, and perhaps for this reason, remembering has been too painful for her. But she will try again.

Bardejov, Czechoslovakia, 1941

'*Move over, Papa, it's my birthday, I want to drive the car.*'

The day is cool with the sun shining. A spring day, full of promise. Cilka has put on her hat and scarf, placed her father's driving goggles on top of her head, determined to drive even if only to the end of the street. Papa has lowered the soft-top roof on his pride and joy: a two-door roaster with brown leather seats and a horn that can be heard miles away.

'*You don't know how to drive a car, don't be silly, Cilka,*' *her father replies.*

'*I can – I bet I can. Mumma, tell him I can drive the car.*'

'*Let her drive the car,*' *her mother says, lovingly.*

'*Now you're being silly. You always spoil the child,*' *her* father says, although they all know it is he who dotes on Cilka. On both his girls.

'I'm not a child,' Cilka protests.

'You are, my diet'a, that will never change.'

'I'm fifteen, I'm now a woman,' Cilka boasts. 'Look, here's Uncle Moshe and he has his camera. Over here, uncle! I want my photo taken driving the car.'

Uncle Moshe greets Cilka, her mother and sister with kisses on each cheek. A manly handshake and pat on the shoulder for her father.

'Are you going to let her drive?' Uncle Moshe asks.

'Have you ever been able to tell her anything? None of us have. Cilka wants to rule the world and she probably will. Set up your camera.'

Cilka wraps her arms around her father's neck, standing on tiptoes to reach.

'Thank you, Papa. Now, everyone get in the car.'

While Uncle Moshe sets up his camera on its stand, Cilka sets about placing the members of her family where she wants them for the photo. Her father is permitted to sit in the front alongside her, her mother and sister are in the back. With her hands confidently resting on the steering wheel, she poses.

With a bang and a flash, the camera captures the moment.

'Where are the keys? I'll take you all for a drive.'

'I'll make a deal with you,' Cilka's father says. 'I promise to give you driving lessons, but not today. Today is your birthday and we will have a lovely day, then celebrate at dinner. For now, we change seats.'

289

Reluctantly, Cilka concedes defeat – one of the few times in her short life she has – and, pouting, moves to the front passenger seat.

Her scarf is flapping in the wind as she is driven through her hometown of Bardejov . . .

Cilka, in Vorkuta, finally falls back to sleep.

CHAPTER 22

'He made it through.'

The words greet Cilka as she enters the ward.

'Mikhail Alexandrovich? Where is he?'

'Bed 1 – we thought you might like to have him as close to the nurses' station as possible. You'll be able to write your notes and still see him.'

'I'll go and say hello.'

Mikhail is sleeping. Cilka looks at him for several moments, her eyes wandering down the bed to where she knows only one leg remains, hidden under blankets. She was present when his right leg was amputated. She touches his forehead, swathed in fresh bandages. Her training kicks in and she picks up his file, scanning it for information on how he fared overnight. Nothing concerning jumps out at her.

When she returns to the desk area, Raisa discusses the other patients and they share out the workload: washing, changing dressings, administering medication. There are two new women on the ward who had a fight the previous night, inflicting nasty injuries on each other. Raisa and Cilka agree to nurse one each to avoid getting caught in the middle of the dispute.

Cilka has barely begun attending to her patient when the words, 'Ambulance going out,' are shouted.

'Go! I'll see to your patient,' Lyuba calls out.

Outside, the ambulance is waiting.

'Do you want to ride up front?' Pavel asks.

'Yes,' Cilka says as she takes hold of the ambulance door. 'After you. Kirill Grigorovich can play with your leg today.'

Reluctantly Pavel climbs into the ambulance, pushing up against Kirill.

'What the hell are you doing?' Kirill demands.

Cilka climbs into the cab, slamming the door shut.

'Let's go.'

With a screeching of gears, the ambulance drives off.

'If we're going to be working together, can we try to get along?' Cilka says, leaning over Pavel and staring at Kirill.

He changes gear, refuses to reply.

'Do we know what we are going to today?' Cilka asks.

'A crane has collapsed and the driver is trapped inside,' Pavel says.

'Only one casualty?'

'I think so, but you never know. Sometimes we've gone to an accident like this and found that the bloody thing came down and landed on ten others,' Pavel answers.

'Who is rescuing him?'

'Depends,' Kirill throws out.

'Depends on what?' Cilka asks.

'Has anybody ever told you, you ask too many bloody questions?'

'Plenty of people, probably everyone who's ever met me.'

The truck bounces over a boulder and Cilka winces as her shoulder slams into the window.

'So you're not going to shut up then, is that what you're saying?'

'I'm not going to shut up, Kirill Grigorovich, so you had better get used to it. Do you want to answer my question? Or should Pavel?'

'Well—' Pavel begins to explain.

'Shut it, I'll tell Cilka I-Have-To-Know-Everything Klein. It depends how dangerous the rescue is. If it's risky, then the supervisors will make the prisoners do it. If not, then the guards will want to make themselves heroes.'

'Thank you,' Cilka says. 'We'll know as soon as we arrive how dangerous it is then. I know you don't like talking to me, Kirill Grigorovich, but it does help if I have even just a little information.'

'Yeah, well, clearly knowing everything didn't stop you being sent here.'

Cilka chortles. 'I never said I knew everything. I just like to know what I'm getting into.'

When they reach the site, there is nothing they can do straight away. Senior guards and supervisors appear from time to time to yell, as prisoners try to untangle the mess that was once the long arm of the crane, now wrapped around the driver's box. There is no glory in this rescue.

For the next two hours Cilka, Pavel and Kirill stand in the cold, stamping their feet, smacking their hands, returning to the ambulance to escape the wind. Several times Cilka climbs up the mangled metal frame of the collapsed crane to wriggle part-way into the cabin to check for signs of life in the driver. Each time she notes his pulse getting weaker, the flow of blood from his head wound no longer gushing, the bandage she has put around the wound soaked in blood.

After her last trip, Cilka returns to the ambulance to tell Kirill to go back to the hospital. On the drive back, Cilka sees the first bloom of spring flowers pushing their way through the frost on the ground. The wind whips them around and still their stalks bounce back, staying rooted to the frozen earth. Cilka has nearly served one third of her sentence. It is unbearable to contemplate how much longer there is to go. Instead, looking at the flowers, she dreams of the light and warmth that soon will come, and with them, time to see Josie and Natia again.

* * *

When she gets back to the ward, Cilka is told Mikhail is awake and has been asking for her.

'How are you feeling?' she asks him, smiling, reassuring.

'Is it gone, my leg? But I can feel it still. The pain is there.'

'I'll get you something for the pain, but yes, Mikhail Alexandrovich, the doctor had to amputate your right leg, but she has done a marvellous job repairing your left leg, and with time it will heal.'

'And I'll be able to walk, how? How, Cilka Klein? How can I live with only one leg?'

'I'm told they can make you a really good lower leg that you will learn to walk on.'

'Really? You believe someone is going to waste money on making a prisoner a leg?' He is getting angry; his voice is raised.

'I'm not going to lie to you, Mikhail Alexandrovich. I don't know if you will be given a different job or whether they will send you home; you won't be able to work in the mines.'

'Is that supposed to make me feel better? That I might now be sent back to Moscow to no home, no family, the one-legged man to beg on the streets?'

'I don't know, Mikhail Alexandrovich. Let me get you something for the pain,' Cilka repeats.

She turns away, not wanting Mikhail to see how their conversation has upset her. Yelena has been watching her and follows her into the dispensary, shutting the door behind her.

'Cilka, are you all right?'

'Yes, I'm fine.'

'No, you're not,' Yelena says gently. 'But that's all right. You know how quickly things can turn bad here, you've seen it before.'

'Yes, but . . .'

'Did I make a mistake putting you on the ambulance run?'

Cilka stops looking at the bottle of medication in her hand, turning to face Yelena. 'No, no, not at all. That's not it.'

'Then what is it?'

'Do you know how long I'm to stay here?'

'I'm not told information like that.'

'Fifteen years. Fifteen years. It feels impossibly long. And then, after that – I don't even remember what life is like outside of a place like this.'

'I don't know what to say.'

'Tell me I will leave here,' she says pleadingly to Yelena. 'That I have the chance to live a life like other young women.' *That I will have friends that don't disappear from my life. That I might find that love exists for me, too. That I might have a child of my own.* 'Can you tell me that?'

'What I can tell you,' Yelena says calmly, 'is that I will do all I can to make that come true.'

Cilka nods gratefully, looking back up at the shelf, seeking another bottle.

'Promise me you will talk to me if you feel any worse than you do now,' Yelena says.

'My father always told me I was the strongest person he ever knew, you know that?' Cilka says, still not looking at Yelena.

'That's a lot to live up to.'

'Yes, it is. But I have always wanted to live up to the expectations of my father, not disappoint him, stay strong no matter what. I don't even know if he's still alive.' She shrugs. 'It's unlikely.'

'A curse and a blessing from your father. I was very young when my father died; I would give anything to have your memories.'

'I'm sorry.'

'There's a patient out there waiting for you. Come on, I'll have a look at him while you give him the medication.'

'What will happen to him now that he only has one leg?'

'We'll get him stable, then move him to a larger city hospital where they can rehabilitate him and hopefully get him a good replacement limb.'

'And then?'

'In the eyes of the State he's still a counter-revolutionary, Cilka,' Yelena says, looking down. 'There's not much I can do about that.'

Cilka picks up the medication, tries again to press down the worry, the sadness and the pain.

CHAPTER 23

The white nights return.

Once again, the women revel in spending Sunday evenings walking around the camp. Trying to feel, for just a couple of hours, they have some small amount of freedom. They know where to walk, where it is safe to go and where to avoid the roaming gangs of men waiting to pounce.

The appearance of Josie and Natia makes some of those evenings the happiest, as Natia shows off her ability to walk. Her attempts to talk entertain them. They play with her wispy hair, fight over whom she likes the most.

The women start to escort Josie and Natia to and from the hut, on the warmest nights, so they can spend time all together away from prying eyes and let Natia run about. They take turns putting Natia in their beds, cuddling her as though she is their own daughter. They kiss her and touch her tiny hands and try to teach her their names.

Josie lets Natia socialise, giving her a nod and a smile if she looks over for reassurance. Josie sits with Cilka on her bed, and Cilka has begun to wrap her arms around Josie, press her face against her hair. Josie takes Cilka's hand and squeezes it. They communicate in this way, instead of saying what they fear, what they know, is coming.

* * *

The light fades quickly this summer. Several of the women stop venturing out. On one warm night, possibly the final gasp of summer, the women escort Josie to the hut with Natia snuggled into her arms. Anastasia has become attached to the little girl and reaches for her.

'Would you look after her for a while, please, Nastya?' says Josie, using the affectionate diminutive for Anastasia. 'I'd like to talk to Cilka.'

Cilka gets off her bed, reaches for her coat, and follows Josie outside.

They don't go too far; there are many people wandering around, and the wind has started up. They find protection beside the hut and huddle against the building.

'Cilka, what am I going to do?' So, they are finally voicing this, Cilka thinks. Beyond the one brief conversation last summer when Josie had told her one of the other mothers, who'd had several children, said they were sent to orphanages when they turned two, they have never given words to the fear. The mother had been broken,

Josie said. Completely blank-faced, barely looking at her child.

Cilka looks away. She has no answer.

'Can you help me, please, Cilka? I can't let them take her away. She's my child.'

Cilka wraps her arms around Josie, letting her sob on her shoulder.

'I can't promise anything, but I'll try. I'll talk to Yelena Georgiyevna, I'll do what I can, I promise.'

'Thank you. I know you can help, you've always been able to,' Josie says, drawing back from the embrace to look at Cilka in such a hopeful, open way that Cilka feels ill. Josie still looks so young, a girl. 'Please don't let them take my baby away.'

Cilka draws her in again, hugs her for a long time. *Please don't let them take you away.*

'Come on,' she says. 'You need to take Natia back to your hut. The wind has picked up and you don't want her getting sick.'

* * *

Cilka speaks to Yelena the next day. Yelena is sympathetic but doesn't think she has any power over the administrators. Both women know there is little chance that they can help Josie and Natia stay together after she turns two, and Josie is forced to return to a general hut without the warm little body to come home to.

Josie will die, Cilka thinks. She will not survive the heartbreak. Cilka has to figure something out.

'Ambulance going out.'

'Coming.'

Tossing the file she is holding to Lyuba and grabbing her coat, Cilka runs from the ward.

Pavel stands holding the passenger door, his big teeth resting over his bottom lip. Seeing her running towards them, he climbs into the cabin. Nothing has changed since their second day together, and so Pavel must sit in the middle.

'Something different today, Cilka,' Kirill offers.

'Wow, speaking first, Kirill,' Cilka laughs.

'No, really,' Pavel says, 'this is serious.'

'Aren't they all? Since when did we decide one accident was more serious than another before we even got there?'

'It's not an accident,' Pavel says. 'We're going to the house of the commandant, Alexei Demyanovich. One of his children is sick and we have to bring him to the hospital.'

'A child! A boy? How old, do we know?'

'I don't know if it's a boy, but it's one of the commandant's children.'

For the first time since her arrival in Vorkuta, Cilka travels on a street outside the compound of the camp and mine. A road built by prisoners. She looks at the houses where families live. Women with small children in tow hurry down the street, carrying bags. They pass several cars. She has seen a car only a few times, when someone important visits the camp.

A guard waves them down, indicating for them to stop.

Piling out, Cilka runs ahead with the guard while Pavel and Kirill retrieve the containers from the back. The front door is open, and the guard leads Cilka into the house and to a bedroom where a girl tosses and screams on a bed. Her mother sits on the edge of the bed, attempting to put a wet towel on her forehead, speaking in a soothing, comforting voice. Cilka recognises her.

'Excuse me, can I take a look at her?' Cilka says as she takes her coat off, dropping it onto the floor.

The commandant's wife, Maria, turns around as she stands.

'Hello, you're . . . ?'

'Cilka Klein. Hello again, what has Katya been up to this time?'

'Cilka Klein, yes. Please, can you help her, she's in so much pain.'

Cilka moves to the side of the bed, bending down to try to examine the girl who continues to thrash about.

'What can you tell me?' she asks her mother.

'She didn't eat her dinner last night and complained of pain in her stomach. My husband gave her something to settle her—'

'Do you know what he gave her?'

'No, I don't know. She didn't come for breakfast. I checked on her and she said the pain was back and wanted to sleep. I left her but when I returned a short while ago, she was like this, and won't say anything. Please, what's wrong with her? You have to help her.'

Maria's jewellery clatters on her wrist as she gestures emphatically.

'Let me have a look at her.'

Cilka attempts to restrain Katya's flailing arms.

'Katya, this is Cilka, I'm here to help you,' she says soothingly. 'Can you please try to lie still and show me where it hurts? There's a good girl. I want to look at your stomach.'

Cilka glances back at the door where the guard, Pavel and Kirill all stand watching.

'You three, get out and shut the door. I'll call you when I want you.'

She turns back to Katya and hears the door close.

'That's better, now let me see your stomach. You're doing well, Katya, you're a brave girl. I know that, we've met before, when you fell off the roof and broke your arm.'

Katya settles somewhat, allowing Cilka to lift her nightdress and look at her stomach. She can see it is distended.

'Katya, I'm going to gently touch your stomach. Tell me when I hit the spot that hurts the most.'

Starting up beneath her ribcage Cilka gently pushes down, quickly moving her hands a few inches at a time. As she moves down to the lower abdomen, Katya cries out.

'What is it, what's wrong with her?' Maria fusses. The room carries the deep, rich smell of her perfume, making Cilka's nose twitch.

'I'm sorry, I can't be sure, but if we get her into the

303

ambulance and to the hospital, the doctors there will be able to diagnose and treat her. I'm going to give her an injection to help with the pain and then we will transport her in the ambulance.'

Cilka can feel how her knees sink into this soft, plush carpet. How nice it would be to lie down in here. To be cared for by a mother, worried over, in this pillow-laden bed.

'I've sent someone to tell my husband. He should be here soon. Maybe we should wait and take her in his car.'

'The sooner we get her to the hospital the better, if you don't mind. I'll ride in the back of the ambulance with her and look after her.'

'All right. I trusted you once before, I'll trust you again. And I would like the doctor to be Yelena Georgiyevna again too.'

'Pavel,' Cilka calls out.

The door opens. Pavel and Kirill stand in the doorway.

'Bring me the medicine.'

Kirill hurries over, placing the drug box on the floor and ripping off the lid.

Cilka quickly locates the medication she wants, fills a syringe and gently injects Katya in the arm. She holds her arm while the pain medication takes effect and Katya settles.

'Get the stretcher, quick, and take the boxes back with you.'

The two return with the stretcher. Cilka and Maria lift

Katya as the stretcher is placed on the bed. Gently they lower her onto it, wrapping her up in blankets from her bed.

'Let's go,' she says to Pavel and Kirill. Turning to Maria, she says, 'Do you want to come with us in the ambulance or can the guard bring you in a car?'

'I want to come with you.'

'You'll need to ride up front. I will be in the back with Katya.'

The guard hands Maria her coat. Cilka grabs hers on the way out of the room as they follow Pavel and Kirill to the ambulance.

Cilka climbs in the back first and helps Pavel slide the stretcher towards her. Kirill has the engine running, shutting the back doors. Pavel hops into the front, the guard holds the door for Maria and helps her sit next to Pavel.

The drive to the hospital is silent, Maria's perfume filling the truck.

Word has reached Yelena that the commandant's daughter is en route. She is waiting for them.

Following a quick examination, she tells Maria she will need to take Katya to surgery straight away. She is certain she has appendicitis, but won't know for sure until she opens her up. If correct, Katya will be back on her feet within a couple of weeks.

'Can I come with you?' Maria asks.

'Well, no, not really, Maria Danilovna. I'll leave Cilka here with you; she can tell you what we're doing.'

'No, I'll be fine while I wait for my husband; I'd rather she was with you.'

'Let's go, Cilka, scrub up.' To the orderlies standing nearby she says, 'Take the patient to the operating room, please. We'll meet you there.'

As Yelena walks off, Cilka quickly speaks to Maria.

'She will be fine. We will have the two of you back together as quickly as possible.'

As Cilka walks from the room she hears the booming voice of the commandant. She takes a moment to watch as he wraps his wife in his arms and she tells him, in a voice thick with emotion, what she knows. Man, woman, child, and the luxury of caring only about one another.

* * *

Yelena tells Cilka she can go and get Maria and the commandant and bring them to Katya, who remains asleep, minus her appendix. Cilka stands at the back of the room while Yelena explains what the procedure involved, the recovery period, and offers to stay the night with her.

Maria thanks her, asking if it would be possible for Cilka instead to stay the night with Katya and her. She's not leaving. The commandant wants his daughter brought home but agrees she can spend one night in her own room here, away from the prisoners. Chairs are brought into the operating room for Cilka and Maria. There will be no more operations today.

CHAPTER 24

Katya wakes several times during the night. Cilka checks on her, and administers further injections for the pain, while Maria reassures her daughter that she will be home soon.

After settling Katya once again, Cilka sits back down, aware that Maria is staring at her.

'Is everything all right?' she asks the wife of the commandant who imprisons her.

'I don't know how to thank you for your kindness, your care. Watching you with Katya overwhelms me. I don't know why you are here, I don't want to know, but will you let me talk to my husband, ask him to help you?'

Cilka doesn't know where to look.

'Do you mean that?'

'Yes, we owe you so much. If it was up to me, you

307

wouldn't spend another night here. Katya is very special to Alexei Demyanovich. Don't tell anyone, particularly our sons, but I think he does have a favourite child, and it's that young girl lying in the bed.'

Cilka stands and walks over to Katya. Looks down at her: fair and pretty, soon to be moving out of girl-hood. Cilka moves a wayward strand of hair from her face.

'I've never had a child,' Cilka says, feeling safe in the warm, quiet room. 'But I am a daughter. I know the love of a mother and a father.'

'One day you will, Cilka, you are young.'

'Perhaps.'

It is too much to reveal to Maria, this well-fed, cared-for woman, that she doesn't think this will happen for her, ever. If it was possible, surely it would have already happened. She no longer functions inside like other women.

'Let me help you leave this place and it could happen sooner. This is only a temporary post for my husband. We may be back in Moscow soon. This may be your only chance to let me help you.'

Cilka sits back down, turning her chair slightly to face Maria, looks her in the face.

'Could I use your offer of help for someone else?'

'Why would you do that?' a clearly perplexed Maria asks.

'Because there is a mother here, in this camp, who is very dear to me. Her little girl, Natia, will be two in a few

308

weeks. As soon as she turns two, she will be taken away and Josie will never see her again. If there is anything you can do to stop that happening, I wouldn't know how to thank you. I would be so, so grateful.'

Maria looks away, overcome at hearing this. She looks at her own daughter and holds a hand across her stomach. Surely she knows what goes on, Cilka thinks. Maybe she has just never allowed herself to think what it is like for the prisoners, the women; their suffering.

Maria nods her head. She reaches out and takes Cilka's hands.

'Give me her details. Natia and her mother will not be separated, if I can help it.'

'Jozefína Kotecka,' Cilka says.

The door to the room opens, Alexei Demyanovich enters surrounded by his bodyguards. He looks at the two women. Cilka jumps to her feet.

'Thank you for looking after my daughter and my wife.'

Katya wakes up at the heavy sound of boots on the wooden floor. Seeing her father, she calls out.

'Papa, Papa.'

Throwing a wink at his wife, Alexei sits on Katya's bed, comforting her.

Yelena appears and examines Katya.

Everyone in the room is smiling. Cilka finds herself in the middle of a happy family occasion and doesn't know how to respond. As Katya is helped into a wheelchair to be wheeled out for the ride home in her father's car, Maria gives Cilka a long hug, whispering that she will take care of Natia and her mother.

As everyone leaves the room, Cilka shuts the door behind them and sits on Katya's bed.

'A mother's love,' she whispers.

CHAPTER 25

Yelena meets Cilka as she arrives at work. 'Come with me.'

Cilka follows.

'Don't take your coat off.'

'Where are we going?'

'Just come with me.'

Yelena walks briskly away from the hospital to the nearby administration building, a three-storey stone building standing beside two similar ones. They head round to the back, a more discreet entrance. A guard outside opens it for them without question. They step into a small reception area. Cilka quickly takes in her surroundings, looking for threats, for anyone who might harm her. She steps forward to be close to Yelena, wanting the security of this woman she has come to trust. And then, there he is. Alexandr stands up from behind a desk. She has not seen him up close for so long. He is thin, like all prisoners, but put-together – composed. His hair neat, his skin clear; his brown eyes have a warm, open expression.

'Wait here just one moment,' says Yelena to Cilka, and she nods to Alexandr and walks away down a corridor behind him and through a door.

'It'll be all right, Cilka,' Alexandr says quietly, clearly noting her distress, and showing he remembers her. He smiles, the corners of his eyes crinkling. Cilka's heart pounds.

Josie has mentioned him a few times and she is always grateful to know he is well. Josie also tells her he writes poems on the corners of pieces of paper, before tearing them off and destroying them.

Cilka goes over to the desk. She manages to speak. 'I hope so, Alexandr,' she says. She looks down and does glimpse scribbles across paper in an expressive hand. She peers back up, cannot help her eyes going to his lips.

'I . . .'

Cilka hears a door close and looks up. Josie! Her friend runs towards her, clearly distraught.

'Cilka, what's happening?'

Yelena is following Josie back into the room.

'I don't know,' Cilka says, heart still racing. 'Yelena Georgiyevna, what's going on?'

'I don't know. Just wait a moment. I was told to bring you here.'

Maria Danilovna walks into the room, Natia in her arms.

Josie cries out and runs to her daughter, stopping herself before she snatches her from the well-dressed stranger's arms. Maria hands Natia over, the little girl clearly happy and calm.

'She's a beautiful little girl, Jozefína,' Maria says. 'Come.' She beckons them back down the corridor. Cilka glances at Alexandr, who nods at her and then sits back at his desk. They go into a dull grey room and Maria closes the door.

Maria turns to Cilka. 'I kept my promise.'

'What's going on?' Josie demands, clutching Natia, terrified.

Cilka strokes Natia's face, then Josie's.

'Josie, this is Maria Danilovna, the wife of Commandant Alexei Demyanovich. You have nothing to fear. She is helping you.'

'Helping me how?'

'Jozefína, I offered to help Cilka Klein after she saved the life of my daughter, not once, but twice—'

'Well it wasn't really me—'

'I'm telling the story, Cilka!' Maria says. 'She saved my daughter's life twice. I asked her what I could do to help her, in gratitude for her care. She didn't ask for anything for herself; she told me about you and asked if I could help you and your daughter.'

'I don't understand, you offered to help her and instead you're helping me?'

'Yes, there is a car waiting outside. It will take you and Natia to the train station and from there to Moscow. A

313

friend of mine, Stepanida Fabiyanovna, will meet you in Moscow and take you home with her. I'm hoping you will take up the opportunity of living with her, earning a small allowance by performing duties and helping in her home.'

Josie, holding Natia, drops to the floor, sobbing, overcome. Cilka bends down beside her, hugging the two of them. Yelena and Maria look on, wiping tears from their own eyes. Natia wriggles free and reaches to put her tiny hands around Cilka's neck. Cilka sweeps the little girl into her arms, holding her close. She kisses her over and over on the face until the little girl bats her away, causing Josie and Cilka to laugh through their tears. Slowly, they all stand up together.

'Mumma,' Natia squeals as she thrusts her arms towards her mother. Josie takes her.

Maria smiles warmly, wiping her eyes. 'I'll leave you to say goodbye properly. Give my best wishes to Stepanida Fabiyanovna. Tell her I will write soon.'

As Maria Danilovna opens the door, Cilka runs after her, surprising herself by wrapping her arms around her. She catches herself, steps back.

'How can I ever thank you?'

'You already have. Take care, Cilka. I'll be checking on you from time to time.'

She gives them all one final nod, and leaves.

The door opens again. It is a guard.

'Time to go. The car is waiting, the train won't.' He holds up a small bag. 'The commandant's wife asked me to give you this; it's some clothes for the little one. I'll put it in the car.'

They walk back into the reception area. Josie quickly runs over to Alexandr.

'Goodbye, Alexandr,' she says.

'Good luck, Josie,' he says, pressing his hands over hers, over the child.

As Josie walks back towards the group, Alexandr locks eyes with Cilka. She turns away, puts her arm around Josie and Natia and walks out into the open with them.

As they reach the car door, Josie looks from Yelena to Cilka. 'I don't want to go. I don't want to leave you.'

Cilka laughs. Josie's words are the most beautiful and absurd she has heard for a long time. She keeps the smile on her face, tries to fight back the tears.

'Get in the car. Go. Find your brothers. Have a good life – for me, for all of us – and make sure that little girl does too. I'll think of you always, and with nothing but happy thoughts.'

One last hug, Natia squeezed between them.

The car door is slammed shut. Yelena and Cilka watch it disappear, neither wanting to move.

'Of all the things I've seen since I've been here, this is what I will remember, what I will cling to when the darkness of this place threatens to envelop me. I don't know how the commandant and his wife have managed it. Someone high up must have owed him a favour. Now back to work, there are other souls to save,' Yelena whispers.

The sun breaks through the thick clouds for a moment. Cilka feels like she is breaking apart. '*Leich l'shalom,*' she whispers quietly, to Josie. *Go towards peace.*

* * *

That evening, Cilka tells the others of Josie and Natia's departure, making light of her role in their release. Tears are shed. Memories relived. Happiness and sadness in equal measure.

The conversation opens up, as it often does these days, about their lives before Vorkuta.

Their reasons for being there are as varied as their personalities. As well as having been in the Polish Home Army, Elena had been accused of being a spy. And then she speaks to them in English, which has everyone in awe of her.

'I knew, of course,' says Hannah, smugly.

For five years they have lived with someone who speaks English. Several ask if she would teach them, just a little. A secret act of resistance.

Other girls from Poland were also charged with helping the enemy, in a variety of ways. None of them mention prostitution. Olga shares again the story of how she found herself on the wrong side of the law for having made garments for a wealthy general's wife. When her husband ran afoul of Stalin and was shot, she was arrested and transported.

Margarethe begins to sob.

'I die a little more each day, not knowing what has happened to my husband.'

'He was taken with you, wasn't he?' Olga asks, as though trying to solve the puzzle aloud.

'We were taken together but sent to different prisons. I never saw him again. I don't know if he is alive, but my heart tells me he is dead.'

'What did he do?' Anastasia asks, having not heard the story yet.

'He fell in love with me.'

'That's it? No, there has to be more.'

'He's from Prague; he is Czech. I call him my husband but that is the problem. We dared to attempt to marry. I'm from Moscow and we are not permitted to marry a foreign citizen.'

Cilka's heart has been racing throughout this whole conversation. She has been here five years and the women know she is Jewish and Slovakian, but nothing of her arrest. Josie had gathered a bit of information from asking Cilka questions, though Cilka never elaborated. She had told her about her friends, like Gita and Lale, wondered aloud with Josie about where they were, whether they were safe. She had told Josie about her mother and sister dying, but had not gone into the details. She is ashamed that she had not told her everything. But if Josie had turned away from her, it would have broken her all over again.

The hut falls into silent contemplation.

'It is time to take my advice again,' Olga says to the group. 'A happy memory. Force it into your head and your heart.'

Bardejov, Czechoslovakia, 1939

'Cilka, Magda, come here quickly,' their mumma calls out.

Magda drops the book she is reading and hurries to the kitchen.

'Cilka, come on,' she says.

'In a minute, let me finish this chapter,' Cilka growls back.

'It's something wonderful, Cilka, come on,' her mother says.

'Oh, all right, I'm coming.'

Holding the book open on the page she was reading, Cilka stomps into the kitchen. Her mother is sitting at the table reading a letter. She waves the letter at the two girls.

'What does it say?' Magda squeals.

Cilka stays standing in the doorway, pretending to read, waiting to hear the news.

'Put the book down, Cilka,' her mother says firmly. 'Come and sit down.'

Cilka splays the book open on the table as she takes a seat alongside Magda, facing their mother.

'What?' Cilka says.

'Aunt Helena is getting married.'

'Oh! That's wonderful news, Mumma,' Magda says. 'I love all your sisters but especially Aunt Helena, I'm so happy for her.'

'What's it got to do with us?' Cilka asks nonchalantly.

'Well, my two beautiful girls, she wants you to be her bridesmaids, to be part of her wedding, isn't that lovely?'

'You mean we get to wear a beautiful dress and have flowers in our hair?' an excited Magda asks.

'Yes, you will both have the most beautiful dresses and I'm sure Aunt Helena would love you to have flowers in your hair. What do you think, Cilka? Do you want to be a bridesmaid, have everyone looking at you and telling you how beautiful you are?'

Cilka looks from her mother to her sister, trying to contain the excitement she feels. She fails. Jumping to her feet, knocking over her chair, she swirls around the kitchen, trying to pull her straight dress out.

'I'm going to be a princess with flowers in my hair. Can my dress be red? I'd really like a red dress.'

'That will be up to Aunt Helena, but you can always ask her. She might say yes, but you will both have to wear the same colour.'

'I'm going to tell Papa.'

Cilka rushes from the kitchen, looking for her father.

'Papa, Papa, Aunt Helena's getting married. She's in love.'

One day, Cilka thinks, it will be my turn.

CHAPTER 26

The winter of 1950–51 is particularly harsh. The hospital is overwhelmed by severe cases of frostbite and other weather-associated ailments. Amputations of lower limbs become common, the survivors immediately shipped off to places unknown, to free up the beds. Pneumonia claims many; lungs weakened from constant inhalation of coal dust no match for the infections that spread through the camp. Cases of pellagra barely make it through the front door – the near-corpses are taken with their peeling skin and put on blankets on the floor near the entrance, ready to be taken out to a truck when they expire.

Injuries increase alarmingly as frozen fingers lose grip on tools; crush injuries rise as weakened prisoners are slow to respond to the dangers of heavy equipment and falling rocks.

Any suspicion of self-harm is verified when doctors question the injured patients. They beg to be kept in the hospital, or at the very least, released from outside work. Some of these self-inflicted injuries are terrible mutilations – among the worst Cilka has seen.

The ambulances struggle to transport the sick and injured, many arriving piled into the back of trucks, or carried in by fellow prisoners.

With the bleak weather, and Josie's departure, combined with the lack of hope, Cilka descends into darkness, again. She refuses her breaks from going out in the ambulance – picking up, dropping off and immediately going back out, endlessly caring for the sick, the injured and dying. She is becoming a stranger on the ward.

The mine supervisors praise her bravery in never refusing to go into a dangerous situation. They say her size and competence make her the best person to enter the mine to look for casualties. That word 'bravery' again – Cilka still thinks she is yet to earn it.

'Ambulance going out.'

'Coming.'

Kirill, Pavel and Cilka race to the mine.

'Not asking what we're facing today, Cilka?' Kirill asks.

'Does it matter?'

'Having a bad day?' Kirill fires back.

'Drop it, Kirill.' Pavel comes to Cilka's defence.

'All right. It's an explosion, so there will be burns as well as broken bones,' Kirill says.

Neither Pavel nor Cilka responds.

Kirill shrugs. 'If that's the way you're going to play it.'

* * *

The chaos is evident as they approach the mine. There is the usual gathering of onlooking prisoners, moving from foot to foot in an effort to keep warm.

Cilka is out of the ambulance before the engine is killed.

'Cilka, over here.'

She joins a group of guards. A supervisor appears.

'Cilka, good to see you. Got a nasty one for you. We were taking explosives into the central drift so we can advance and one of them went off unexpectedly. We've got at least six prisoners in there and about the same number of guards. We've also got our explosives expert in there. He was going to be setting the dynamite. He's the top man around here. Shit, there will be trouble if he's not all right.'

Cilka starts walking towards the entrance to the mine.

'Pavel,' she calls out, 'bring the box. Come on, hurry up.'

The supervisor runs after her, 'Cilka, you can't go in yet. They haven't declared it safe.'

She's heard it all before.

'And who's going to declare it safe, standing up here?'

With no answer, Cilka turns to Pavel. 'I can't make you come with me, but I'd like you to.'

'Cilka, you heard the man – the walls could collapse around us.'

'There are men in there. We have to try.'

'And get killed ourselves? I don't think so.'

'Fine, I'll go in by myself. Hand me the box.'

Pavel holds out the box, hesitates, then pulls it back towards himself. 'I'm going to regret this, aren't I?'

'Probably,' she says with a small smile.

'Definitely,' says the supervisor. 'Look, I can't stop you, but I can advise against it.'

'Come, Pavel, let's go.'

'Here, take the big lamp,' the supervisor says.

As Cilka and Pavel descend in the lift, the lamp barely penetrates the dust rising and swirling around them. They step out into the darkness and inch forward for several minutes before beginning to call out.

'Can anybody hear me?' Cilka shouts. 'Call out if you hear me so we can find you. Is there anybody here?'

Nothing. They walk deeper, getting closer to the blast site as the ground underfoot becomes an obstacle course, littered with rocks and boulders. The path narrows.

Pavel stumbles, slipping on a jagged rock and screams as much from the fright of falling as from being hurt.

'Are you all right?'

His string of expletives bounces off the walls. As the echo dies down, they hear a cry.

'Over here, we're over here.'

'Keep talking, we're coming,' Pavel calls out as he and Cilka hurry in the direction of the voice.

Their combined lights illuminate several men waving and calling to them. As they arrive, Pavel asks who is in charge. A guard sitting beside an unconscious man identifies himself.

'Tell me who we have here and what you know of the others,' Cilka says.

There are six of them – three guards, two prisoners and the explosives expert who is unconscious. Their helmets were knocked off in the explosion, the lights went out at the same time and they can't see to tell how badly injured they all are.

Cilka asks if any of them can stand and walk out themselves. Two say they think they can even though they are badly hurt. One reports he has a broken arm as bone has pierced his shirt and coat.

Using the lamp, Cilka and Pavel do a quick examination of the men. The explosives expert's breathing is ragged, and he has a head wound. She asks Pavel to check on another unconscious man. It only takes him a moment to report that he is dead. He was one of the guards.

Cilka concentrates on the explosives expert. Besides the head wound, he seems to have been hit in the chest by something; a depression tells her he has several broken ribs. Cilka has the able-bodied men help her lie him straight. She administers a drip into his arm, and roughly bandages his head.

'What of the others?' she asks the guard. 'We were told there were about twelve of you down here.'

The guard tells her to shine her light further ahead. When she does, she sees that the path is mostly blocked by rock from the explosions.

'They will be on the other side of that,' he explains.

'Have you tried calling out to see if any of them respond?'

'It will be a waste of time. They were about a hundred metres in front of us, going ahead with the dynamite when it went off. They would have taken the full force of the first explosion, then there were two more. They didn't stand a chance.'

'All right, I'll let you report that when we get out. For now, let's see who is capable of helping the other men walk out of here. I need at least one to help Pavel carry our expert here.'

'I can help,' the guard says.

'I can help,' one of the prisoners croaks, coughing.

'Thanks.' Turning to the other prisoner: 'Can you keep an eye on him?' she says, nodding towards the injured man. 'He's got a badly broken arm.'

'I've got him,' the prisoner answers.

Cilka holds the lamp up towards the way out and the shuffling, wincing men start to follow it. Pavel, behind her, eases his arms under the unconscious man's shoulders, taking a firm grip around his chest. Cilka picks up the medication box, places the intravenous bottle of fluid on top, and follows the workers along the long, claustrophobic corridor and eventually into the open door of the lift cage.

She looks back. Through the sooty swirl of the lamplight she can see that Pavel is struggling with the weight of the man. She hears rumbling. *No.* Dislodged rocks break away spewing out clouds of dust. She hears Pavel scream.

Cilka hears yelling, and the lever of the lift clicking up, the cage door slamming. She coughs and coughs, ears ringing. She collapses, her head hitting the hard caging of the lift wall, her body vibrating as it starts its slow ascent.

* * *

'Cilka, Cilka, squeeze my hand.' Yelena's soothing voice drifts into Cilka's semi-consciousness.

Hand, feel hand, squeeze, she tells herself. The small effort of obeying this command sends shock waves of pain through her body and she lapses back into unconsciousness.

* * *

The sound of someone crying out stirs Cilka awake. Without opening her eyes, she listens to the familiar sounds of doctors and nurses going about their work, of patients calling out for comfort, calling out in pain. She wants to call out for both.

'Are you with us, Cilka?' she hears Raisa whispering. She feels Raisa's breath on her cheek; she must be leaning over her.

'It's time to wake up. Come on, open your eyes.'

Slowly, Cilka opens her eyes. The world is a blur.

'I can't see,' she whispers.

'You may have blurred vision, so don't panic, Cilka. You're going to be all right. Can you see my hand?'

Something flashes in front of Cilka, a movement. It could be a hand. Cilka blinks several times, and each time she does so her vision clears a little until she can identify fingers; yes, it is a hand.

'I see it, I see your hand,' she mumbles weakly.

'Good girl. Now just listen while I tell you how you are, then you can tell me how you feel. All right?'

'Yes.'

'You have had a nasty blow to the back of the head requiring twenty stitches. I can't believe you made it out of there, when the whole tunnel was collapsing. What are you made of?'

'Stronger stuff than you thought.'

'We had to cut some of your hair away, I'm afraid, but it will grow back. Now, you are bound to have a headache and we don't want you talking, feeling like you have to do anything.'

Cilka opens her mouth to speak. *Pavel.* She is remembering the last moments in the mine. She gurgles his name, in distress.

'It's all right, Cilka,' Raisa says.

'Pavel . . .'

'I'm sorry, Cilka. He didn't make it.'

And it is my fault, she thinks. I made him go in.

She closes her eyes.

I am cursed. Everyone around me dies or is taken away. It is not safe to be near me.

'Cilka, you have grazes and bruises on your upper back where the rock landed, you must have been bent over when it happened. They are nothing serious and are healing nicely.'

She tries to breathe. It doesn't matter about her.

'How are the other men?'

'Oh, Cilka. Only you would ask about others before yourself. Thanks to you, the workers who came out before you are mostly fine.'

Cilka is relieved they are not all dead. But, Pavel. She should have been more careful.

'Now,' Raisa says. 'Here is how you are going to be treated, and I want your promise that you will do as we tell you. I want none of your interfering, even if you do think you know more than all of us put together.'

Cilka says nothing.

'I said, promise.'

'I promise,' she mumbles.

'Promise what?'

'To do as I'm told, not to interfere and think I can heal myself.'

'I heard that,' Yelena says, having snuck up on them. 'How is our patient?'

'I'm—'

'I'll do the talking, you've just agreed to keep quiet,' Raisa says.

'I said nothing about keeping quiet.'

'My question has just been answered. Cilka, tell me how you feel? Where does it hurt?'

'It doesn't.'

Yelena huffs. 'I want you to stay lying flat for another twenty-four hours. Try not to move too much, let your body heal, particularly your head, I suspect you have been badly concussed and only rest will heal that.'

'Thank you,' Cilka manages.

'Get some rest. I got word back to your hut that you were injured but are going to be all right; I know how close you are to the women there and I thought they might be worried.'

Hannah certainly will be, she thinks. But the last container Cilka got for her will last for a while.

Cilka's thoughts turn back to Pavel and a tear escapes and runs down her cheek.

* * *

The next day, Cilka opens her eyes to find a strange man leaning over her. Before she can say anything, he grabs one of her hands and kisses it.

'Thank you for saving my life, you are an angel. I've been watching you sleep, hoping you would wake up so I could thank you.'

She recognises him as the explosives expert from the mine.

Lyuba appears beside him. 'Come on, back to your own bed. I've told you, you can't keep coming over here. Cilka needs her rest.'

'But—'

'Lyuba, it's all right, let him stay for a moment,' Cilka croaks.

'Thank you again.'

'How are you? You didn't look too good last time I saw you,' Cilka says.

'So I've been told. But I'm much better, I'm going back to my hut tomorrow, so I must be.'

Cilka manages a smile. 'It's been good to see you. Look after yourself.'

As the man goes back to his bed, Lyuba reappears in front of Cilka.

'I hear your quick actions, and directions, saved him and the other workers. He won't stop going on about it.'

'But, Lyuba, I dragged Pavel in, and now he is dead.'

'You needed help, and it was his choice.'

'He came in because he cared about me. I see it now.'

'Well then he'd be glad you made it out.'

'Can I see her?' Kirill appears behind Lyuba, who steps aside.

'How you feeling?' he asks, with genuine concern.

'I'm so sorry, Kirill. I'm so sorry,' Cilka says, close to tears.

'It wasn't your fault, what happened to Pavel.'

'But he only helped because I asked.'

'He would help you even if you didn't ask. I guess you'll have to ask me, now.'

'I don't think I want to do this anymore, go out with you, without Pavel.'

'Don't say that. Of course you'll be back, you just have to get better.'

Cilka sighs. 'I don't think I can be the one who risks other's lives.'

'Cilka Klein, mostly, you don't tell others what to do, they risk their lives because you *don't* ask. That's why they want to help you. Don't you understand that?'

Cilka looks at Kirill, seeing him differently. The bravado he has shown her, even the contempt he has shown towards her, has gone.

He briefly touches her hand with his big hairy one. 'Get better, I'll come and check on you in a couple of days. And Cilka, Pavel wasn't the only one who cared about you.'

Before Cilka can respond, Kirill walks away.

* * *

Cilka doesn't keep her promise. Over the next ten days as she recovers, she is growled at, yelled at, threatened with being tied down. She is most active at night when staff numbers are low. Several times she attempts resuscitation on patients she hears having trouble breathing. Mostly she just visits other patients and comforts them.

Her injuries heal, her headaches reduce and the stitches are removed from her scalp. She hides the continued pain in her back, not wanting to prolong her stay on the ward, and asks Yelena to release her so she can go back to the hut. She shouldn't be taking up one of these precious beds.

'You can go soon,' Yelena tells her.

* * *

A few days later, as Cilka and the medical team emerge from surgery – Cilka's first since she has been back on her feet – the camp long since closed for the night, they are met by several senior camp officers. The officers enquire about the explosives expert and are relieved to hear he is doing well and will, after a few more days of care, be able to resume his duties. Cilka tries to slink away from the conversation, moving to the back of the group. As she tries to leave the room, one of the men calls out.

'Nurse, please stay where you are.'

Cilka freezes. She doesn't know what she has done wrong but no good has ever come from being spoken to directly by a camp commandant. When the doctor has finished his report, the commandant walks over to Cilka. Tall, slim, the cap on his head resting off to the side, he resembles someone she once knew, someone who used her. She starts to shake as memories she fights hard to bury flood back.

'Are you the nurse who went into the mine and saved the injured men?'

Cilka can't answer. He repeats the question.

'Yes,' she stammers. 'I went in, but it was the doctors who saved the patients.'

'That's not what I heard. Your bravery saved many men and I want you to know we are grateful.'

'Thank you, I was just doing my job.'

'What's your name?'

'Cilka Klein, sir.'

'Are you a registered nurse here?'

Before Cilka can answer, Yelena butts in. 'Cilka has been trained here by many senior doctors and other experienced nurses, her skills are exceptional and we're very grateful to have her.'

The commandant acknowledges the comments.

'Nevertheless, you are a prisoner here.'

'Yes,' Cilka murmurs, her head lowered.

'Do you live in the nurse's quarters?'

'I live in Hut 29.'

The commandant turns to the doctor. 'She may move into the nurse's quarters.'

With that, he leaves, his entourage trailing behind him.

Cilka slides down the wall that had been holding her up, trembling.

Yelena helps her to her feet.

'You must be exhausted. It's been quite a time for you. Let's find a bed here for you to sleep in for one more night. I don't want you going back to your hut tonight, and tomorrow we'll talk about moving you.'

Cilka allows herself to be led away.

CHAPTER 27

Cilka wakes up on the ward and can see clear blue skies outside the window. Sunrise has been creeping forward, and the coming light makes her think about the women in her hut even more.

When Yelena comes in, Cilka tells her, 'I'm so grateful for the offer to sleep in the nurses' quarters, but I've decided I want to stay where I am.'

Yelena looks at her, stunned.

'If it's all right, I'd like to stay with my friends.'

'Where you are unsafe . . .'

Cilka knows that Yelena is aware of what happens at the night, in the camp – she has seen the injuries. Cilka understands why it might seem unfathomable.

'Where my friends are,' she says again. Olga, Elena, Margarethe, Anastasia. And, she thinks fearfully, if Hannah has told them, then I need to face up to that. To her. 'I don't expect you to understand.'

Yelena takes a deep breath. 'It's your decision and I'll respect it. Should you change your mind . . .'

'You'll be the first to know.'

She has to go back because the women Cilka shares a hut with have become her family. Yes, they don't always agree. There have been many fights, some of them physical, but that is what large, complex families endure. She remembers the arguments and pushing and shoving that went on between her and her sister while they were growing up. But the cooperation, and the sharing, outweighed the conflict. Women had come and gone, but the central unity of the hut remained, with the gruff Antonina Karpovna an integral part.

* * *

When Cilka enters the hut the women look at her sadly. They know, she thinks. She could walk straight back out, but she forces herself to stay, to face them.

'Oh, Cilka,' Margarethe says. 'Olga has gone.'

'What do you mean, gone?' Cilka asks, forcing a deep breath.

'They took her away this morning as we were going to work. Her sentence was up.'

'But I didn't get to say goodbye,' Cilka says. She doesn't know if she can fit any more missing inside her.

'She said to say goodbye to you. Be happy for her, Cilka. She will be able to go back to her children.'

Anastasia enters the hut, joins them. 'Cilka! Did they tell you?'

'Yes,' Cilka replies. 'I'll miss her.'

Anastasia wraps her arms around Cilka.

'We missed you.'

* * *

The hut is unusually quiet that night, Olga's empty bed a constant reminder that she has gone, and they are left behind.

Several men come after lights out, including Boris. He is subdued. Cilka lies quietly beside him.

'Don't you ever want to talk about us?' he finally asks.

'I don't know what you mean by us.'

'You and me, what we mean to each other. You never tell me how you're feeling.'

'What do you care? You just want my body.'

Boris leans on one elbow, trying in the dark to see Cilka's face, to read her expression, look into her eyes.

'What would you think if I told you I'm in love with you.'

Cilka doesn't respond for several moments. He waits.

'That's a very nice thing to say.'

'I really thought about it when you were away, in the hospital. And what do you feel for me?'

Nothing, she thinks. I have merely tolerated you. And not for the first time, the kind, attractive face of Alexandr comes into her head. But she should not tease herself like this.

'Boris, you are a very nice man; there is no one in this camp I would rather have lying with me,' she says, able to make out his ruddy nose, the wetness on his lips in the half-light. She looks back at the ceiling.

'But do you love me?'

'I don't know what love is. If I was to allow myself to fall in love with someone, I would have to believe there was a future. And there isn't.'

But she does know that it is possible for her to be drawn to someone, in the way she has heard people speak about. It is also cruel to be so drawn to someone in a place like this.

'How can you be sure? We could have a future together. We won't spend the rest of our lives here.'

It is better to feel nothing, she thinks.

'Do you see that empty bed over there?'

Boris peers into the dark.

'No.'

'Well, there is an empty bed. Olga slept there every night since the day we arrived here.'

'Yes . . .' Boris says, uncertain.

'Do you know why she was here?' Cilka's voice rises, eliciting a 'shut up' from the darkness.

'How could I know why she was here when I don't even know why you're here?'

'She was Russian and she fell in love and tried to marry a man from Prague. That is against your laws. For that they were taken away; she ended up here and she has no idea what happened to him but she suspects he is dead.'

'What does that have to do with us?'

'I am from Czechoslovakia and you are Russian.'

'Things can change,' he says plaintively.

'Yes, they can, but right now this is our reality.'

Boris snuggles into Cilka, his passion gone, seeking comfort. Cilka tolerates it.

* * *

Boris's affection, and his abuse, remain constant; the injured and sick remain constant; the friendships in the hut remain quietly expressed through the sharing of resources, through the consoling of one another over their conditions, their losses. Margarethe, Anastasia, Elena and Hannah remain, but Cilka does not feel as close to them as she had to Josie. Hannah reminds Cilka, whenever possible, that she could disrupt the peace of the hut, that she could reveal all. And Cilka still cannot face that. Cilka remains connected to Yelena, even if it remains mostly unsaid – expressed through looks and gestures across a patient's bed, across the ward. And though she tries to deny the feeling to herself, Cilka looks out for Alexandr – a figure smoking, his eyes closed in momentary pleasure, near the adminis-tration building. In snow, through rain, in brief sun – his face turned up to the light. When she sees him, her heart leaps, but still she hurries on, thinking that to let in such longing can do no good.

All this continues as the seasons change – darkness to light, white nights to long dark winters. Cilka's nightmares still often wake her: emaciated bodies, whistling doctors, the commandant's black, shiny boots. She grasps for the good memories, but they are getting further and further away. She fantasises about Josie and Natia's life, about Lale and Gita's. She imagines them safe and warm and holding each other. She endures.

CHAPTER 28

Vorkuta Gulag, Siberia, June 1953

Another white-night summer. The first few Sunday evenings of venturing out 'after dark' lack the enthusiasm and enjoyment of summers past. Their eighth summer, eight years of their lives stolen.

There is an echo of restlessness throughout the camp. As summer reaches its peak, Cilka overhears talk on the ward of a strike. Men in one area of the camp are refusing to work. That evening she tells the others what she's heard.

A level of excitement spreads through the hut at this rumour. Elena has heard nothing in the sewing room where she now has a job, thanks to Olga's lessons. She and Cilka are entreated to find out all they can.

The next day, Cilka asks Raisa what she knows. In a

hushed voice, Raisa tells her she has heard other workers have gone on strike.

Out on the ambulance that day, something Cilka still does along with ward duty, though not as often, she sees several dozen men sitting on the ground outside one of the administration buildings.

Kirill slows down to stare at the extraordinary sight of men sitting around during the day. Several guards stand nearby, watching.

'Well, that's different,' Fyodor – the ambulance officer Cilka is now often paired with – comments.

'Haven't you heard?' Cilka says. 'They're on strike, they're refusing to work.'

'Maybe we should join them, I'll turn the ambulance round,' Kirill says.

'Keep driving, it's not as if it's true hard labour you're doing,' Cilka fires back.

'I love it when you're feisty, Cilka Klein, I'm surprised you're not one of the ringleaders running the strike.'

'How little you know me, Kirill.'

'Oh, I think I know you pretty well.'

'Excuse me, there's three of us here,' Fyodor chimes in.

* * *

Back on the ward, the staff gossip is all about the growing strike and how the authorities will handle it. The options available to settle the dispute seem limited and likely to end in an increased workload at the hospital. Nobody knows if there is a specific aim to the unrest, or a new group of prisoners influencing the older ones, men still with the energy to protest at the way they are treated.

That evening, Elena shares what she knows. The strikers want better living conditions, she says. The women look around their hut, which they have made into the best home they could. An old jug containing a few flowers sits on a nearby table, embroidered artwork is tacked to walls, and they each have a bed, something they know is a luxury.

'What else?' someone asks.

'They want the barbed wire removed from around the camp and they want us to remove the numbers from our uniforms; they say it is degrading.'

This last demand causes Cilka to rub her right hand over the coat sleeve of her left arm, thinking of the number permanently stamped onto her skin.

'Oh, and we should be allowed to write letters home to our families once a month.'

'Anything else?' Margarethe asks.

'I heard something about demands for political prisoners,' chimes in Anastasia, 'but I didn't take much notice.'

'Why not? It affects us,' Margarethe says.

'We're not all political prisoners,' Anastasia says.

'We are all victims of an unjust, harsh dictator,' Elena pronounces.

'Elena, don't say that. Not even here,' Margarethe whispers firmly.

'She can say what she wants,' Hannah says proudly.

'I'm not interested in politics; I've never voted or

marched or protested,' Anastasia says. 'I stole bread so others could eat.'

'Can we all stop talking like this? It can only get us into trouble,' Margarethe says.

Cilka nods. 'Let's not say or do anything to get us into any more trouble than we are in just by being here.'

'That's your preferred way to do things, isn't it, Cilka? Just lie down and take it,' says Hannah.

Elena glares at Hannah.

'It's all right, Elena,' Cilka says. 'Anger is what we feel when we are helpless.'

Hannah pushes herself violently off the bed and spits at Cilka's feet, before storming out of the hut. Elena balls her fists and goes to follow her.

'Don't,' Cilka says. 'Let her go.'

* * *

Over the next few days, the unrest grows. The number of prisoners on strike reaches the thousands. Calls for the ambulance at the mine cease as the prisoners down tools. The machinery grinds to a halt. Thousands of prisoners sit in the compound, no one threatening to escape its confines. Just a passive, peaceful sit-down.

An orderly regales Cilka, Raisa and Lyuba with his version of a speech made by one of the leaders of the uprising.

'No matter our nationality or where we are from today, our fate is sealed. Very soon, brothers, we will know when we can return to our families.'

Raisa and Lyuba listen before hurrying away, anxious not to be involved.

'What else did he say?' Cilka asks, fired up. She may not have a family to go to but she could look for Josie, for Gita. Does she dare hope?

'Not much. He was asking everyone to stay sitting and not cause trouble, give the pigs no reason to attack us.'

'Us? Were you sitting with them?'

The orderly looks sheepish.

'For a while. I'm with them, I support them, but my work here is important.'

'Good for you,' Cilka says to him.

The rumours are rife. Cilka soaks up all the information she can. Each evening she relays what she knows. Elena does, too. Clandestine groups have been forming since the death of Stalin in March of this year; communication between camps has increased, spreading plans for a mass strike at Gulags across Siberia. A month earlier, they were told, strikes had occurred in East Berlin, and this convinced the organisers in Vorkuta to do something about their living and working conditions. Hannah has begun to sit very quietly during these conversations.

The doctors working with Cilka discuss the non-violent nature of the strike, grateful bloodshed has been avoided. So far.

* * *

'They've stormed the jail!' an orderly runs into the ward screaming one morning.

The staff gather around him. His news is scant. Hundreds of men have stormed the area housing maximum-security prisoners and have released many. The newly freed prisoners have joined the others and the sit-in has resumed.

Five days later, guards move on the prisoners. Cilka is advised not to leave the hospital. Prisoners have erected barricades and concerns grow that the guards and camp authorities may be planning retaliation.

Cilka is terrified for her friends, hoping they are safe. And she fears for Alexandr, too.

The next day, the stalemate is broken.

'Prepare for casualties,' Yelena warns the staff.

Gunfire reverberates around the camp. Within minutes, Cilka and her colleagues are overrun with prisoners bringing in wounded men, and some women. The ward is awash with blood. The initial chaos is organised by one of the doctors like a military operation. No one gets past the treatment area at the front of the ward without being assessed by medical staff. Cilka works without stopping.

They keep coming. Many are dead on arrival and are quickly taken away by those who carried them in. Those with life-threatening injuries are sent immediately for treatment, the others ordered to wait in the reception room outside.

Like all the medical and nursing staff, Cilka is threatened verbally and pushed around by panicked men insisting she treat their comrade first. With no one to ensure their safety, she and her colleagues stand up for themselves, looking for and getting support from nearby prisoners.

With no change in the light outside, Cilka doesn't know when day becomes night becomes day again.

'Take a break, have something to eat and drink,' a blood-splattered Yelena tells Cilka and Raisa, who together are bandaging the same badly wounded man.

'There's too much still to do,' Raisa responds.

'Take a break, then come and relieve Lyuba and me,' Yelena says, and it's the first time Cilka has heard her raise her voice like that. 'It's the only way we are going to cope. We have to look after ourselves.'

Cilka and Raisa get themselves a cup of tea and hunk of bread, bringing it back onto the ward. They sit with the less injured awaiting their turn for treatment. No one talks. Cilka dozes.

She is startled awake. Several men in uniform storm into the ward, guards hurrying behind them.

'Who's in charge?' one of them bellows.

Yelena approaches them. 'I am.'

'I want to know the name of every *zek* in here. Get me the list.'

'I'm sorry, I don't have a list. We've been too busy treating them, saving their lives, to ask them their names.'

Yelena receives a fierce slap to her face, sending her sprawling.

'I'll be back in an hour and I want the name of every single person.'

Cilka crawls over the floor to get to Yelena as the uniforms leave the ward.

'Are you all right? The bastard. How dare he hit you!'
She helps Yelena to her feet.

'Didn't see that coming,' Yelena says with a brave smile.
'How can I help?'

'Get paper and a pencil and get the names please, Cilka.'

'But what if they're unconscious?'

'Then make them up.'

The Vorkuta Uprising is over. Two weeks of a bloodless standoff ends with dozens dead, hundreds injured.

As Cilka obtains the names of the prisoners who are conscious and makes up names for those who aren't, she is flooded with conflicting emotions. Talking quietly to the men who can answer her questions, she draws strength from their defiance and attempted resistance. Many of them are proud of the wounds they obtained while fighting for what they see as a just cause – better working and living conditions.

When looking at the severely wounded – many that she knows will probably not survive – she is wracked by grief for their failed resistance; grief for the loss of Pavel; grief at the departure of her friends, Josie and Olga. She can only hope they are somewhere safe. Hope that the best efforts of the doctors and nursing staff will save some of these lives that hang in the balance. Hope that one day another uprising will lead to a better outcome and they can all go home.

She gets to the furthest beds and drops down when she sees a familiar face.

'Hannah!'

Hannah looks at Cilka through half-closed eyes.

The doctor nearby looks over. 'Bullet wounds, Cilka,' he says, and gives her a sorrowful look.

Hannah croaks, 'Help me, Cilka.'

There's a lot of blood, but Cilka can see the wounds are in Hannah's arm and chest.

'I'll be back,' she says, and she runs to the dispensary. She returns with a rubber tourniquet and gauze. She lifts Hannah's blood-covered arm, causing her to howl, and tightens the tourniquet. Then, with her left hand and the gauze bandages, she applies pressure to the chest wound. She is not sure how long ago Hannah was injured, but she can see why the doctor may have moved on to patients with a better chance of surviving.

Cilka pushes Hannah's hair back from her forehead. She is covered in cold sweat.

The two women hold each other's eyes. Despite everything, at this moment Cilka finds herself willing Hannah to live. She knows why she has become brutalised in this place, why she let addiction take hold. Now, lying before her, Cilka can see only her bravery, her humanity.

'Hannah . . .'

Hannah draws a pained breath over bloodied teeth. 'I couldn't stand by, Cilka, and let the men have all the fun.'

'You are so strong, Hannah,' Cilka says.

There are cries and moans all around them.

Hannah takes short, sharp breaths. She reaches out with her non-injured arm and grasps the front of Cilka's apron.

'Cilka,' Hannah says, her voice choked with blood, 'you are strong too.'

Tears well up in Cilka's eyes. She takes Hannah's hand from the front of her apron, curls her fingers around it. With her other hand she keeps the pressure on the chest wound. Trying, failing, to stop the bleeding.

Hannah squeezes her hand back.

'Just keep making sure—' Hannah says, gasping for air – 'you do not let them break you.' She pushes these last words through her teeth, fiery and tough. 'Please . . .' she says. 'Say goodbye to Elena for me.'

'Hannah . . .' Cilka says, tears rushing now down her cheeks, her lips. 'We need you.'

'I'm not afraid,' Hannah says, and closes her eyes.

Cilka sits with Hannah as her breaths come further and further apart, and then not at all. She cries for the loss of a person of such strength and integrity. Hannah may not have liked Cilka, or been able to understand what it had been like in that *other place*. But Cilka respected her. Everyone affected by war, captivity, or oppression reacts differently – and away from it, people might try to guess how they would act, or react, in the circumstances. But they do not really know.

Once she has composed herself, and washed the blood from her hands, she picks the list back up and completes her task.

She hands the list of names to Yelena.

'I hope this will do,' she says.

She needs to get back to the hut to break the news.

'Ah, hope, now that's a word we must use more often here,' Yelena replies. She looks up from the list, at Cilka. She frowns. 'Cilka, are you all right?'

Cilka nods. It is too much to explain. 'I just have to get back to my hut.'

'You may go,' Yelena says.

* * *

Life in the camp and in the hospital slowly returns to normal. Despite the white nights, no one risks being outside in the evenings due to the increased guard presence along the perimeter fence, and the sense that the guards are still jittery.

The hut mourns Hannah. Though she was always finding ways to get under her hut-mates' skin, she was admired, especially now that the women see what she used to do for them all. Elena takes it the hardest, beating herself up for not knowing her plans, for not being by her side.

Cilka learns that the prisoners who survived the uprising face no further punishment. They go back to their huts, to their jobs, their lives returning to normal. Rumours circulate about some prisoners removing the patches identifying them by a number. They are getting away with it, no attempt is being made to force them to sew it back on.

When entering the hospital one day, Cilka is relieved to look across the yard and see the familiar tall, confident figure of Alexandr, closing his eyes and breathing out smoke into the frosty air.

She gets to work, the sight sustaining her for days, like food.

CHAPTER 29

The dark returns.

There's a blizzard howling outside and only one man braves it to enter Hut 29. Boris. He is distraught. He has learned he is to be released in a few days' time and is trying to pull strings to have Cilka released too, so they can start a life together.

Cilka says nothing as he regales her with plans of moving back to his home, of his family there and how he will get a job and he can provide for Cilka and the family he wants to have with her. Cilka feels sick. She has to think of something.

She runs her fingers across his scalp as he snuggles into her.

He tells her he loves her.

Cilka is thrown back to another place, another time.

351

Auschwitz-Birkenau, 1944

'You know I care about you, don't you?'

'Yes, Commandant Schwarzhuber,' Cilka replies meekly.

'I'd do something about my feelings for you if I could. You know that, don't you?'

'Yes, sir.'

'Don't call me sir here, in bed. Use my name, Cilka.'

'Johann.'

'It sounds so lovely coming from your lips. You do like me, don't you?'

Cilka forces her voice to sound loving. He doesn't see the tears she wipes from her eyes as she tells the biggest lie of her life. A lie that will allow her to stay alive.

'Of course I do, Johann.'

Tentatively Cilka runs her fingers through his hair. He purrs like a kitten, snuggling into her chest.

'Johann?'

'Yes, little one.'

'I've never asked you for anything in all the time we've been together, have I?'

'Mmm, no, I don't think you have, why?'

'Could I ask you for just one thing?'

'I suppose so. Yes, if I can give it to you. What is it you want?'

'It's not for me.'

'Then who?'

'For my friend, Gita. She likes this man, just as I like

you, and it would be good if he could have his old job back, he was very good at it.'

'What's his job?'

'The Tätowierer *– he was the* Tätowierer.'

'Mmm, I have heard about him. Do you know where he is?'

'I do.'

'Then why don't we pay him a visit tomorrow?'

'Thank you, Johann. Thank you very much.'

Cilka clears her throat and swallows back her tears. There is no use for them in this place.

* * *

Aware that Boris is stroking her face, running his hands down her neck, Cilka forces herself to find that voice again.

'Oh, Boris, I don't know what to say. I care so much for you; you have been so important in my life here.'

'But do you love me, Cilka?'

She clears her throat. 'Of course I do. You have been my saviour.' She marvels at his inability, now and always, to read the tone of her voice, her body language, the things that don't lie. She doesn't believe in miracles, in love.

'I have to take you with me. I want you with me. I can't bear the thought of any of those animals putting their hands on you. They tell me they are lining up to take you as soon as I go.'

The words stab Cilka like a knife and she clutches her

chest. Boris interprets her groan to be the pain of sadness that he is leaving. He holds her, gently whispering his love and how he is going to take care of her.

* * *

At the mess the next morning, Cilka, Elena and Anastasia sit together over their gruel.

'I heard everything last night,' Anastasia says to Cilka.

'Don't worry your head about it, Anastasia,' Cilka says. She needs to solve this on her own.

'Heard what?' Elena says.

Anastasia says, 'Boris is being let out.'

Elena stops eating for a moment. 'Cilka, you have to move into the nurses' quarters.'

'We'll work it out. I can't leave all of you.'

'Cilka, don't be stupid!' Elena says, hitting her with her spoon. 'We all have husbands, or protection,' she says, sending a subtle wave to Antonina across the hall. 'You will be eaten alive. Even Antonina or your fancy doctor won't be able to save you.'

Anastasia's lip wobbles. 'Cilka, I will miss you so much, but Elena is right. We will try to see you on the white nights – like Josie, remember?'

Cilka stares at her gruel. Considering.

* * *

Cilka wades through knee-deep snow to the ward after rollcall, and seeks out Yelena.

'Can we talk?'

354

'Of course, Cilka.'

'Can you please move me, now, today, into the nurses' quarters? I can't continue sleeping in the hut,' she blurts out.

'Are you hurt?' Yelena asks.

'Not yet, but I might be if I stay where I am. Please help me.'

Cilka still feels terrible about leaving her friends, but it is true that they are all now protected. Her being there won't change a thing. They don't need her for extra rations either, as most of them now have better jobs.

'Calm down. Of course we'll help you. You will go to the nurses' quarters with Lyuba when you have finished your shift this afternoon,' Yelena says. 'Do you want to tell me what happened? I thought the women you live with care for you.'

'They do. It's not them, it's Boris.'

'The pig who forces himself on you.'

'Yes. He told me last night he is being released and that other men are lining up to take me.'

'That's enough, Cilka. No one is taking you. No one will harm you ever again as long as I can help it.'

CHAPTER 30

L iving in her new home, with a bed, a small chest of drawers, fresh clothing, makes Cilka's daily life easier. It is access to a shower that breaks her, reducing her to a sobbing heap crumpled under the water, where Raisa finds her, cradles her, dries, dresses and puts her back to bed.

Each evening, Cilka returns to the barrack that she shares with twelve other nurses, and if she sees a bed unmade, it is soon made. The floor is swept, sometimes several times a day, the personal keepsakes and photos belonging to each nurse dusted and arranged on their drawers. Keeping busy in this way helps with the intense missing of her friends back in the hut and makes her feel she can contribute something to her new living companions.

She has been in Vorkuta for eight years. Eleven years

have passed since she left her home town of Bardejov, bound for Auschwitz, still an innocent child.

Her father, dear Papa, occupies much of her thoughts. Knowing her mother and sister have died has allowed her to grieve, remember them. She is tormented by not knowing if her father is alive or dead. *Why can't I feel his loss, mourn his death; why can't I rejoice, knowing he is alive waiting for me to come home?* Neither of these emotions rests with her. Only the unknown.

A week into her new situation, during a break, Yelena sits down with her. She tells her about a patient she treated a couple of days ago with a burn on her arm. When she asked the patient what happened, she was told it was self-inflicted. The patient identified herself as Elena and asked Yelena to pass on a message to Cilka.

Boris had come looking for Cilka, planning to take her away. When Elena told him Cilka had taken a turn for the worse and was back in hospital and not expected to live, Boris had flown into a terrifying rage and smashed up her empty bed. Elena wanted Cilka to know that the wood had kept them warm that night. Her message was a warning, however: Cilka must stay away from Hut 29. Other men have come looking for her, bad men . . .

Cilka is horrified that Elena had to do that to herself to get a message to her.

'Did they say any more? Are the women all right?'

'Yes,' Yelena said. 'She said not to worry, they are all fine.'

'Am I really safe? Can they not find me here?' Cilka asks.

'You're safe, none of those men would dare venture near the staff quarters. In all my years here, I've never seen anyone cause any trouble. We have our own protection.'

It starts to sink in for Cilka: even on the white nights, she may not ever be able to see her friends. She is safe. They are safe enough. But again, she is separated from those she has become close to. Is there to be no lasting relationship in Cilka's life?

Not that they ever knew her completely.

'Can I ask how Petre Davitovich is?' Cilka asks, because at least she can know there is the possibility for others, in here, to have something lasting.

She will not let herself entertain the fantasy of the tall, brown-eyed Alexandr.

'Oh, he's wonderful, he's—' Yelena catches herself. 'What do you know about Petre Davitovich and me?'

'Just what everyone else here knows, that you two see each other, and we are so happy for you.'

'Everyone knows?'

Cilka laughs. 'Of course we do. What else do we have to gossip about in here?'

'Break's finished. Come on you, back to work.'

* * *

On her ambulance trips throughout that winter, Cilka notices that the number of prisoners working at the mine seems to be dwindling. Fyodor tells her there have been a lot of prisoners released in the past few weeks and not so many new ones coming in. They discuss what this means, and whether they might also be freed – they've heard of prisoners being released early. Cilka can barely let in the thought, the hope.

Soon it is spring; the days are lengthening. Cilka notices more flowers than usual. They poke their heads above the snow and ice, waving in the breeze. Cilka's steady routine, the time passing, and the freshness of spring bring her a level of relative calm, despite the deep ache she still feels for her losses and how much she misses her friends. And her secret longing. The ache is as much a part of her daily life as the harsh elements, hard bread, and the call of 'Ambulance going out!'

One day they stop outside a cluster of buildings that include food storage and laundry supplies. They are met and waved into a section Cilka hasn't been in before but quickly identifies as the sewing room. Long tables with barely room between them for someone to sit in front of the machines.

Cilka looks around and sees a hand waving at her and Kirill and Fyodor.

'Over here.'

Cilka walks over and jumps at a gentle tap on her shoulder. 'Hello, stranger,' a beaming Elena says.

'Elena!' The two women hug. Cilka doesn't give Elena a chance to answer any of her questions, as she fires one after another. 'How is Anastasia? How is Margarethe?'

'Slow down, let me look at you.'

'But—'

'Anastasia is fine, Margarethe is well. Everyone misses you so much but we know you can only be safe away from us. You look well.'

'I miss you all so much. I wish—'

'Cilka, we have a patient here, will you take a look at him?'

Cilka registers Fyodor and Kirill attending to the man lying on the floor, groaning, clutching his chest.

'What's wrong with him?' she says, walking over but holding onto Elena's hand, to bring her with her, to spend as much time with her as possible.

'Chest pains,' Fyodor replies.

Cilka crouches down, Elena with her, and introduces herself to the patient and asks some general questions. His answers indicate there is nothing she can do but get him to the hospital as quickly as possible for the doctors to assess.

'Load him up,' she tells the men. She lingers over a last hug from Elena, then follows the stretcher outside, jumping into the back of the ambulance. She glances one more time at her friend before giving the patient her full attention. She again asks the questions she knows the doctors will want her to answer on arrival.

On her way back to her living quarters that afternoon she stops and picks as many flowers as she can carry. Placed in pots, jugs and somone's mug, they greet the other nurses on their return.

* * *

The white nights are back. Cilka and the nurses take their evening walks outside. Occasionally, Cilka thinks about risking a visit to the general compound to see her friends, to wander between the huts, share in the laughter that only comes at this time of year. And could she, finally, find the words? Something within her still closes over at the thought. She knows that she would be recognised by some of the men and boys, that she is still not safe, and so she stays away. She does not see Alexandr on those evenings – perhaps their shifts are out of sync – but she often glances to the administration building anyway, just in case.

She is almost grateful when the winds return, the sun goes down and her temptations are no longer a threat. But then winter arrives with a vengeance. With the new concessions gained at the expense of dozens of lives in the fateful uprising a year ago, work grinds to a halt on many days as prisoners are no longer expected to work in the bitter cold, with temperatures well below freezing, and constant darkness. Many days, the prisoners cannot leave their huts – the snow piled so high throughout the camp that even walking to the mess for meals is not possible. The road between the camp and the mine is blocked, making it difficult for either trucks or the train to collect the coal needed throughout the Soviet Union.

Futile attempts are made by prisoners to shovel snow away from their huts and create a path to the mess. Some succeed, but many give up as more snow arrives faster than they can clear it.

Paths are created between the medical and nursing staff quarters and the hospital.

The injuries presenting for Cilka and the others to treat now often arise from brutal beatings as bored men and women forced to stay indoors for days on end release whatever energy they have in physical violence. Cilka hears of, and sees, some beatings that are so severe the loser doesn't survive. Like caged animals with nothing to live for, the prisoners turn on each other. Cilka's gently flowering optimism starts to shrink back down inside her. This is always, she thinks, the way people will treat each other.

Poor sanitation, as the prisoners become reluctant to venture outside for the most basic of human bodily functions, leads to illness and this also fills the ward. The doctors often lament that they are wasting their time treating patients who will return all too soon with the same symptoms, the same ailments. And then the weather lifts and the temperature rises the few degrees needed for the prisoners to be sent back outside, to work.

* * *

'Ambulance going out,' Fyodor shouts.

'Coming,' Cilka replies, grabbing her coat and the new, softer scarf Raisa gave her recently.

'Where are we going?' Cilka asks as the ambulance turns away from the front gates.

'Not far, just to the other side of the administration building,' Kirill tells her.

'Another heart attack. One of the commandants doing it with someone he shouldn't have?' Cilka jokes.

Fyodor and Kirill stare at her, taken aback.

Several men stand around, blocking their view of the patient. As Cilka walks towards them she notices a piece of timber lying nearby, covered in blood.

'Get out of the way,' Kirill calls.

They step aside and Cilka sees a man lying on the ground, not moving, the blood draining from him turning the white snow all around him an ugly shade of red. As Fyodor and Kirill advance towards the man, Cilka freezes, fixated on the blood-stained snow.

Auschwitz-Birkenau, 1944

The loud pounding on the door of Block 25 wakes Cilka. Disorientated, she looks around the room. She has been dreaming, and it takes her a moment to remember where she is. Crawling out of her bed, she takes the coat that doubles as an extra blanket and pulls it on, then slips her feet into the boots waiting for her next to her bunk and pulls on her thick gloves.

Opening the door from her single room out into the large room where dozens of women have just spent their last night on earth, she screams at the pounding door, 'Coming, we're coming.'

She walks between the two rows of bunks, screaming at the women: 'Get up, get up and get out of here!'

She shakes each of the bodies awake, giving them a gentler, last message with her eyes. In between her screams, loud enough for the SS to hear, she softly mumbles and whispers – prayers, an apology, a frustrated sort of rumble. Not enough to bring herself to tears. And not looking at them in the eye. She can no longer do that. The women in Block 25 know what fate awaits them. No one speaks or resists; an eerie calm surrounds them as they file into the middle of the room.

As Cilka opens the door, the blinding sunlight reflects off the powdery snow surrounding the building. She hears the engine idling on the truck waiting just outside the fence.

The women wait behind her, the keeper of the death block. 'Get out!' she screams. 'Come on, you lazy bunch, get moving, quicker.'

She holds the door open as one by one the women exit the block and walk between the SS officers guiding them to the back of the truck. The last woman is struggling to walk; a gap has opened up between her and the woman in front. Cilka sees the nearest SS officer pull his swagger stick from its holder on his belt and advance on the woman. Cilka gets to her first, screaming at her as she slips her arm around the woman, half dragging her towards the truck. The SS officer puts his stick away. Cilka doesn't let up on her screaming until she has helped the woman onto the truck. The doors are slammed shut, and the truck drives off. The SS officers wander away.

Cilka stands watching the truck leave. She is completely

hollowed out, though she feels bile in her throat. She doesn't see the prisoner until she is a few feet away.

'Murderer,' the prisoner hisses at her.

'What did you say?'

'You heard me, you murdering bitch. You have as much blood on your hands as they do,' she says in a shaking voice, pointing to the departing truck.

The woman walks away, turning back, glaring at her.

Cilka looks from her to the truck as it rounds a building out of sight, to her hands.

She tears at her gloves. Using her teeth, she frees her fingers, throws the gloves to the ground and drops beside them. Burying her hands in the snow, she grabs handfuls of it, rubbing each hand furiously, desperately, tears streaming down her face.

'Cilka, Cilka,' a panicked voice calls out.

Her friends Gita and Dana run to her. Reaching down, they try to lift her up, but she fights them off.

'What's wrong with you, Cilka?' Dana pleads.

'Help me wash it off, make it go away.'

'Cilka, come on . . .'

Cilka holds up her hands, now red from the cold and the vicious rubbing.

'I can't get them clean,' she wails.

Dana takes one of Cilka's hands and rubs it with her coat to dry and warm it up before pulling one of the discarded gloves on.

'Cilka, we've got you. It's all right.'

Gita helps her to her feet.

'Come on, let's get you back in your room,' she says.
'The blood, can't you see the blood?'
'Come on, back inside before you freeze,' Gita says.

* * *

'Cilka, are you all right, we could do with a hand here,'
a worried Kirill says.

'All this blood,' she says, staring at the ground.

'Cilka.' Fyodor touches her arm gently. She flinches.
Then sound and light and air come back to her. She swallows, takes a breath.

She focuses on the unconscious man lying at her feet.
Though his face is covered in blood, she thinks she knows
who it is.

No, not him. Please.

'Get the stretcher, Kirill. I can't see his injuries,' she
manages to say. 'We'll load him up and I'll get a better
look in the ambulance.'

Once the man is on the stretcher, Cilka walks beside
him as he is carried to the ambulance. A prisoner joins
them.

'Is he going to be all right?'

'I don't know yet. Do you know his name?'

'Petrik – Alexandr Petrik,' the man says as he peels off,
walking away.

CHAPTER 31

'Check Bed 13 and record the time of death,' Yury Petrovich says to Cilka the next morning as he starts his rounds on the ward.

What he doesn't realise is that Cilka has been checking Bed 13 all night.

'Surprised he's still with us. I expected him to die overnight,' Yury says.

'All right,' Cilka says, trying not to reveal any emotion in her voice. After all, she does not really know Alexandr, has barely spoken with him.

Cilka reads Alexandr's notes again as she walks back over to Bed 13. She looks down at his unconscious figure. His face is badly swollen, she can see his nose and left cheekbone are broken. She pulls back his right eyelid, gently, noting his pupils are pinpointed and swim in liquid.

It is strange to be touching him after all this time, and in these circumstances.

'Oh Alexandr, what did you do to deserve such a beating?'

She pulls back the blanket covering him and examines his chest. Dark purple bruises cover his entire abdomen. She softly runs her hands over his ribs. None feel broken. She examines his legs. Multiple bruises and a badly swollen, twisted left knee. No obvious broken bones.

'Why isn't Bed 13 being actively treated?' she asks Lyuba. 'I'm seeing lots of bruises and swelling and his face is smashed up, but no major broken bones.'

'I'm not sure,' Lyuba answers. 'But . . .' she lowers her voice, 'I heard he was caught smuggling written material out of the camp, and they think he had been doing it for some time.'

'Who said that?'

'An officer was here earlier this morning, asking about him. He left when he was told he wasn't going to make it.'

Cilka remembers the scribbles on the edges of the paper at his desk in the administration building. Did the doctor assign her this man because he knew she wouldn't just let him expire, while the official notes would make the authorities think they didn't have to do anything further?

'I'm going to clean his face up a bit and see if I can find a head wound.'

'He's your patient,' Lyuba says. 'Just be careful.'

Cilka tends to her other patients before returning to Alexandr. She is trying not to be too obvious about her attentions. As she cleans away dried blood and removes splinters of timber from his scalp, she talks to him softly. She continues washing his chest and looking closely at the injuries there. She straightens his twisted left leg and thinks she feels a tremor of resistance, a reflex to the pain that a conscious person would make.

She goes outside with a bowl and returns with packed snow from a spring flurry. Placing a towel under his knee, she packs the area with snow, holding it in place with another towel. She records all his vital signs, none of which tell her he is currently losing his battle to live.

Throughout the day she monitors Alexandr, replacing the icy snow when it melts into a pan. She notes the swelling around his knee has subsided a little.

That evening she hands his care over to the night nurse who, on looking at Alexandr's file, asks Cilka what she's been doing. The patient is not for active care. Cilka tells her she has been doing basic nursing care only, has administered no medication or done anything contrary to what she has been taught.

'Well don't expect me to do the same,' the nurse responds.

'I don't,' Cilka says, knowing she has to be careful.

She finds it hard to leave the hospital. She will come back as early as she can in the morning.

Alexandr remains unconscious for the next four days. During the day Cilka washes him, talks to him, packs snow around his injured left knee, checks for reflexes. There aren't any. At night he is ignored.

'How much longer are you going to continue caring for Bed 13?' Yelena asks on the fifth day.

'Until he wakes up or dies,' Cilka answers.

'We weren't sure he'd live this long; what's your secret with him?'

'Nothing, I just clean him and talk to him. The swelling around his face and head is going down, there's this gentle face under there,' Cilka says. Knowing she can be open with Yelena, she says, 'I've met him before, you know. There's just something about him.'

'Cilka, how many times have we told you not to get attached to your patients?' Yelena scolds.

'I just want to give him the best chance to live. Isn't that what we're here to do?'

'Only when there is hope of survival. You know that. I bet you can't count the number of patients you have cared for who have died.'

'Whatever the number is, I don't want there to be another,' Cilka says with more anger than she intends.

'All right. Let me know if you want me to look at him, or if anything changes with him.'

Cilka goes back over to Bed 13.

'Well, Alexandr, you're getting me into trouble. Now I need you to do one of two things. Wake up or . . . No. Just the one thing, wake up. I want to hear your voice again.'

'Ambulance going out.'

Cilka returns with two patients from an accident – a truck has skidded in the mud and overturned. She is kept busy for the rest of the day. She leaves the ward exhausted. Nothing has changed with Alexandr.

The next morning Alexandr is where she left him. As she begins her morning ritual of washing his face, he says quietly to her, 'I thought you'd given up on me.'

Cilka jumps up, gasping.

'Yelena Georgiyevna!'

Yelena is at the bedside in an instant. 'What's wrong?'

'He's awake, he spoke to me.'

Yelena leans over Alexandr. Lighting a match, she flicks it back and forth in front of his eyes. He blinks several times. The only other person Cilka has ever known to have eyes of such a dark brown they appear almost black was her friend Gita. Gita's face flashes before her.

Cilka leans over Alexandr, peering into his eyes.

'I'm glad you're back,' she says.

'Cilka. I believe we have met before.'

Yelena looks at Cilka with a half-grin. 'Cilka, will you continue caring for this patient? I think you know what is needed.'

'Thank you, Yelena Georgiyevna. I'll call you if I need you.'

'You have a beautiful voice, Cilka, I've enjoyed our conversations.'

'What conversations?' Cilka says playfully. 'I've been doing all the talking.'

'I've been answering. Could you not read my thoughts?'

Cilka blushes, 'I don't even remember what I said to you.'

'Would you like me to tell you?'

371

'No, I would not. Now lie still and let me look at your injuries.'

Over the next six days, Alexandr's injuries fade and heal. It is only when an attempt is made for him to stand and walk that the extent of the injury to his knee becomes obvious. The joint will not flex or bend without pain.

When Cilka has a spare moment, she assists Alexandr onto his feet and, with his arm around her waist, supports him as he adjusts to weight-bearing and slowly, painfully walking a few steps.

Two weeks pass and Alexandr is still on the ward.

Having spent the best part of the day at an accident scene at the mine, and assisting in surgery, it is the end of her shift before Cilka gets back to Alexandr.

'Can you stay and talk?' he asks when she tells him she has come to say goodnight.

'I guess I could stay for a little while.'

Cilka grabs a chair, places it at the head of the bed and, after propping Alexandr up on more pillows than he is entitled to, she sits with him. They talk. They laugh quietly.

'Cilka,' a nurse says.

'Yes?'

'The patient needs his rest and so do you. Time to go.'

'I'm sorry. I'm leaving now.'

'I'll see you tomorrow, Cilka. Sweet dreams.'

The next morning Cilka asks Yelena if she can have a private word.

'Come into the dispensary,' Yelena says.

Yelena shuts the door behind them, leans against it.

'It's going out on the ambulance . . . ' Cilka says shyly.
'What about it?'

'It's, just, well, I was wondering if I could take a break from it and work in the ward for a while.'

'He has to leave here sooner or later, Cilka.'

'Of course he does. He's getting better every day, I know that.'

'Do you want to stop the ambulance run until he is discharged?'

'It's not about Alexandr being on the ward.'

'I see. It's about you no longer wanting to risk your life. I think I understand.'

'I wonder if I've done it for long enough.'

'You've taken more risks, not all of them calculated, I fear, than anyone else I know. Consider yourself no longer on the ambulance run.'

'Perhaps just one more so I can say goodbye to Fyodor and Kirill. I've become quite fond of them.'

'In a brotherly way.'

'Of course.'

'And Alexandr? You care for him, don't you?'

Cilka doesn't answer.

'It's all right, you're allowed to feel something for a man. It makes me happy to see you thinking about a future.'

'How can I think about a future while I'm here, really?'

'You can, and I think you do. Get back to work. Once more out on the ambulance.'

As Cilka goes to leave the room, Yelena embraces her. 'I'm happy for you,' she whispers in her ear.

Cilka doesn't have to wait long for her final ambulance run. That afternoon she travels with Fyodor and Kirill to yet another mine collapse. This time she is cautious and asks the supervisor to declare the tunnel safe before she ventures in. The two men caught in the collapse cannot be resuscitated and are left for the truck to take their bodies to the mortuary.

On the drive back to the hospital Cilka tells Fyodor and Kirill she won't be accompanying them anymore. The other nurses will be rotating that role.

Kirill goes silent. Fyodor is gracious and tells Cilka how he has enjoyed being in her company and watching her work.

As they arrive back at the hospital, Fyodor gives her a warm brotherly hug and a kiss on the cheek. Cilka turns to Kirill, expecting the same. He stands away from her, looking at the ground.

'Kirill, I'm sorry if you don't like my decision to stop the ambulance run. Will you say something?'

'Is there anything I can say to make you change your mind?'

'No. No, nothing, this is what I want, for me.'

'And what about me? Have you considered what I might want?'

'Kirill, what are you saying? What has my decision got to do with you?'

'Obviously nothing,' he says, with barely concealed fury. 'See you around, Cilka Klein.'

'Kirill, wait. Can't we at least be friends? Kirill, please, don't leave like this.'

Without a backward glance, Kirill walks away, leaving Cilka stunned. *What is it he was saying? What is it he wasn't saying?*

CHAPTER 32

'Two more days, that's all I can keep you for, I'm afraid,' Yelena tells Alexandr and Cilka.

'Thank you, we'll make the most of them, won't we, Cilka?'

Cilka blushes. 'I have work to do,' she stammers as she rushes away.

'She'll be back,' Yelena tells Alexandr with a wink.

Cilka spots Kirill at the nurse's desk.

'Kirill, hello, it's nice to see you back,' she says as she approaches.

'What's going on there?' he snarls at her.

Perplexed, Cilka looks where Kirill is indicating, back at Alexandr. 'What do you mean?'

Does Kirill know something about who attacked Alexandr? Cilka wonders. If so, is there a risk he'll tell the person who beat him up that he's alive? Her heart races. No, Kirill is Cilka's friend. He wouldn't.

'You and him, what's going on?'

Ah, Cilka thinks. This is something else entirely.

'I think you should leave now, Kirill, I have work to do.'

* * *

At the end of her shift, Cilka takes the chair that has become a witness to her and Alexandr's growing friendship and sits beside him.

He has spoken quietly about his past, and his arrest. He had been translating for the Soviet administrators but feeding back information to the resistance fighters. When he was caught he was brutally tortured, made to sit on a stool for days until he was completely numb, starving, soiled. He gave up no names.

He wrote poetry in his head. And, after spending time in another camp and doing hard labour, when he got the role in the administration building he could not help writing some of the poems down. Sometimes he would disguise the true words of the poem inside paragraphs of propaganda. And then he realised he could do this with information too. With every piece of written material leaving the camp being checked over, he suspects a savvy counter-intelligence officer caught on.

'And here I am. But my poems have never been about happy things,' he says to Cilka. 'Now I have met you, they will be. And I look forward to sharing them with you.'

Cilka looks him in the eye. Trusts she may be able to share with him too.

'There is something else I have to tell you,' Alexandr says seriously.

Cilka stares at him. Waiting for more.

'I've fallen in love with you.'

Cilka stands, knocking the chair over. Those few words are so large, so overwhelming.

'Cilka, please, stay and talk to me.'

'I'm sorry, Alexandr. I need to think. I need to go.'

'Cilka, stay, don't go,' Alexandr calls out.

'I'm sorry, I have to.' She forces herself to look at him again. 'I'll see you in the morning.'

'Will you think about what I said?'

Cilka pauses, looking deep into his dark brown eyes.

'I'll think about nothing else.'

* * *

Cilka knocks on Raisa's bedroom door, in the nurses' quarters. The nurses share rooms and the prisoner nurses are in a larger dormitory within the barracks.

'Come in,' a sleepy Raisa calls out.

Cilka opens the door, stands in the doorway, doubled over.

'Are you all right?'

'I'm not feeling well, I don't think I should go on the ward.'

'Do you want me to take a look at you?' Raisa asks,

throwing her legs over the side of the bed to sit on the edge.

'No, I just want to sleep.'

'Go back to bed. I'll get up and start your shift. I'm sure the others will overlap and cover you.'

'Can you tell Yelena Georgiyevna I think I'd better be off for two or three days? I don't want to spread whatever it is I have to the patients.'

'No, you're probably right. Go back to sleep and I'll have someone bring you something to eat in a few hours and check on you.'

Cilka closes the door and returns to her bed.

Auschwitz-Birkenau, 1944

The footsteps in the block and then the knock on her door startle Cilka. She remains lying on her bed. The knock comes again.

'Come in,' she says, barely above a whisper.

The door slowly opens. A face pokes into the room.

'Lale! What are you doing here? You shouldn't be here,' Cilka cries out.

'Can I come in?'

'Of course, come in. Shut the door, quick.'

Lale does as he's been told. Leaning against the door, he looks at Cilka, who is now sitting on her bed looking back.

'I had to see you. I had to say thank you in person, not through Gita.'

'It's dangerous, Lale. You shouldn't be here. You don't know when one of them will come here.'

'I'll take the risk. You took a bigger one asking for me to get my job back. I need to do this.'

Cilka sighs. 'I'm glad it worked out. It was breaking my heart seeing Gita so upset, not knowing if you were alive, then hearing where you were working.'

'Don't say any more, I can't bear hearing how it would have been for her. My stupidity got me into trouble. Sometimes I wonder if I will ever learn.' He shakes his head.

'She loves you, you know.'

Lale raises his head again. 'She's never said that to me. I can't tell you what it means to me hearing it.'

'She does.'

'Cilka, if there is anything that I can do for you, within the limits of my ability right now . . . you just have to get a message to me.'

'Thank you, Lale, but I can take care of myself,' she says.

She sees his face twist, like he is trying to find the right words.

'What you are doing, Cilka, is the only form of resistance you have – staying alive. You are the bravest person I have ever known, I hope you know that.'

'You don't have to say that,' she says, shame curling through her.

'Yes, I do. Thank you again,' he says.

She nods. He leaves the room, leaves Block 25.

CHAPTER 33

'Cilka, Cilka, wake up.'

Yelena shakes Cilka gently, waking her from a dreamless sleep; Cilka is disorientated. She pulls the blankets up to her chin, attempting to hide, to escape the threat she feels closing in.

'Cilka, it's me, Yelena. You're all right, I just need you to wake up so I can talk to you.'

Cilka registers the voice. Drags herself from sleep. 'Yelena Georgiyevna, what time is it? What's going on?'

Cilka moves over so Yelena can sit on the bed beside her.

'It's early morning but I need to talk to you. Something's happened to Alexandr.'

Cilka stares at Yelena, but no words come.

'During the night someone came into the ward and beat

him up. We don't know how it happened, but he was found unconscious a short while ago.'

'How? How could this happen?' Cilka sits up, fully awake. 'Where were the nurses, the staff? How can someone get beaten up in a hospital?'

'Slow down, I don't have all the answers. There was only one nurse on duty, and it was a busy night for her. At one point she went for a break and that must have been when someone came in.'

'But didn't another patient see something, say something?'

'We're still trying to find out how this happened. The nurse came and got me and I wanted to come and tell you straight away. He's been taken to the operating room for assessment. Get dressed and come with me.'

With gowns wrapped around their clothes and wearing masks, Cilka and Yelena enter the operating room and approach the table where Alexandr's beaten body lies. Raisa stands beside him. She looks at Cilka with sadness and compassion. Cilka gently touches Alexandr's shoulder. She can't bear how vulnerable he looks. Yelena puts her arm around Cilka.

'What can you tell us, Raisa?' Yelena asks.

'Must have been two of them. I'd say one of them held something, maybe a pillow, over his head, while the other beat him with a piece of wood, judging by the splinters I'm finding.'

'And nobody heard anything? What about the patient beside him?' Cilka blurts out.

'Can't answer that, Cilka. We'll have to make enquiries but we have to make a plan, too . . .' She looks at Yelena.

Yelena explains. 'Someone obviously wants him dead and there's no way of knowing if it's someone—' she brings her voice right down – 'on the inside, or even connected to the authorities.'

'Do you think it's the same person as before?'

'If they found out he's still alive somehow, that's highly possible.'

'But how would they—' She stops. She's worried she knows the answer.

Raisa says, 'Right now, we need to help Alexandr. We might have more answers for you later.'

'What are his injuries?' Yelena asks again.

'He was unconscious when found. He has been hit around the head but I think he's unconscious from being suffocated. Nothing on his body, thankfully, is broken. I'm so sorry, Cilka,' Raisa says. 'Why don't you leave us, and we'll get you when we're finished here.'

'I'm not leaving,' Cilka says angrily.

'All right,' says Raisa.

Yelena eases Cilka a pace or two away from the table.

'We have to work out how to protect him,' Cilka says.

* * *

Several hours later, Cilka accompanies Alexandr from the operating room to the far corner of the ward, where a screen is placed around his bed. A chair is brought for Cilka and she insists she will be his nurse. Neither Yelena nor Raisa argues with her. Food is brought to her, which she barely touches. The hot, calming tea she devours.

Yelena checks on the two of them regularly. As the day ends, Yelena tells Cilka she has spoken to the man in the bed next to Alexandr and found out more.

The patient next to Alexandr had been threatened by two men when he woke to the sound of wood thumping on flesh. He had received one punch to the mouth to intimidate him into silence. He was told he wasn't to say anything to alert the nurse after they left in case Alexandr wasn't yet dead. The man was shaken and very upset. Whoever it was that carried out the beating must have been waiting in the reception room outside, which is unstaffed at night. They may have bribed or threatened the guards outside the building, and Yelena is reluctant to question them in case she draws attention to the fact that Alexandr is still alive.

Yelena then confirms the plan they started hashing out overnight.

She speaks quietly. 'We've changed his file to say he has died and created another file using the name of a recently deceased patient, amending the record to say that patient had been healed. So as far as the hospital records are concerned, Alexandr died from his injuries as a result of a beating. We will keep the screen around his bed for a while and work out the next step. We've told the patient in the next bed that he is contagious and not to come near him.'

'Thank you,' Cilka says, mind racing. That buys some time, but what's next?

'It is the best we can do for now, Cilka.'

When Yelena leaves, Cilka places her head on the pillow beside Alexandr's.

* * *

The next morning, Cilka wakes to see Alexandr looking at her. For several moments their eyes are locked, wordlessly conveying their feelings for each other. They are interrupted by Raisa.

'I see you are both awake. Now, which one should I look at first?'

Cilka smiles. 'Him, of course.'

Raisa tries to explain to Alexandr his injuries and how he is to be treated. Cilka can't help herself and constantly interrupts with her positive spin on his recovery. Alexandr says nothing, nodding, looking grateful but worried, echoing Cilka's true thoughts.

* * *

Days pass as Alexandr slowly recovers behind the screen. His bruises fade, but movement still causes him pain. When Cilka runs into Kirill going in and out of the reception area she tries to act friendly and natural, politely declining his advances without making him angry, not wanting to draw any unnecessary attention to the screened area on the ward. She suspects it was him who either assaulted Alexandr or alerted the original attacker to the fact that he was still alive, but she has no way to prove it.

Alexandr happily accepts the pain of getting out of bed

to walk with his arms around Cilka as she helps him. They are told Cilka is not the best nurse to be assisting him, their difference in height more of a hindrance to his recovery than a help. This is not the only advice they ignore. Each night Cilka is found sitting slumped in a chair, her head on his pillow, sound asleep. She has barely left his side since the beating.

The number of patients in the hospital has begun to slow, and word reaches the staff that numbers in the Gulag are reducing significantly. Prisoners are being released early on the orders of General Secretary Khrushchev, who has succeeded Stalin. He is reaching out to the West. The stain the Gulag system has placed over his empire is becoming known, and appeasement is required to continue talks with non-communist countries.

Alexandr is able to walk on his own now, and the screen has become conspicuous, drawing questions from patients and staff about how bad the 'infection' is behind it. They need to work out the next step.

'Cilka, can I see you a moment?' Yelena calls one morning.

'I'll be right back,' Cilka tells Alexandr.

Yelena steers Cilka into the dispensary.

'Nothing good ever happened in this room. What is it?' a concerned Cilka asks.

'Do you trust me?' Yelena asks.

'More than anyone I've ever known, besides my family.'

'Then I need you to trust me now. Alexandr will be discharged in two days' time . . .'

'No, you can't. You promised,' Cilka cries.

'Listen to me. Not out into the prison population where someone would notice he's not the dead man whose name and number we've assigned him. He will be discharged to a hut nearby, where he will be safe. I want you to trust that I'm doing all I can to help.'

Cilka is speechless. This is a good thing. He will be safe. But again, someone is being taken away from her.

She tries to smile. 'You are so good, Yelena Georgiyevna. I am grateful. *He* will be grateful.'

Yelena looks troubled, in a way Cilka has never seen before. She is always stoic, practical and positive.

'Cilka, there's something else.'

Cilka's heart sinks.

'I've put in a request to move to Sochi, where they have built a new hospital.'

She reaches her arm out for Cilka, but Cilka flinches. She doesn't know what to say. Yelena deserves to be somewhere better, after the years she has voluntarily put into this awful place. But what will Cilka do without her?

'Cilka?'

Cilka can't look at her. She is holding everything back. She has never had any choices. Everything has simply happened *to* her. No matter how much she wants it, she can never hold on to people. She is alone. Completely alone in the world.

'Cilka, you have to believe I am doing everything I can for you too.'

Cilka pushes her feelings down inside her, looks up at Yelena.

'Thank you, Yelena Georgiyevna, for everything.'

Yelena holds her eyes.

It feels like goodbye.

* * *

The women of Hut 29 are all she has left. Cilka keeps thinking about Lale in Birkenau, how he had told her she was brave. How other people have told her she is brave. How Alexandr has opened something up in her, making her want to live, not just stay alive.

And she knows there is one more brave thing she has to do.

She talks to the trusties who act as guards for the nurses' quarters, gives them her stash of extra food, and they agree to escort her that night – a Sunday – to the hut. She needs to talk to the women.

As they walk through the compound, she can see men eyeing her from a distance, but they do not approach. She opens the door to the hut, while the guards wait outside.

'Cilka!' Margarethe rushes towards her, enveloping her. 'What are you doing here? It's dangerous.'

Cilka begins to shake. 'I need to talk to you all.' She looks around. There are a couple of new faces, but the hut is still mostly women she recognises, including her oldest hut-mates, Elena and Margarethe.

'Please, sit down,' she says.

'Is everything all right?' Elena says.

'It is,' Cilka begins. 'Well, I have met someone, and I

388

feel something for him, and I may lose him yet, but I never even knew I would be able to feel something for a man, because of everything I have been through.'

The women sit politely. Elena gives Cilka an encouraging look.

'You all shared your pasts with me, your secrets, and I was too afraid. But I should have reciprocated. I owe it to you.'

She takes a deep breath.

'I was in Auschwitz,' Cilka says. Margarethe sits bolt upright. 'The concentration camp.'

She swallows.

'I survived because I was given a privileged position in the camp, in the women's camp in Birkenau. A bit like Antonina. But . . .'

Elena nods at her. 'Go on, Cilka.'

No one else speaks.

'I had my own room in the block. A block where they would put the—' she struggles to say the words – 'sick and the dying women, before they would take them to the gas chambers to murder them.'

The women have their hands over their mouths, unbelieving.

'The SS officers, they put me there, in that block, because there were no witnesses.'

Silence. Complete silence.

Cilka swallows again, feeling light, dizzy.

Anastasia starts to cry, audibly.

'I know that sound, Anastasia, it is so familiar to me,'

Cilka says. 'I used to get angry. I don't know why that emotion. But they were all just so helpless. I wasn't able to cry. I had no tears. And this is why I have not been able to tell you all. I had a bed, I had food. And they were naked and dying.'

'How . . . how long were you there?' Elena asks.

'Three years.'

Margarethe comes to sit near Cilka and holds out a hand. 'None of us know what we would have done. Did those bastards kill your family?'

'I put my mother on the death cart myself.'

Margarethe forcefully takes Cilka's hand. 'The memory is giving you a shock. I can tell by your voice. And you're shaking. Elena, make a cup of tea.'

Elena jumps up and goes to the stove.

The rest of the women remain quiet. But Cilka is now too numb to think about how her words have been received. There's an exhaustion taking over her.

Such a small space of time has passed, but the words have been so large.

When Elena returns with the tea, she says, 'Hannah knew, didn't she?'

Cilka nods.

Margarethe says, 'I hope this isn't more of a shock, Cilka, but many of us had guessed that you had been there. You being Jewish, not talking about your arrest.'

Cilka begins shaking again. 'Really?'

'Yes, and things you would say here and there.'

'Oh . . .'

'You survived it, Cilka,' Elena says. 'And you will survive here too.'

Anastasia, the youngest, still has her hand over her mouth, silent tears falling down her cheeks. But none of them has reacted as Cilka had always played over in her mind, had always feared. They are still beside her.

And so maybe she can tell Alexandr, too. Maybe he can know her, and still love her.

'I'd better go,' Cilka says.

Elena stands with her. 'Come back again, if you can.'

Cilka lets Elena put her arms around her. And Margarethe. Anastasia still seems too shocked.

Cilka goes out into the night, dizzy and trembling.

* * *

'Good morning,' Cilka greets the receptionist as she heads towards the ward. She has one more day with Alexandr. She doesn't know yet how she can possibly say goodbye. Will she dare to promise that she will try to find him, many years from now, on the outside? Or should she just accept her fate, her curse?

But though she is losing him, losing Yelena, and though she has lost everyone dear to her, Alexandr has kindled a fire within her.

Not to anger, but to something like hope.

Because she never thought she could fall in love, after all she's been through. To do so, she thought, would be a miracle. And now she has.

'Cilka,' the receptionist says.

Cilka turns back.

'I've been asked to tell you to go to the main administration block, they want to see you.'

Cilka pulls her hand back from the door to the ward. 'Now?'

Alexandr is just inside. She could say good morning, first. No, she'll get this out of the way and then have the day with him before he is discharged. A day where she can tell him everything, and then never speak of it again.

* * *

Entering the administration block, Cilka is confronted by several other prisoners, all men, standing around complaining about why they are here. She reports to the only person looking official, behind a desk.

'I've been asked to report here,' she says with a confidence she doesn't feel.

'Name.'

'Cecilia Klein.'

'Number.'

'1-B494.'

The receptionist rifles through several envelopes on her desk. Taking one, she looks at the number printed on it. 1-B494.

'Here, there's a small sum of money in there and a letter to hand to the guard at the gate on your way out.'

Cilka doesn't take the offered envelope.

'Take it and get out of here,' the receptionist snaps at her.

'Where am I going?'

'First to Moscow, then to be deported to your home country,' the receptionist says.

Home?

'I am to go to the train station?'

'Yes. Now get out of here. Next.'

The bulb in the ceiling blinks. Another piece of paper. Another moment where her life is decided for her.

'But I can't just leave. There are people I need to see.'

Alexandr. Will he be released? Released under the dead man's name. How will she find him?

Her chest aches, feels like it's collapsing in on itself.

Yelena, Raisa, Lyuba, Elena, Anastasia and Margarethe – if she could get to them . . . She needs to say goodbye!

Klavdiya Arsenyevna is there, overseeing the prisoners' release. Cilka has seldom seen her since moving into the nurses' quarters. Now the guard steps forward.

'You are lucky, Cilka Klein, but do not test my patience. You are to leave immediately, not to go anywhere but the front gate. Or I can arrange for a guard to drag you to the hole if that's what you would prefer?'

Cilka takes the envelope, shaking. The men behind her have all gone quiet.

'Next,' says the receptionist.

* * *

Cilka hands the letter to the guard at the gate, who barely glances at it, indicating with his head for her to move on. Slowly, she walks away, looking around for someone to stop her, tell her it's all a mistake. The few guards she passes ignore her.

On she walks, down the only road she sees. Alone.

The heavy clouds roll in. Cilka prays it doesn't snow today.

In the distance she can see small buildings. Homes, she thinks. She walks on. Aching with sadness, but dizzy, also, at the strangeness of this freedom. This road in front of her. One foot, the next. What do people do with this?

Walking down a street with houses and a few shops, she peers into windows. Women with children, cleaning, playing, cooking, eating, look out at her suspiciously. She catches the rich smells of stew, and baking bread.

She hears a familiar sound, a train slowly pulling in behind the buildings, and hurries towards it. By the time she reaches the railway line, the train is disappearing. Her eyes follow the tracks to a small station. She goes to it. A man is in the process of closing and locking the door to a small office.

'Excuse me?'

The man pauses with his key in the door, stares down at her.

'What do you want?'

'Where was that train going?'

'Moscow, eventually.'

'And among the released prisoners, did you happen to see a man . . . tall, slight bruising on his face . . .'

The man cuts her off. 'It was full, there were many men. I'm sorry, I wouldn't be able to tell you.'

Cilka opens the envelope stuffed in her coat pocket. She pulls all the money out.

'Can I have a ticket for the next train, please?'

Josie and Natia are in Moscow. If all the trains went to Moscow, then in Moscow she could look for them, and eventually also, for Alexandr. If only she could remember the name of Maria Danilovna's friend. It will be very difficult to track her down. But she can try. She will.

'It's not due yet, but all you need is your release paper and movement order.'

'When will it come?'

'Tomorrow, come back tomorrow.'

Cilka is totally deflated, exhausted, desperate.

'Where will I stay?' she says, close to tears.

'Look, I can't help you. You'll just have to do what all the others like you have done, find somewhere warm to hole up in and come back tomorrow.'

'Can I stay here somewhere?'

'No, but look out for the police, they patrol day and night looking for your type, you prisoners – some of them have caused trouble stealing from shops and homes while waiting for the train.'

Cilka is crushed. She turns away, walks back to town.

* * *

Other prisoners have also been released and been told by the stationmaster to return the next day. They wander the streets. They get into trouble with the locals. Blood is spilled. Cilka doesn't offer to help, choosing to stay apart.

She still doesn't believe she is free. Maybe the world is just a wider prison, where she has no family and no friends and no home. She has – had – Alexandr. Is her life to be spent wondering about him the way she wonders about her father, about Gita, about Josie? How will she really find Josie in a huge city like Moscow? At least she knows Yelena will be safe. But she didn't get to say goodbye, to hug her, to thank her properly. She feels wrenched in two. She spends the night behind a shop, curled up in a doorway in an attempt to keep out of the icy wind.

* * *

She hears the commotion of dozens of people yelling before she hears the train. The fog in her head clears with the realisation night has become day. Her transport out of Vorkuta is pulling in to the station.

She joins the others, running, all heading to the same place. The train has beaten her to the station and stands waiting, its engine running. She is pushed and jostled and knocked to the ground several times. Picking herself up, she keeps moving. The queue for the doors is long. The stationmaster has left his room and walks up the line of waiting passengers, checking their papers. No ticket is handed over. Cilka takes the form from her pocket and holds it out for him.

The stationmaster's hand reaches for it.

'Thank you,' she says to him.

With one hand on hers, he smiles down at her and nods encouragement.

'Good luck out there, little one. Now, get on that train.'

Cilka rushes towards the open carriage door. As she is about to step up into the train, she is pushed heavily aside by two men wanting to board ahead of her. The compartment is looking very full. She reaches her arms into the scrabble, desperately trying to get a hold on the doors so she can swing in. The train whistle calls, warning them all to get on board. There is yelling and pushing in front of her, and a man falls from the pack, back off the carriage steps and lands on the ground, twisted beside her.

'Are you all right?' she says, letting go of the door and reaching down to him. People continue to shove and swarm around them. He looks up and beneath the hat are the startled brown eyes of Alexandr.

'Cilka!'

She reaches under his arms to help him up, her heart thumping wildly in her chest.

'Oh, Alexandr. Are you all right?' she repeats, her voice choked with tears.

He winces as he stands, the stream of people behind them thinning out. Her hands are still under his arms.

The train whistle sounds again. She looks to the door. A small gap has opened in the crowd.

'Let's go!' she says. Her hand goes to his and they climb onto the train together, Alexandr's foot clearing the platform just as it starts moving.

In the carriage, Alexandr puts his arms around Cilka.

She weeps, openly, into his chest.

'I can't believe it,' she says.

She looks up into his eyes, soft and kind.

'I can,' he says. He strokes her hair, wipes the tears from her cheeks. In his eyes she can see everything he has been through, and, reflected, her own eyes and everything she has been through.

'It is time to live now, Cilka,' he says. 'Without fear, and with the miracle of love.'

'Is that a poem?' she asks him, smiling through her tears.

'It is the beginning of one.'

EPILOGUE

Košice, Czechoslovakia, January 1961

The bell dings on the café door and in walks a glamorous, tanned woman with a heart-shaped face, painted lips and large brown eyes.

Another woman, with curls in her hair and showing her curves in a lively floral dress, stands up from a table to greet her.

Gita walks towards Cilka, and the two women, who have not seen each other for almost twenty years, embrace. They are so different to how they were back then: now they are warm and healthy. The moment is overwhelming. They pull back. Cilka looks at Gita's lustrous, curled brown hair, her plump cheeks, her shining eyes.

'Gita! You look incredible.'

'Cilka, you are beautiful, more beautiful than ever.'

For a long time, they simply look at each other, touch each other's hair, smile, tears leaking from their eyes.

Will they be able to talk about that *other place*? That time?

The waitress comes over and they realise they must look a sight – pawing at each other, crying and laughing. They sit down and order coffee and cake, sharing more looks, delighting in the knowledge that these are things they were not allowed, that it is still a daily miracle to have survived. These simple pleasures will taste different, for them, to anyone else in this café.

First Cilka asks about Lale, and is delighted to hear about how he and Gita found each other in Bratislava after the war, what they went through after that, and how they have settled in Australia. Gita only stops smiling when she says that they have been trying a long time for a baby, with no success. She touches her stomach, reflexively, under the table, as she says this.

'Alexandr and I, too, have had no success,' Cilka says, reaching out to clutch her friend's other hand.

And then, working backwards, Gita asks – voice lowered, huddling in closer – if Cilka would like to talk about the Gulag.

'It is where I met Alexandr,' Cilka says, 'and made other friends too.' It is too hard to articulate the relentless bone-chilling cold, the constant flow of sick and injured and dead prisoners, the rapes she again endured, the humiliation and pain of being imprisoned there, after the *other place*.

'Cilka,' Gita says. 'I don't know how you could bear it. After everything we'd already been through.'

Cilka lets the tears run down her cheeks. She never speaks about this with anyone. No one around her, other than Alexandr, knows she was in Auschwitz, except for her only Jewish neighbour who had been hidden as a little boy all throughout the Shoah. And few people know she was in Siberia. She has done her best to put the past behind her, create a new life.

'I know the people who came in after us, to Birkenau, they just didn't understand what it had been like, to be there for so long.' Gita continues to hold Cilka's hand. 'You were sixteen, and you had lost everything.'

'We were faced only with impossible choices,' Cilka says.

The sun shines in through the café window. The past is seen through a muted grey light – cold, and never as far away as they'd like. The images and smells are near the surface of their skin. Every moment of loss.

But they turn their faces to the sun coming in.

Gita brings the conversation back to Lale, to their business ventures, and to the Australian Gold Coast where they holiday. She spoons cake into her mouth, closing her eyes with pleasure, the way Alexandr still does when he smokes or eats. And Cilka joins in, talking of the present, of living.

They lift their glasses and toast, '*L'Chaim.*'

NOTE FROM HEATHER MORRIS

'Did I tell you about Cilka?'

'No, Lale, you didn't. Who was Cilka?'

'She was the bravest person I ever met. Not the bravest girl; the bravest person.'

'And?'

'She saved my life. She was beautiful, a tiny little thing, and she saved my life.'

A brief conversation, a few words thrown at me one day while I was talking to Lale about his time in Auschwitz-Birkenau as the Tattooist of Auschwitz.

I returned to the topic of Cilka many times with Lale. I held his hand as he explained to me how she saved his life and what she did to be in a position to save his life. He was distraught remembering, and I was shocked. This was a girl who was sixteen years of age. Just sixteen. I became captivated by Cilka, unable to understand or comprehend the strength someone of her age must have had to survive the way she did. And why did she have to be punished so harshly for choosing to live?

I listened to Gita on her Shoah tape talking about Cilka (though she does not use her name), the roles she had in the camp, including in Block 25, and how Gita felt she was judged unjustly. 'I knew the girl who was the block *alteste*. She lives now in Košice. Everyone says she was this and she was that, but she only had to do what the SS told her. If Mengele told her this person has to go to Block 25, she would take her in, you know? She couldn't cope with so many people. But those people don't understand who haven't been there the whole time. And didn't go through the stages of what's going on. So they say, one was bad, one was good, but this I told you – you save one, and the other one had to suffer. Block 25, you couldn't get out anybody.' She also mentioned how she had visited her 'after' in Košice, and Lale also told me that she had.

I searched testimonies of other survivors for reference to Cilka. I found them. Did they bring me comfort? No, they did not. I found conflicting comments such as: she did bad things to survive; she gave me extra rations when she found out I came from the same town as her; she yelled and screamed at the condemned women; she smuggled me food when I was certain I would die of hunger.

A picture of a very young woman surviving in a death camp, submitting herself to the sexual advances of not one but two senior SS officers, was emerging. A story of bravery, compassion, friendship; a story, like Lale's, where you did what you did in order to survive. Only the consequences for Cilka were to be imprisoned for another ten years in the coldest place on earth – Vorkuta Gulag, inside the Arctic Circle, Siberia.

With the release of *The Tattooist of Auschwitz* floods of emails, messages, arrived from around the world. The vast majority of them asked the question 'What happened to Cilka?'

With the support of my editors and publishers I began the research that would lead me to uncovering the story that has inspired this novel.

I engaged a professional researcher in Moscow to uncover details of life in Vorkuta – the Gulag where Cilka spent ten years.

I travelled to Košice, and at the invitation of the owners of the apartment where Cilka and her husband had lived for fifty years I sat surrounded by the four walls Cilka called home. The owner told me she felt Cilka's presence in the apartment for many months after she moved in.

I sat and talked to her neighbours Mr and Mrs Samuely, both in their nineties. They shared stories of living next door to Cilka and her husband for many decades.

I met another neighbour who shared the name Klein. He told me he and Cilka were the only Jewish people in the building. They would speak softly together on significant Jewish days of celebration.

At the town cemetery I visited the graves of Cilka and her husband and paid my respects, placed flowers, lit a candle.

With translators and one of my publishers, I travelled to Sabinov, an hour's drive north of Košice, where we got to see the birth extracts of Cilka and her sisters (see the Additional Information below for details).

We were shown the marriage certificate of her parents and learned the names of her grandparents.

In Bardejov, where Cilka and her family had lived and were transported from, we read reports from the school Cilka and her sisters attended. They all were rated excellent for behaviour and manners. Cilka shone in both mathematics and sport.

I wandered through the streets of the old town. Stood outside the home where Cilka once lived, ran my hand along the remnants of the city wall, that protected the residents for hundreds of years from invading enemies, unable to protect Cilka from the request to submit to the Nazis. Such a beautiful place, a peaceful place – in 2019.

I am comforted by the knowledge Cilka spent nearly five decades with the man she loved and, according to her friends and neighbours, had a good life. Mrs Samuely told me how Cilka would talk about her love for her husband with the female friends in their circle. She would be teased by the other women who did not share such passionate feelings of love towards their husbands.

When writing of the rape, yes there is no other word for it, in Auschwitz-Birkenau, I found very little documented in the filmed testimonies. What I did find were papers written more recently when *female* interviewers spoke to survivors about this subject. How they uncovered the deep shame these women had lived with for many decades, never speaking of the abuse, never being asked the question 'Were you ever sexually assaulted by the Nazis?' The shame is ours, not theirs. They lived for decades with the truth, the reality of what happened to them, buried deep within.

Time is up. It is time these crimes of rape and sexual abuse were called out for what they were. Crimes often denied as they were not 'official Nazi policy'. I found specific mention even of Schwarzhuber as a 'smirking lecher' (from a female inmate physician) and I have read, in one testimony: 'it was rumoured she [Cilka] received [SS Unterscharführer Taube]'. While millions of Jewish men, women and children died, many lived and carried the burden of their suffering, too ashamed to mention it to their families, their partners. To deny it happened is to stick your head in the sand. Rape is a long-established weapon of war and oppression. Why should the Nazis, one of the most vicious regimes the world has ever known, forswear this particular form of cruelty?

I was humbled to have Lale Sokolov in my life for three years and hear his story first hand. I did not have this luxury with Cilka. Determined to tell her story, to honour her, I found a way to weave the facts and reportage of her circumstances in both Auschwitz-Birkenau and the Vorkuta Gulag with the testimonies of others, particularly women.

To navigate the fictional and factual elements required to create a novel, I created characters based on what I discovered through reading and research into what life was like in these camps. There is a mix of characters inspired by real-life figures, in some instances representing more than one individual, and characters completely imagined. There are more characters based on real life figures in the Auschwitz-Birkenau sections, as I learned about them from Lale.

History never gives up its secrets easily. For over fifteen years I've been finding out about the amazing lives of ordinary people under the most unimaginable of circumstances. It's a journey that's taken me from the suburbs of Melbourne, Australia, to the hills of Slovakia to the railroad tracks at Auschwitz-Birkenau and the buildings beyond. I've spoken to people who lived through those terrible days. I've spoken to their family and friends. I've seen meticulous records from Yad Vashem and the Shoah Foundation and handwritten documents in civil archives dating back to the nineteenth century. They all paint a picture, but sometimes that picture isn't clear and often the details don't all line up. The challenge of working with history is to find the core of what was true and the spirit of those who lived then.

Days before *Cilka's Journey* was due to go to the printers, new facts were uncovered concerning her parents. They didn't relate to her time in the Nazi or Soviet camps, but they did shed new light on this remarkable woman and where she came from. It was a reminder to me that the story of *Cilka's Journey* is far from fully told, even with the book you hold in your hands.

Stories like Cilka's deserve to be told, and I'm humbled and honoured to bring it to you. She was just a girl, who became a woman, who was the bravest person Lale Sokolov ever met.

ADDITIONAL INFORMATION

Cecilia 'Cilka' Klein was born in Sabinov, eastern Slovakia on 17 March 1926. Her mother was Fany Kleinova, née Blechova, her father Miklaus Klein (b. 13 January 1895). Cilka was the youngest of three daughters of Miklaus. Olga was born to Miklaus and Cecilia Blechova on 28 December 1921. It appears that Cecilia Blechova (b. 19 September 1897) died on 26 March 1922, and that Miklaus then married Cecilia's sister, Fany Blechova (b. 10 May 1903), on 1 November 1923. Miklaus and Fany had two daughters, Magdalena, 'Magda', born 23 August 1924 and Cecilia, 'Cilka', and Fany would have also raised Olga as her own daughter. Cilka was named for her aunt, and Olga was both her and Magda's cousin, and their half-sister. In the fictional narrative, Cilka's sisters are represented as one character, Magda.

On the registry of birth for each of the girls, Miklaus is listed as 'non-domiciled', meaning that he was Hungarian. Czechoslovakia was created at the end of the First World War, when the Austro-Hungarian empire ceased to exist, and eastern Slovakia sat on the border of this newly created nation and Hungary. Miklaus Klein was born in the northern Hungarian town of Szikszó, 100 miles south of Sabinov. Miklaus was never during his life regarded as a Czechoslovakian citizen.

At some point before 1931 the family moved to Bardejov, where each of the girls attended the local school. The family are known to have lived in Klastorska Street and Halusova Street. Miklaus's occupations on his daughters' birth certificates and their school records vary wildly – he is a salesman, a tradesman, an industrial business employee and latterly a driver. It seems that he worked for a Mr Rozner in Bardejov, possibly as his driver.

When the Second World War broke out, Germany annexed what is now the Czech Republic. Hungary sided with the Germans and what is now Slovakia capitulated. While people at this time would have still identified themselves in an official context as Czechoslovakian, the country was divided in two and Hungary also took control of an area in the south-east. This meant that the fate of the Jewish people of Czechoslovakia varied according to which part of the country they were living in. The Jews of Hungary were sent to the camps in 1944.

In survivor testimonies, people from the area often refer to themselves as 'Slovakian' or 'Slovak', and so in the narrative I have used both Czechoslovakia and Slovakia/ Slovak depending on official or personal context. Likewise, people from the Czech region might identify themselves as 'Czech'. And Slovakian and Czech were, and are, separate (but very similar) languages. Both are West Slavic languages and are closely related to Polish. When visiting Cilka's home town of Bardejov I learned that she would also have understood Russian, through exposure to the Rusyn dialect.

In 1942, the Nazis set about rounding up the Jews of the region of Slovakia. All Jewish people in Bardejov were ordered to go to Poprad from where they were put into cattle wagons bound for Auschwitz. Miklaus and the three girls entered Auschwitz on 23 April 1942, where Cilka was given prisoner number 5907. There is no record of Fany Kleinova having gone to Auschwitz, but witness testimonies, and Lale Sokolov, describe Cilka having seen her mother put on the death cart at Birkenau. In reality they most likely all left Bardejov on the same date and waited in Poprad for transports. Cilka's occupation at the time of her entry to Auschwitz is listed as 'tailor', her older sisters are 'housewives'. In the novel, I have imagined the daughters going earlier than their parents, as this happened in many instances, where each Jewish family was ordered to send able-bodied young people (over the age of sixteen) to go and work.

The entire family, bar Cilka and her mother, are listed in the Yad Vashem Archive as having been murdered in the Shoah. We do not know when Miklaus, Fany, Magda and Olga were murdered, but we do know that only Cilka survived Auschwitz. (In one record I have uncovered Cilka too is listed as having been murdered in Auschwitz, but this is also the case with Lale Sokolov, and we know that both survived and made it back to Czechoslovakia.)

At the end of the war the Russians liberated Auschwitz-Birkenau, and it seems that at this point Cilka was taken to Montelupich Prison in Kraków, possibly after going through an NKVD filtration/interrogation point (this has been simplified in the novel) where she was given a sentence for collaboration, which I understand is because of her role in Block 25, and being pointed out as having 'slept with the enemy'. This is how Lale understood it.

From there she made the long, arduous journey to Vorkuta, in the Arctic Circle. Certain aspects of her time there I have taken from reportage: her job in the hospital; being taken under the wing of a female doctor; going out on the ambulance. Alexei Kukhtikov and his wife are loosely based on real people. Kukhtikov was director of both of Vorkuta's prison camps, Vorkutlag and Rechlag, and during his time there commissioned the building of a children's hospital (built by prisoners, of course).

Upon her release, I believe Cilka was sent to either Pankrác or Ruzyně Prison, both of which are in Prague, before eventually returning to Czechoslovakia. There is an entry on her birth certificate in 1959 granting her Czechoslovakian citizenship. Cilka was back home, and life with a man she loved, whom she met in the Gulag, could begin. Alexandr is an entirely fictional creation, and

I have not included the name of the man she met in Vorkuta and subsequently married, in order to protect the privacy of his descendants. Cilka and her husband settled in Košice, where Cilka lived until her death on 24 July 2004. They never had children, but those I have met who knew them spoke of their great love for one another.

Heather Morris, October 2019

AFTERWORD BY OWEN MATTHEWS

Vorkuta – The White Hell

Cilka's last sight of the Auschwitz-Birkenau death camp would have been of the wrought-iron sign erected over the gates: *'Arbeit Macht Frei'* – Work Brings Freedom. The first thing she would have seen on her arrival in the Soviet Gulag camp at Vorkuta was another sign: 'Work in the USSR is a matter of Honour and Glory.' Another declared that 'With an Iron Fist, We Will Lead Humanity to Happiness.' A taste for sadistic irony was just one of the many traits that Nazi Germany and Stalin's USSR shared.

Both Hitler's concentration camps and the Soviet Gulag existed for the same purpose – to purge society of its enemies, and to extract as much work from them as possible before they died. The only real differences are one of scale – Stalin's Gulag was far larger than anything

Hitler ever conceived – and of efficiency. Stalin certainly shared Hitler's genocidal tendencies, condemning entire ethnic groups, such as the Chechens, Crimean Tatars and Volga Germans, to mass deportation, death marches and forced labour. But where the Germans used Zyklon-B poison gas, Stalin preferred to let cold, hunger and over-work do their lethal work.

Over eighteen million people passed through the Gulag system from 1929 until Stalin's death in 1953, according to the Soviet State's own meticulous records. Of those, modern scholars estimate that some 6 million died either in prison or shortly after their release. Like Hitler's concentration camps, Stalin's Gulag housed both political prisoners and common criminals – as well as people condemned for belonging to politically unreliable nations, such as Poles, Jews and Ukrainians, or to the wrong class, whether wealthy peasants or pre-Revolutionary aristo-crats. In the closing days of the Second World War the Gulag population was swelled by German war criminals and ordinary German prisoners of war, as well as hundreds of thousands of Soviet soldiers who had chosen surrender over death and were therefore presumed to be collabo-rators with the enemy. During Cilka's time in Vorkuta her fellow prisoners included the commander of Germany's Sachsenhausen concentration camp Anton Kaindl; famous Yiddish, French and Estonian writers; Russian art scholars and painters; Latvian and Polish Catholic priests; East German Liberal Democrats and even a British soldier who had fought with the Waffen-SS British Free Corps.

Alongside the intellectuals and war criminals were a large population of murderers, rapists and even convicted cannibals.

Nobel-prize-winning author Aleksandr Solzhenitsyn, the Gulag's most famous victim and its most dedicated chronicler, described Stalin's system of forced labour camps as the Gulag Archipelago. The word is appropriate, as the camps spread across the Soviet Union's eleven time zones like a string of interconnected islands. There were Gulags in Russia's biggest cities, some housing German prisoners of war serving as slave labourers, and others where imprisoned engineers and scientists toiled in high-tech prison laboratories. But most Gulags were located in the remotest corners of the Siberian north and in the far east – indeed whole swathes of the USSR were effectively colonised by State prisoners who built dozens of brand-new cities, roads, railways, dams and factories where there had previously been just bleak wasteland.

Vorkuta was such a colony, both in the sense of a penal settlement and a tiny island of life in a hostile, unexplored territory. In the late 1920s, Soviet geologists identified vast coal deposits in the frozen taiga wilderness, an area too cold for trees to grow, where the Pechora River flowed into the Arctic Sea. The region was some 1,900 kilometres (1,200 miles) north of Moscow and 160 kilometres (99 miles) above the Arctic Circle. Soviet secret police lost no time in arresting a leading Russian geologist, Nikolai Tikhonovich, and setting him to work organising an expedition to sink the first mine in the area. In the early summer of 1931, a team of twenty-three men set off northward from Ukhta by boat. Prisoner-geologists led the way, ordinary prisoners manned the oars, and a small secret police contingent was in command. Paddling and marching through the swarms of insects that inhabit the tundra in summer months, the party built a makeshift camp. 'The heart compressed at the sight of the wild, empty landscape,' recalled one of the prisoner-specialists, a geographer named Kulevsky. 'The absurdly large, black, solitary watch tower, the two poor huts, the taiga and the mud.' The beleaguered group somehow survived their first winter, when temperatures often fell to forty degrees below zero and the sun did not rise above the horizon for the four-month-long Polar night. In the spring of 1932, they sank the first mine at Vorkuta, using only picks and shovels and wooden carts.

Stalin's Purges – the mass arrests of suspect Party members and of politically unreliable wealthy peasants – began in 1934 and provided the mass of slave labour needed to turn this desolate site into a major industrial centre. By 1938, the new settlement contained 15,000 prisoners and had produced 188,206 tonnes of coal. Vorkuta had become the headquarters of Vorkutlag, a sprawling network of 132 separate labour camps that covered over 90,000 square kilometres – an area larger than Ireland. By 1946, when Cilka arrived, Vorkutlag housed 62,700 inmates and was known as one of the largest and toughest camps in the entire Gulag system. An estimated 2 million prisoners passed through Vorkuta's camps between 1931 and 1957 – an estimated 200,000 of them perished from disease, overwork, and malnourishment in the Arctic conditions.

By the 1940s, Vorkuta had been connected to the rest of Russia by a prisoner-built railway. There is still no road to Vorkuta, even today. A brand-new city had been built on the unstable permafrost – the deep-lying soil that never thaws, even in the height of summer. The city boasted a geological institute and a university, theatres, puppet theatres, swimming pools and nurseries. The guards and administrators lived lives of comparative luxury. 'Life was better than anywhere else in the Soviet Union,' remembered Andrei Cheburkin, a foreman in the neighbouring nickel-mining Gulag of Norilsk. 'All the bosses had maids, prisoner maids. Then the food was amazing. There were all sorts of fish. You could go and catch it in the lakes. And if in the rest of the Union there were ration cards, here we lived virtually without cards. Meat. Butter. If you wanted champagne you had to take a crab as well, there were so many. Caviar . . . barrels of the stuff lay around.'

For the prisoners, however, the living conditions were shockingly different. Most lived in flimsy wooden barracks with unplastered walls, the cracks stopped up with mud. The inside space was filled with rows of knocked-together bunk beds, a few crude tables and benches, with a single sheet-metal stove. One photo of a women's hut does show single beds, and embroidery strung around the hut, as in this narrative. In photographs of Vorkuta taken in the winter of 1945 the barracks are almost invisible – their steeply sloping roofs come almost to the ground so that the snow accumulating around them would insulate them from the bitter Arctic cold.

Almost all survivors speak of the 'terrible heavy smell' that pervaded the barracks. Few Gulags had any kind of laundry facilities, so filthy and mildewed clothes would lie drying along the edge of the bunks, the tables, and on every available surface. At night, prisoners use a *parasha* – a communal bucket – in place of a toilet. One prisoner wrote that in the morning the parasha was 'impossible to carry, so it was dragged along across the slippery floor. The contents invariably spilled out.' The stench made it 'almost impossible to breathe'.

In the centre of most of Vorkutlag's hundred-plus camps was a large open parade ground where the prisoners stood to attention twice a day to be counted. Nearby was a mess hall, where prisoners were fed a daily soup made of 'spoiled cabbage and potatoes, sometimes with pieces of pig fat, sometimes with herring heads' or 'fish or animal lungs and a few potatoes'. The convicts' area was usually surrounded by double rings of barbed wire, patrolled by Alsatian guard dogs, and surrounded by guard towers. Beyond the wire were the guards' barracks and administrators' houses.

Who were the guardians of this nightmare world? 'Where did this wolf-tribe appear from among our own people?' Alexander Solzhenitsyn asked. 'Does it really stem from our own roots? Our own blood? It is ours.' Some of the guards in the Gulag were themselves former prisoners. Many more convicts served as *druzhinniki* – the prisoner trusties who were given extra food for their role in keeping order in the camp and informing on potential troublemakers.

Most guards, though, were professional secret policemen who volunteered for the service. The men drawn to serve in the Soviet secret police, in the famous phrase of its founder, Felix Dzerzhinsky, could be either 'saints or scoundrels'. Clearly the service attracted more than its fair share of sadists and psychopaths, as witnessed by the memoirs of camp guard officer Ivan Chistyakov, who described 'the bunch of misfits' who were his drunken subordinates. He called the Gulag a 'madhouse shambles' and often dreamed of exposing his fellow officers' 'illiteracy' and 'misdeeds'. Perhaps the most chilling psychological insight offered by Chistyakov's diary is the portrait of a humane man conforming to an inhuman system. 'I'm beginning to have that mark on my face, the stamp of stupidity, narrowness, a kind of moronic expression,' he wrote. 'My heart is desolate, it alarms me.' And the diary is also a chronicle of the essential selfishness of human suffering: Chistyakov often lamented for himself but rarely for the inmates, whom he described as lazy and dishonest. 'Today . . . I had to imprison one woman, there's some muddle about an escape, a conflict with a phalanx leader, a knife fight,' wrote Chistyakov. 'To hell with the lot of them!' But it is they, not he, who were being starved and worked to death.

'To do evil a human being must first of all believe that what he's doing is good,' wrote Solzhenitsyn. 'Or else that it's a well-considered act in conformity with natural law.' Chistyakov offered no justification for the slave-labour system that he was helping to run – only insight into the banality of evil. He, and hundreds of thousands of other officers, were only following orders, and the inhuman system of which he was a part seemed to Chistyakov as inexorable and invincible as the crushing frosts and the buzzing summer flies.

In the frozen hell of Vorkuta, male prisoners were expected to work ten-hour days – reduced in March 1944 from twelve hours after too many work accidents began to impair productivity – down jerry-built and desperately unsafe coal mines. Records for the year 1945 list 7,124 serious accidents in the Vorkuta coal mines alone. Inspectors laid the blame on the shortage of miners' lamps, on electrical failures, and on the inexperience of workers.

Camp life was no less harsh for the tens of thousands of women imprisoned in Vorkuta. Though spared the mines, female prisoners were nonetheless expected to perform heavy physical labour, hauling coal and water, digging ditches, working in brickworks, carrying supplies and building barracks. The women's quarters were separated from the men's by walls of barbed wire – but prisoners mixed freely during the day. Many camp guards, and also the more powerful trusties, kept women prisoners as servants and mistresses. They were often referred to as camp 'husbands' and 'wives'. Rape by fellow inmates and guards was prevalent. A 1955 report noted that 'venereal disease, abortions and pregnancies were commonplace . . .

pregnant women were sent to a special camp where work was lighter. A mother was allowed to stay with her child for two years, after which it was placed in a special nursery and the mother returned to her original camp. She received photographs and reports of the child's development and was occasionally permitted to see it.' The same report noted that out of 1,000 female inmates at Vorkuta's Brickworks No 2., 200 were suffering from tuberculosis.

In the harsh conditions of the camps, prisoners formed tribes in order to survive. Poles, Balts, Ukrainians, Georgians, Armenians and Chechens all formed their own national brigades, slept separately in national barracks, and organised celebrations of national holidays. Adam Galinski, a Pole who had fought with the anti-Soviet Polish Home Army, wrote that: 'We took special care of the youth . . . and kept up its morale, the highest in the degrading atmosphere of moral decline that prevailed among the different national groups imprisoned in Vorkuta.' Jews, however, were a special case – they lacked the common language and common national identity to form a coherent tribe. Many Jews – such as the influential Yiddish writer Der Nister, who died at Vorkuta in 1950, had been imprisoned for celebrating their Jewish identity. Yet they found themselves taunted and persecuted for their ethnic association with the Jewish Bolsheviks such as Genrikh Yagoda, who had created the Gulag system.

For ten months a year, the intense cold was a constant, lethal companion of Vorkuta life. 'Touching a metal tool with a bare hand could tear off the skin,' recalled one prisoner. 'Going to the bathroom was extremely dangerous. A bout of diarrhoea could land you in the snow forever.' And prisoners were woefully badly equipped to deal with the brutal climate. In Vorkuta, according to camp records, only 25 to 30 per cent of prisoners had underclothes, while only 48 per cent had warm boots. The rest had to make do with makeshift footwear made from rubber tyres and rags.

The Arctic summer of Vorkuta, when the scrubland bloomed with scarlet fireweed and the low-lying landscape turned into a vast bog, was scarcely more bearable. Mosquitoes and gnats appeared in huge grey clouds, making so much noise it was impossible to hear anything else. 'The mosquitoes crawled up our sleeves, under our trousers. One's face would blow up from the bites,' recalled a Vorkuta inmate. 'At the work site, we were brought lunch, and it happened that as you were eating your soup, the mosquitoes would fill up the bowl like buckwheat porridge. They filled up your eyes, your nose and throat, and the taste of them was sweet, like blood.'

Escape was unthinkable. Some of the remoter camps had no barbed wire, so unlikely was the possibility of prisoners ever making it across hundreds of kilometres of wilderness to freedom. Those that did attempt escape did so in threes – the third prisoner coming along as a 'cow' – food for the other two in case they didn't find any other nourishment.

Former prisoners frequently recall their time in the Gulag as a season in another world, one with its own climate, rules, values and even language. As Solzhenitsyn wrote, the 'Gulag was a universe' with its own speech and codes. For camp administrators, pregnant women were 'books', women with children were 'receipts', men were 'accounts', released convicts who remained in exile were 'rubbish', prisoners under investigation were 'envelopes', a camp division was a 'factory'. *Tufta* was the art of pretending to work, *mastyrka*, the art of malingering. There was a rich underground culture of tattoo designs for politicals, addicts, rapists, homosexuals, murderers. The slang of the Gulag soon spilled back into mainstream culture and became the slang of the entire Soviet Union; the rich vocabulary of Russian obscenity developed mainly in the camps.

Occasionally, the tormented slave labourers of the Gulag rose against their masters. The Vorkuta Uprising of July–August 1953 was one of the bravest, and most tragic, of such uprisings. Stalin died in March 1953, and his chief policeman Lavrentiy Beria was arrested shortly afterwards after a Politburo power struggle. On a warm July day, the prisoners of one Vorkuta camp downed tools, demanding that inmates have access to a state attorney and due justice. Convicts in neighbouring camps, seeing that the mine-head wheels in the rebel camp had stopped spinning, joined the strike. Top brass from Moscow was sent in – the State Attorney of the USSR, and the commander of the Internal Troops tried to reason with the strikers. On July 26 prisoners stormed the maximum-security punitive compound, releasing seventy-seven of its inmates who had been kept in solitary cells that spelled death in wintertime. Days later, the authorities finally acted, massing armed troops to open fire on the rebels, killing sixty-six and wounding 135.

The Vorkuta Uprising changed nothing – but in Moscow, the political climate was shifting. The winner of the struggle to succeed Stalin, Nikita Khrushchev, ordered the release of hundreds of thousands of political prisoners. Later, he would denounce Stalin's crimes at a secret session of the Communist Party, and decree the re-examination of most of the political cases of the Great Terror. By the end of 1956, over 600,000 victims of the Terror would be officially – posthumously – pardoned.

Released prisoners were given a small sum of money and travel orders to other parts of the USSR. The vast majority remained *limitchiki* – forbidden to live within 101 kilometres of any major city, largely to limit the political fallout of their stories on the Communist faith or urban citizens. The remaining foreign prisoners, mostly German prisoners of war, were finally allowed home. A few found their way to the US and testified to Congress about the horrors of the Gulag.

Today, around 40,000 people still live in Vorkuta – many the descendants of convicts or camp guards, plus a few hardy nonagenarian women who were imprisoned there and never left. In Soviet times, Vorkuta miners and residents enjoyed a generous state subsidy for enduring the harsh conditions. Those subsidies disappeared with the end of Communism, but nonetheless most of the population stayed. In the 2000s a new gas pipeline was built, bringing new prosperity and a new generation of workers. Every year on 31 October residents meet at a monument to the victims – a small space filled with a mass of rusty barbed wire on the spot where investigative geologist Georgy Chernov pitched his tent in 1931, effectively founding the city.

But the most enduring monument to the victims of the Gulag remains in the printed words of the survivors – the stories of their lives and their battle not just to live but to retain their humanity. Reading a simple litany of horrors quickly ceases to be meaningful. As Boris Pasternak wrote of the man-made famine that killed millions in the Ukraine in the early 1930s, 'There was such inhuman, unimaginable misery, such a terrible disaster, that it began to seem almost abstract, it would not fit within the bounds of consciousness.' Reading about the Gulag begins to seem like a story of another planet, too distant for comprehension.

But listen to how Varlaam Shalamov, a writer who survived seventeen years in Kolyma in the Soviet Far East, defined what it meant to feel fully human in the Gulag. 'I believed a person could consider himself a human being as long as he felt totally prepared to kill himself,' a character says in one of Shalamov's 'Kolyma Tales'. 'It was this awareness that provided the will to live. I checked myself – frequently – and felt I had the strength to die, and thus remained alive.' Both he, and Cilka, lived. And that was their victory.

The last word must go to Alexander Solzhenitsyn. 'I dedicate this to all those who did not live to tell it,' he wrote in the foreword to his classic study, *The Gulag Archipelago*. 'And may they please forgive me for not having seen it all, nor remembered it all, for not having divined all of it.'

ACKNOWLEDGEMENTS

Lale Sokolov – you gave me your beautiful story and shared with me what you knew of Cilka Klein. Sending you my heartfelt thanks for inspiring me to write *Cilka's Journey*.

Angela Meyer, on a visit to Lale's hometown of Krompachy you sat with me on a window ledge into the small hours of the morning, solving the world's problems and drinking Slivovitz. You encouraged me to make Cilka's story my next project. You have been with me every step of the way as my friend and editor in telling this story. You are simply brilliant, funny, dedicated to telling stories well. From the bottom of my heart – thank you.

Kate Parkin, Managing Director of Adult Trade Publishing, Bonnier Books UK. How many authors get to call their publisher a friend? I do. Your guidance, wisdom and support past, present and future is with me always. Thank you so much.

Margaret Stead (Maverick), fellow Kiwi, fellow traveller, Publishing Director, Zaffre, Bonnier Books UK: *Mauruuru*. What a talent, what a person to have on my team.

Ruth Logan, Rights Director, Bonnier Books UK, thank you for making Cilka's story fly to all four corners of the globe, ably assisted by the amazing Ilaria Tarasconi.

Jennie Rothwell, Assistant Editor, Zaffre, Bonnier Books UK, your eagle eye in producing the highest-quality content makes my writing better than it would/should be. Indebted.

Francesca Russell, Publicity Director at Zaffre, and Clare Kelly, Publicity Manager at Zaffre, thank you for keeping me busy and arranging for me to share the stories the team at Zaffre all work so hard to release.

There are others at Zaffre to thank for their brilliant work in art, marketing and sales. Nick Stearn, Stephen Dumughn and his team, and Nico Poilblanc and his team. Thank you all very much. The Slivovitz is on me.

There are many wonderful people at St Martin's Press in the United States who have been involved in developing the story and getting it to print. I need to mention a few here, with full acknowledgements being given in the US edition.

A woman who met me at an elevator in New York with the biggest smile and arms ready for an embrace, the President and Publisher of St Martin's Press, Sally Richardson. Thank you. Thank you. This welcome soon extended to publisher extraordinaire Jennifer Enderlin. Again, my sincere thanks. The rest of the team, please accept my thanks, your names and roles will be broadcast in the US edition.

Benny Agius (Thelma), General Manager, Echo Publishing, you are a shining, bubbling beacon, holding me together on many occasions. Someone I can laugh with, share concerns with when my life is pulled in many directions. Thank you for being there.

Dakujem (thank you), Lenka Pustay. You got caught up in the spell of learning all you could about Cilka. Your time, effort and stubbornness to not leave any stone unturned in the pursuit of this information has been a joy to be on the receiving end of.

Anna Pustay – *Dakujem*. You started me on my journey to Krompachy. You embraced Lale's story and became attached to Cilka's story in the same way. You are a beautiful lady.

The people of Košice who knew Cilka, invited me into their homes and shared stories of Cilka and her husband. Mr and Mrs Samuely; Valeria Feketova; Michael Klein – *Dakujem*.

My friends in Krompachy to whom I have become so attached, who have assisted me in many ways with *Cilka's Journey* – Lady Mayor Iveta Rusinova; Darius Dubinak, Stanislav Barbus and the always smiling driver who delivered me safe and sound to so many destinations around the countryside, Peter Lacko – *Dakujem*.

For her outstanding research uncovering life in the

Gulags, in particular Vorkuta, professional researcher Svetlana Chervonnaya in Moscow – Thank you.

Thank you so much Owen Matthews for your brilliant afterword on the Soviet Gulag system. You have condensed academic research into a readable, easily understood description of this time and place.

Friends and family who supported me on my journey writing *Cilka's Journey* who I am so happy to have in my life. I love them all dearly. My big brother John Williamson who sadly died before the book was released, but whom I consider a far superior writer to me, and for whose support to write I am eternally grateful. Ian Williamson, Peggi Shea, Bruce Williamson, Stuart Williamson, Kathie Fong Yoneda, Pamela Wallace, Denny Yoneda, Gloria Winstone, Ian Winstone.

To the people who matter the most to me who sometimes lose out as I devote time to research, writing and travelling – my children and grandchildren. Ahren and Bronwyn, Jared and Rebecca, Azure-Dea and Evan, and the beautiful little people to whom I am just Grandma – Henry, Nathan, Jack, Rachel and Ashton. You are my life, my world.

Alyth and Alan Townsend, thank you for providing me with accomodation in my soul city – Christchurch, New Zealand, to write *Cilka's Journey*. We go back a long way.

And especially the man of my life for forty-six years. Steve, it seems lately you are missing out the most in this crazy journey of mine. Thank you for your love, your understanding, your unquestioning support and yes, I know, you are my biggest fan.

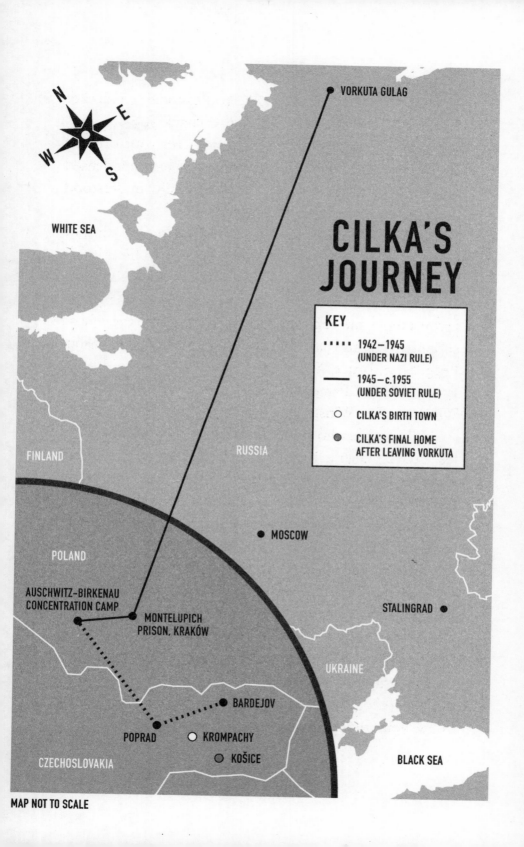

Do you have a story to tell?

Discover more moving stories,
and share yours with Heather at:

www.yourstoriesofhope.com